Heartland
Weddings

Print ISBN 978-1-62416-238-1

eBook Editions:
Adobe Digital Edition (.epub) 978-1-62416-503-0
Kindle and MobiPocket Edition (.prc) 978-1-62416-502-3

Published by Barbour Publishing, Inc., P.O. Box 719, Uhrichsville, Ohio 44683, www.barbourbooks.com

Our mission is to publish and distribute inspirational products offering exceptional value and biblical encouragement to the masses.

 Member of the
Evangelical Christian
Publishers Association

Printed in the United States of America.

Heartland
Weddings

Two Contemporary Romances Under One Cover

JENNIFER JOHNSON
CATHY LIGGETT

BARBOUR
PUBLISHING

A WEDDING SONG IN LEXINGTON, KENTUCKY

by Jennifer Johnson

Dedication

This book is dedicated to my husband, Albert. I will always remember the first time I saw him. I was a sophomore (cheerleader). He was a senior (quarterback). He was sitting on the football bench, his head ducked down—he'd just been hit in the back and was catching his breath. I'd never seen him before, but I knew he was The One. (From that moment, the poor boy didn't have a choice but to like me back. It's true— I'm quite persistent.)

I love you, Al!

Chapter 1

*In order to plan your future wisely, it is necessary
that you understand and appreciate your past.*
JO COUDERT

The floorboard creaked. Megan McKinney leaped from
the office chair, her stapler clattering to the ground.
Ignoring it, she twirled away from the copier and toward
the front door of the law office. At the sight of a client, she
placed her hand against her chest to still her racing heartbeat. She forced a smile. "Sorry 'bout that. I didn't hear the
door."

The red-haired woman rolled her eyes then stared at
long, manicured fingernails. "Obviously."

Megan sat and straightened in the chair. Dumb machine
jammed up papers more than it copied them. Clients often
scared the life out of her, coming in when she was elbow-
deep in yanking out documents.

She forced a smile as she took in the woman's lime-
green, spring sweater, the shape enhanced by modern medicine, and the white capris that exposed the lace outline of
some very skimpy undergarments. No doubt about it, the
redhead was here for Justin.

Megan raised her eyebrows. She had to give the woman
credit: the silver rhinestone sandals were the most adorable

she'd ever laid eyes on.

Lifting her chin, Megan prepared herself for the woman's tirade if she wasn't the younger Frasure's scheduled appointment. She had endured more than her share of self-centered fashion plates since coming to work for the law offices of Frasure, Frasure, and Combs six months ago.

"You gonna tell Justin I'm here?" The woman offered a quick glance of contempt and placed her hand against her chest. Megan noted the gargantuan marquise diamond on her left ring finger. Engagement ring. No wedding band.

Megan bit back the urge to ask the woman if her fiancé would also be available for the appointment. She shook her head. None of her business. "Let me check. What is your name?"

"Never mind, darlin'."

At the syrupy-sweet shift in tone, Megan followed the woman's gaze and saw that her divorce-turned-adoption-attorney boss, Justin Frasure, had opened his office door.

Megan gritted her teeth and forced a smile. Justin furrowed dark, thick eyebrows above chocolate-drop eyes. His stunning and impossibly delicious looks never failed to send a shiver down her spine and then a wrinkle of disgust to her nose. She couldn't stand men like him.

He motioned for the redhead to enter his office. Megan looked away until she heard the door shut behind him.

Sucking in her gag reflex, she twirled her chair toward the computer screen. She highlighted Justin Frasure's latest appointment as an indication that the client had shown up. *Something tells me that woman isn't here for adoption advice.*

She clicked a few buttons on her keyboard and switched

to the university home page. With a huff, she typed in her username and password. Still no posted grade from her spring class. She logged off, and Justin's appointment book flashed on the screen.

Her stomach turned. *Justin Frasure must have run out of the hot divorcees in the city. Added engagees to his list instead.* She wrinkled her nose. *Is there such a word as* engagees?

The last secretary had warned Megan he would hit on any pretty woman who crossed his path and that Megan, as quite the "adorable cutie," would be a prime target.

But he hadn't hit on Megan. Hadn't even flirted with her. Not that Megan cared. She didn't want the man's attention. Not in the slightest. After dating Clint Morgan in high school, she and God had enough issues to work through when it came to trusting men.

Besides, what did she care about who came into the law office? Scooping up the nonurgent messages she'd taken throughout the day for the three lawyers, she made her way to the office mailboxes outside their doors. She'd cringed when she'd placed Justin's messages in his box, remembering how one woman with a strong southern accent had whined incessantly because she couldn't speak with that "handsome, young lawyer" directly.

Megan bit back the growl that threatened almost every day she worked. Nothing upset her more than a man who played women. The Holy Spirit nudged her heart. She shouldn't judge him. The Bible told her to pray for those who got on her nerves. Maybe, not in so many words, but she knew her flustered feelings wouldn't change the guy's behavior. She blew out a long breath. *Forgive me, God. Bless*

Justin. She gulped. *And the redhead.*

Okay, so maybe her heart didn't feel the silent prayer she'd sent upward, but it was the best she could do for now. She made her way back to the desk and flopped into the seat. The heart could be deceitful. Obedience was the key. God had proven that time and again.

Shaking away the thought, she focused on the letter the elder Frasure had given her to type. She glanced at the clock. Only two more hours to work, and then she'd be off for a three-day weekend.

She finished the letter, e-mailed it to Mr. Frasure for final approval, then checked the college website again to see if the grade for her education class had been posted. She sighed when the space remained blank. "Well, my professor has to post by Monday," she whispered as she scooped a pile of folders in her arms and headed to the filing cabinet.

The door to Justin Frasure's office opened, and the redhead walked out, shutting the door hard. Frustration, or more like fury, seemed to etch her brow and purse her lips as she nodded toward Megan and headed for the front door. Megan placed the last file in its appropriate place. She stood to her full height and flattened the wrinkles from her blue checkered skirt.

She rarely talked with Justin. It was Mr. Combs and Justin's father who seemed to need her assistance the most. But Mr. Combs was on a cruise with his wife, and the elder Frasure was with a client—a very attractive client who would probably be with him awhile. It had only taken a week for Megan to realize the acorn didn't fall far from the Frasure tree.

She exhaled a long breath. She had no choice but to remind Justin she wouldn't be in the office the next day. Glancing toward the door, Megan hoped his mood didn't mirror the client's.

Forcing herself to lift her chin in confidence, she knocked on the doorjamb, cleared her throat, then opened the door. The younger Frasure's head snapped up from whatever he was studying at his desk. His eyes flashed, ready for confrontation. She sucked in a breath, realizing she hadn't waited for him to invite her in.

Then his expression softened, and his entire body seemed to exhale. Megan swallowed and balled her fists at her sides, willing her legs to stay strong beneath her. The man was sinfully attractive. It wasn't fair.

She cleared her throat again. "Mr. Frasure?"

"I've told you to call me Justin." His voice, though deep as Mammoth Cave was long, whispered to her like a butterfly kiss on her cheek.

"I know." She nodded as she reminded her brain to continue to send the message to her legs to stay upright. "But you're my boss, and I feel it's appropriate. . ."

His lips curved up ever so slightly on the left side, as if he found her determination for propriety, or possibly her discomfort at being in his office, somewhat humorous. "All right, Ms. McKinney. How can I help you?"

"I just wanted to remind you I will not be at work tomorrow."

A shadow fell across his face, and he looked down at his desk. "I'd forgotten." He picked up his iPhone from the desk and punched something into it. He looked at her again. "I remember now. You asked for a personal day. Do you mind my being nosy about it?"

Megan shook her head. "Not at all. I'm going on a canoeing field trip with my sister's sixth-grade class. I went with her last year. It's a lot of fun. The water is calm, practically unmoving, or so it seems, and only waist-high in most areas. We all have to wear life jackets the entire time, so it's very safe for the students. It has to be. Her school takes eighty students each day with only eight or nine chaperones. But, it's. . ." She clasped her hands in front of her waist as she realized she'd become quite animated in her description of the trip. She cleared her throat. "It's a lot of fun."

A full smile curved his lips. "Sounds like it." He leaned back in his chair. "I haven't been in a canoe in years."

"It's nice." She took a step back from his door then lifted her hand in a hesitant wave. She had no idea why the man made her so nervous. "I'll—I'll see you Monday."

"Okay."

Unclenching her fists, she rubbed her clammy hands together.

"Hey, Megan."

She turned at Justin's voice, realizing that may have been the first time she'd heard him say her given name. If only his voice wasn't as enticing as his looks. The man had been entirely too well formed in his mother's womb. "Yes?"

"Your blue outfit really accentuates your eyes."

He looked away from her and focused on his computer screen. For a moment, Megan felt glued to the carpet. She stared at Justin, her jaw dropping slightly. Blinking twice, she found her voice. "Thank you."

Once again having to force messages from her brain to her legs and feet, she turned on her heels and headed toward her desk. *Did he just hit on me? Was that flirting?*

She gnawed the inside of her cheek. He acted as if he'd merely stated facts, no emotions, no ulterior motives. She shut down her computer and grabbed her purse out of its cubby. *I'll believe it was simply an observation, a kind observation. Nothing more.*

Megan awakened early, made some coffee, then walked onto the back deck with her java, devotional, and Bible to enjoy the sunrise. She was a natural early riser, and God never ceased to amaze her with the beauty of His creation each new day. Having been raised on a small farm in southeastern Kentucky, she missed the smell of cattle, freshly cut grass, and honeysuckle blooming in spring. She missed watching the sunrise over trees and through hills.

And yet she and her sister, Marianna, had managed to find an apartment in the midst of Lexington that overlooked a well-groomed, nature-filled park. The sun rose just as spectacularly here. Megan sat in the black patio chair and took a sip of her cream-filled coffee. The warmth covered the slight nip of the early spring air, and she couldn't help but grin.

The back door opened, and Marianna stepped onto the deck. Her sister's long blond mane reminded Megan of the bird's nest they found every year in the dogwood tree in front of their parents' house. Though alike in so many other ways, Marianna had never learned to appreciate the glory of a sunrise in the morning. Megan met God in the morning. Marianna preferred the night.

Megan waved to her sister, younger by three short minutes. "You're up early."

Marianna groaned as she flopped into the chair beside Megan. She folded her legs up onto the seat, wrapped her arms around her calves, and dropped her chin on her knees.

Megan laughed. "Happy birthday, sis."

Marianna wrinkled her nose and grinned. "Happy birthday to you, too. What a great way to spend our twenty-fourth birthday—in a canoe with a bunch of sixth graders."

"Are you kidding?" Megan nudged her twin sister's arm. "This trip is a blast."

Marianna grabbed Megan's coffee cup off the patio table and took a sip.

"Hey!" Megan grabbed it back from her. "I don't want your cooties in my coffee. I'm telling the teacher."

Marianna rolled her eyes. "I am one of the teachers. We'll have a lot of fussing and tattling today. They're eleven- and twelve-year-olds, you know."

"Oh I know." Megan nodded. "And you love every minute of it."

Marianna started to grin, but a yawn took over, and she swiped her eye with the back of her hand. "You're going to love teaching, too. Did you get your grade back yet?"

"Not yet." Megan stared out over the park, so peaceful and still. Only an occasional bird chirped. A squirrel raced from one tree to the next. She knew God wanted her to use the musical talent He'd given her. She'd always assumed it would be through contemporary Christian music, but when she'd had the opportunity to work with her twin in the school system over the last year, Megan realized she wanted to teach children as well.

Marianna dropped her legs out of the chair then wrapped her hands around her bare arms. "It is absolutely freezing out here. I'm going in." She hopped up, stepped through the door, and looked back at Megan. "First dibs on the shower."

Megan shook her head and waved her hand through the air. "You always take a shower first, and you always use all the hot water, too."

"You know what they say: the early bird gets the worm."

"I got up a full hour before you."

"But you sit out here on the deck, enjoying the nippy fifty-degree weather."

Megan laughed. "Go get your shower, and save me some water."

Marianna shut the door, and Megan turned back toward the park. She picked up her Bible and turned to the scripture she'd read every birthday since she was sixteen. Her Sunday school teacher had insisted the teens memorize it. She opened to Jeremiah, *"For I know the plans I have for you,"* declares the Lord, *"plans to prosper you and not to harm you, plans to give you hope and a future."*

She shut her Bible and sucked in a long breath. That year had changed her life. Having gone to church every Sunday with one of her neighborhood friends, she'd accepted Jesus into her heart when she was fourteen, and

He was her Savior, her Redeemer from sin. Accepting Him was the best choice she'd ever made.

But sixteen? Sixteen was a year she'd never forget. It changed how she looked at things. What she thought. What she felt. God was still working on her heart and mind, getting her through the hurt and confusion.

She closed her eyes and whispered into the breeze. "You've brought me so far, precious Jesus. Keep loving me. Keep molding me. I am Your clay."

The phone rang inside the apartment. Megan opened her eyes and spied one of the elderly neighbors as he puttered down the sidewalk, his small poodle on a leash in front of him. The phone rang again. Megan gripped the arms of the chair.

Marianna was in the shower and wouldn't be able to answer it. Megan knew who it was. She knew she should answer it. God would want her to answer it.

Pushing herself away from the chair, she walked toward the rings. Even if everyone she knew would agree with her right to ignore the call, Megan would obey the Spirit.

She'd obey, and maybe one day her heart would follow her actions. She walked through the door and glanced at the caller ID. Just who she'd expected. Sucking in a breath, she grabbed the phone off the receiver. "Hello, Mom."

Chapter 2

*No one ever choked to
death swallowing his pride.*
HARVEY MACKAY

Gripping the sides of the canoe, Colt Baker jerked his head around at the sound of a bloodcurdling scream. What in the world would be causing such a ruckus?

In an obvious attempt to get the canoe turned around, his niece paddled her oar feverishly on the right side. "Colt, come on. Something's gotta be wrong. Looks like Miss Megan, and she's got Stephanie with her."

In just a few strong strokes of his paddle, Colt maneuvered them around, and he and Hadley headed back toward the still squealing teacher. This couldn't be good. Stephanie was impulsive and often too physical. She showed little affection and frustrated easily. But Hadley had a soft spot for the autistic child, and she was often able to settle the girl down.

As they drew closer, Colt spied the young, blond-haired teacher in the back of the canoe holding Stephanie tightly against her chest. To his surprise, Stephanie wasn't fighting the teacher, but both of their paddles had fallen into the creek. Several canoes filled with students floated around them, but no one tried to hand the paddles to the twosome.

17

"What's going on?" Hadley yelled before Colt had the chance.

"A snake's in their canoe," one of the boys said. Colt remembered the kid had been one of the "tough" guys in Hadley's class, always bragging, sometimes bullying. He sure looked scared out of his mind over a snake—which Colt had to admit was a good thing. It could be a cottonmouth that found its way into the canoe, and if it struck one of them, they'd have a hard time getting the victim to a hospital quick enough.

Colt looked back at the teacher and Stephanie, realizing it wasn't the teacher howling; it was his niece's young friend. He guided their canoe closer to the boys. "Hadley, I want you to hop in their canoe. I'll go get the snake."

The smaller boy reached out to take Hadley's hand. His eyes were as big as his fists, and the poor guy was drenched from head to toe, probably having "accidentally" fallen into the water as many of the students had.

"No, Uncle Colt." Hadley shook her head and pushed the boy's hand away. "Stephanie's about to lose it. You need me over there to calm her down."

"Her teacher can calm her down."

"That's not our teacher. That's Ms. McKinney's sister. Stephanie probably don't know her at all."

Colt looked at the woman who seemed to be gripping Stephanie so tightly the child was likely losing oxygen. He could see the woman was saying something in Stephanie's ear, probably trying to calm the girl. But fear wrapped Stephanie's expression, and her hands trembled. At any moment, the girl could snap and try to jump out of the canoe, possibly making the snake strike her or the woman. "Okay, but you will stay as far away from the snake as possible, you hear?"

Hadley nodded. " 'Kay."

"I'm in front." Colt grabbed ahold of the boys' canoe and pushed his way toward the front while Hadley weeded her way around him. With as few strokes as possible, they paddled toward the canoe. Colt knew he couldn't call out to the woman that they were there to help. Stephanie might panic. Instead, he sat up as tall as he could to see inside the canoe. Relief washed through him when he saw the reptile.

"Not poisonous," he whispered to Hadley. He could almost feel his niece's sigh of relief behind him. "Big black snake. Must've got in before we started."

"Thank the Lord."

Colt grinned at the sound of true thanksgiving in Hadley's voice. "Once we get just a tad closer, on my three, you grab the side of their canoe, and I'll grab the snake and hop out."

Silently they drifted a few feet closer. He turned and nodded to Hadley. He lifted one finger. Two fingers. "And three!"

In one swift motion, he jumped up, grabbed the black snake with his hand around the head, his pointer finger pressed against its bottom jaw and his thumb firm against its top, and then jumped into the water with it. The everybit-as-healthy-as-he-expected snake's body fought to take flight along the water, but Colt tightened his hold. If he released the critter, the kiddos would freak, and he'd have a string of flipped canoes and screaming twelve-year-olds to deal with.

He trudged through the waist-high water to the muddy bank. Glad he'd worn his work boots, he dug the strong heels into the mixture of mud and rocks until he'd made his way out of the water. After walking several yards away from the students, he released the snake into a grassy area, watching as it slithered through the field.

He wiped his brow with the back of a saturated sleeve. "Poor feller probably hadn't expected so much activity today. All he'd done was take a nap in an unused canoe."

He turned around and saw that Stephanie had climbed into the canoe behind Hadley. She held tight around Hadley's waist, her face, even her glasses, pressed against his niece's back. "Uncle Colt," she hollered. "I'm going to take Stephanie back to the starting spot. You come back with Miss Megan."

Colt looked at the woman sitting alone in the canoe. Her already pale complexion had drained of all color. Shocking blue eyes peered at him with intense emotion. He walked back to the bank and into the water. Without a word, he pulled the canoe over to the side and got in behind the frightened woman.

He wanted to pat her shoulder to assure her everything was all right but didn't want to startle her with his soaking wet hands. She was as spooked as a wild buck, but she was also as pretty as a field full of daisies. His insecurities flared like he was in the sixth grade all over again.

"It'll be all right." He managed to speak the four words as he paddled back toward the starting point. The woman Hadley had called Megan didn't say anything the entire ride. He couldn't help but wonder why Stephanie had been in the canoe with her to begin with. Stephanie often had a resource teacher with her on field trips. In his thinking, the canoe trip would warrant a teacher coming specifically for Stephanie. It seemed odd the science teacher's sister would be the one taking care of an autistic child.

Not that this Megan had done anything wrong. By all appearances, she seemed to have kept Stephanie as calm as could be expected. The more he thought about it, the more surprised he was that Stephanie had gotten into the canoe with Megan at all. Usually she would only venture with someone she knew well.

He paddled up the concrete bank, and Hadley's science teacher, Ms. McKinney, helped her sister out of the canoe. Their resemblance was striking.

Ms. McKinney wrapped her arms around her sister. "Oh Megan, I can't believe that happened."

"How's Stephanie?"

Colt looked at Megan. The concern in her tone was evident.

"She's fine. Are you okay?"

"I'm fine. I knew it wasn't poisonous. I just couldn't get Stephanie to settle down."

The frustration in her voice made him want to defend her. "Normally a special needs assistant or a chaperone goes with Stephanie." He glared at Hadley's teacher, even though his words were intended for Megan. "Don't be upset with yourself. You shouldn't have been in that situation. She should have gone with someone she knows."

"I was her chaperone."

Colt looked at the woman who hadn't uttered a peep the

full thirty minutes he'd paddled upstream. She crossed her arms in front of her chest and glared at him. "I thank you for helping me. I needed it. But I do know Stephanie. Her mother asked me to be her chaperone today. Please do not insinuate my sister is not doing her job."

Before Colt could respond, the woman stomped toward the restroom facility. He looked at Hadley's science teacher. Embarrassment swelled in his gut and tightened his throat.

She clasped her hands in front of her. "I can assure you, Mr. Baker, I would never do anything to put a child in danger. My sister has been Stephanie's music teacher this entire school year. They are actually very close. The snake was more than Stephanie is used to handling, and—"

Colt raised his hand. "When a man's in the wrong, he should swallow his pride and 'fess up. I assumed something without knowing the facts. I'm sorry."

Ms. McKinney's cheeks tinted pink, and she nodded. "Thank you." She pointed toward the picnic area. "Hadley and Stephanie are already eating lunch if you'd like to join them."

"I think I will." Though he'd already eaten his fill of humble pie, Colt sauntered toward his truck, took his lunch cooler out of the back, then made his way to Hadley. It wasn't his fault he'd thought Stephanie didn't know the teacher's sister. Hadley hadn't known. It was an honest mistake, and he took pride in being a guardian who cared about the well-being of his niece and her friends.

He sighed. That didn't make him feel better. He pulled the wet T-shirt away from his chest, but once released, it clung to his frame again. Being wet didn't help either. But at least the sun shined bright and warm. It wouldn't be long before he dried.

He sat beside Hadley and opened his lunch. "How are you doing?"

Hadley smiled at Stephanie, exposing deep dimples in both cheeks. "Much better now."

"Hi, Colt," Stephanie said as she dipped her chin so she could peer at him above the rim of her glasses.

Colt lifted his fist, and Stephanie knuckle-bumped it with her own. She giggled then wrapped both hands around her sandwich.

"How are you doing, Stephanie? You having fun?"

"There was a snake, Colt." Stephanie's thick, dark eyebrows rose, the right higher than the left.

Hadley put her hand on Stephanie's shoulder. "Yep, but it's gone now. Right?"

"Right!" Stephanie waved her right arm in an exaggerated motion. "All gone."

Pride swelled in his heart for his niece. The sandyhaired, green-eyed cutie was hardly bigger than a fencepost, but her heart was as big as a barn. And she had spunk and fight in her. The girl handled a horse better than most men. And yet her heart was as tender as a mare's for her foal. He loved the girl with every breath in him.

Colt took a bite of his sandwich. Out of the corner of his eye, he saw Ms. McKinney's sister exit the restroom. He could tell by the damp strands of hair around her face and neck that she'd washed up. He wanted to talk to her, to apologize for accusing her sister. Instead, he watched as she sat at a far table with Ms. McKinney and several teachers.

She and her sister sat side by side on a bench that faced him. He could tell they were identical twins—both with light skin, blue eyes, and long blond hair, but Megan had a deeper dimple in her left cheek when she smiled, and her eyebrows seemed to be a shade darker.

"Ms. Megan's awesome." Stephanie's words interrupted Colt's thoughts.

"She's a good piano teacher?" Hadley asked.

"Miss Megan's the best. She's awesome."

"I'd like to learn piano someday," Hadley said. "Maybe you could show me."

Stephanie moved her fingers through the air like she was playing the instrument. "You go like this."

Colt smiled as Hadley laughed and mimicked Stephanie's motions. Maybe it wouldn't be such a bad idea for Hadley to start taking piano lessons. His niece loved to sing, and it was often too quiet in their big family farmhouse with only the two of them.

He gathered up his, Hadley's, and Stephanie's garbage and headed toward the trash can. It would give him an excuse to talk to Megan and apologize to her. As he made his way toward the picnic table, one of the teachers stood up and motioned for the students' attention.

"When you can hear my voice clap once."

A clap sounded from the teachers and many of the students.

"Clap twice," she added.

This time almost all the students clapped twice and faced her. In a matter of seconds, the entire picnic area grew silent with all sixth-grade faces staring at their teacher.

The woman raised her hands in the air. "Today is a very special day. It's Ms. McKinney and her sister, Megan's, birthday. Let's sing happy birthday to them."

The students cheered and then began the birthday chorus. The sisters were petite enough that a couple of the girls walked toward their science teacher and her sister and wrapped an arm around their shoulders with ease.

Once the song ended, the students and teachers made their way out to the open area for a few games. Megan stayed at the picnic table, cleaning up the mess. Colt walked to her and grabbed some items off the table.

"I'm sorry for my assumption."

Megan jumped and placed her hand on her chest.

Heat warmed Colt's cheeks. "Sorry. I guess I should have let you know I was here."

Megan smiled, exposing the deep dimple on the left side. "I think I'm still a little jumpy about the snake." She pitched several wrappers into the trash. "It's okay. I was a bit shaken for Stephanie." She turned and peered into his eyes. "I really am grateful you helped us. I don't know how I would have gotten her to calm down."

"It was nothing." His stomach knotted up talking to her. It had been a long time since he'd felt anxious talking to a woman. He cleared his throat. "Well, Stephanie's been bragging about you being a terrific piano teacher."

Megan smiled again. This time he noted the beautiful white teeth and a twinkle in her eyes. "She teaches me more than I teach her, and that's the truth. Music is her gift."

Colt rubbed his hands against his pants then clasped them together. "I was wondering if you'd be interested in

25

giving lessons to my niece, Hadley. She's the one who got Stephanie out of the canoe."

"I know who Hadley is. I help with my sister's class every chance I get. I'd love to give her lessons." Megan reached into a side pocket on her lunch bag and pulled out a card.

Colt raised his eyebrows. "You keep business cards on you? Even when canoeing?"

She shrugged and grinned. "You never know when you'll need them."

Colt laughed out loud as he flicked the card. "I suppose you're right." He put the card in the front pocket of his jeans. "I'll give you a call this week."

"I'll look forward to it."

He watched as she walked toward the open area to join the students and teachers in their game. He was the one who could hardly wait.

Chapter 3

No battle plan survives
contact with the enemy.
Colin Powell

A horn blew from outside the apartment. The front door swung open. "You're being kidnapped!"

Megan jumped up from the couch and smacked her hand against her chest. "Amber! You scared the life out of me. What are you talking about?"

Marianna ran down the hall and into the living room. "What's going on?"

Another friend, Julie, pushed past the petite brunette. She wore an orange and red party hat on top of her short dark curls. She blew a whistle that hung from her neck. "Amber already told you what's going on. You're being kidnapped. Get your shoes."

Amber raced to her and looped her arm around Megan's. Julie rushed to Marianna and grabbed her hand. "Let's go."

Still in a daze, Megan slipped on her flip-flops and allowed herself to be pulled out of the apartment. She gazed back at Marianna. "Grab a key."

With her sister's eyebrows still raised and her jaw dropped open, Marianna nodded and reached for her purse despite Julie's nudging to get out of the house.

Once shoved into the backseat of Amber's car, Megan looked at Marianna as she clicked her seat belt across her waist. "Did you know about this?"

Marianna shook her head. Amber and Julie slid into the driver's and passenger's seats and began a chorus of an off-key rendition of "Happy Birthday to You." As understanding dawned, Megan and Marianna laughed. Megan smacked the seat. "Of course."

"Should have known they'd do this," said Marianna.

Amber winked into the rearview mirror, and the twins joined the singing. When the chorus ended, Marianna chimed in with a new chorus about smelling like a monkey.

Megan shook her finger in front of Marianna's face. "I don't think so, little sister."

Marianna stopped and dipped her chin, zeroing in on Megan with a deadpan expression. "Really? You're still trying to call me 'little sister'?" She lifted up three fingers. "Three minutes is nothing."

"It's something on the birth certificate." She pointed to her chest. "Makes me the oldest. The more mature."

"Whatever. You sound really mature right now."

Julie twisted in the passenger's seat and flicked both of them in the knee.

"Ow!" they squealed in unison.

"I can't believe you two still fight over three minutes. Every year it's the same thing."

Megan shrugged. "She just can't stand that I'm older."

"Babies have more fun."

Amber interjected, "Well, we're all going to have fun tonight."

Megan grinned at her sister as she trailed her fingertips along her pinned-up hair. She glanced down at her clothes, thankful she'd chosen a matching shirt and pair of shorts after returning home from the canoe trip and taking a shower. "Julie, Amber, you two are crazy."

Marianna added, "You definitely surprised us."

Megan looked at her sister, who still hadn't taken a shower. A giggle welled up inside of Megan and spilled out. She pinched her nose. "What was that you said again? Something about *me* smelling like a monkey? I was worried about not having on any makeup, but at least I don't stink."

Marianna wrinkled her nose and shoved Megan with her elbow. Megan pushed her back then shifted away from her sister, rolled down the window, and stuck her head out.

Amber looked at them from the rearview mirror. "Now, now, birthday girls. Do I need to call your mother?"

Megan bit her lip as she rolled the window back up. The one conversation with Mom had been enough.

Julie turned in the passenger seat. "We couldn't let your birthdays pass without some kind of celebration."

"I hope we're not going anywhere where people will have to smell me," Marianna huffed. She glared at Megan with obviously feigned offense.

"No worries. We can sit outside." Amber pulled into the parking lot of Megan's favorite frozen yogurt shop.

Megan rubbed her stomach. "Orange Leaf! I hope they have fresh blackberry topping tonight."

"Since it's our birthday, I'm getting confetti cake yogurt." Marianna pinched her thumb and finger. "Maybe a smidgen of red velvet, too."

"Not me." Megan shook her head. "I'm getting my usual—coconut, pineapple, and pomegranate."

Marianna jumped out of the car. "I love this place. I don't care if I do stink. . . ."

Amber grabbed Marianna's arm. "Hold on, flash. Julie and I are buying you all's dessert."

Julie added, "Yeah. We know you're going on your annual birthday shopping spree with each other tomorrow, but we wanted to do something for you today."

Megan hugged Julie then Amber. "You two are the best. What a great way to end our birthday."

Marianna opened her arms. "Will you risk a hug from me, too?"

The friends laughed and shared a group hug. Megan had spent a good deal of the afternoon flustered over the incident with Stephanie and the snake. She was thankful for friends who knew just how to make her smile.

"Surprise!"

Megan opened one eye and glanced at the alarm clock on her nightstand. Seven was way too early to rise on a Saturday morning. Surely Amber and Julie hadn't come for a second birthday kidnapping.

She rolled over in bed and stretched her arms. She could hear someone talking to Marianna in the other room. She grimaced. Didn't sound like their friends.

"Wake up, Megan."

Her mother stood inside the door. The voice had sounded happy coming from her sister's room. Not so much now.

Megan blew out a sigh. "Hey, Mom."

Her mom forced a smile. Really, it was ridiculous. If the woman didn't want to spend time with her, it wouldn't break Megan's heart.

"I want to take you girls to breakfast. Maybe a little shopping."

Marianna wrapped arms around their mother from behind. Their mom's face lit up, and she laughed as she turned to give Marianna a hug.

"I love surprise visits," said Marianna.

Their mom patted her arm. "Me, too. Go get dressed."

Marianna ran off, and Megan heard the bathroom door shut. That was great. She'd have to wait half of forever for her sister to get out.

Her mom clapped her hands. The smile was gone from her face. "Let's go, Megan."

Megan pushed herself to a sitting position. She loved the morning. Maybe not this early on a Saturday. Especially after they'd spent a good deal of the night watching romantic comedies on the DVD player. Still, normally she liked an early morning wake-up call.

But not when it was her mother glaring at her from the bedroom door.

"I'm coming. Give me a second."

Her mom left the doorway. Within moments, she heard the coffeemaker brewing. She loved her mother. At least she tried to. But it was pretty obvious she didn't want to spend time with Megan as she did with Marianna.

That was fine. Don't feel obligated. Megan wasn't overly thrilled with the idea of spending her birthday fussing with her mom either.

Once Marianna finished, Megan took her turn in the bathroom. Within half an hour, they were ready and heading to breakfast. Marianna selected her favorite restaurant. It wasn't Megan's choice, but she hadn't expected her mom to ask. It didn't matter anyway.

Megan seated herself at the table across from Marianna and her mother. They busied themselves discussing wedding plans. Discontent niggled at Megan's heart. She wished her relationship with her mother wasn't strained. It hadn't always been this way.

Eight years ago everything changed, and though Megan knew in her mind she should forgive her mother, her heart felt otherwise.

Her mother hadn't forgiven her either. Hah. What a laugh! Megan had done nothing to warrant her mother's anger. Well, she did date the guy her mother didn't like. Truth be told, her mom had said she wasn't allowed to date Clint. But really, was that such an offense that would warrant eight years of a strained relationship? Talk about holding grudges.

"So, how are things going for you, Megan?"

Her mother's voice sounded tight, and she stuck her nose in the air. The pompous attitude may have worked in her office before she retired, but it didn't intimidate Megan.

"You know she finished her last class," said Marianna. "All she has left is student teaching."

Megan grinned at her sister. Ever the peacemaker

between her and their parents. "She's right. I can even student teach on the job if I'm hired."

"Really?" Her mother fluffed her short, red curls then adjusted the collar of her short-sleeved blouse.

"Yep. Maybe she'll get a job at my school." Marianna dipped her head. "Wouldn't that be great, Megan?"

It would be wonderful. She hoped she could work in the same building as her sister. She preferred the elementary students, but she wouldn't turn down a job at the middle school.

Her mother pursed her lips then focused again on Marianna. Though Megan enjoyed discussing wedding preparations with her sister, she had no inclination to make small talk with her mother. When she was younger, she'd tried to win her parents' affections again. After high school, she'd determined to seek God's approval.

If her parents wanted to reconcile, she'd be willing, but she wouldn't alter who she was to bow down to them.

Are you really willing to reconcile?

She shifted in her seat at the niggling of her spirit. God wanted her to forgive them, even without their request. And she tried. At least she wanted to try. But forgiveness didn't happen easily. Especially when it wasn't requested.

Megan twisted in her seat as she scanned the restaurant. Where was their waitress? They'd been here—she looked at her watch—a full ten minutes. She was ready to get this day done.

"In a hurry, Megan?" Her mother's sarcastic tone grated on her nerves.

As a matter of fact, this is not how I planned to spend my day. She bit the inside of her mouth, thankful she hadn't said the words aloud. "No. Just hungry."

Her mother studied her, and Megan determined not to look away from her scrutiny. A piece of her hoped to see a sliver of reconciliation, some sort of desire to make amends in her mother's gaze. As usual, it wasn't there.

Their waitress arrived, and Megan let out a long breath. She did wish things were different between them.

Megan pushed through the front door of the law office. After a mostly wonderful weekend, Monday had arrived faster than she'd hoped. The morning with her mother had been tiresome, but she and Marianna had shopped to exhaustion once she left. She'd purchased a couple of adorable outfits to start a school year—if she landed a position.

Sunday had also been filled to the brim with activities: Sunday school and church service, choir practice, and children's church in the evening. Going to work would provide her a bit of rest after such an eventful weekend.

"What in the world?" Her gaze took in the oversized arrangement of white daisies and pale pink roses. Her heartbeat sped up as she gently touched the satin bow wrapped around the neck of the clear vase. The last time she could remember receiving flowers was when she'd gone to her senior prom. *And as I recall, I picked those up myself since my date was just a friend.*

She bit her bottom lip as she pulled the card off the

prong. Who would have sent her flowers? Her mind raced with the possibilities. There was that new guy at church who had paid a lot of attention to her, but he also got her and Marianna mixed up often enough that she felt pretty sure he wouldn't have been investigative enough to find out where she worked. She grinned. He'd have probably put the wrong name on the front as well.

She read the single word written in black ink on the marbled white card. It was definitely her name written on the front.

It could have been her sister. She scrunched her nose. She doubted it would have been Marianna. Rent was due in less than a week, and her wedding was only a couple of months away.

A face popped into her mind. The guy from the canoe trip. What was his name? Colby? Cody? Colt.

That was it. Megan could tell the guy felt bad about accusing her sister of being incompetent as a teacher. He'd asked her about giving his niece piano lessons, and then on the trip back to the school, he seemed to search for things to say to her or Marianna. He probably sent flowers to her sister as well.

It was silly to keep guessing. She pulled back the envelope flap.

"Good morning, Megan." The senior Frasure's deep voice boomed through the room.

Megan sucked in her breath and placed the card against her chest. Either she'd become jumpy the last few days or people around her had grown bent to scare the life right out of her. "Good morning, Mr. Frasure."

He motioned toward the flowers. "Lovely arrangement. Must be from some young fellow who has his sights set on you."

Megan's cheeks warmed. Very few men had sought her out in a romantic way. She figured she was pretty enough. Marianna received her share of attention until her engagement with Kirk. But Megan wasn't interested in dates or boyfriends. And she must have put off some kind of antiman vibe, because she hadn't gotten any offers in a long time.

"So, who're they from?"

"I don't—"

Mr. Frasure opened his hand to stop her. "Sorry, Megan. That's none of my business." He pointed toward his office door. "I need you to get your notepad. I have a couple of letters that need to go out first thing this morning."

Megan bit back a sigh as she put the card on her desk and scooped up her notebook. The senior Mr. Frasure had to be the only businessman in the United States who still wanted his secretary to shorthand a letter before it was typed. Mr. Combs and the younger Frasure communicated with her almost solely through e-mail messages, an occasional phone call, or even dictation.

She grabbed a pen from the tray and started to follow him to his office.

He stopped midstep and turned toward her. She bumped into him, gasped, and jumped a few steps back. "I'm so sorry, Mr. Frasure. I didn't expect you to stop."

He waved away her apology. "Not a problem. While I get settled, run into the conference room and get me a cup of coffee."

Megan nodded, placed her pad and pen on a seat, and walked to the room the lawyers used for talking to clients and other attorneys. She measured the coffee, filled the filter, and poured two bottles of water into the pot.

While it brewed, she straightened the eight cushioned, brown, leather chairs sitting around a long, rectangular mahogany table. Various fake plants sat in small and large pots around the perimeter of the plain room. The only other furniture in the room was an oversized, ornate bookshelf that held more legal manuals and books than seemed necessary to exist. Her bosses seemed to have every legal reference book written, except a Holy Bible—the most important reference of all.

Not that it surprised her. The senior Mr. Frasure only dated women who were twenty years or more his junior, and he never dated the same woman longer than six months. At least that's what the previous secretary told her, and so far Megan had seen two young women come and go from his life. Mr. Combs was married and seemed to be happy enough, but he spent every opportunity given to him on the golf course. And the junior Frasure—Justin's reputation preceded him, as well as the steady flow of beauties who continually sought his expertise.

Megan huffed as she picked up the coffeepot and poured the hot brew into an oversized ceramic mug. She needed to be a godly witness to the men she worked for. She scrunched her nose. Even if they were the kind of men who turned her stomach.

She headed back toward Mr. Frasure's office. She tripped on the plush carpet when she spied her younger boss inspecting the paperweight on her desk. Breathing a sigh of relief that the coffee hadn't spilled; she straightened her shoulders and lifted her chin before Justin realized she was in the room.

She cleared her throat. "Hello, Mr. Frasure."

He gazed at her and smiled. He looked amazing in a pinstriped charcoal suit and deep red satin tie. His eyes, so dark and mysterious, beguiled her like the spider drew the fly. Once caught in the web, the fly could never escape, and more than once since she'd started working here, Megan feared falling for the handsome lawyer.

He pointed to the paperweight she'd received the first week she and Marianna visited the church a year ago. "Do you go to church here?"

She nodded.

"Do you like it?"

She nodded again. Her throat seemed to have filled with cotton, and her mind shifted to blank. She couldn't seem to get words of any kind to form.

His eyes danced with humor, and she would have sworn he bit the inside of his cheek to keep from laughing at her. "Do they have Bible studies?"

He lifted his hand before she could nod again. "Wait. That's another yes or no question. I'm a lawyer. I should know how to interrogate people better."

He cleared his throat as he straightened his shoulders. "Ms. McKinney, on which night of the week does this church"—he pointed at the paperweight again—"have a Bible study that I could attend?"

He winked, and Megan felt her legs turn to rubber,

as they seemed to have a habit of doing in his presence. Swallowing, she forced her mind and mouth to work together at the same time. "I go to Bible study on Thursdays."

"Is it a Bible study I could attend?"

She shrugged. "There are about fifteen of us. It's a singles' class."

"Perfect. What time does it start?"

Megan furrowed her brow. She wanted to be a witness to her bosses, but she really didn't want any of them joining her Bible study. She allowed herself to be vulnerable with her group. They were close, and each of them was seeking God's will with their whole heart, not looking for their next date.

Conviction welled in her spirit. How could she be so arrogant? So pompous? It wasn't *her* group. It's was God's group. *Forgive me, Lord. Justin wants to learn more about You, and I'm being selfish. About a Bible study group!*

She looked into his eyes. He seemed genuinely interested to know more. Warmth filled her, and she felt a smile lift her lips. "We meet at seven. It would be wonderful if you could go."

"Great. I believe I will." He placed the paperweight back on her desk then started toward his office. He turned toward her again. "Your flowers are pretty. Who are they from?"

"I still haven't had a chance to read the card."

"Well, read it." He opened his office door, stepped inside, then shut it behind him.

Megan glanced at the senior Frasure's office door. Any

minute he'd be stomping down the hall looking for her. *This will only take a second.*

Plucking the card once again off the prong, Megan smiled as excitement welled within her. She opened the envelope flap and pulled out the card. Her jaw dropped. Only two words were written on the card. "Happy Birthday."

She swallowed the knot in her throat and the fear that clenched her heart. Why would this man send her flowers? What were his intentions? His motives? His. . . She blinked at the questions swirling through her mind. She gazed at her youngest boss's office door as she spoke the last word on the card. "Justin."

Chapter 4

Temptation is like a knife that may either cut the meat or the throat of a man; it may be his food or his poison, his exercise or his destruction.
JOHN OWEN

Justin walked into the small fitness center and looked up at the clock above the mirror-covered wall. He had thirty minutes before his buddy, Kirk, arrived to lift weights. Plenty of time to run three miles on the treadmill.

He nodded to the dark-haired desk attendant as he shoved his iPhone and keys into a wooden cubby. The large gym he'd used since college had metal lockers with combination locks. He looked around the small open facility. There was no need for locks here. He could see the cubbies from anyplace in the building.

He stepped onto a treadmill, put in his earphones, then plugged them in so he could watch the Reds' game on the TV in front of him while he ran. Releasing a sigh, he realized he'd miss the familiarity of his old gym, but he wanted to help Kirk get back into a workout routine, and his friend felt uncomfortable in the larger facility. Justin selected a challenging course of speed and inclines, and soon lost himself in the rhythm of the workout.

The changes he'd made in his life proved more difficult than he'd expected. But God knew that, and Kirk had told him his faith wouldn't be without challenges.

His mind drifted to his meeting with Sophia the week before. She was a temptation to him. And she knew it.

Memories of dates they'd spent together poured into his mind, and he pushed the button to speed up his run. He'd pushed himself at the gym a lot since he'd given his life to Christ two months ago. God wanted to be first in his life, but women were his weakness.

And two months was a long time.

He yanked the earplugs out and pumped his fists harder in sync with the run. Staring up at the ceiling, he asked God for the strength to think of something else. Anything else.

Work. He was busy at work. Two couples were coming into the office the next day to sign adoption papers. One of the couples had been foster parents to their son for three years. Tomorrow they would finally become his legal parents. He and Megan had spent hours combing through the documents to ensure the signing would take place without a hitch.

The three miles complete, he slowed his pace to a fast walk. He wiped the sweat off his forehead with the back of his hand. Thinking of Megan was dangerous territory, too.

There was something about her. She was pretty but not gorgeous like most of the women he noticed. Still, she invaded his thoughts at the oddest moments. She was easy to be around with her sense of propriety and efficiency at work. She didn't bat her eyes or flip her hair over her shoulder like most of the women he knew. She intrigued him. Her faith was apparent in more than just the paperweight on her desk.

He turned off the treadmill and stepped down. He took a long swig of water and tossed the empty bottle in a nearby trash can. He didn't need to think about Megan either.

"I don't believe we've met."

A soft hand touched his elbow, and Justin flinched. He looked at the woman and inwardly sighed. Tight black and pink fitness getup. Legs as long as his. Silky dark hair pulled in a ponytail. Emerald green eyes. *God, is this some kind of test?*

He forced a smile and extended his hand. "Justin. I just joined."

Her nails tickled his wrist before she shook his hand. "Brandy." She pointed to the logo on her too-tight shirt. "If you ever need anything, you just let me know. I work Tuesdays and Thursdays."

Justin nodded, trying to act uninterested. The woman smelled delicious, nothing like a person who worked at a fitness club.

She lingered, apparently waiting for his response. He wished he still stood close to the treadmill. He could have stepped back on as if starting the second half of his workout.

The front door swung open, and Kirk walked inside. He waved to Justin, blew out an exaggerated breath, and shoved his keys in a cubby. "Sorry I'm late, man. Traffic was a killer."

Justin sent up a silent prayer of thanks, nodded to Brandy, then headed toward his friend. "Perfect timing."

Kirk squinted his eyes. "What's going on?"

Justin tilted his head to motion behind him. Kirk looked past him, and Justin punched him in the arm. "Don't look."

Kirk gaped back at him. "Brandy hit on you?" He shook his head. "Man, she is so hot."

"What would your fiancée say if she heard you say that?"

"She'd say, 'Man, she *is* hot.'"

Justin growled as he made his way to an open weight bench. Kirk followed behind him. "Seriously, I want to trade temptations."

Justin added weight to the bar then lay back on the bench. "How can you even begin to compare your addiction to mine? Video games don't waltz up to you after a workout and start up a conversation."

"Are you kidding? Every time I walk past the electronics section of a store or even turn on my computer, a little voice in my head says, 'Come on, just one game.'" He shrugged, tapped his temples with his fingertips, and lifted his eyebrows. "It's evil."

Justin laughed at Kirk's dramatics. "Nowhere near the same as a live person."

"I don't know about that. Mine's even in my house."

Justin let out a long breath. "I suppose you're right. Temptation is temptation, and yours is no less than mine."

Kirk sobered. "But I do have a big support system. God. Marianna. My family. My Bible study group."

"I have you and God."

"You could join my study."

Justin wrinkled his nose and shook his head. He'd tried to visit Kirk's church once, but something just seemed off to him. Maybe it was the fact he'd dated the preacher's wife in high school. Sure, it had been thirteen years, but it still felt weird.

"Yesterday you mentioned a Bible study you planned to try out."

"They meet tonight."

"You going?"

"I think so. My secretary goes there, and. . ." Justin laughed when Kirk ducked his chin and peered at him. He lifted his hands in surrender. "I promise it's on the up and up."

"What church is it?"

Justin told him the name, and Kirk nodded. "That's where Marianna used to go. She switched to my church when we got engaged. Her sister still attends, and she loves their Bible study."

"That's great." Justin patted the top of the bar. "But if we don't start working, I'm not going to make it."

Kirk growled. It had only been a few months since Justin reconnected with his high school sweetheart. But Justin knew as soon as Kirk muttered, "I do," his friend would give up the gym membership.

"Marianna had better appreciate all I'm doing for her."

Justin switched places with Kirk and stood behind the bar to spot while Kirk completed his reps. "When am I going to get to meet this girl?"

"Soon. She's been nuts teaching middle school and planning the wedding. But she's anxious to meet you."

"I'll try not to steal her away."

"Not funny, man."

Justin laughed as Kirk lay back against the bench and frowned. "You used to love to work out in high school. Remember baseball conditioning?"

Kirk grimaced as he pushed the bar up until his arms were straight. He dropped it onto the bar. "That was before I discovered how delicious pastries and sodas are. I've changed quite a bit since high school."

Justin nodded. His friend was not the same guy he'd known during his teen years, and Justin was thankful he'd run into the metamorphosed version.

Justin rubbed his hands together to ensure his palms weren't as damp as he feared. Normally he was a man of stoic confidence, one people sought out for assistance and assurance. But he was out of his natural element.

Standing outside the megachurch's front door, he realized he had no idea where the Bible study would be located in such a massive building. He'd visited here once before, years ago, with a woman who'd needed his assistance through a nasty divorce. He flinched at the overpowering memory of his motive for attending church with her. She was yet another woman he needed to seek out to ask forgiveness.

Sophia had taken his apology just as he'd anticipated she would. The gorgeous redhead walked into his office assuming he wanted to start up their relationship again, but when she'd learned he only wanted to apologize, she'd flown into a rage.

Her nostrils flared as she pierced her cool blue eyes into him. "You called me over here for what?"

He'd tried to explain again he'd accepted Jesus into his heart, and though he didn't deserve her forgiveness, he wanted to apologize for the way he'd treated her.

She'd jumped to her feet. "Don't flatter yourself, Justin." The anger that lit her eyes shifted to one of seduction as she placed her hands on his desk and leaned toward him. "I make my own choices." She leaned closer to him and raked one hand through his hair.

Shivers raced through him at the light scratch of her fingernails, and he forced himself to stare only into her eyes. She was a temptation to him, and she knew it.

He'd cleared his throat and forced his gaze away from hers. "I just wanted to apologize. I won't bother you anymore."

She'd stood there for what was probably only a few seconds more but seemed like an eternity. He didn't want what he'd had with Sophia, and too many other women. He wanted God's peace and contentment in his life, not just momentary satisfaction.

Snapping back to reality, he reached for the church's door handle then hesitated. *You've changed me, God, and yet I still feel as if I'm not good enough to walk into Your house.*

"You're not, but I am."

He pulled open the door and walked inside, remembering his dad's words that the church walls would fall in if he stepped inside one. Justin shared the sentiment until he'd reconnected with Kirk. His friend led him to the Lord and assured him the walls should fall in on everyone.

A welcome desk sat to his right, but no one was in the lobby. Heavy oak doors he remembered led to the sanctuary were closed in front of him. Long halls extended on his right and left as well as more entrances to the worship area and stairs that led to the balcony.

He looked around for some kind of poster or map. But he didn't even know where the class met. His thumb rubbed the hard new leather of his Bible. He gritted his teeth. He could have planned this better. Asked Megan how to get to the class or if she'd meet him in the lobby. Aggravation swelled in his chest, and he turned and headed for the door.

Megan opened it and gasped when they made eye contact. "You came?"

Embarrassment warmed his neck and cheeks. What was wrong with him? He hadn't acted this way since he was in middle school. He cleared his throat and nodded. "I did."

He watched as she bit her bottom lip. He couldn't read her expression. Was she simply surprised? A little apprehensive? Or upset? An ache twisted his stomach at the idea she wouldn't have wanted him to join her class. He knew she was a Christian. Her faith was evident, and he'd hoped her Bible study would teach him more about his faith.

Her lips curved into a genuine smile, and the heaviness in his gut lightened. She motioned to him. "Come on. We'll go together."

He fell into step beside her. His gaze took in the various children's paintings of crosses and flowers covering the walls. The sign on the first door was labeled nursery, then toddlers, then twos, all going up chronologically. A bulletin board was covered with pictures of children hunting Easter eggs in the back of the church's property.

One particular picture caught his eye. It was of Megan sitting on the ground with her legs stretched in front of her. She had a basket filled with candy between her legs. Two boys and a girl sat around her, pillaging through the goods. But Megan was looking up, smiling at the camera with her right cheek twice its normal size, obviously stuffed with candy. She looked so happy and carefree and innocent. It yanked at his heart.

"I'm glad you came."

Justin snapped from his reverie. Megan's voice was softer than usual, and for a moment, he wondered if she felt obligated to say it. Then she looked up at him, and his heartbeat sped at the fullness of her smile.

He gripped the Bible tighter in his hand. "I've been looking forward to it." He opened his arms wide. "This is all so new to me, but I know I need to find a church."

Megan shifted her weight and studied him. Under her intense scrutiny, he had to resist the urge to adjust his polo's collar. Finally, she nodded. "I think you'll like our group. We have a lot of fun together."

She opened the door, and Justin followed her inside. The room was bigger than he'd expected. According to the sign on the door, it normally housed eight-year-olds. He assumed the sign was accurate by the children's materials lining the walls. Metal chairs were set up in a circle.

Justin looked around at the women in the room. One slightly plump, shorter lady with flaming red hair and bright pink glasses. Another woman, average-length blond hair, crooked teeth, possibly blue eyes, just kind of plain. There was another woman with highlighted brown hair. She was already seated, but if Justin guessed right, and he usually did, he'd say she was probably a little taller than average, five feet seven or five feet eight.

Megan interrupted his analysis. "Justin, this is Kat. She's our discussion leader this week."

Justin took in the dark-haired woman. Deep brown eyes. Small button nose. And lips that would make Angelina Jolie envious.

Kat extended her hand. "We're glad to have you."

Before Justin could respond, voices sounded from the doorway. Justin looked as a tall brunette and a strawberry blond walked in and took seats beside each other.

He swallowed the knot in his throat as he glanced around the seven women in the room. *God, is this some kind of joke?*

He cleared his throat and addressed Megan. "Is this a girls' Bible study?"

Megan narrowed her eyelids. "Are you looking for a girls' only Bible study?"

The insinuation behind the question stung, but he knew his reputation preceded him. It was one of the reasons he'd determined to apologize to the women he'd treated as little more than momentary amusement. The truth of the reputation was why he needed to drown himself in God's Word. He stared into her eyes, hoping she'd see the truth. "No. I'm not."

Kat said, "I'm sorry about this, Justin. The guys had a makeup baseball game tonight. Their Tuesday night game was rained out."

Justin cocked his head. "Baseball?"

Kat nodded. "Yep. Started two weeks ago. They could use a few players."

Justin opened his mouth to offer to play. It had been four years since his last college game. He missed it something fierce.

"Maybe Justin will play. He's really good. Played in college."

Megan's comment stunned him. It was the first time he'd heard her call him by his given name, and he couldn't imagine how she knew he'd played in college.

Kat's expression brightened. "You did?"

He nodded but looked back at Megan. "How did you know that?"

"Your picture's on your dad's wall."

He pursed his lips. He'd forgotten. For some reason he kind of hoped she'd known because she wanted to know, not because the picture was right in front of her face. He shook his head. He didn't need to be thinking like that. He was avoiding his temptation.

Kat smiled. "Terrific. I know they'd love to have you." She clapped. "But for tonight, it'll just be you and us girls."

Justin glanced around the room once again. Just what he needed to encourage his faith. A Bible study filled with a bunch of women.

Chapter 5

*Nobody, who has not been in the interior of a family, can
say what the difficulties of any individual of that family may be.*
JANE AUSTEN

Megan twisted the wire around the tulle pew bow. She stuck her hand through each loop and twisted the material into a shape Marianna wanted. Once satisfied, she handed it to Marianna to attach the silk yellow Asiatic lilies, orange Gerberas, baby's breath, and deep red ribbon. Her sister's wedding color choices were bolder than Megan would have selected, but she had no doubt her sister would pull off one of the most beautiful celebrations she'd ever seen.

Megan clenched and unclenched her fists then wiggled her fingers to relieve the stiffness. "How many more?"

Marianna pointed to each as she counted. She wrinkled her nose as her lips spread into a sheepish grin. "Only thirty-five."

Megan huffed as she let her head fall against the back of the chair. "There is no way we'll finish all these today."

"I know, but I thought maybe we'd get half of them done."

"Ten more?"

Marianna pushed the tulle closer to Megan. "Yep. That's

all." She twisted the wire, connected two of the flowers to a red bow. "It's not too bad. Especially since you aren't taking any classes right now."

Megan folded the tulle, making uniform loops. She'd finally gotten her grade for her spring semester class. An A, just as she'd expected. The only thing left was student teaching, and if a music position opened over the summer and she landed the job, she was eligible to complete her student teaching on the job.

Megan peered at her sister. "I do have other things to do today."

"Like what?"

"I'm going to Hadley's house. Her uncle asked me to give her piano lessons."

"I forgot. The day of the canoe trip, right?"

Megan nodded as she twisted wire around another bow.

Marianna clipped most of the stems off two of the orange flowers and attached them to a large yellow lily. "He's really protective of Hadley."

Megan snorted. "I could tell."

Marianna set down the flower arrangement. She brushed a stray hair away from her eyes. "What I mean is you must have made a great impression for him to ask you to teach Hadley. I've never had a parent, especially a man who isn't even the girl's biological dad, be so involved in what we're teaching and how we're teaching it."

Megan growled. "Great. So, he's going to be a pain in the neck?"

Marianna shook her head. "No. He isn't rude or intrusive, but he is involved. And he's a Christian. And he's good-looking."

"Where are her parents?"

Marianna shrugged. "I don't know the details, and even if I did, you know I couldn't tell you. Confidentiality." Marianna shuffled her eyes as she reached across the table and pushed Megan's arm. "I do know he's rich."

Megan's cheeks warmed. "Marianna, I can't believe you would say such a thing."

Marianna laughed, and she rubbed her hands together as if she'd just found the fictional pot of gold at the end of the rainbow. "Well, he is."

"You know I'm not interested in dating."

Marianna sobered, and Megan shifted in her seat. She knew what was coming. Part of her wanted just to get up and go to the restroom or go get a drink from the kitchen. She didn't want to hear any lectures. Though Marianna stood beside her during the worst time of her life, her sister had no idea how bad it was to live it.

Marianna's voice softened. "It's been eight years, Megan. Maybe it's time."

All that time had passed, and yet when Megan closed her eyes and allowed her mind to travel back, she could still recall every detail. Even the smell of Cajun leftovers. She hadn't touched spicy food since.

Megan shook her head. "No. I don't think so."

She stared at the mass of flowers, tulle, wire, and clippers sprawled on top of the table. She knew Marianna studied her, her expression a mixture of frustration and pity. Megan noticed the calendar hanging on the refrigerator. She looked back up at Marianna. "When are we supposed to have the fittings for the bridesmaid dresses?"

The diversion worked. Marianna jumped out of her seat and walked to the refrigerator. She moved her hands across the dates on the calendar. The thing was covered with appointments and sale dates of various wedding items.

Marianna tapped the calendar. "Here it is. Next Monday, five o'clock." She looked back at Megan. "Once you get a little bit of sun, I know you'll love the color."

Megan bit the inside of her mouth to keep from responding. She still couldn't believe her sister was forcing her to wear a strapless yellow dress. Megan was pale as a ghost. Yellow was the last color she would ever choose to wear. And her shoulders were covered with freckles. Which was why she enjoyed keeping them covered.

Of course, Marianna's two bridesmaids were both tall brunettes with killer long legs and willowy shapes. They'd look gorgeous in the light color. Megan would look like a short yellow cupcake.

The only redeeming facet of the dress was the thick red sash around the waist. She just wished the whole dress could be that color. But Megan would be a good sister. She wouldn't mention that her sister had condemned her to a lifetime of embarrassing photos and memories. It was Marianna's day, and Megan wouldn't fuss about what she had to wear.

"You know Mom's coming for the fittings."

Marianna's voice interrupted Megan's thoughts. Megan knew she would. They'd seen a lot more of their mother since Marianna's engagement, which was to be expected. Megan knew her emotional estrangement from her mom and stepdad was not what God wanted, but she couldn't forgive them.

Marianna continued, "Bill wants to come with her."

Megan sighed. "I'm not surprised."

"You need to make amends."

Megan frowned at her sister. "They don't mind that our relationship is superficial. They don't care that—"

"But you're the Christian."

Megan smacked her hand on the table. "I get tired of being the one who has to forgive and forget. They've never once apologized to me, and you know they were wrong."

Marianna averted her gaze and picked at one of her fingernails. Megan knew her sister. She was trying to figure the right words to say to make Megan change her mind. Well, this was too big. God should understand why she couldn't just forgive and forget.

Marianna opened her arms. "You're right. They owe you an apology. But you may never get it."

Megan squeezed her eyes closed. Why did God ask her to forgive people who didn't deserve it, didn't even want it? A fresh wave of realization of Jesus' covering of her sin washed over her. She hadn't deserved forgiveness, and yet God granted it to her.

But God was bigger than her. He was God, after all. The Maker of heaven and earth and all of creation. He had a lot more power within Himself to draw from. And yet He still wanted her to forgive. She knew scripture said it. Knew God commanded it. But she didn't feel it. And she didn't want to.

Wind whipped through Megan's hair as she drove the old country roads that led to the small town of Midway. She tapped the top of the steering wheel. Her fingers still ached from making pew bows with Marianna earlier in the day. And they were only half through with the pew decorations. She cringed at the thought of starting up on them again.

Megan turned a curve and slowed to a near crawl behind an oversized tractor. She allowed her gaze to sweep the countryside. She'd missed the beauty of her mountains and hills in eastern Kentucky, but the rolling pastures of Midway were just as breathtaking.

She passed a farm with several horses grazing. An ornate white barn with a gray roof and black-trimmed doors and windows sat a thousand feet or more away from the road. She lifted her brows. "Haven't seen many houses nicer than that barn."

She glanced at the GPS suctioned to her windshield. If the gadget was right, she'd stay on this road for two more miles. She lifted her pointer finger in the air and spoke in a monotone voice. "Then I'll arrive at my destination, on right."

She laughed at herself as she continued at a speed that would challenge a turtle. Two cars had slowed behind her, but with so little traffic on the road, she didn't expect the farmer would pull over and allow them to pass.

Passing another horse farm, she drank in the whitewashed brick walls on each side of the entrance. Portfolio antique verde lights hung on the brick walls on each side. Though the decorative wrought-iron gate was closed, Megan still spied the house that looked as if it had been copied off the pages of *Gone with the Wind* and planted in the small town of Midway. She whipped her hair over her shoulder, threw back her chin, and proclaimed, "After all. . .tomorrow is another day."

The GPS jabbered at her, and she looked at the entrance to her destination. Though not as gaudy, the brownstone and wrought-iron entrance opened up to a two-story white vinyl farmhouse with a charcoal roof and deep red shutters, an oak front door, and a wraparound porch.

She shifted into PARK, scooped the piano books and her purse off the passenger's seat, then reached around to the outside of the car to open the door. She sucked in a deep breath as she shoved the door closed with her hip. "Marianna was right. Definitely rich."

She had taken just a couple of steps toward the house when Old Yeller raced across the yard barking at her. Megan bit back a squeal as she booked it to the front porch. She loved dogs, and golden labs had been one of her favorites since reading about this one's twin as a girl. She clenched her jaw when the massive creature leaped onto the porch and bared his teeth at her.

"Old Yeller!" A male voice sounded from behind the house. Colt walked around to the front and patted his thigh. "Get over here, boy."

Megan blew out a breath and offered a weak smile when the animal nestled against Colt's leg then sat beside him. "Your dog?"

Colt nodded. "Yep."

Megan loosened her grip on the piano books. The canine winked, an involuntary motion she was sure, but adorable just the same. The dog panted heavily but remained obediently beside his master. He looked up at Colt.

"His name's Old Yeller?"

"Don't you think he looks like him?"

"Definitely." Megan lowered her hand palm up and started to bend down. "He won't hurt me, will he?"

"I'd reckon not. Old Yeller's about the sweetest dog I've ever owned."

Colt patted the dog's side, and Old Yeller walked to Megan and sniffed her hand. Once Megan had received a slobbery lick, she petted the animal's head and neck. Old Yeller moved closer, and Megan fought the urge to wrap her arms around the dog's thick neck.

Megan stood and wiped her hand on the side of her denim capris. "Is Hadley ready?"

Colt looked at his watch. "She should be back any minute. She's been practicing her barrel racing."

Megan lifted her eyebrows.

Colt cocked his head. "It's a rodeo sport where the competitor rides around three barrels in a cloverleaf pattern as fast as she can without knocking them down."

Megan shifted her weight. "I know what it is. I just didn't know girls did it, especially girls as young as Hadley."

Colt scoffed. "Well sure. Hadley's one of the best in the nation." His lips parted into a smile that would outshine John Wayne. "You should go with us to a rodeo sometime."

Heat crept up Megan's neck as she realized how accurate her sister had been in describing Colt as quite a hottie. She knew he was just bragging about his niece. He wasn't asking her on a date. Besides, it was Hadley's barrel-racing, sweat-flying, steed-stomping rodeo he was talking about, not some moonlit ride on a pair of tame horses. "Well, I—"

"That was some ride."

Megan turned and saw Hadley stomping toward the porch, patting her hands against her jeans. Old Yeller bounded down the steps and ran around the girl until she bent down and petted the canine.

"You were supposed to be back half an hour ago to allow time to clean up." Colt frowned and crossed his arms in front of his chest.

Hadley looped her fingers through the waist of her jeans. "I know, Uncle Colt, but Fairybelle was riding like a champion, and I had to let her keep practicing at that pace."

Megan watched as Colt's expression softened. She had a feeling the preteen had her uncle wrapped snugly around her pinkie finger.

He pointed toward the house. "Get on in there and clean up quick. I'll show Miss Megan the piano."

Hadley grinned as she rose up on tiptoes and kissed her uncle's cheek. She waved to Megan. "Be right back."

Megan's heartbeat sped at being left alone with Colt again. She wished Hadley had listened to her uncle and been ready when she arrived. She also wished Marianna hadn't cursed her into noticing Colt's good looks.

Colt didn't make a move to guide her inside. He just sort of stared at her. Which made no sense. What did he want her to say? Surely he couldn't tell she thought he was quite the cutie. She inwardly growled. She had news for him. There would be no baring of the soul, no admission of his good looks.

He waved toward the house. "Come on in."

Megan rolled her eyes at her own dramatics as she

followed the man into his home. Listening to her sister go on about Colt Baker had her mind all in a tizzy. The man wasn't that good-looking. Just because he had dirty-blond hair, blue eyes, and the swagger of a true homegrown cowboy didn't mean he was any more than the average Joe she passed each day on the street.

She rolled her eyes at her wayward thoughts as she followed Colt through the living room and down a hall. The house didn't look like a bachelor pad. Though a bit dated, the décor was one of the more feminine Americana styles she'd seen.

He guided her into a room, and Megan gasped. The walls were covered with books and Victorian figurines. Dusty rose-colored drapes and an elegant swag cascaded from the top of the window. Beside a tall lamp sat an ivory satin-covered wingback chair. But it was the Victorian baby grand that stole her breath.

She gestured toward the instrument. "Does it work?"

"Tuned and ready."

She placed a hand on her chest and nodded toward it. "May I?"

"Yeah. Give her a whirl. Let's see how she sounds."

Megan sat down on the bench. She caressed a few keys before placing her hands in position. But what to play? Something Victorian would be best. She searched her mind. She knew little from that era by heart, but there was surely something she could play a few chords of.

She remembered a song she'd learned in high school. Her fingers danced across the keys, and she threw herself into "The Dying Poet" by Gottschalk. She didn't think with her brain, just allowed her fingers to remember the notes. The soothing melody filled her and reminded her of a time of happiness and innocence.

When she finished, she stared at the black music holder. She'd learned the piece just before she'd started the tenth grade. Things were easier then. Good and bad was absolute. Life wasn't tainted.

"Am I gonna learn to play like that?"

Hadley's question broke Megan's reverie, and she twisted in the seat. She rubbed her hands together and smiled at the girl. "Absolutely."

She glanced across the room at Colt. He was leaning against a bookshelf, his arms folded across his chest. Surprised pleasure etched his features, and she looked away from him. He really shouldn't look at her like that.

Chapter 6

Generosity is giving more than you can,
and pride is taking less than you need.
KHALIL GIBRAN

Colt blinked and shook his head as he pushed away from the bookshelf. He didn't know enough about Megan to be swept away into some kind of strange ooshy-gooshy land just because she played a few chords. She reminded him of his mom. For a moment, he was the proverbial fly stuck to the wall, entranced by Cozette Baker who sat at the piano playing an elaborate tune. Her husband, Wade, leaned against the doorjamb, mesmerized into a deep calm after a laborious day on the farm. Colt knew his mother's playing soothed his dad's soul. He hadn't realized how much it comforted his own. He missed her. His mom. And his dad.

With a wave of emotion threatening to rise out of his chest, Colt retreated from the room and headed to the front door.

"That was so pretty, Megan. Play another."

Hadley's awe-filled voice filled the foyer, and Colt wasn't able to make it to the door fast enough. Another rhythm pealed from the piano. He recognized the old hymn "When the Saints Go Marching In."

A low growl slipped through his mouth. That was the *perfect* song to uplift his spirits. One about when God's children left this world to meet Him in the heavens. He sucked in a deep breath then stepped out into the warm spring air and lifted his gaze to the cloud-dotted sky. "God, I miss Mom and Dad."

Growing up, life had been perfect. Better than anything shown on old television sitcoms. His dad, the hardworking farmer, and his mom, the doting wife and mother, raised his brother and him in God's majestic Kentucky countryside. They'd attended their small country church each time the doors were opened.

Then things changed. His brother befriended Tina. They started drinking and doing drugs. She got pregnant. Then came Hadley. Then Mom and Dad's car accident.

He pushed the spiraling gyro of hard recollections from his mind. No reason to dwell on them. He had a farm to tend. Horses and Hadley to raise. And God and his church stood beside him. Past was past. And he wasn't going to allow a few tunes on a piano to set him off to wallowing in sadness about things that couldn't be altered.

His big yellow dog meandered up the stairs and nudged his leg, begging for attention. "Hey, Old Yeller." Colt bent down and petted his buddy, who'd been around nearly as long as Hadley. A constant companion through the ups and downs of the last decade. "Let's say we go check on the horses."

Old Yeller barked and took off toward the stables. Colt had finished his chores early and had planned to stay in the house for Hadley's first piano lesson. He wouldn't go far. Wouldn't stay out too long. But he'd get away for just a bit. Get his thoughts and feelings back in check. Next time Megan came for a lesson, he'd be better prepared to hear the old piano come to life.

He thought of the young woman sitting on the piano bench. Though most of it was pulled back in a ponytail, blond wisps framed her face. Complete serenity etched her expression when she closed her eyes and dug into that first song. She felt the music with every fiber of her body, and it stirred something primitive within him.

He smiled. She was a good woman. Not like Tina. He could trust Megan with Hadley. She loved God. He could just tell it. Only a relationship with Jesus could cause such a peace in a person. He picked up his pace toward the stable. She was someone he could be proud of. Call home about. Even if there was no one but him and Hadley left to answer.

More than an hour passed. He pushed the saddle back on the rack. He'd gotten so wrapped up in oiling the thing he'd forgotten to check his watch. Megan may have gone ahead and left. He hoped not. She hadn't been paid. And he hoped she'd let him know Hadley was alone before hitting the road.

He took long strides toward the house. But she may have had somewhere she needed to go, and he couldn't fault her if she'd gone. People who were late grated on his nerves.

He glanced down at his watch again and gritted his teeth. Fifteen minutes was a long time to wait when a person had somewhere to go.

Reaching the back door, he barreled in without stamping the dirt off his feet. He pulled off his ball cap, walked through the mudroom, coming to a halt at the kitchen door. Hadley and Megan stood over the island countertop. Hadley wore his mother's pink-and-white polka-dotted BEST GRANDMA apron. She shaped a chunk of prepackaged cookie dough into a ball. Megan placed a ball of dough on the cookie sheet.

A knot formed in his throat, and he swallowed it down. It had been a long time since he'd seen a woman in the kitchen—outside of Hadley, and he most certainly couldn't call her a woman. He cleared his throat. "Sorry I'm late. Got caught up with stuff in the barn."

Hadley and Megan looked at him. A blush swept across Megan's cheeks, and Hadley stuck out her bottom lip into a dramatic pout. "Uncle Colt!" She jabbed her hands onto her hips. "If you'd have waited ten more minutes, we'd be done with our surprise."

He raised his eyebrows and made eye contact with Megan.

She placed a ball of dough onto the cookie sheet then wiped her hands on a paper towel. "Hadley wanted to bake you some cookies. She said they're your favorite."

Colt's heart raced. Her shy gestures and deep blue eyes cantered on his senses like a horse in competition. "That was awful sweet."

Hadley smacked her hand against her thigh, causing

him to shift his attention back to his niece. She wrinkled her nose and wiggled her shoulders and head from side to side. "Yeah, but you had to go and ruin it and come back too quick." She stuck out her lower lip. "You never let me surprise you."

Colt bit the inside of his lip. The older Hadley got, the more dramatic she became. Some days the young'un would set off to stomping through the house and crying for no reason he could figure at all. It was as if turning twelve had caused some kind of weird metamorphosis in the girl about which no one had given him fair warning.

Having been raised with just himself and his brother, Colt didn't know what to expect as a girl got older. He knew there were things young ladies dealt with that boys didn't, and he figured he probably needed to look into finding out more about those things, but Hadley was only twelve. Not even a teenager yet. Surely he had a few more years before he needed to start initiating uncomfortable talks with his niece.

A wave of nausea swirled in his throat at the thought. Raising the girl on his own was more than he'd bargained for. Not that he regretted or begrudged it. He loved her more than just about anything in the world. In fact, he couldn't think of a thing he loved more. Still, he hadn't the faintest clue what to do with these emotional outbursts.

She shouldn't be mad at him for showing up too soon when he was a full fifteen minutes late coming in from the barn. Hadley picked up the cookie sheet and shoved it into the oven with a bit more force than necessary. The kid made no sense.

Actually the whole thing was quite comical. He pulled out a stool from underneath the island and lowered himself down onto it. "Well, Hadley, I'm sorry for showing up too soon, even though I'm fifteen minutes late."

She glared at him. "Don't make fun of me, Uncle Colt. I was wanting to do something nice for you."

Megan placed a hand on Hadley's forearm. "Why don't you play the tune I taught you? He'd probably like to hear it."

Warmth swelled up in Colt's chest as he drank in the ease with which Megan handled his niece. Her voice was calm. Her expression sincere.

Hadley tumbled right into Megan's charms. Her expression softened, and her eyes lit up when she looked back at Colt. "You wanna hear?"

Colt stood and motioned toward the piano room. "Absolutely."

Hadley pushed away from the counter and raced away. Colt noticed Megan set the timer on the oven before following his niece. Hadley's impulsive behavior and mood shifts didn't seem to faze the piano teacher. She took his niece in stride, and he wished he'd made himself stay and watch the lesson. See them interact. Spend a little time with Megan.

He knew Megan was a Christian. And from what little he'd seen, she seemed to be a good influence on his niece. The girl needed a woman's influence. A woman who loved the Lord and lived for Him. Megan might be the answer to his petition to God for help with Hadley.

She might be more than that.

The idea wrapped itself around his brain. He hadn't been looking for a woman in his life. He'd been filled up with farmwork and Hadley. But now he'd met Megan and seen her in action with his niece. Thoughts and feelings were coming to him that he couldn't recall the last time he'd pondered. To his surprise, the notions set kinda good with him.

He followed Megan to the piano room. She surely wasn't hard to look at. Small frame with curves in all the right places. Blond hair, shiny and as soft looking as fully ripened wheat. Eyes so blue they shamed the sky for color.

Megan turned to him. He stopped short and felt heat rising in his neck. It was a good thing she couldn't read his mind.

"She already knows the keys and where to place her hands. Teaching her will be a snap."

Colt nodded. He wished he knew something clever to say. He'd never known exactly how to act in front of a woman. Hadn't been overly worried about it anyway. He reached into his back pocket and pulled out the check he'd written to her. "Here. Before I forget."

Megan accepted the money. "Thank you."

A broken tune sounded from the piano, and Colt focused his attention on his niece. Though she stopped and started over several times, he recognized the tune. The same one Megan had been playing when he'd walked out. Only Hadley didn't add the extra melody to "When the Saints Go Marching In." She played the tune simply.

After several moments of starting and restarting, pausing and moving her fingers to correct notes, Hadley finished the song, looked over at Colt, and smiled. "Whaddaya think?"

Now she wasn't mad at him. Now she was smiling, eyebrows lifted, expression in anticipation of his approval. The kid never failed to confuse him. He walked to his niece and patted her shoulder. "Sounds great. I can't believe you got through the whole chorus after only one lesson."

Hadley's smile lit up the room. It surprised him how such simple praise from him meant so much to her. The older she got the more he tried to remember to tell her when she did a good job. She seemed to need the reminding.

But it wasn't in his nature to always be spouting off one compliment after another. To his thinking, less meant more. He tended to enjoy seeing the results of his hard work. He didn't need to talk about it. Didn't need a pat on the back. But Hadley sure did. The girl wore him out with her neediness lately. Still, he wanted to encourage her. And she was a good kid—when she wasn't being moody.

Colt turned to Megan. "She's doing great."

"Like I said, she already knows a lot. Hadley may be the easiest student I'll ever have."

Hadley jumped off the piano stool and raced to Megan. She wrapped her arms around her. "I'm glad Uncle Colt asked you to come. Stephanie says you're the best, and I know it's true."

Colt took in the affection Hadley already felt for Megan. She'd always been a loving child, quick to give hugs, but he could see she really liked Megan. He sent a silent prayer of thanks that God had brought her into their lives. Hadley needed a female influence.

"Do I have to wait until next Saturday?" Hadley looked from Megan to Colt. "Couldn't I have two lessons a week?

Maybe she could come on Tuesdays, too?"

Colt glared at his niece. "Hadley! I'm sure Megan has other things to do than come over and—"

"Actually," Megan interrupted him, "I wouldn't mind at all giving you two lessons a week. On one condition."

Hadley clasped her hands and bounced on her heels. "What?"

Megan looked from Hadley to Colt. A slight blush colored her cheeks and she bit her bottom lip. The mixture of mischief and hesitation in her expression drew him. He couldn't wait to hear the condition.

"What?" Colt and Hadley asked together.

She blew out a breath. "I used to ride horses when I was a girl living in eastern Kentucky. Could we maybe work out a trade, the extra hour lesson for an hour of riding?"

Colt's jaw dropped. That was what she wanted—to ride horses? The woman couldn't be more perfect for Hadley. Or him. "Are you serious?"

She wrinkled her nose and shifted her weight from one foot to the other. "Yeah."

Hadley snorted. "Well sure. We can do that." She motioned outside. "We can go out there right now. I'm always open to a horse ride. I didn't know you rode horses."

Megan chuckled. "It's been awhile. I may be a bit rusty, but hopefully it's like riding a bike. It'll come back to me."

Colt motioned to the door. "You wanna go now?"

"I would love to." Megan shook her head. "But I can't. My sister's getting married in July. We've been working on some decorations, and we still have a ton to do."

She picked up her purse from the settee and gave

Hadley another hug. Colt wished she'd offer one to him, but he wasn't going to hold his breath. Maybe another day.

He followed her to the door. "So, we'll see you Tuesday?"

"Sounds great. What time?"

"You can come for dinner if you'd like," Hadley answered.

Megan shook her head. "That's awfully sweet of you, but I'm having a dinner with a friend. Would six be too early?"

"Sounds good to me," said Hadley.

Megan looked at Colt, and he nodded. He wished she would come to dinner as Hadley had suggested. He hoped her plans weren't with a date. Here he'd been having all these thoughts of her being a perfect mate for him, and he didn't even know if the woman had a boyfriend. He hoped she didn't.

"Okay. I'll see you then." Megan waved and walked down the sidewalk.

Hadley looked up at Colt. "I really like her."

"I can tell."

"She'd be good for you, too."

Colt didn't respond. He ruffled her hair then walked away from the door. The oven beeper sounded, and Hadley ran to the kitchen. Saved by the bell. He didn't want his niece to see he thought she was right.

Chapter 7

Character is doing the right thing when nobody's looking.
There are too many people who think that the only thing that's
right is to get by and the only thing that's wrong is to get caught.
J. C. WATTS

Justin looked at his reflection one last time in the full-length mirror. He appeared comfortable in his newly pressed khakis and bright melon polo. A fresh shave and a recent haircut completed the look. The last time he'd felt so nervous was when they'd gone to trial for the Jones's divorce proceedings. He'd had to squelch more than one bloodbath with those two arguing over their five million dollars in family assets.

At the time, he'd dug into the case, anxious to make Mrs. Jones the victor and him a benefactor of the win. Now it hurt to think he'd been so excited and consumed in helping the desolation of a thirty-five-year union. Some moments he still wondered if Mrs. Jones would have been willing to try counseling if he had suggested it.

But past was past. He couldn't change it. And God had forgiven him. He picked up the brown leather study Bible he'd been making good use of and headed downstairs. He hadn't told Megan of his plan to visit her church. She probably assumed as much since he'd gone to Bible study on

Thursday, but he'd been busy on Friday, and they hadn't really talked about Sunday morning services.

He hadn't wanted to discuss it with her anyway. This was something he needed to do on his own. Free of women. His stomach churned when he thought of the possibility of running into Amy. He hadn't seen her in years, but she had once attended the church, and she might still be there.

Memories of his relationship, if he could call it that, with the woman flooded his mind. She was beautiful. Her husband had an affair. She didn't want the divorce, but her husband did. She'd talked about her faith and cried for God to help her. She'd been vulnerable but determined. Then succumbed.

And Justin had congratulated himself for it.

Justin clamped his eyes shut and pressed the Bible against his chest. "God, I can't do it. The walls will fall in if I walk through those doors on a Sunday morning."

A scripture from 2 Corinthians washed through his mind, *"Therefore, if anyone is in Christ, the new creation has come: The old has gone, the new is here!"* He couldn't fathom why God would save him. Why He would choose him. His sin was so ugly. So arrogant. So self-serving. When he thought of the way he'd treated people, especially women, it sickened him to his core.

Learn to fellowship with believers. He'd read Paul's books over more times than he could remember. Paul claimed to be the worst of sinners, seeking out the destruction of Christians, encouraging the stoning of Stephen. And yet when Paul gave his life to Jesus, he changed. Radically. Completely. And without hesitation.

Opening his eyes, Justin grabbed his keys off the foyer table. He had to go to church. Had to hear God's Word. He didn't deserve the right to walk through those church doors, but God had given the grace, and he could not deny his Lord.

Justin made his way out of the house and to the car. Christian music pealed from the speakers as he drove the short distance. He just had to make it through today. Sit in the back. Talk to as few people as possible. Just take the first step. Going alone felt so different from going the one time with Kirk. His nerves surprised him.

He pulled into the parking lot and watched as people walked into the church. A family with a little boy and infant. A teenage girl and a woman who was probably her mother. An elderly couple. A middle-aged man.

He waited as the flow of members and visitors became more sporadic. Glancing at his watch, he knew the service started in less than five minutes. But he wanted to wait until the very end. Normally he ate up attention from people. Looked for a pat on the back or a word of praise for showing up. Today he just wanted to slip in. Be invisible.

See if Amy was there.

If she was, he would need to apologize to her. If not today, soon. She might smack his face or laugh at him. Spit on him maybe. He would deserve all of it. She had been a conquest. And he had won. His gut churned anew at the memory.

Pushing the thought away, he opened the car door and stepped out. The church doors had shut. Hopefully the men who were standing there welcoming people inside had already gone to their seats.

He walked up the stairs and opened the large wooden door. An older woman with graying light brown hair stood beside the door that opened to the sanctuary. Her dark red lips parted into a welcoming smile as she handed a bulletin to him. "We're happy to have you."

He accepted the paper and nodded. "Thank you."

She pointed to the left side. "There are some open seats in the back."

He went inside. To his relief, the congregation was standing and singing a song he didn't recognize. It had a contemporary beat, but he hadn't heard it on the radio. He assumed there were many songs he wouldn't recognize. "Amazing Grace" maybe, but that might be it.

The words to the song were displayed in large letters on a screen in the center of the wall. A tall red-haired man stood behind the pulpit singing with a fervor Justin had witnessed from a television worship leader when he'd been a boy shuffling through stations. The man waved his right hand back and forth to the beat of the music. As a kid, Justin thought the guy on TV looked goofy. But this man obviously sang with his whole heart.

Justin slipped into an empty pew in the very back of the room. His plan to go relatively unnoticed was working until the music stopped and the worship leader invited everyone to "reach around and shake someone's hand."

He cringed but plastered a smile on his face as one person after another made his or her way to him to greet him and shake his hand. He hadn't seen Megan. Or Amy. In truth, he didn't want to run into either of them.

They finally sat down, and Justin went ahead and opened his Bible to the passages listed in the bulletin. Music started again, and he looked back to the front.

Megan was there. Alone. She held a microphone. She was going to sing?

"I'm not going to play today." Her voice reverberated through the room.

A grunt of disapproval washed over the congregation, and Justin looked around. People could act like that in church? Someone could speak from the pulpit and the congregation could respond, and with a negative sound? He thought old men stood behind the pulpit and preached the truth about hell, and the congregation listened. Maybe a few of the older men said, "Amen" or something, but there wasn't any actual interaction.

Megan continued, "But I'm still going to sing."

Laughter and applause sounded from the people, and Justin looked around again. This church was nothing like he expected. Completely different from Kirk's. He settled back in the pew and studied his firm's administrative assistant. He'd never heard Megan sing. He knew she played piano. Figured she must be pretty good, because she had a degree in it. He probably should have assumed she sang, but he'd never put much thought into it. She wasn't the kind of girl he went after.

She was pretty enough. Not gorgeous but pretty. She wasn't flashy like the girls he dated. Didn't have a husband or a boyfriend whom he needed to best and steal her away from. He inwardly growled. How he hated the man he was. He thought it might take the rest of his life to restore his reputation. And he wouldn't be able to do it. God would have to.

The background music continued, and then Megan joined in. Her voice little more than a whisper, she sang of forgiveness. The music flowed softly, like water trickling across a creek bed, and Megan's voice, gentle yet sure, added the message to the flow.

As the song progressed, the music crescendoed, and Megan's volume rose as she sang of God's triumph over our mistakes and the strength of His restoration. Her voice mastered confidence and beauty and conviction. He felt the words, the sound, the truth to the depth of his being.

As the song ended, Justin watched her. Megan transformed when she sang. Her face, her voice, her body language. All of it spoke of a woman completely overwhelmed with adoration for God. How had he never really noticed her?

He had no intention of *really* noticing her now. He was focused on the Lord and building a relationship with Him. He needed to spend time making God the true Lord of his life.

Still, Megan stirred something in him. It was different than he'd felt with other women. It was pure. Holy. He didn't want from her. He wanted to give to her. It was a different feeling than he'd ever known. Even though he didn't know what to make of it.

For now, Justin didn't need to dwell on it. The song had given him the confidence he needed to sit in the church. He was a sinner, but he was forgiven. He could start anew.

The preacher walked to the pulpit. The man was younger

than Justin had anticipated. He wore a white button-down shirt and green striped tie and brown pants. His sandy-colored hair was cut short, but he wore a mustache and wide goatee. He looked more like a dressed-up Harley Davidson rider than a preacher.

Then the man spoke, leading the congregation in prayer. Justin knew he was a man following God. Humble. Sincere. Honest. Immediately Justin wanted to hear the message this man would deliver.

With his eyes still closed, he felt someone slip into the pew on the far side away from him. To his surprise, his heart raced at the thought of Megan sneaking in from the back and choosing a seat close to him.

When the prayer ended, he glanced to the end of the pew. The couple looked at him and nodded. Then recognition dawned. It was Amy. And the husband Justin helped her divorce.

The sermon was agonizing. Justin didn't hear a word the preacher said. Instead, he battled over whether he should talk to Amy. Was she married to the man again? Did he know about her and Justin?

She was on his list of women to whom he planned to apologize—but at church with her ex-husband, boyfriend, husband, whatever the guy was? Justin wasn't sure this was the most appropriate venue.

The service finally ended. *God, what do I do?* He glanced at Amy. The guy had already stood and made his way to Justin. With his pointer finger, he poked Justin's shoulder. "What are you doing here?"

Justin's old nature, which hadn't had much time to

change, erupted, and he grabbed the man's finger and pushed it away. "Attending a church service."

"I know what you did." Fury laced the man's eyes and etched his jaw. He balled his hands into fists. "Did you come here to see my wife?"

Justin cocked his head. He owed Amy an apology, but if this guy thought Justin would sit by and allow himself to be pummeled, he'd learn real quick that white-collar workers could fight as well. Especially when provoked. "Ex-wife?"

"She's my wife again. No thanks to you."

Justin's brow puckered. "If I remember correctly, she came to see me because of you."

The man pulled back a fist, and Justin readied himself to lay the guy flat on his back.

"Timmy, please." Amy grabbed the man's arm.

Justin simmered when he looked at Amy's face, etched with embarrassment. His mistreatment of her haunted him more than any other. He wished he could change it. She was a Christian woman going through a very hard time. And he'd taken advantage of her.

Justin looked at her, hoping she could see how much he meant the words. "Amy, I'm sorry."

Timmy bristled up again. "Do not talk to my wife."

"What's going on?"

Justin turned and saw Megan standing behind him. She held a Bible and some other materials against her chest.

"Nothing. We're leaving." Timmy grabbed Amy by the arm and, before another word could be spoken, ushered her out of the church.

Justin let out a long breath. He'd been nervous about

attending church, but he hadn't expected to make a scene. He glanced back at Megan, expecting her to inundate him with questions. Instead, she studied him. He felt uncomfortable, which didn't sit well. Normally he was the epitome of confidence. He shrugged. "Sorry 'bout that."

"Didn't look like you caused it."

"Oh, I did."

Megan cocked her head, and Justin grew more ill at ease at her scrutiny. He wanted to explain himself to her. He needed to be honest with her. For her to know the truth— the whole truth—and still accept him.

"So Megan, who's your friend?"

Justin looked at the owner of the masculine voice. Up close, the pastor looked even younger than he had at the pulpit. He might even be in his twenties.

Megan pointed to Justin. "This is one of my bosses, Justin Frasure."

Justin accepted the pastor's extended hand. She motioned to the minister. "Justin, this is Pastor Wes."

"It's good to meet you."

"You, too. We're glad to have you here this morning. In fact, we've got some church baseball practice later this afternoon. Could use a few more members. You interested?"

"I'm actually already planning to be there. Kat told me about it at Bible study Thursday night."

Pastor Wes smiled. "Terrific." A young woman grabbed his arm, grinned at Megan and Justin, then pulled the pastor away.

Megan chuckled. "That's his wife. She probably needs help with their twins."

Justin looked at her. He needed someone to talk to. To tell him the church wouldn't spontaneously combust because he'd attended a service. "Would you be willing to have lunch with me?"

Megan's eyebrows rose, and she took a step back. "Well, I. . ."

"I could really use someone to talk to." He clasped his hands. "If you're not busy."

Megan adjusted the Bible and other materials in her arms. She didn't answer right away, and Justin wished he could take back the invitation. She looked down then nodded just a bit. "Okay."

He held up his keys. "I can drive and then bring you back to the church."

Megan shook her head. "No. I'll drive myself. Where would you like to go?"

They decided on a restaurant, and Justin followed her to the parking lot. He had no idea why he'd invited her to lunch. She was probably the last person he needed to talk to. He didn't spill his guts on a regular basis. Until recently he didn't have guts to spill. He'd spent his life not caring about people or how they felt.

Now he'd invited Megan, his secretary, to have lunch with him so he could talk with her. She'd just shown up too soon after the confrontation with Amy's husband. He didn't need to share anything with Megan. He'd just take her to lunch, and he'd see her the following day at work. One lunch. No problem.

Chapter 8

Stolen kisses are always sweetest.
LEIGH HUNT

Megan squirted a dollop of hand sanitizer into her palm, rubbed her hands together, then dropped the bottle back into her purse. She placed her purse on the booth close to the window. She glanced to the front of the restaurant where Justin had taken their flashing pager. He placed it in the basket then collected the two trays containing their individual size pizzas and chopped salads.

They'd chosen to eat at one of her favorite places. Not only did she love the "smashed" tomato sauce on their pizzas and the homemade vinaigrette dressing on their salads, but she also adored the atmosphere of the place. On one side, a brick wall was painted green and trimmed in red. Videos of Italy scrolled across a large-screen television. Large windows covered two walls, allowing for natural light. The kitchen area was open, and she could watch as the cooks placed pizzas in the oven set over 800 degrees. They served real Italian pizza, and she loved it.

Justin arrived at the booth and placed the trays on the table. He smiled as he slid into the seat across from her. Man, the guy was entirely too good-looking. And that melon polo looked amazing against his naturally dark skin.

She felt like the ugly duckling sitting across from him. But having already reached adulthood, she felt fairly confident she wouldn't be changing into a swan anytime soon.

He extended his arms across the table and opened his hands. "May I pray?"

Nervous about touching her boss, just the two of them, at lunch, in which he insisted on paying, she rubbed her thumbs against her fingertips beneath the table. Her nerves were ridiculous. She lifted her hands and placed them in his. "Of course."

She bowed her head and listened to his petition to God. His heartfelt words and humble offerings to her Savior melted away any uncertainty she had about lunch with him. She knew what happened between him and Amy. The whole church knew.

Timmy had confessed all his sins in a couples' Bible study he'd agreed to attend with Amy. The only problem was he'd confessed all hers as well. She didn't know Amy well, but she knew enough about her to know she was a private woman with a very sensitive spirit. Megan couldn't imagine she'd have wanted her failures to be publicized. Megan sure didn't.

When he finished the prayer, Megan opened her eyes and looked at Justin. He was a changed man. A lot different than he had been when she first started working in his office. For a moment, she wondered if Clint would have been different if he'd accepted the Lord.

The thought sickened her, and she wrinkled her nose and swallowed back the bad taste in her mouth. That guy was vile. Treacherous. Deceitful. Manipulative. The pressure of his knee against her leg washed over her anew. She touched the spot as her body trembled, and she forced the memory from her mind.

"You okay?"

Megan straightened in the seat and lifted her chin. "Mm-hmm." She pierced her fork through the salad then shoved a bite into her mouth. She nodded, hoping he'd erase the concerned expression from his face. She swallowed and pointed her fork at the dish. "My favorite salad in the world."

Justin took the bait. "I like it, too."

She wiped her mouth with the napkin. "So, what did you want to talk about?"

Justin pushed his fork through the salad. He seemed hesitant, uncertain. She'd never witnessed those qualities in him before. She hoped he didn't want to talk about Amy. It wasn't any of her business, and it wasn't as if he needed to clear the air between them so they could build a relationship together. She had no inclinations for a relationship, and most especially with a man who'd studied as many women as he had law books. Even if he had changed.

He looked up at her, and her stomach fluttered at the intensity of his gaze. "You have a beautiful voice, Megan."

She hadn't expected him to say that. She cleared her throat. "Thank you."

He leaned back in the booth. "That song was like a wave of peace, like a. . ." He crinkled the napkin in his hand. "I'm not good with pretty language. More of a law guy, you know."

He winked at her, and her heart dropped to her ankles.

Inwardly she picked it up, shoved the organ back in place, and hammered some boards around it. There was no way she'd allow this man's words to get to her.

He continued, "It was what I needed to hear. God's forgiven me. Just like the song says. I'm restored, and I need to move on from this place. Forgive myself and move on."

Megan didn't know what to say. She watched as he looked down at his plate. He picked up the knife and cut off a piece of his pizza. She noticed his hand trembled. Not much. No one would notice unless the person was studying him.

But Justin Frasure did not tremble. He was strength and certainty. He was the spider who seduced the fly.

He glanced back up at her. "I'm not the same person I once was. Do you believe that?"

Megan swallowed. It was almost as if he asked for her forgiveness. But he'd done nothing to her. He didn't need her approval, and she couldn't give it. It wasn't her place. Her heart was untouched by him, and it would stay that way.

His dark brown eyes searched hers. They reminded her of a puppy begging his owner for a pat on the head or a rub on the belly. She couldn't simply not answer him. Sucking in a deep breath, she determined to state the facts of what she'd seen in him. Facts only. No feelings. The heart had a way of being deceitful, and she wouldn't be tricked by it again. She nodded. "I have seen a change in you."

Relief washed his features. "I'm so glad. I've worked so hard."

Megan lifted her hand and shook her head. "Justin, it's

not about your work. You can work as hard as you want. God does the changing."

Her words pricked her spirit. Her sister's comment about it being time to move on from the hurt eight years before flooded her mind. Megan had worked hard to build the walls, layers of them, around her heart. She loved her sister, her friends, and the kids she worked with in church. Once she became a teacher, she knew she'd adore those children just as much. But her parents, her old boyfriend—even though he was dead—and any man who'd dared to look at her since, she'd pushed away, placing an invisible barrier between herself and them.

She was safe that way. She'd put in a lot of work building her safe haven. She hadn't allowed God any changing.

Emotions warred within her. She couldn't stay here with Justin. Couldn't sit here and give him advice she'd only just realized she wasn't heeding. But she couldn't forgive. Surely God wouldn't require it of her. Some things were too sacred, too pure.

Clint didn't deserve it. He didn't even need it. He was dead. Her parents didn't want it. They didn't care. Didn't even know they needed to be forgiven. They still blamed her.

She thought of her Christ, who was punched and mocked and placed on a cross for the world to see. And He'd done nothing wrong. He'd loved. He'd served. He'd come to save. And they had killed Him.

And He forgave.

But why did He do it? They were unworthy. He'd hung on that cross because of her sins as well. She was unworthy. She didn't deserve salvation, but Jesus had given it to her.

And she was to be like Him. God commanded it. But how? She loved the Lord, read her Bible, served in His church. She'd forgiven the guy who'd rear-ended the car she'd driven off the lot only one day before. She'd forgiven Marianna more times than she could count for taking long showers and leaving her with cold water. She'd forgiven the woman who'd neglected to pay her for her son's piano lessons before they moved to another state. She'd forgiven many people for various reasons over the years since she'd become a Christian.

But Clint and her parents. It was too hard, and they weren't sorry.

Visions of a movie she'd watched about Jesus's crucifixion streamed through her mind. Soldiers wagering for Christ's clothes. Mocking Him with looks, laughs, and even blows. And Jesus forgave them.

Open her heart to everyone. That's what God wanted her to do. To be a vessel He could use. To be willing to be hurt. To love unconditionally.

She smacked her napkin atop the table. *Fine, Lord. You win. I forgive everyone, and I'm moving on with my life.*

She stood and walked over to Justin. Without a word, she leaned over, grabbed his cheeks in both her hands, and pressed her lips against his.

Shaven, his cheeks were soft against her fingertips, but not as soft as his lips. His mouth was perfect. Inviting. Delicious. An arrow of pleasure shot through her, and she deepened the kiss.

Realization of her actions punched her gut, and she opened her eyes. His were closed, and he seemed to enjoy her touch as much as she did his. Her brain jolted, and she jumped away from him as if he were the 800-degree oven at the other end of the restaurant. She pressed her hands against her lips. Heat washed over her, and she shook her head. He was a man. He was a womanizer. He was her boss. "Mr. Frasure."

"Megan." Though surprise still filled his expression, he didn't seem upset she'd flung herself at him. He reached for her hand.

She brushed him away. "Mr. Frasure, I am so sorry."

Before he could respond, she raced out of the restaurant. Shoving her hand in the bottom of her purse, she rummaged for her keys. "How hard can they possibly be to find? I have a big pink monogrammed key chain attached to them, for crying out loud."

She yanked out the key chain as she reached the car. Her hands trembled when she tried to stick the key in the lock.

"Miss Megan."

Megan jumped and squealed at the sound of her name. She placed her hand on her chest and looked at Stephanie and her mom. She forced a smile to her lips. Lips that still felt the pressure of Justin's against them. "Hi, Stephanie. How are you?"

Her voice was too high. Even to her own ears.

Stephanie tapped the side of her face with her palm. Something she did when she felt nervous or unsure of a situation. "Are you okay, Miss Megan?"

Megan let out a breath and forced her nerves to calm. "I'm fine, Stephanie. May I have a hug?"

Stephanie smiled, and she wrapped her arms around Megan. Hugs always worked with the autistic child. For her, they affirmed everything was okay. Megan waved as Stephanie and her mother walked to the department store beside the Italian restaurant.

She turned back to her car. Justin stood in front of it. Heat rose up her neck and cheeks again. She hadn't even seen him leave the restaurant. He stepped closer to her. "Megan."

She looked to the heavens as she opened the car door. "Please, Mr. Frasure."

"Do not call me Mr. Frasure."

She looked at him, noting the hurt in his eyes that she addressed him formally. She dipped her head. "Justin."

"We can talk about this."

Her strength returned as she shook her head and looked back up at him. "No. I promise there is nothing to talk about. I have no idea why I did it. I don't just go up to men and kiss them. I don't even date."

He drew his eyebrows together. "What do you mean you don't date?"

"Just what I said. I don't date. Period. Ever. I haven't in eight years. I don't plan to ever again. I apologize for my actions. That was not like me."

He placed his hand against his chest. "I'm not offended, Megan. You don't owe me an apology."

"I don't want to date you."

"Did I ask you to date me?"

Megan shook her head. "No. Of course not. I'm the one who—I shouldn't have. I don't know why I did it. I don't. . ."

He lifted his hands in surrender. "Okay. I get it."

"I don't want to give you the wrong impression."

"'Kay." He smacked his hand against his thigh. "You don't like me. I get it."

"I'm sorry, Mr. . ."

He glared at her, and she cleared her throat. "Justin." His name slid through her teeth with a mixture of frustration and pleasure.

He nodded. "Okay. I'll see you tomorrow at work."

She slid into the car and turned the ignition. She felt his eyes on her even as she pulled out of the parking lot. *God, what in the world possessed me to do that? You're talking to me about forgiving people, and I jump up and kiss Justin?*

She drove toward the apartment. She was one mixed-up, crazy woman—that's what she was. The memory of his lips against hers still niggled at her mouth. It was the first kiss in eight years, and she couldn't believe how delicious it had been. So different from the one years ago.

The one before it had been insulting and suffocating and too-often haunting. She hadn't realized until moments before a kiss didn't have to be that way.

She didn't want to think about it. She couldn't think about it. Not only was she not going to get involved with a man, but she most certainly would not get involved with a man who'd dated more women in Lexington than lived in her small hometown. Okay, maybe that was an exaggeration, but the truth was Justin Frasure was an experienced man.

Even if he had changed.

Megan pulled into her driveway. She had other things to think about. Like getting the children's church lessons ready for the evening service. She still needed to run by the grocery and pick up snacks and drinks for the kids.

She also needed to look at her closet. She needed to find the least attractive thing she owned and press it to wear to work tomorrow. She wasn't glamorous and gorgeous like the women who'd strolled through the law office doors many times before. Still, she had no intention of leading the youngest lawyer at the firm to believe she was dolling up for him. Justin Frasure was the last thing she wanted.

Chapter 9

We can decide to let our trials crush us,
or we can convert them to new forces of good.
HELEN KELLER

Megan tied the oversized red bow around the back of the waist of the bridesmaid dress. She dropped her hands to her sides and twisted left to right in front of the full-length mirror to drink in her reflection.

The design was adorable. The strapless sweetheart cut enhanced her chest and cinched in her waist. The slight flair of the skirt stopped just above her knees, a length that accentuated her muscular calves. If only the dress weren't yellow and she didn't have a smattering of freckles covering her shoulders.

Marianna assured her she would be able to get a tan before the wedding. But first of all, Megan worked every day until five. Her chances of getting in the sun were limited to weekends. And second, she flat-out refused to go to tanning beds. She was scared to death of them.

Once, as a teenager, she'd ventured to Forever Tans in their small hometown. She'd paid for just one visit. Donned the sunscreen and her bikini. Reclined on the bed and placed the eye protection goggles over her lids. Took a deep breath and pulled the top of the bed halfway over her body.

The bulbs turned on, and she'd practically jumped out of her skin. She'd reached for the handle on the lid and realized it had closed on top of her. She pushed the thing off and jumped out. It was like lying in a cooking coffin. A tan wasn't worth it. She'd put her clothes back on, walked out, and hadn't gone back.

She peered at her reflection in the mirror. No. She'd probably look just like this when it came time to walk down the aisle ahead of her sister.

"Hurry, Megan. Everyone's already out here." Marianna's voice sounded from the runway area at the back of the store. She appreciated the relative privacy the boutique had for brides and their parties to model dresses. Sure, people could still see them if they wanted, but a person would have to be purposeful or downright rude to be able to do it.

Megan already knew what her mother would say about the dress. Sucking in a deep breath, she pushed open the changing room door and walked out to join Julie and Amber.

Marianna clapped her hands when the three of them stood side by side. "You all look beautiful."

Megan glanced at Julie and Amber. One of the seamstresses pinned the fabric around Amber's waist to make it a bit tighter. The pale yellow color harmonized with the dark skin and hair color of both of their friends. Megan glanced at her mother. Her expression spoke volumes.

She remembered one of the skits she'd watched on *Sesame Street* as a girl. Four shoes—three small tennis shoes and a great big boot—sat on the ground while some off-camera guy sang for the audience to try to figure out which of the things was not like the other, and to try to figure it out before he finished the song. Well, today Megan was the bridesmaid who didn't belong.

"Are you going to try to get a bit of a tan, Megan?" her mother asked.

Megan studied the woman. Light red hair, cut short and curly, framed her face. Her skin, much lighter than Marianna's and Megan's, would have been washed away in the pale yellow dress if she'd been the one to have to wear it. Worse than Megan. She'd have thought her mom would have a little bit of mercy on her.

But it was her mother. Mrs. I'll-say-what-I-want-when-I-want-and-make-no-apologies-for-it.

Megan sighed. "Probably not. I work until five Monday through Friday."

"Have you thought about going to a tanning bed?"

Megan shook her head.

"It's not a cooking coffin, Megan."

Megan shook her head again. She wasn't going to get back in a tanning bed. Not even for her sister's wedding. She looked at her friends with their gorgeous darker skin color then down at her own white-as-snow legs. She'd just be the bridesmaid who looked a little different. She was the maid of honor, after all. It was okay she wouldn't look the same.

"What about a spray tan?" said her mom.

"Last time I had one, I was orange. Though it would go with Marianna's colors, it's not a shade I prefer for my skin."

Marianna jumped in. "Mom, look how beautiful the style fits Megan. Her calves look amazing." She pointed toward the top of the dress and arched her eyebrows. "My sister's got a killer body."

Megan squinted at her. "We have the same shape."

Marianna shrugged. "What can I say? We both have killer bodies."

Megan, Julie, and Amber burst out laughing, and Megan noticed her mom chuckled a bit as well.

"They all look beautiful if you ask me." Her stepfather, Bill, placed his arm around her mother's shoulders. "I can't believe one of our girls is getting married."

Megan couldn't believe he sounded so sentimental. He'd been their stepfather since they were toddlers. In truth, he'd been the only father they'd known. Both of them called him Dad. He'd never been cruel, but he hadn't been overly close with them either. He worked a lot, and when he was home, he watched television.

"I can't believe it either." Her mother reached across her chest and touched his hand on her shoulder.

"Well, I can't wait," Marianna squealed. "Only sixty-three days." She swatted the air. "But who's counting."

"Obviously you are," Julie laughed. "Have you decided on our shoes?"

Marianna clapped her hands. "Actually I have. Be right back."

She raced to the shoe section of the store. Megan pursed her lips together when her sister returned with a very loud red, orange, and yellow floral high heel. She didn't know how they were twins. No way. Not in a gazillion years would Megan pick those gaudy shoes for someone to wear in her wedding.

Amber grabbed it from Marianna's hand. "Oh, they're so cool. I've never seen anything like them."

Megan agreed with her there.

Julie touched it. "Feel the texture. They're so soft."

Megan didn't care how soft the disgusting things were. Baby's bottom. Kitten fur. They were still revolting.

"I've got a surprise for you." Marianna pressed her hands against her chest. "The cost is on me. I'm so thankful y'all were willing to pay for the dresses that Kirk and I agreed to buy your shoes."

"That's so sweet." Julie hugged Marianna.

"Yes, thanks." Amber joined her. "I'm going to have to find an outfit to wear these shoes with. They are so cool. So unique."

Megan joined her friends in hugging her sister, but she wasn't feeling the same excitement over Marianna's gift. She was just thankful she didn't have to fork over the cash for the atrocious footwear.

Marianna whispered in her ear. "I know you hate them."

"I don't hate them."

Marianna grinned. "Yes, you do."

Megan slid her arm through the crook of Marianna's. "You know I'll wear anything you want for your day. I'm so happy for you."

"I know that." Marianna kissed Megan's forehead. "You are the best twin sister a girl could ever have."

"Wearing this." She pointed to the dress then the shoes. "And those. Uh yes, I am the best sister ever."

Marianna laughed. "You really look beautiful. Your skin is flawless."

"Freckles?"

"Your freckles are adorable. I'm sure Hadley's uncle would think so."

Megan elbowed her sister. "Whatever! I have no interest in Colt Baker."

"You should."

Julie called from the bridal dress section of the store. "Marianna, I know your dress is still being altered, but why don't you try on the floor model so we can see all of us together?"

Their mother stood and walked in Julie's direction. "That's a marvelous idea. Here, let me help you find it."

Marianna's face lit up. "I'm coming."

She raced off the platform, and Amber and their dad followed behind. Megan stepped down and plopped into the chair her mom had left. The last thing she needed to do was encourage Colt. She still couldn't believe she'd kissed Justin yesterday.

She'd tossed and turned most of the night, fretting over how she would behave in front of him at work. Worry niggled her brain over how he would act with her. To her relief, he'd spent the best part of the day out of the office. He'd said he had court, but she had no idea who for. She logged their cases, and it was no one she knew of.

Maybe he was meeting up with some woman and he'd only been playing the part of a Christian. Maybe it was all some weird act.

Shame washed over her at the ugly thought. He'd given her no reason to believe his faith wasn't genuine. She was the one who'd behaved less than appropriately, flinging herself at him at lunch after church.

She didn't want to think about Justin. Marianna was right. Colt would be a better match for her. A solid Christian. Raising his niece on a farm. Didn't seem to have a sordid past. Very protective. She couldn't imagine him disrespecting a woman.

She also couldn't imagine herself in a relationship with him. She didn't want a man. Any man. Sordid. Solid. Stable. Or surly. She didn't want to partner up with anyone.

She was destined to be single. She'd finish school and find a job as a music teacher. Love her students. Love her nieces and nephews. And one day die a contented old maid. That was her plan. And neither Colt Baker nor Justin Frasure was going to alter the plan she determined for her life.

"We found it." Marianna's face shone with delight as she made her way to the fitting room. Their mother followed close behind, and normally Megan would join to help. But she wasn't sure what her mom would say. Besides, it would be good for the two of them to have a little time together.

Dad sat in the chair beside her. She crossed her legs, twitching her foot. Not wanting to be stuck alone with her dad, she scanned the shop for Julie and Amber. They hadn't followed her mom and sister into the fitting room. But they couldn't be too far.

"How are things going, Megan?"

"Good." She continued to scan the room. It was just as she feared. He would start talking to her.

Their conversations had been limited since their blowup when she was almost seventeen. As soon as she'd graduated, she'd hightailed it out of their house and never looked back. Of course, she saw them on holidays. And on occasion, Marianna would drag her to their hometown to visit. But Megan kept to herself. Listened to conversations between Marianna and Mom. Dad usually stayed in the TV room anyway.

"You still working at a law firm?"

He was looking at her. She knew he was. Why he wanted to start a big old conversation now after all these years, she had no idea. "Yep."

"Still in school?"

"Mm-hmm."

"Finished for the summer?"

She nodded.

"So what are your plans?"

She glanced at him then studied the hem of her dress. She wasn't going to get away with not talking to him. Praying for God to give her peace and patience, she said, "Well I hope to get a job this summer so I can do my student teaching while I'm actually working. It's the only thing I have left to complete the program. And since I already have a degree, I could complete my student teaching on the job."

He nodded, and Megan was surprised to see he genuinely seemed interested. "You have any prospects?"

"I have applied for an opening in an elementary school in Lexington. I haven't gotten a call about an interview yet, but school isn't out for the summer until next week either."

"They wait until school's out to start interviews?"

Megan shrugged. "That's what I hear."

Her dad patted her shoulder, and Megan tensed. "I hope you get the job."

She looked into his face, and she could tell he meant it. "Thanks."

"Here we are." Her mom guided Marianna out of the fitting room.

Her sister was a vision in the sleeveless, sweetheart-cut dress. The fit was tight around her top and waist and loosened only a bit around her hips. It then flowed down over her legs and into a long train. Unlike the decorations and the styles she'd selected for the bridesmaids, Marianna's dress was simple elegance. It was something Megan would pick for herself.

Though that would never happen.

Julie and Amber appeared from whatever corner they'd been hiding in. They stepped onto the platform with Marianna. Megan couldn't deny the dresses flattered the wedding gown. Marianna had an excellent eye.

Her mother nudged Megan out of the chair. "Go on up there with them. Let me look at you all together."

Megan joined her sister and friends. She grabbed Marianna's hand. "You are absolutely gorgeous."

"Thank you."

Their mom waved her hands. "Okay. Stand in the order you'll be in at the wedding. Let us get the whole effect."

Megan stood beside her sister, then Julie, then Amber.

"Breathtaking," said their dad.

Mom grabbed Dad's hand. "You all look so beautiful."

They turned to look at themselves in the mirror. Megan couldn't help but smile. She still looked like the one that didn't belong, but she couldn't deny the overall picture was lovely.

Julie made her way to Marianna. She pulled back her hair to get a better visual for what it would look like in just a little over two months. "You're going to be the most beautiful bride ever."

Tears glistened in Marianna's eyes, and Megan felt such excitement for her sister. Kirk was a wonderful, godly man. He would be a good husband. One day the two of them would have a passel of children, and Megan would have the opportunity to spoil them all rotten.

Amber stood beside Marianna. "This dress flatters you so much." She turned toward Megan. "You'll have to get a similar one when you get married."

Her mother huffed. "She can't wear white."

Megan heard Marianna draw in her breath. Megan's mother might as well have jabbed a knife through her stomach. Julie and Amber didn't know the past. They had no need to know. Megan had spent eight years trying to forget. More time than usual of late.

Megan lifted her chin and straightened her shoulders. The look of confused shock on Julie and Amber's faces made her nauseous. She nodded to Amber. "Thank you. Marianna does look gorgeous, doesn't she?"

Marianna smiled. Megan knew her sister well enough to know it was forced. She clapped her hands. "I'm starving. Let's get out of these dresses and get some lunch."

Megan snuck a peek at her parents who were deep in conversation before she turned to head back to the dressing room. Julie and Amber seemed to have forgotten her mother's outburst as they giggled back to their rooms. Or maybe they'd simply decided to ignore the comment.

Megan walked into her room and shut and locked the door. A slight knock sounded. Megan stared at the door-knob. "Yes?"

"Are you okay?" Marianna's voice, laced with concern, was a little above a whisper.

"Of course. I'll be out in just a minute." She sucked back the sniffle, determined not to let anyone know the hurt of her mother's words.

Silence sounded from the other side, and Megan thought Marianna had moved on. Then another whisper followed. "I'm sorry, Megan."

This time she heard the rustling of dress fabric and knew her sister had made her way to her own dressing room. Megan pulled at the thick red bow tied in the back. She turned toward the mirror. A single tear slipped down her cheek. She brushed it away with her finger. She was sorry, too.

Chapter 10

Conflict is inevitable,
but combat is optional.
Max Lucado

Justin lifted his baseball glove and bat out of the trunk of his car. It felt good to hold the equipment again. At first, he'd been a little rusty at the practice on Sunday afternoon.

Could have been because it had been years since he'd picked up a bat. Or because of Megan's kiss. He pressed his lips together at the memory of it. They didn't have some passionate, fire-brewing exchange. And yet it had churned something inside his gut he didn't know needed stirred.

He'd pondered what it could mean. Maybe the kiss was different because he was a Christian, determined to live for the Lord and not his temptations. Or because he didn't whisk her off her feet and take her back to his place. Maybe it was because she let him know point-blank she hadn't meant it and wasn't interested.

Whatever it was, that kiss haunted him.

He'd avoided Megan yesterday at work. Spent most of the day running errands, met a few clients in a coffee shop. Today he had to go to the office. Seeing her tightened his chest. Even in a long skirt that appeared a couple of sizes too big and a crazy, ruffled floral top, she'd looked so cute, he'd wanted to scoop her up and at least kiss the tip of her nose.

He shook his head. This wasn't good. Not good at all. Women were his weakness. His greatest temptation. When he'd committed himself to the Lord, he'd promised to develop and grow his relationship with Jesus for a while. Then he'd consider trying to build one with someone of the opposite sex. He hadn't been a Christian long enough. Only a few months. There was still so much he needed to learn about God and faith and trust and sacrifice. He still had too many women to seek and offer an apology.

"There you are."

Justin looked to his left. Kirk and a blond woman wearing sunglasses and a ball cap walked toward him. Justin waved. The girl looked so much like Megan. Same height. Same build. He even noted the same hair color spilling from the back of her ball cap. He needed to get a grip. He spent too much time thinking about his secretary.

Kirk motioned to the woman. "Justin, it seems like it's taken forever to get the two of you in the same place. But I want you to meet my fiancée."

"It's about time." Justin extended his hand. "It's a pleasure to meet you."

The woman took off her sunglasses, and Justin dropped the bat and glove to the ground. "Megan?"

The woman laughed, and Justin instantly realized she wasn't Megan. Megan had a dimple in her left cheek. The look-alike extended her hand. "Megan's my twin. I'm Marianna. How do you know my sister?"

Justin blinked. He hadn't known Megan had a twin. Of

course, he hadn't known she sang until Sunday. The woman had worked in his office for more than half a year and there was so much he didn't know about her. Too much he wanted to know. He accepted her hand. "She works for my firm."

"You're Justin? Justin *Frasure*?" She shook her head. "How could I not have put this together before now?" A look of contempt flashed across Marianna's face, and her smile wavered, but she recovered and kept it plastered to her lips.

"Guilty as charged." Justin studied the woman's face, wishing he could ask what Megan had said about him. He'd been a scoundrel. He couldn't and didn't deny it. But he was a new man. Something in him needed Megan to know that. More than any other person on earth. What had his secretary told her sister? Had she mentioned the kiss? Didn't twins tell each other everything?

"This is great." Kirk's response broke Justin's concentration. He looked away from his friend's fiancée. "Megan is Marianna's maid of honor. You're my best man. And the two of you already know each other."

Marianna frowned. "You'd told me his name was Justin." She shoved her hands in her pockets. "You probably told me his last name. I just didn't put it together."

"No problem, honey." Kirk wrapped his arm around her shoulder. "It's great they already know each other. Especially since I took so long selecting my groomsmen." He laughed and spread his arms. "It's kinda hard to pick stand-ups when God, Marianna, youth, and video games are a guy's life."

Justin continued to study Marianna. He couldn't read

her expression. He picked up his equipment off the ground. "I'd better start warming up."

Justin started toward the field when Kirk continued, "Marianna and I will be cheering for you on the bleachers. I always rode the bench while you made all the plays anyway."

Justin chuckled at his friend. "You were a better cheerleader than any of the girls."

Kirk squinted. "Don't be comparing me to the cheerleaders."

Justin laughed and continued toward the field.

"Wonder why Megan didn't come," Kirk said to Marianna.

"She's riding horses with Colt and his niece."

Marianna's response sent prickles of jealousy through Justin. Who was this Colt fellow? Megan had never mentioned him. 'Course, it was nearly every day Justin learned something new about the woman who wouldn't leave his thoughts. Was she dating this horseback rider? And if she was, why did she kiss Justin, and why did she say she wasn't interested in a relationship at all?

"Oh, I don't think so."

Justin looked up and saw Amy's husband, Timmy, barreling toward him. Justin sighed. He glanced at the bleachers and for the first time noticed Amy sitting on the bottom row. Her gaze was trained on her husband, and a look of fear marked her face.

He wished he could apologize to Amy. Really apologize. One of her complaints about her husband, besides his constant infidelity, had been his volatile temper and willingness to make a scene when he was mad.

Justin looked at Timmy, who was now only a few yards away from him. The man obviously hadn't changed. Trying to settle the guy down, Justin extended his hand. "I don't want any trouble, Timmy."

Fire seemed to shoot from Timmy's eyes. His face had morphed through more shades of red than Justin thought possible. It had been a few years since Justin had to use his fists to calm a fellow down. Admittedly it was because Justin had stolen away the guy's girlfriend. But if he had to defend himself, he would.

"You don't want any trouble?" Timmy spat through his teeth. "What are you doing here?"

Justin pointed to the baseball bag. "Came to play ball."

Timmy pointed to the dark blue T-shirt Justin wore. It didn't say the church's name on it, like Timmy's did, as Justin had been late to join, but it matched in color. "Play for *my* church." He pointed to his chest. "Oh no. I don't think so."

Justin wondered where Timmy had been during the afternoon practice on Sunday. If he'd shown up then, they could have gotten past this with a little more privacy. He knew Timmy felt he should move on to another church, but he'd probably run out of places to worship if he had to avoid every woman from his past. No. He wouldn't leave. He'd sinned. There were consequences for those sins, but he'd also changed.

Amy had been willing to forgive Timmy. He didn't understand why Timmy felt what happened between her and Justin was any different.

"What's going on, guys?"

Justin looked to his right. He hadn't noticed Pastor Wes stood beside him.

Timmy motioned to Justin. "He's not playing with us."

Pastor Wes nodded. "Yes, he is."

Timmy squinted. "Do you know who he is?"

Justin balled his fists. He'd had just about enough. He was trying to be patient with the guy. Understood why the man wouldn't want to hang out. Even understood why the guy didn't want Justin around his wife. But this needed to be hashed out in private. Not after a church service and not before a church ball game.

Pastor Wes nodded again. "Yes, Timmy. I do know who he is, and he's playing on our team. God's changed his life. Just as he changed yours."

Timmy's expression blanched, and for a moment, Justin thought the pastor's words had gotten through to the man. His jaw tightened and his face hardened again. He pointed to his chest. "If he stays, I leave."

"He's staying."

Timmy glared from Pastor Wes to Justin then back to the pastor. He shoved his glove under his arm. "Fine."

He stomped toward the dugout, picked up his gear, and motioned to Amy. She hopped off the bleachers and hustled behind him.

Justin frowned at Pastor Wes. "I'm really sorry about that. I could leave. He has reason to hate me."

Pastor Wes stroked his goatee as he peered at Justin. "Justin, I counseled Timmy and Amy before their divorce. I counseled Amy through the divorce. She spent nights at our house with my wife comforting her, encouraging her in the

Lord. I know exactly who you are and what you've done."

Embarrassment swelled from the pit of his stomach to the top of his head. The ugliness of his own sin that Jesus washed away flooded him anew. The reality of all he'd done hit him in spurts, like when he was confronted with someone who'd hurt from his past actions. Sometimes the reality overwhelmed him. Like now.

It was the reason he studied Paul so thoroughly. Paul claimed to be the chief of all sinners. Justin would argue he was worse than Paul. Still, Justin related to the apostle from scripture. He knew what it was to be the worst of men and then be changed.

"A lot of the sin heaped on Christ on that cross came from me."

Pastor Wes patted his shoulder. "Me, too, brother. But we don't have time for a share fest." He nudged Justin toward the field. "Let's go warm up."

Justin followed the pastor to the team. They were tossing balls back and forth. This church team was not going to be anything like the last team he played for in college. Several of the players were over fifty and some well over two hundred pounds. These were just a bunch of members getting together to have a good time.

Brian, one of the guys who'd been at the Sunday practice, motioned to him. "Wanna catch?"

"Sure." Justin picked up a ball and tossed it to Brian. He caught it and threw it back.

"Heard you went to Bible study Thursday night."

"Yep."

"I'll be there this week." He pointed to two guys a ways

across the field. "Rick and Mike, too. Had to miss 'cause of a makeup game. Guess you already know that."

"That's what Kat said."

Brian's face turned red, and Justin wondered if he and the teacher had a bit of a thing going. Brian changed the subject. "I'm glad you came. We need more players."

"Looks like you lost one when I came."

Brian didn't comment, and Justin wondered if he and Timmy were friends. Maybe it really aggravated him to be warming up with Justin instead of Amy's husband.

Brian threw the ball again. "I've been praying for Timmy. He's having a hard time. Just lost his job."

Justin didn't respond, but he felt for the guy. A lot of people had been losing their jobs. Caused stress on the families. Made people angry. 'Course, Justin understood why Timmy was angry with him. Justin had no notion of being friends with the guy and his wife. It wouldn't be proper. Even though their divorce had been final when Justin dated Amy, he'd crossed a line that couldn't be uncrossed.

But he couldn't avoid everyone he'd ever known before becoming a Christian. He'd have to move to another state, and he didn't feel God asking him to do that. No. He'd stay in Lexington. Live his life now for the Lord. And deal with consequences of his past as they came. Like dealing with Timmy.

Something in his heart twisted, and he felt an urge to pray for Timmy and Amy. After a quick silent prayer, he inwardly committed to keep them in his daily petitions. They would never be friends, but he could still pray for them.

Brian passed the ball again. "Can you play shortstop?"

Justin threw the ball back and shrugged. It wasn't his strongest position. In fact, with all the bending and squatting involved, and having not played for years, he felt pretty confident he'd be downright atrocious in the position. But he'd do what was needed. "Sure. If that's where you need me."

Brian caught the ball and tossed it into his gloves a few times. "Well, I know you're better as pitcher, but Timmy was shortstop, and all the other guys haven't really played it or are too out of shape." Brian elbowed one of the overweight older guys beside him.

The guy, Jerry, puffed out his chest and sucked in his gut. "Who you calling overweight?" He rubbed the top of his bald head. "And I ain't old."

Justin and Brian laughed.

Jerry guffawed as he shook his finger in the air. "Your day's coming, boys." He patted his belly. "It takes years to build up this physique, but it comes just the same."

Justin laughed again. Jerry was probably the same age as his dad, and the senior Frasure was most likely in better shape than Justin. He had to be, chasing after all the women Justin's age.

A thought traipsed through his mind. If he wasn't spending his senior years chasing women, if he was settled down, would he allow himself to put on a little weight? Embrace losing his hair? Would he be happy like that?

As those thoughts weaved through Justin's mind, Jerry's wife jogged out onto the field with a cold bottle of water. The slightly plump, graying woman handed it to him then rose on tiptoes to kiss his cheek.

An older version of Megan flashed through his mind. He might downright enjoy seeing her jog out to bring him water and kiss his cheek. If she looked at Justin as Jerry's wife had looked at him, he wouldn't mind if she added a few pounds and a bit of gray splashed through her hair.

He pushed the thought away. He needed to focus on baseball. The game was about to start. Making his way to the dugout, he glanced over to the stands. He wondered if Megan attended the games. Obviously she didn't. Besides, Marianna said she'd gone horseback riding with some guy named Colt.

The idea still grated on his nerves. He needed to push this fancy toward his secretary out of his mind. It wasn't time. Maybe a year from now. Once he was stronger in his faith. He spent time in the Word every day, but he still worried he'd mess up.

He glanced at Marianna and Kirk. The woman watched him, a look of wariness in her expression. He knew she'd seen the exchange between him and Timmy. He wondered how much she'd heard. He wondered what Megan had shared with her.

He wanted to defend himself to Megan's look-alike, to tell her he was different than his reputation. That he wouldn't be unkind to her sister. That he cared about her.

He shook his head. What was he thinking? Only moments ago, he admitted he needed nothing to do with a relationship with any woman. And his constant thoughts about Megan made her an even worse possibility.

The feel of her lips against his pressed on his mind.

Why it haunted him he didn't know. It made no sense. He just wanted to stop thinking about it. He looked around the field. He needed this game to get going. He watched the players from the other team take the field. If the game didn't hurry up and start, he was going to have to do something. Run around the field. Punch a wall. Something. His hands itched for movement. His feet tapped against the ground. He couldn't take it any longer.

The umpire shouted, "Play ball!"

Relief washed over Justin. He had something to occupy his mind.

Chapter 11

One of the hardest things in life is having words in your heart that you can't utter.
JAMES EARL JONES

Colt rode his steed at a slower pace than Megan and Hadley. Thunderbolt would have been happy to ride at a faster pace, and truth be told, Colt wouldn't have minded riding alongside Megan. But he held back.

"There is this one guy."

Colt perked up at Hadley's words. She was in sixth grade. Boys should still have cooties.

"Tell me about him," answered Megan.

"He's mean to me. He pushed me into the locker. Told me I was ugly."

Anger balled in Colt's gut. A teacher should have been around to witness a boy pushing his niece. He'd have to make a trip to the middle school. He blew out a breath. School was almost out, and Hadley had gotten mad at him several times for sticking his nose in her business.

Megan laughed, and he frowned. His niece's mistreatment was hardly cause for happiness. Her voice was light. "I remember when boys used to do that. Next thing I knew they wanted to be my boyfriend."

Colt leaned back in the saddle and smiled. Now that

he thought about it, he'd picked on a cute blond in middle school. Emily Watson. She'd been a full three inches taller than him and wore the same red shirt every day. He'd pinched her, even poked her with his pencil to get her attention. She'd run off and told the teacher, and he'd had to stay in during break.

"I don't think he wants to be my boyfriend," said Hadley.

"I bet he does, but since it sounds like he's not being very kind, I'd ignore him if I were you."

"I can't. He sits behind me in science."

"Ask to be moved."

Hadley shifted in the saddle. "She'll get mad at me."

"Trust me. I know the teacher. She won't."

Colt grinned as he recalled the science teacher was Megan's twin.

"You wanna race?" asked Hadley.

"Definitely."

Before Hadley could say, "Go," Megan shot off. Colt laughed as Hadley shouted, "No fair."

Colt laughed as she kicked Fairybelle in the haunches and took off after her piano teacher. Megan handled the boy discussion well. He would have threatened to call the school, and Hadley would have thrown a fit, and they'd have battled for the rest of the day. Already, the situation was nearly resolved.

He thought of Megan sitting with Hadley on the piano bench. He'd forced himself to stay close while Megan taught the second lesson of the week. The memories of Mama playing niggled at him once again, but he'd determined to keep himself inside and listen.

Hadley already loved Megan McKinney. She'd talked about little else since the lesson on Saturday. Even wanted to know what church she attended, thinking Colt might take her for a visit. The girl needed a woman in her life. He knew the time was coming when she'd have personal questions Colt wouldn't know how to answer. If he even knew the answers.

Hadley and Fairybelle beat Megan and Daisy with ease. Of course, it wasn't really a fair race. Daisy was the most laidback horse he owned. Docile. A bit past her prime.

With it being so long since Megan had ridden a horse, he didn't want to chance one with too much spunk. Though watching her now, he was pretty sure she could handle Thunderbolt if he let her. She'd been right. Horseback riding must be like riding a bike. Something one never forgot.

The girls slowed their pace, and soon Colt had caught up with them. He glanced at Megan. Her hair blew around her face, and her cheeks were deep pink and her eyes bright from the exertion of the ride. She sucked in a deep breath and looked at Hadley. "You beat me."

Hadley grabbed the reins in one hand and swatted the air. "Of course. Was there any doubt?"

Colt laughed at his niece's teasing. "I reckon it would have been a fairer race if we'd given her a horse that could hold a candle to Fairybelle."

Daisy whinnied, and Colt reached over and petted her neck. "You're a good girl, Daisy. But truth is truth."

This time Megan and Hadley laughed. Colt drank in

the sincerity of Megan's expressions. She enjoyed this ride through his land. A real country girl at heart. Someone who thrived on breathing in the land God created.

Hadley guided her horse to the left. "Let's go this way."

"What's this way?" Megan asked.

Colt didn't respond. He knew Hadley had prepared a surprise for her piano teacher. He'd been thrilled with the idea when his niece suggested it. Give him more time to talk to the woman.

"You'll see," said Hadley.

The trail thinned between trees and bushes, and Colt moved behind Megan with Hadley taking the lead. He sucked in the delicious smells of late spring. With June just around the corner, the land had been fully replenished with spring showers and mid-May sunshine.

He was proud of his land. It boasted some of the richest soil in all of Kentucky. He raised strong, healthy cattle, always turning a good profit when time came to sell. And his horses were some of the best in the nation. He'd had five make it to the Kentucky Derby, and he rarely wanted for investors to buy a filly or a steed from him.

Yes. God had been good to him. True, he'd inherited the land. It was his grandfather's father who'd done the hardest work, starting the farm from next to nothing. He had gone to an early grave, having put so much blood, sweat, and tears into this land.

But Colt had done good by the land as well. Even got his degree in agriculture. He knew what to grow, when, and how. He'd plotted the land into sections, placing cattle and horses in the best areas at the best times, all the while allowing each section a rest after a few years of labor of keeping up livestock and vegetation.

The land would be here long after him. It was his duty before God to care for it properly, and he'd always done just that. He'd been a good son to his parents. Done right. Not been a burden. They'd gone to their graves knowing the land would be cared for. Now it was Colt's responsibility to ensure the next generation took pride in the land as well.

He looked up at Hadley. She cared for the land and for the animals. But she didn't really know farmwork. She knew rodeos and barrel racing, how to care for horses. But not cattle and crops. Besides, he kinda wanted to be able to pass the farm on to a son. One who would carry on the Baker name.

To do that, he'd need a wife. One who served God and wasn't afraid of hard work. One who'd uphold the family's good name. His gaze shifted to Megan.

"We're almost there," Hadley called from the front.

He couldn't wait to see Megan's face. Confident Hadley's scheme was one the piano teacher would appreciate. The trees thickened, and he pushed a bush away from his foot. The land opened up, and he saw the clearing. An old oak tree with a swing tied to one of the strongest branches sat beside his favorite pond.

He looked at Megan, wanting to note her first reaction. Her eyes opened wide as she scanned the land. He knew it was a breathtaking sight, and the expression on her face said all he'd expected. She loved it.

Megan placed her hand on her chest. "This place is amazing."

Colt hopped off his horse and grabbed the reins in one hand. He held up his free hand to help Megan off the horse. She accepted it, and Colt felt a moment of thrill to be holding Megan's soft hand in his. She put her weight on the left stirrup then swung her right leg over the horse and stepped down to the ground.

Hadley grabbed Megan's hand away from his, and he had to bite back a growl at his niece. "Come here. Let me show you."

Colt tethered the horses, allowing them to drink, then followed the girls around the tree.

Hadley pointed to the closed wicker basket and cooler they'd brought to the spot just a bit before Megan arrived. "Colt and I made lemon cake today. Remember when we were making cookies for Colt? You told me it was your favorite. I hope it's good. Colt and I never made it before."

Colt's cheeks warmed when Megan looked at him, an expression of appreciation and awe on her face. Hadley hadn't had to do much convincing to get him to do something kind for Megan. Right now, he wanted to feel the softness of her hand in his again.

Hadley continued, "We put some pops and waters in a cooler. I didn't know what you like to drink, so there are several different kinds."

He watched as Megan took in the quilt that was already laid out on the ground. Then she scanned the view of the pond and the land around them. She shook her head. "I don't know what to say."

Hadley rubbed her belly. "Say you're ready for some cake. I'm hungry."

Megan smiled. "Sounds good to me." She walked to the wicker basket, opened it, and lifted out the cake. She popped off the plastic lid. "Mmm. It smells and looks wonderful."

As if on cue, Colt heard barking in the not-so-far distance. In the blink of an eye, Old Yeller had bounded out of the woods and made his way to Megan.

"Now wait a minute, Old Yeller." Colt smacked his thigh, and the dog reluctantly meandered to him. "You have to wait your turn." He looked up at Megan and smiled. "The dog has a terrible sweet tooth."

Megan's laugh filled the air and blew through the leaves and grass. It was a beautiful, honest sound. She addressed his dog. "Then I'll be sure to save a good-sized piece for you."

Old Yeller barked his obvious appreciation.

Hadley handed him his favorite soft drink then placed the caffeine-free drink Megan selected beside her. He took the piece of cake Megan offered him. Old Yeller sat beside him with a filled paper plate as well. His was gone before Colt had time to get the fork to his mouth.

Megan swallowed a bite. "This is really good." She looked from him to Hadley. "I'm impressed."

Hadley beamed. "Thanks."

Colt took his bite. It was pretty good. Moist like it should be. The icing wasn't homemade, but it was a good brand. He wasn't a big fan of lemon, but it tasted like it was supposed to.

Hadley swallowed a bite. "So what do you think of this place, Miss Megan?"

"It's the most beautiful place I've seen since moving away from home."

"Where did you live before?" Hadley asked.

"I lived in a small hollow in Pike County." She lifted her hands in the air. "The trees grew every bit as big as this one. The hills rolled all around us. There were ponds and trails and perfect hiding places around every nook and cranny." She focused on Hadley, and Colt drank in her enthusiasm. "Marianna and I even found tombstones dated all the way back to the mid-1800s."

"Sounds like a neat place to grow up."

"It was a lot of fun."

Hadley had a quizzical look on her face. "So why'd you move?"

Colt watched as a flash of pain raced through Megan's eyes. She missed her mountains.

Megan twisted a paper towel in her hands. "Marianna"— she nodded to Hadley—"Miss McKinney, and I had to go away for college."

She nodded and averted her gaze for a moment. It was more than that. Colt could tell it was. He wondered what had happened that she'd left her beloved country, but now wasn't the time to ask. She obviously didn't want to share the whole truth with Hadley.

As usual, Hadley's interest shifted, and she hopped to her knees and looked at Megan. "I'm going to go swing. Wanna go with me?"

Megan pointed to her plate. "I'm going to finish your delicious cake first. You go on over there."

Hadley scurried off, and Colt felt a mixture of relief and trepidation to be alone with Megan. He searched for what to say. He could ask her about school. She'd said she had attended college. Maybe ask about her church or her hobbies or. . .

"Hadley is a total sweetheart."

Colt nodded as he looked at Megan. Hadley was definitely a safe way to start a conversation between them. "She is."

"She's picking up the piano super fast."

"Yes. You said she would." Colt gnawed on the inside of his cheek. His stomach turned, and his hands clammed up. Hadley should be an easy subject. But she was a woman, and his one-on-one experience with women was a list about as long as his fingers. Nope. Not that long. It included Hadley and his mom. And maybe Emily Watson. She had agreed to go with him to their eighth-grade dance.

He wanted to talk about more stuff with Megan. Get to know her. He wiped away the sweat beading on his brow. But talking to a woman was hard.

Maybe he should just be honest. Throw himself out there. He hadn't really thought about needing a woman in Hadley's life before, but he must not have had his eyes open wide enough. Hadley needed a woman. He swallowed. He'd just come out and ask about her passions and dreams. How she'd feel about living on a farm again. His farm maybe.

Whoa, Colt. Now let's slow down those thoughts. Get to know the woman a bit first.

He cleared his throat. "Didn't you say you were in school to be a music teacher?"

She nodded.

"I'm assuming you're done with classes for the summer."

She nodded again and swallowed down a bite of cake.

He watched her wipe her mouth and take a quick drink of pop. "Yeah, I am. All I have left is student teaching, but I can do that on the job. In fact, I have an interview on Thursday for an elementary school." She wrinkled her nose. "I haven't told Justin yet, and I listed him as a reference. I better do that tomorrow."

A flash of heat skidded through his veins. "Justin?"

Megan shoved her empty paper plate into the bag they'd brought for the trash. "He's my boss."

Colt nodded in understanding, but something about her calling the man by his first name upset Colt. He tried to shake the feeling away. For all he knew, Justin was a fifty-year-old married man with a passel of kids and grandkids. "I forgot where you said you work."

"Frasure, Frasure, and Combs Law Offices in Lexington. I've been there about seven months. Planned to stay longer. I didn't know I could work and complete my student teaching at the same time." She wrinkled her nose again. "They'll probably be a bit bummed if I get the job."

Colt had a questioning look on his face. "Why?" He realized his query could be construed that he didn't believe her to be a good employee. He opened his mouth to explain, but she'd already started to answer.

"They've had several secretaries come and go."

"They're hard to work for?"

Colt remembered his first farming job that wasn't on this farm. His dad had wanted him to see what it was like to work another man's land. The guy was a bear to work for, demanding, never satisfied. He'd worn Colt plum out. Looking back, he wondered if the old guy and his dad planned it that way to ensure Colt wouldn't be a difficult boss when the day came for him to hire help.

Megan shook her head. "No. The work isn't bad. It's just that. . ."

Megan paused, and Colt's interest piqued. He could see she fished for the right thing to say. He appreciated she wasn't someone who just sought out ways to bad-mouth her boss. Still, Colt wanted to know more about this Justin guy.

Megan clasped her hands. "In the past, there have been a lot of girls."

"Girls?"

"Well, women really. I mean, Combs is married, so not him, but. . ."

Colt felt his blood pressure rise. What was Megan trying to say exactly? "And this Combs fellow? He's Justin?"

She shook her head. "No. Justin is one of the Frasures. He's the son. He and his dad aren't married, and they. . ."

Megan clapped her hands together and sat up straighter. "You know what, let me tell you about Justin. He's a new Christian. He seems to be very genuine in his faith. He's even joined the Bible study I attend at my church. That's Justin." She stood, and a smile split her lips as she motioned toward Hadley. "I think I'll join her on the swing."

Colt watched Megan leave. So, Justin was a womanizer who'd suddenly found faith and decided to join Megan's Bible study. Colt wasn't an idiot. He knew how men thought. Megan was a sweet, innocent, beautiful woman, and Justin wanted to take advantage of her. He just might have to look into this Justin Frasure.

Chapter 12

Never be afraid to trust an
unknown future to a known God.
CORRIE TEN BOOM

Megan's heart raced as fast as a filly straight out of the gate at the Kentucky Derby. She'd hoped. She'd prayed. She'd even procrastinated the last two hours of work on the chance the senior Frasure or Mr. Combs would walk through the office front door. Didn't they have work that needed to be finished? Where could they be at all hours of the morning?

She looked up at the pewter-finished antique clock on the wall. Her interview was scheduled for 11:30. She still hadn't told her bosses about it, hadn't asked if she could take her lunch half an hour before her regular time.

Normally this type of hesitation would be the action of an irresponsible employee, one who didn't care or take pride in her work. That wasn't the case for Megan.

She had no choice. She had to avoid Justin.

They'd said only a few passing words since their Sunday afternoon lunch in which she had plastered a big one on his lips. Heat warmed her cheeks. She still couldn't believe she'd done that. Not that it hadn't been delicious. Mind consuming. Toe curling. But what kind of weird entity had

126

momentarily taken over her body and caused her to act so out of character?

She glanced at his closed office door. He hadn't come out, and no one had gone in since he'd arrived at 8:00. It was now 10:30, and she really needed to be on her way in around thirty minutes.

Perspiration dotted her upper lip. She was being ridiculous. Nearing a panic attack over speaking with a man she wasn't supposed to like and didn't want to have anything to do with. *Though he does seemed to have changed.*

She pounded her fist against the top of her thigh. It was that kind of thinking that kept getting her into trouble. Shaking her head, she jumped to her feet and pushed away from her desk area. She had no more time to waste.

He probably wouldn't want to discuss her momentary lapse in judgment anymore than she did. In fact, it was probably the reason he'd holed himself up in the office all morning.

Lifting her shoulders and chin, she made her way to the door and knocked. She could do this. She was a grown woman. Who had a degree. Who paid her own bills. Who didn't need a man in her life.

"Come in."

Justin's voice was entirely too delicious. Deep as a bass drum. Confident as a steady rhythm. Her knees weakened, and she touched the doorjamb to ensure her vertical position. She opened the door then bit the inside of her cheek to keep from swooning over the lamination of his pearly whites.

"Do you need something, Megan?"

"Uh. . .well, yes." She cleared her throat. The mixture of embarrassment over their last meeting and the anxiety over telling him about the interview nearly overwhelmed her.

He pursed his lips and folded his hands together, placing them on his desk. "We need to discuss Sunday. I haven't spoken with you, because I didn't want you to feel uncomfortable."

Megan waved her hands. "No." She shook her head. "That's not what I came here to talk about." It was the absolute last thing she wanted to talk about. Though she'd enjoy thinking about it later.

He leaned back in his chair. "Okay. What is it?"

The motion tightened the button-down shirt against his entirely-too-bulky chest. She blinked several times. What was happening to her? An alien with a crush on dark-haired lawyers had slipped into her room in the middle of the night and slithered into her body and taken over. It was the only explanation she could think of.

Megan looked above the man. She studied the framed diploma on his wall. "I need to take an early lunch today. Leave at eleven, and I won't be back until one. I should have asked earlier, but. . ."

What could she tell him for the "but"? *But I was waiting for your dad or Mr. Combs to come into the office? I didn't want to talk with you because the kiss that you didn't give me, but I slobbered all over you, haunts me during the night and a good part of the day.* She stood with her mouth agape. She had no answer for the "but." None she was willing to voice anyway.

Justin waved his hands in front of him. "You don't have to explain."

She clamped her mouth shut. He'd saved her from the horror of whatever explanation she'd have tried to come up with.

Justin studied her, his expression full of interest and concern. "However, may I ask what's going on?"

She swallowed again. She had to tell him anyway. He may be getting a call in the next few days. In fact, she hoped he would. "I have an interview."

"What?" His face twisted into a myriad of shock, concern, and regret. "Why? Because of the kiss?"

Megan waved her hands. She really didn't want to talk about the kiss. She'd already said she didn't want to talk about it. Didn't want to think about it. Couldn't the man take a hint? "It has nothing to do with that. You know I've been taking classes to get my certification to teach music."

Justin nodded.

"I have an interview for a music position at an elementary school."

His eyebrows drew together in a straight line. "I didn't think you were finished with classes."

"Technically I'm not. However, I am allowed to complete my student teaching while on the job. If I'm hired."

He lifted and lowered his chin in slow motion as if filtering the information through his mind. He didn't look happy. She knew it was because it would be a nuisance to train a new assistant if she left. But a part of her wanted him to be upset it would be her leaving.

He turned back to his computer. "Of course, you can take a longer lunch."

His tone was gruff. He was more than just upset. He

was mad at her. But surely he understood her goal was to get a job as a teacher, and she'd have to try for opportunities as they presented themselves.

In fact, he had no right to be angry. As long as she gave a good notice, it was her life. He had no part of it. Even if he had been trying to take up residence in her brain.

She bit her lip. He was one of her references. Crud. She still hadn't told him. She'd listed all of the lawyers, as she wasn't sure which would be available to answer a reference call. It wouldn't do her any good if Justin answered it all cranky because he didn't like the thought of replacing his secretary. The very thought of her missing out on a job opportunity because Justin gave her a bad reference. . .

She shook her head and inwardly groaned. Just tell him already.

"I also listed you as a reference."

She clasped her hands together, willing herself not to fidget as he turned back around to face her. His brows rose, and a mischievous smile spread across his face. "Does that mean I could give you a bad reference to keep you from getting the job?"

Megan gasped. Justin was a scoundrel. Surely he wouldn't do such a thing. She'd been a good employee the last several months, taking almost no time off, finishing work on time or early. She even kept the office straightened up and clean, even though a woman came in to clean thoroughly once a week.

Justin winked. "I'm just teasing you, Megan. I couldn't possibly give you a bad report. You're an excellent employee."

His praise warmed her all the way to the soles of

her feet. "Thanks, Justin."

He lifted one eyebrow. "No Mr. Frasure, huh?"

"I—well—" He was Mr. Frasure. It was the way she should think of him. The way she wanted to think of him, and yet *Justin* repeated itself over in her mind. Especially when she thought of his lips against hers.

"I'm still just teasing, Megan." His face shifted to a more serious expression. "I want you to call me Justin."

She nodded. She didn't trust herself to respond. She walked out of the room and scooped her purse out of the drawer. She needed out of the office. It didn't matter that it was seventy-five degrees outside and a cool sixty-eight in the building. His office was entirely too hot.

"Where are you?" Megan yelled as she threw open the front door of the apartment. She tossed her purse and briefcase on the couch. "Marianna!"

Marianna walked out of the kitchen, wiping her hands on a dish towel. "What is it?"

Megan opened her hands and twirled in a circle. Her heart felt as if it would burst through her chest. She envisioned her classroom filled with children looking at her, their expectant gazes waiting for instruction.

Okay, so maybe Marianna's classes had never behaved in that way the times Megan visited, but elementary kids would be different. She wouldn't have paper wads and rubber bands hurling across the room. She inwardly chuckled.

It would be their bodies flopping all over the place, probably.

She pushed the thought away. Only happy thoughts at this moment. "I think I nailed the interview."

Marianna wrapped her in a hug. She released her and squeezed Megan's arm. "I knew you would do great. There was no doubt."

Megan noted the fingerprint of flour on her sister's face and knit her eyebrows. "What are you doing?"

"Making fried chicken." Marianna ducked her chin. "Or something like it."

"*You* are cooking?"

"I'm trying. Kirk loves his mom's fried chicken, so I got the recipe from her, and. . ."

Megan pointed at her sister. "And you're trying to make it."

Marianna rolled her eyes. "I've got to learn to cook sometime. Kirk won't marry me if he finds out how pathetic I am in the kitchen."

"He already knows you're a wretched cook."

"I know. Isn't he wonderful?"

Megan laughed. "Is it edible?"

Marianna looped her arm around Megan's. "Everything is ready, so let's go find out. You can tell me about the interview while we eat."

"I'm going to change first."

Megan walked to her room and changed into a pair of gray stretchy shorts and an old I Love New York T-shirt. She washed her hands before joining her sister in the kitchen/dining room. She had to admit the food actually smelled delicious. She was starving, so she hoped her senses weren't being deceived.

Marianna pulled a plate from the cabinet and handed it to Megan. "Tell me all about the interview."

Megan dipped mashed potatoes from the stovetop onto her plate. "I think I answered the questions well. They asked why I wanted to be a music teacher, and I told them about my love for music and getting to work with you."

Marianna nodded, and Megan spooned a good helping of green beans from the pan. "The principal had already spoken with your principal. Remember I listed her as a reference?"

"You're kidding? They must have looked into you before you even got there."

Excitement bubbled up inside her. "That's a good thing, don't you think?"

"Absolutely."

Megan speared a piece of fried chicken and put it on her plate. It actually looked pretty good. Her sister might have started to develop some culinary abilities after all these years of living on their own. She walked to the table and sat across from Marianna. "Justin acted a little weird when I told him I had an interview. But I expected that. I wanted to speak with his dad or Mr. Combs."

"Justin?" Marianna squinted. "You mean Mr. Frasure?"

Heat blazed up Megan's neck and cheeks. She hadn't wanted to call her boss by his given name, and she'd been adamant about keeping their relationship on a professional level. Until she kissed him. Even though it hadn't meant anything, she couldn't seem to go back to thinking of him as Mr. Frasure.

Megan shoved an oversized bite of potatoes into her mouth, hoping to mask the blush she knew was forming on her entirely too-white skin. "Yes. That's who I mean."

"I met Justin."

Megan's interest piqued, and she looked at her sister. "You did?"

"You'll never guess who he is."

"Who?"

"Kirk's best man."

Megan choked on the mashed potatoes. She coughed and patted her chest then took a long drink. "The guy from high school?"

"Yep."

Megan's hands grew clammy as she thought of spending so much time with the boss she wanted to avoid. He was Kirk's best man. She was the maid of honor. They'd see a lot of each other in the next two months.

Marianna was staring at her. Megan wanted to believe she had no idea why, but the girl was her twin. Since birth they'd been able to sense things about each other.

Marianna shook her head. "You can't like him."

"I don't like him." Megan dabbed her mouth with the napkin. She was determined not to like him.

"You wanna know where I met him?"

Megan shrugged, feigning indifference. "I don't care."

"I met him at the church softball game. Kirk wanted to go to support him. He's encouraging him in his new faith."

"That's terrific. He's been coming to our Bible study."

Marianna continued to study her, and Megan knew her face had to be the same color as the fire hydrant in front of their apartment. "Timmy was there, too. For a while."

Megan cringed. She'd seen Timmy try to confront Justin at church. She wondered how much worse it might have been on the ball field, but she didn't want to act overly interested either.

"Timmy and Amy left, and I think you know why."

"Yes, I know why."

Megan tried to act as if her sister's words didn't bother her. She shoved a bite of green beans into her mouth and forced herself to chew them. She didn't want to be attracted to Justin. Didn't want to think about him all the time. The only time she wasn't thinking of him was when she was with Colt and Hadley. She'd have to find a way to spend more time with them.

"Megan, you can't fall for him."

Megan smacked her hand on the table. She did not want to have this discussion with her sister. "Have I said one word to make you believe I like Justin Frasure?"

"You don't have to. Remember we had concerns about Clint, and—"

Megan stood, pushing the chair away from her so hard it fell to the floor with a thud. "I remember Clint every day of my life." She clenched her fists. "Every day. Do not mention him to me."

Marianna opened her mouth to speak. Megan noted the apology in her sister's eyes, but Megan didn't want to hear it. She lifted her hand to silence her sister and stormed to her room.

She shut the door and locked it then fell on top of her bed. How could Marianna say that? She knew what happened with Clint. Knew what he took from her. Even knew Megan had kept the shame to herself for three long months until Clint was killed in a car accident. Marianna knew the horrible things her parents said when Megan finally told.

Tears welled in Megan's eyes. She'd spent too many days of her life wrapped in sorrow over that man. He wasn't even a man. He was a sixteen-year-old boy.

Justin was wrong in every way. She didn't want a man in her life. She wanted to be free, to be safe. She would never feel safe with a man.

Megan sat up in her bed and wiped the tears from her eyes. She'd had eight years to cope with it, and she would not allow herself to go to that wretched place of hopelessness again. No. She was stronger than that. God made her stronger. She would not think of Clint or Justin. A relationship was the last thing she wanted.

Chapter 13

Trials, temptations, disappointments—all these are helps instead of hindrances if one uses them rightly. They not only test the fiber of character but strengthen it.

JAMES BUCKHAM

A relationship was the last thing he wanted. Justin shoved the gearshift into PARK and hopped out of the car. He couldn't stop thinking about Megan's interview. Wondering how it went.

He didn't want her to get the job, but he should. He should be happy she might be able to do what she'd been working toward the whole time he'd known her. But the thought of walking into work and not seeing her—a growl escaped his lips.

This attraction he felt wasn't good. He'd promised to spend time, months of time, building his relationship with the Lord, resisting his greatest temptation—women. But Megan was different. He didn't simply want a physical relationship with her. He enjoyed talking to her. Something inside him turned when he listened to her sing. He wanted to understand what she was thinking. He wanted to know she was thinking of him.

He shook his head. Thoughts like this were dangerous. He didn't need a woman in his life, and she deserved someone who wasn't him. He'd mistreated too many women to deserve someone so purely devoted to God.

He spied Kirk through the gym window and waved. Walking inside, he nodded to the young woman at the desk. What was her name? Bridget? Brittany? Brandy. That was it. He looked away from her. A knockout from head to toe, she was the kind of woman he'd always gone after. Someone he appreciated physically but cared nothing about in any other way. From the way she looked at him, the feeling seemed to be mutual.

He looked away from her and headed toward Kirk who'd already started his workout on the treadmill. Justin noted his friend had a full twenty minutes on him.

Kirk pointed to his watch. Sweat rolled down his forehead as he panted through his words. "Gotta get done quick tonight. Taking a shower here. Marianna's picking me up at six."

Justin programmed the machine for the workout he wanted. "I wondered where your car was."

"She dropped me off. We're going to dinner then back to her place to stuff invitations." Kirk ducked his chin and scowled.

Justin wrinkled his nose. "Sounds like a lot of fun."

"It'll be a blast."

Justin laughed at his friend's sarcastic tone. "Better you than me, friend."

The workout on the treadmill picked up, and Justin's heart rate accelerated. It felt good to get his blood pumping. Took his mind off watching Megan walk out that door and head to an interview.

"Your day will come," Kirk said. "But I'm glad you're focusing on God first. How's Bible study going?"

"Terrific. It's great to study scripture and make friends with people who want to encourage my faith." Justin didn't mention his favorite part of the study was being able to see Megan. She knew so much about scripture. She felt everything they studied to the depth of her being. Her passion for God and for learning more about Him drew Justin. He wanted to learn more about her. Discover when it was she became so impassioned about deepening her walk with the Lord.

He wanted what she had. But he also wanted her.

The kiss traced through his mind. How many times had he thought of it? The kiss played constantly on a loop that tracked through his mind, and it didn't make sense that he pondered it more than he remembered his various escapades with multiple gorgeous women. It was the simplicity, the honesty, the sincerity of Megan that made him keep going back to that one moment.

Kirk tapped his arm. "You still with me?"

Justin looked at Kirk. "Yeah, just got caught up in thinking about Bible study." Well, that was partly true.

"I said I was glad you're finding more accountability partners."

"Yeah, after all the beat downs I'm getting from confessing my sins to every woman I've ever known"—Justin blew out a breath—"I've needed the encouragement."

"What are you studying?"

"Paul, which is terrific for me. I feel like a modern-day Paul."

"How so?"

"I'm the worst of sinners whom God mercifully chose to save."

Kirk's workout slowed to the cool-down stage. He grabbed his towel off the side of the machine and wiped his face while he slowed to a walk. "That's true for a lot of us. Not just you."

Justin nodded. His workout accelerated, and he pushed through the programmed mountain climb. He tried to focus on the workout, keep his mind off his secretary.

Kirk's machine stopped. "I'm going to go ahead and start lower-body strengthening. We'll work on upper-body when you finish."

"Sounds good." Justin focused on the workout. He wished it was Thursday. He'd be able to see Megan at Bible study. He could ask how the interview went.

"Hey, Justin. How's it going?"

He looked beside him. Brandy had gotten on Kirk's treadmill. She walked at a leisurely pace. He noticed the flirtatious smirk on her face. *Give me strength, Lord. I'm feeling weak.*

Justin acknowledged her then turned his attention back to the workout. He tried to recall the 1 Corinthians scripture he'd determined to memorize. "*Do you not know that in a race all the runners run, but only one gets the prize? Run in such a way as to get the prize. Everyone who competes. . .*"

He always forgot the exact wording at that point. It was something about going into strict training for a crown that would last. He closed his eyes. He'd read the passage again when he got home. It was the strict training part of the passage that drew him. He knew he'd have to be disciplined, very determined, in order to win his battle with the flesh. Kirk warned him he might always fight the temptations, but the longer he was obedient, the easier the fight would be.

God, I'm counting on that.

"So, how have you been Justin? Work going okay?"

Justin glanced at the bombshell beside him. *Is this some kind of joke from You, Lord, or a playing of the devil?* Justin knew the answer. God didn't play jokes. Situations like these were something else Kirk warned him about. As long as Justin was trying to live for Christ, the enemy would throw in distractions to dissuade his faith.

Justin sighed. It would be rude to outright ignore her. He glanced down at the time left on his workout. The cooldown started in two minutes. He'd be off this machine and working on strength and tone in only six minutes. He could make it that long. He looked at Brandy. "It's been a good week. Everything's fine."

"Great. It's been busy here. Everyone wanting to shrink a few inches before heading to the beach." She leaned toward him. "Not going to happen for most of our clients. You gotta put down the doughnut if you're going to lose the weight." She nudged him with her elbow. "Know what I mean?"

Justin cringed at her critical attitude. Though he knew only months ago he would have laughed and added his own sentiments to the comment.

He focused on the machine. Four minutes left. Maybe if he didn't talk to her, she would go away. He almost chuckled aloud. That sounded like his philosophy for finishing his math homework when he was a kid. It never worked.

"I get off at six." Brandy's voice was sultry. Way too enticing. "Would you like to grab a bite?"

Justin blew out a breath. He didn't need to finish his cooldown. There were only three minutes left anyway. He glanced at Brandy. Wow. The woman's hair fell in cascades over her shoulders. It looked so soft and silky. And the expression in her eyes. A welcome invitation. Justin swallowed back the knot in his throat. He shook his head. "Sorry. I have plans tonight."

It was true those plans involved picking up a deli sandwich and heading back to the house to watch whatever was on the television. But he didn't need to go into those details. He needed to get away from her. He stepped off the machine and headed toward Kirk.

Justin jingled the car keys. He hadn't completed the workout he'd planned, but he didn't want to stay at the fitness center once Kirk left. Not with Brandy working today. Kirk was finishing his shower, and Justin had already called good-bye to him.

Walking toward his car, he spied Megan sitting in her vehicle in the parking lot. He shook his head. That wasn't Megan. It was Marianna. Kirk's fiancée. Justin still couldn't get over his best friend's future wife was Megan's sister. It was going to be a tough couple of months trying to keep his thoughts on friendship while working with Megan.

"Hey." He waved to Marianna then made his way to the car.

To his surprise, she got out and headed toward him. She wore a smile, but it was forced, and Justin could see the look of disapproval in her gaze. She gripped the strap of her purse once she stood beside him. Justin wiped his still-sweaty forehead with the palm of his hand.

She glared up at him. "I need to talk to you."

Justin studied her. "Okay."

"My sister works for you."

"Yes, I know." His brow wrinkled. He thought they'd already discussed this. Her lip trembled.

"Amy and I were good friends."

His stomach twisted. So that was what this was about.

Marianna continued, "When she remarried Timmy, she kinda stepped away. We don't talk as much."

Justin didn't respond. He knew where this was going. She might as well get her feelings out now so they could make it through the wedding preparations in relative peace. He hoped.

She shifted her feet as her voice became stronger. "She confided in me about things. Lots of things."

That was it. Just as he figured. She knew all about his darkest hour. Sure, he'd dated many women with whom he'd been their divorce attorney, but Amy was by far his lowest moment.

"I'm not the same person."

She lifted her hand to stop him. "I know God changes people. I don't deny that. Kirk says your faith is real." She squinted as she crossed her arms across her chest. "You can be as real and as Christianlike as you want. Change the world. Write books. Speak in schools about how God got ahold of your life and made you a better man."

She paused, and her nostrils flared. "Just stay away from my sister."

Aggravation swelled inside him. He'd just spent the last hour working out in the presence of a beautiful temptation, and he'd walked away from her. Besides the fact he hadn't made the first move on Megan McKinney. Although it was probably a good thing her sister couldn't read his thoughts.

He thrust out his chin. This woman had no right to talk to him in such a way. She knew only what she'd been told about him—which was probably largely true. Still, she didn't know the person he'd become. He'd only seen Marianna twice. And from what he knew of her from Kirk, she was supposed to be this amazing Christian woman. The expression on her face at that moment was anything but Christian.

"Marianna, you don't know me."

"I know enough."

Justin bit the inside of his lip. He wanted to light into her. To use a few choice words to tell her she needed to mind her own business. A few months before, he'd have waylaid her with a verbal fury that would have sent her home crying. *God, calm my thoughts. Guide my words.*

It was good she was protective of her sister. A quality he admired in people. He cleared his throat. "I can assure you I have the utmost respect for Megan."

She glared at him, and he knew she wanted to hear more. She wanted to hear he didn't like Megan, that he didn't think about dating her or kissing her at all moments of the day. Again, he realized it was a good thing she couldn't read his mind.

"She's dealt with enough, Justin. Her last boyfriend had 'changed.'" She put up her pointer and middle fingers on both hands and made quotation marks. "It was a lie. He. . ."

She paused, and Justin found himself needing to know what the guy had done to Megan. Marianna shook her head. "He hurt her. She hasn't dated since."

He puffed out his chest. Whatever happened in the past had nothing to do with him. She had no right to judge him when she hadn't bothered to give him a chance. "Not that it is any of your business, but I can assure you. . ."

Her expression softened, and her eyes took on a pleading look. "That was eight years ago, Justin. She hasn't even gone out on a date since she was sixteen."

"That's got nothing to do with me."

"You don't know my sister."

"But—"

"Heed my words. Stay away."

Justin felt as if he'd been punched in the gut. Questions that needed answers swirled through his mind. What could the guy have done that she'd stopped dating completely? He remembered her words at the restaurant of not being interested in ever dating. But why had she kissed him? Was he the first guy she'd kissed since she was in high school?

Kirk walked out of the fitness center, and Marianna pierced Justin with a pleading look not to share what they'd been discussing. It wasn't the first time a woman wanted him to keep his mouth shut when her fiancé, husband, boyfriend, or whoever caught them talking.

Marianna didn't have to worry. He wouldn't tattle that she'd just slammed his character, and he had no desire to talk about Megan. Even though he did want to know what happened to his secretary.

Kirk wrapped his arm around Marianna and planted a quick kiss on her forehead. "She talking your ear off about the wedding?"

Marianna giggled and punched his arm. "You're the only one I do that to."

Kirk let out an exaggerated sigh. "Don't I know it."

She punched him again, and he laughed.

Justin motioned toward his car. "I'd better get going. You two have fun licking invitations."

Kirk groaned and looked at Marianna. "You did get the wet pads, right?"

"Of course I did. We can't really lick over two hundred invitations."

Justin slipped into his car, thankful he didn't have anything to do with a wedding. The very idea of being dragged around from one frilly place to another to pick out dresses, flowers, and fancy cards made his stomach ache.

He thought of Megan. She was the only woman in the world he could imagine being willing to do such awful things with. She'd be simple but elegant, and she wouldn't get all bent out of shape about things that didn't matter.

Marianna's words flooded his mind. Someone had hurt Megan. A primal urge to find the man and rip him to shreds welled up within him. He didn't know how the guy had hurt her. Broken up with her just before prom? Cheated on her with her best friend? Whatever it was, he couldn't stand the idea of someone hurting her. But who was he to talk. . . ?

He pushed the ridiculous notions from his mind. The last thing he needed was a relationship. Unless it was with God.

Chapter 14

The weak can never forgive.
Forgiveness is the attribute of the strong.
MAHATMA GANDHI

Megan tried not to think about the job interview as she drove the scenic route to Colt's house. Only a few days had passed. It would be at least a week more before she heard anything.

And yet each day she found herself growing more anxious. She wanted the job. More than she realized.

She drove down the long lane leading to Colt's house. She hoped Hadley would enjoy the new music book she'd brought with her. The preteen was nutty about the latest teen Nickelodeon shows, so Megan brought one of the more popular current tunes to play on the piano.

She parked the car, but Hadley shot out of the front door of the house before Megan had time to get out of her vehicle. The girl's eyes were swollen, and tearstains streaked her cheeks. She yanked open Megan's door and shoved a partially wadded letter in Megan's face. "Look at this. Read it."

She dropped the note in Megan's lap and covered her face with both hands. "I hate Uncle Colt. I hate him." She raced away from the car and toward the barn.

Megan sat, flabbergasted, as she picked up the note and read it. The sound of horses' hooves caused her to look up and see Hadley riding Fairybelle toward the pond at a pace that made Megan's stomach twist.

She skimmed through the letter. Pain for the girl who was so much more to her than just a student laced through her heart. Today they wouldn't get much piano playing accomplished, but Megan would be a shoulder for the girl to cry on when she returned. But why did Hadley say she hated Colt? It wasn't her uncle's fault.

"Shouldn't have let her check the mail today."

Colt's slow, sad voice made Megan jump. She placed her hand against her chest and got out of the car. "You scared the life out of me."

"Sorry." Colt took the paper from Megan's hand.

Megan felt instant compassion for the blond-haired giant. A true, rough-around-the-edges farmer, Colt was doing his best by his niece, even though it was painfully obvious he had no idea how to handle the pain in this letter.

She grabbed his hand in hers and squeezed. "It's not your fault her father died." Sadness welled inside her. He had been Colt's only sibling as well. "He was your brother, too. I'm surprised Hadley hadn't mentioned it. The child is so open, and the letter said he died a month ago."

"She didn't know."

Megan frowned. "Hadley didn't know?"

Colt nodded.

Megan tried to figure out what he meant. She must have missed some crucial information. "But her mom's letter said you'd taken care of all the arrangements and—didn't

Hadley go with you?"

Colt shook his head. "No. I didn't want her to know. Didn't want to upset her."

What a ridiculous thing to think. Did he plan to protect her from life? The child couldn't hide from heartache. Especially pain that directly affected her. At some point, she had to learn to cope with hard things.

Megan looked in the direction Hadley had raced off on her horse. How could Colt not tell her? Not give her the opportunity to say good-bye? No wonder Hadley was so upset with her uncle. Megan peered up at the man. "Well, she's upset now."

"I should've checked the mail."

Megan's mouth fell open. He still wanted it to be a secret. So he planned never to tell the child her biological father was dead. Even if the man had never uttered a single word to Hadley, he was her father, and she would always be tied to him. "You just weren't going to tell her?"

Colt looked down at her, his gaze ablaze with anger and frustration. "The last time her dad, my brother"—he pointed to his chest—"saw Hadley was when she was four months old. He stayed long enough to beg my parents for cash and didn't even so much as look at his daughter. So, yes, I didn't tell her because I didn't want to upset her."

Megan searched for the words to say, to help him understand that even though the man hadn't been a part of Hadley's life, he was still the girl's biological father, and she'd want to know. An old wound peeled open inside Megan's heart when she thought of her own father. The one she hadn't seen or heard from since she was in kindergarten.

Megan's words were little above a whisper as she tried to keep her own emotions at bay. "She would still have wanted to know, to have gone with you."

Colt shook his head. His eyes blazed with contempt, and his jaw was set tight. "Hadley's mother, if that's what you want to call her, never should have sent this letter. She's a no-good alcoholic and drug addict. Maybe worse than my brother. Do you know how he died?"

Megan shook her head.

"It's disgusting. Vile."

Megan bit her bottom lip. Colt was angrier than she'd ever seen. His hands shook with the fury inside him. She didn't answer, but she knew the dam of his attempt at control was about to break, and she'd learn more than she probably wanted to know.

Colt twisted the ball cap Megan only just realized he'd held in his hand. "Hadley's father got so drunk and high on pills he went into the bathroom to vomit. But he passed out and drowned in the commode."

Megan's stomach turned at the mental image. She noted Colt's fury was quickly turning to a deep-seated sadness. A hurt that he'd carried alone for over a month.

"Colt, I'm sorry."

He raised his hand. "Now, you think I should have told Hadley all that?"

"Not all that, just. . ."

He pierced her with his gaze. "Not any of it. It's my job to protect Hadley. I've made a commitment to my parents and the Lord to raise her in Him, to shield her from the filth that was"—he lifted up the letter—"and still is, her biological parents."

Megan felt deep sorrow at his arrogance and unforgiveness, and yet she knew his heart's intention was to protect Hadley. And she didn't know what it was like to deal with a drug addict as such a close relative, but she did know what it was like to wonder about an absent biological father.

Megan cleared her throat. "You're a good uncle, Colt. God has blessed Hadley with you, but you should have told her that her father died."

Colt started to say something then clamped his lips, wadded the letter in his hand, threw it down, and walked back to the house. Megan picked up the note and read through it again. Hadley's mother, Tina, said she'd written once before and asked if Hadley would contact her.

Megan's heart constricted. Another reason for Hadley to be mad at Colt and for Colt to be worried about Hadley. Megan knew contact with her biological mother could be detrimental for the preteen. Especially if the woman was still abusing drugs and alcohol. Colt probably had every legal right to keep Hadley and the woman away from each other. And Megan would not try to encourage him to allow a relationship that would be unsafe for Hadley.

She glanced back down at the note. The woman's pleadings seemed so honest and genuine. It was no wonder Hadley felt so much anger toward her uncle. But the woman's true emotional and physical state couldn't be observed through a letter.

Megan closed her eyes and lifted her face to the heavens. *Oh God, help Colt and Hadley. What a hard situation. Give Colt the ability to put away past hurt. Show him how much, if any, relationship he should allow for Hadley and her mom.*

The old wound that had only been superficially closed rubbed against her insides. *And God, be with my dad wherever he is.*

More than an hour passed, and Hadley still hadn't returned from the pond. At least Megan assumed that's where she'd gone. Colt tried to pay her for a piano lesson that didn't happen and send her on her way, but Megan would have no part in it. The man had said precious little to her since their discussion when she'd first arrived, but in her spirit, she knew she couldn't leave.

He felt he'd done the right thing by keeping his brother's death from Hadley. And she loved that he had such a protective nature toward his niece. But Megan agreed with Hadley. He should have told her.

She clasped her hands. "Colt?"

"What?"

"I want to go find Hadley."

"Why?"

"To talk to her."

"She's okay."

Megan placed her hand on Colt's shoulder. He acted like a little boy who wasn't willing to share his favorite toy with a friend. Well, she had news for him. Hadley was not a toy. "Colt, she is not okay."

"She should be. I was protecting her from them."

"I know you think you were protecting her, but you

should have told her the truth."

Megan held her breath when Colt turned and peered at her. He was going to throw her out, but she determined she would fight to stay. Hadley needed her, and Colt was acting like a spoiled brat.

"Fine," he muttered as he looked away.

Megan patted his shoulder before she walked out of the house and headed to the barn. Once she had the saddle on Daisy, Megan hefted herself onto the horse and nudged her in the flanks. Not the most excitable of animals to begin with, Daisy simply did not feel the same compulsion to check on Hadley.

Finally reaching the clearing, Megan breathed a sigh of relief when she saw Fairybelle tethered to a tree. Hadley sat beside the pond's bank, her legs folded up against her chest, her chin propped on her knees.

Megan hopped off the horse and approached her young friend. Hadley didn't move, but Megan noted the darkened tear streaks trailing down her dirty face. She sat beside her young friend and waited for Hadley to talk.

Megan drank in the serenity of the place. It was a good place to clear her head. The calm water and just an occasional *kerplunk* of a fish or frog or some small creature moving around in the water. Birds chirped overhead, and crickets sang on the ground around them.

"I thought you'd have left by now." Hadley's voice was low. She sounded like a wounded cat who'd barely managed to escape a fight with her life.

"No. I was waiting for you."

"I don't want to play today."

"I don't blame you."

Hadley didn't respond again, and Megan waited. She prayed God would give her the right words to say. Words that would comfort. That wouldn't encourage Hadley's anger toward Colt. Misguided as Megan believed he was, she appreciated his want to protect his niece. His motives were correct, and in truth, Megan didn't know the whole situation. She only knew how desperately she'd always longed to know her own biological father.

"He should have told me."

Hadley sounded more tortured than angry, and Megan still waited. She inwardly begged God for wisdom in how to speak. With no answers coming, she stayed silent.

"I don't even know how he died." Hadley turned toward Megan. The pain etched across her features stabbed at Megan, and she grabbed the preteen's hand in hers. Hadley went on. "I know when it was, though. Last month Colt said he had to take care of some business with the farm. He let me stay with my friend Callie. I was so excited to stay with her for three nights in a row. If I'd have known. . ." Hadley made a fist and punched the ground.

"I don't have all the answers, but I know this for sure"—Megan stroked the girl's long, matted hair—"Colt loves you. He had the best of intentions. He wanted to protect you."

"Uncle Colt always wants to protect me, and I know he loves me. But sometimes he's just too proud to tell me the truth about things." Hadley looked at the ground. "My dad was an embarrassment to the family. But he was still my dad."

Megan sucked in her breath. The child understood things well beyond her years. Probably because she was left by her parents. She'd been raised in the most loving and caring environment possible, but the knowledge that her biological parents had left her still stung to the depths of her heart.

Megan looked out over the water. "You know, I don't know my dad either."

"I thought your mom and dad lived out in eastern Kentucky."

"Mom and stepdad."

"Oh."

Hadley was quiet, and Megan knew the preteen studied her and tried to figure out what Megan was thinking. Megan turned toward her young friend. "It's hard when someone who should care about you isn't a part of your life."

Fresh tears swelled in Hadley's eyes, and she looked back at the ground. "That's why I should have been there to say good-bye."

"Maybe you should have." Megan wrapped her arm around Hadley's shoulder. "You need to talk to Colt. Not yell. Talk. He loves you." Megan cupped Hadley's chin and lifted her gaze to hers. "And you need to forgive Colt."

A wave of realization washed through Megan, and she knew she needed to heed her own advice. It was time to forgive her mom and stepdad for their reaction. They'd been wrong, just as Megan knew Colt had been wrong, but Megan still needed to forgive them.

Just as Colt might not realize Hadley needed the opportunity to say good-bye to her father, her parents may not realize their reaction had been wrong. But what they thought or believed didn't matter. What mattered was that she needed to forgive. Truly forgive.

Megan bit her bottom lip. The thought of it weighed on her heart. There was a ridiculous comfort in carrying the unforgiveness within her. It gave her reason to be angry with them, to keep their relationship at a distance. Forgiveness would make her vulnerable. It would tear down the wall.

And yet God required it.

And the wall hurt. It was heavy.

To the depths of her soul, she knew whatever God required, He would provide what was needed to make it through. He would help her vulnerability. He would make something beautiful in place of that wall. If she'd let Him.

God, help me let You heal me. I'm like the father in scripture who begged for help with his unbelief. Release me from my need to stay safe behind the wall of unforgiveness. Help me to forgive.

"She didn't tell me she loved me in the note."

Hadley's quiet words interrupted Megan's thoughts. Megan nudged closer to Hadley and wrapped both arms around her. She'd noticed that as well. She'd even reread the note a couple of times, hoping she'd simply missed the words. "I'm sorry, Hadley."

Hadley lowered her head against Megan's shoulders. A new stream of tears flowed, wetting Megan's shirt. She was quiet while the young girl cried. Megan simply stroked Hadley's hair and rubbed her back. After several moments, Hadley sat up and wiped her eyes. "I'm ready to talk with Uncle Colt."

Megan nodded and stood to her feet. She helped Hadley up as well. She prayed that Colt would be ready and willing to talk with his niece.

Chapter 15

Sometimes the heart sees
what is invisible to the eye.
H. JACKSON BROWN JR.

Megan dropped the pen and stretched her fingers. Her sister's wedding was going to kill her. She wasn't sure she could make it through the next several weeks of preparations. Marianna and Kirk were supposed to have finished the invitations more than a week ago. They should have been in the mail, yet here Megan was helping her sister write out addresses.

Marianna put her cell phone on the table. "Kirk's going to be here to help in fifteen minutes."

Megan nodded. She hoped the guy would hurry up. She'd written her parents' address and the addresses of various potential guests on fifty envelopes, and now her fingers felt as if they would fall off.

"He's bringing Justin," Marianna added.

Megan's heartbeat sped up, and she inwardly chided herself. The man had really begun to get under her skin. He was attentive in Bible study, asked questions, and made valid points. His prayers seemed heartfelt and honest.

Even at work, he'd taken on an ethical persona Megan never would have dreamed possible. It wasn't as if he wasn't a decent lawyer before. He was good—if a person defined good as someone who got you a healthy sum of money from the spouse you were ditching. But now, as an adoption lawyer, he showed compassion for the soon-to-be parents and a diligent tenacity to help them find a child to adopt.

She'd found herself more drawn to him than ever, which meant she avoided him every chance she got. She knew a man could change. Scripture was full of changed men. But she didn't want a man, let alone one with a past that required a change.

Marianna sat beside her and placed her hand on Megan's. "He wouldn't be good for you."

Megan pulled her hand away. "Why do you keep saying that? I have never said I like him. I don't want a man in my life. No man."

Marianna didn't move. She stared at Megan, and though she didn't want to, Megan shifted under the scrutiny. "When Clint said he'd changed, we all believed him."

Megan smacked her hand against the tabletop and peered at her sister. "Really, Marianna. You're going to bring him up today of all days?"

She stood and turned toward the bathroom. She saw Marianna glance at the calendar on the wall. Megan heard Marianna's gasp, and she knew her sister understood.

Megan shut the bathroom door and turned on the faucet. She could hear Marianna's apology from outside the door, but she didn't respond. This was the hardest day of the year. Every year. In the past, she'd spent the day curled up in a blanket in her bedroom, watching hours of television. Of course, she'd make sure it was stupid programs that would never remind her of the anniversary of that day.

She cupped her hands under the water then splashed her face. Today she'd determined to get up, to get dressed, to spend the day with her sister. To forget. It had been eight years. It was time. Way past time.

She'd tried to call her parents a few times since the evening she'd spent with Hadley. Her own advice nipped at her conscience, and she needed to attempt to make things right. Each time the answering machine blared back at her. They'd returned her calls but when she was at work and unable to answer. Tears filled her eyes, and she stared at her reflection in the mirror. "God, it's over. It's been over. Help me not to go there again."

As soon as the words left her mouth, she relived Clint's hand gripped around her arm so tight she'd had bruises for several weeks. The remembrance of his breath against her mouth sent a shudder through her body, and she splashed water on her face again.

Marianna pressed against the door. "I'm sorry, Megan. Let me in."

Megan didn't respond. She couldn't. She swallowed and squeezed her eyes shut, willing the smells and visions from the past to leave her mind. Maybe she wasn't ready to join the living on this day. Maybe she needed to slip into her pajamas and get in bed. Sleep away the memories.

Marianna's voice sounded against the door again. "Kirk and Justin are here."

Megan opened her eyes. She had to collect herself. How would Marianna explain her sister locked up in her bedroom? She didn't want her to explain. Didn't want any-one to know. Past was past. And she was over it.

She patted her face with a towel then grabbed the make-up from behind the sink. While taking deep breaths, Megan reapplied mascara and added some blush to her cheeks. She ran the brush through her hair. If she just pretended today was any other day, she'd be fine.

After taking several deep breaths, she walked out of the bathroom. She could hear Justin's deep laugh from the kitchen. A chill swept through her. She didn't understand why he seemed to suck her under his spell. Today was the worst of all days, and yet the sound of Justin's laugh charmed her like a cobra out of a wicker basket.

She wouldn't think about it. She would ignore him, and when everyone left, she'd slide into her jammies and enjoy an evening of chocolate and television. She was pretty sure she'd saved several episodes from Shark Week.

Plastering a smile to her lips, Megan walked into the kitchen and waved. Justin had taken the seat beside hers. Of course. Acting nonchalant, she sat down and started ad-dressing an envelope.

Justin smiled at her. She hated his straight, white teeth. "How are you doing today?"

Megan didn't look at him. "I'm fine."

She was as fine as a haunted person could be. Her cell phone rang, and Megan excused herself. She walked into the living room. She didn't recognize the number on the screen. "Hello."

"Hi, Megan. This is Tammy Carey, the principal at. . ."

Megan's heart beat in her chest. She tried to understand

what the woman was saying. *God, please let me get this job. I gotta get away from Justin.*

She frowned at the ending thought of her prayer. She wasn't sure God would approve of her last petition. Justin had been only gentlemanly to her. It wasn't his fault he made her act cuckoo.

"I'd like to offer you the position if you're still interested."

"Really?" Megan's voice raised two octaves higher than normal.

"Really."

Megan grabbed a paper and pen off the end table and wrote down all the information she needed about signing contracts and new teacher induction and contacting people at the board of education. She could hardly believe it was happening. She was actually going to be teaching students in the fall.

"Thank you so much, Mrs. Carey. I'm really excited about this opportunity."

"We're pleased to welcome you aboard."

She said good-bye to her new boss and pressed the paper with the information of all the things she needed to do against her chest. For the first time in eight years, this date had something good connected to it.

She closed her eyes and pushed out her chin. "God, it's a new start. The perfect day for a change."

Megan walked back into the kitchen, her heart drumming a rhythm of a new start. She placed her phone on the counter. "That was Principal Carey. I got the job at the elementary school."

Marianna jumped out of her chair and raced to Megan,

wrapping her in a hug. "I just knew you'd get it."

Kirk extended his hand. "Congratulations."

Megan watched Justin. He smiled, but she could tell it didn't fully reach his eyes. His chest rose and fell in a long breath. "Well, that's call for celebration."

Megan sat beside him and lifted up an envelope. "I've got an idea. We'll address envelopes."

Marianna giggled. "Sounds like a lot of fun to me."

Justin shook his head. "I know you ladies already made dinner in the slow-cooker, but why don't I treat all of us to dessert?"

Kirk wrinkled his nose. "No can do, man. Marianna and I start our couples' counseling tonight."

Megan watched as Justin raised his eyebrows. He'd obviously not heard of counseling before the wedding.

Marianna said, "The pastor requires it for every couple before they get married."

Kirk added, "We'll discuss what we both expect from the marriage. Who pays which bills. Who cleans and does laundry." He shrugged. "We talk about expectations before the vows. Doing that limits the after-the-honeymoon surprises."

Megan watched as Justin chewed on the information. He started to nod. "That sounds like a terrific idea." He turned toward Megan, and she held her breath. "I could still take you out for dessert."

She noticed her sister's warning look from across the table. Megan jutted out her chin. Marianna had no right to pass so much judgment on Justin. He'd been in no way inappropriate toward her. If anything, Justin should be afraid of her. She was the one who smacked a kiss on him.

Besides, she wanted to celebrate. To wrap herself around a new reason to remember this day. God was blessing her with a teaching position even before she had her full credentials. A dessert and maybe a coffee sounded wonderful.

She looked at Justin. "I would love to." She scrunched up her nose. "It's going to be hard telling my boss about my new position."

Justin pursed his lips and nodded. "It's going to be hard for your boss to hear the news. Wonder how long you'll stay with your office."

"August 1st."

"A little less than two months."

Megan saw sadness etch his features. Was he simply sad he'd be losing a good employee, or was it more? She didn't want to admit it. Berated herself for it. But a part of her wished it was something more.

Her mind knew life was easier, safer when she kept relationships at a distance. But there was something about Justin. He drew her.

Me and every other single, and married, woman in Lexington.

She didn't want to think of Justin in that way. She just wouldn't think about it at all. She addressed another envelope and stuck the invitation inside. She knew Marianna stared at her, waited for her to look up so she could scold her acceptance of the offer with her eyes. Well, she wasn't in the mood for Marianna's scolding.

They finished the envelopes and ate the slow-cooker lasagna. Marianna had found the recipe online. Megan had been sure it would be disgusting, but to her surprise it wasn't too bad. As she placed her plate in the dishwasher, Justin touched her arm. "Are you ready?"

Megan nodded. For a moment, she wished she'd declined Justin's offer. Part of her longed for her jammies and chocolate. But she'd told him she'd go. She waved to Kirk and Marianna, making sure to avoid eye contact with her sister.

Justin touched the small of her back as he guided her to the car, and a mixture of trepidation and pleasure washed through her. She listened as Justin talked nonstop about a couple he was working with who were about to receive their baby from Ukraine. They reached the quaint café, and Justin made his way to open the car door for her before Megan even realized what he was doing.

It felt an awful lot like a date. Not a friendly celebration. She wished she'd driven her own car. There was comfort in knowing she could leave anytime she wanted. She looked up at Justin, and the kindness in his expression settled her.

They walked inside, ordered their desserts, then made their way to a small table in the corner. Megan watched as Justin's expression changed when he saw a woman at a table a little ways from theirs. She tried not to consider who the woman could be and opted to try conversation. "Thanks for bringing me."

Justin's gaze softened. "I'm happy for you. Even if it's bad for me."

As he fidgeted with his napkin, Megan caught him sneaking another look at the woman. A long sigh slipped from his lips. "Megan, I'll be right back."

Her forehead creased with concern as she watched him walk toward the woman. The woman didn't look pleased to see him. As Justin spoke, confusion wrapped the woman's face. She shook her head. The woman wanted Justin to leave. It looked like the woman said, "Fine," before Justin walked back to Megan. The woman watched him and scowled when he sat across from her. The disgust in her expression was apparent, and Megan shifted in her seat.

"What was that about?"

Justin studied her, frustration etching his brow. "You really want to know?"

Megan nodded, though she wasn't sure she did.

"I'm not the man I used to be." He traced his finger along the brim of the cup. "And one of the things God wants me to do as a new creation is apologize to those I've hurt."

Megan studied her chocolate brownie à la mode. She knew what he meant. It sickened her. "The women?"

"Yes."

Justin's voice was barely above a whisper, but she felt the force of it like a tornado wreaking havoc on a town. What was she doing having dessert with this man? He was the last man in the world she should ever sit with at the same table.

She sneaked a peek at the woman, who boxed her dessert in a Styrofoam container. Being in the same room as Justin must prove too much for her.

Megan chewed the inside of her cheek. The woman was gorgeous. Like breathtaking. Sickening. Long, straight blond hair. A body that required a lifestyle of diet and exercise. Megan wondered what dessert the woman could possibly be eating that would allow her to look so beautiful.

"Most of them aren't accepting my apology."

Megan looked back at Justin. He twirled his fork around his cheesecake. He gazed across the table at her. "I'm sorry to have done that in front of you. I haven't been able to get in touch with her. She was the last woman I needed to speak with, except Amy, but we both know how that's going."

He stopped and locked her gaze with his. He probed her mind for her thoughts, for her opinion of him. She averted his gaze. Knowing he'd held so many women twisted her insides. Saddened her more than it should.

"When I saw her," he continued, his voice just above a whisper, "I knew the Holy Spirit wanted me to ask forgiveness. It's hard. . . ."

He stopped and shoved a bite of his cheesecake into his mouth. Megan felt too sick to try hers. "So, there have been a lot of women?"

"More than I'd like to admit."

"Why?"

"Would you like the honest answer?"

Megan blinked.

"I wasn't a Christian, Megan. Even Christians struggle with sin, but when you aren't saved. . ."

Nausea twirled in Megan's gut. She didn't want to hear the answer. Couldn't stomach the words. She excused herself from the table and walked to the bathroom. The sickness she felt earlier. The memories. They swarmed her as she stared at her reflection. She grabbed a paper towel out of the dispenser and wiped her face. *God, get me out of here.*

Chapter 16

Love me when I least deserve it,
because that's when I really need it.
SWEDISH PROVERB

Megan opened her eyes and stared at the ceiling. Somehow she'd made it through the rest of the dessert date with Justin. He'd taken her home, she'd slipped into bed, and mercifully God had allowed her a romp through dreamland.

Turning over in bed, she tucked her arm under her head. The bright sun sneaked through the cracks of the blinds. It was Saturday, and her only plans for the day were to clean the house, do some laundry, and study her Sunday school lesson. The apartment complex's pool had opened a few weeks ago. Maybe she'd slip down there and try to get a bit of a tan before Marianna's wedding.

The awful June date was behind her for an entire year. She smiled when she realized now she had something different to connect to the date. She'd gotten the job as an elementary school music teacher. Thankfully she had the whole summer to seek advice and plan her lessons and discipline tactics. She had plenty of time to study several of the books she'd read over the last few years. *I will need to call the university Monday and find out how to set up on-the-job student teaching. And I need to write a resignation letter.*

Her insides clenched as a wave of regret washed through her when she remembered Justin's reaction. He'd tried to act as if he didn't care, but she had seen the disappointment in his eyes. She was a hard worker, efficient. But she wondered if it could be something more. Berated herself that part of her hoped it was.

She thought of Justin's expressions when he returned to the table after speaking with the blond at the café. His reaction to her questions repulsed her.

She released a long breath and pulled herself up from the bed. Today was not a day to think such things. It was a new start. The past was gone, and she could dwell on things to come. Positive things. A bright outlook.

Marianna flung open Megan's door, her expression full of sadness and concern. "We have to go to Pike County. Now. Get dressed."

Megan scratched her arms. The last thing she wanted to do was make a trip to see the parents. Sure, she'd tried unsuccessfully to get in touch with them, but today was not the day she planned to focus on that. "What? Why?"

"Apparently Dad is sick. Really sick."

Megan squinted. "What do you mean?"

Tears welled in Marianna's eyes. "Mom called. He has cancer. Liver cancer. They didn't tell us because they hoped he'd make it past the wedding. They didn't want me to worry while I planned. . ." Marianna flopped onto the edge of the bed and placed her face in her hands.

Megan walked to her sister and wrapped her arms around her shoulders. His coloring had seemed a bit off when they visited for the fitting. In fact, Megan remembered thinking it kind of weird he wanted to be there with a bunch of girls for it. And she'd been surprised at how kind he'd acted.

Megan's heart beat faster, and her head began to ache. She and her sister's relationship with him had grown strained after Clint. It had been the same with their mom. Now that she thought about it, Megan remembered her mother seemed especially weary at the fitting. Megan swallowed back emotion. "What did Mom say?"

"He's not going to make it to the wedding." Marianna looked up at Megan. "And she was crying."

Megan scrunched her eyes closed, willing the tears to stay inside. She knew their mother. The woman held things inside. She didn't show pain. Or worry. She was stoic. Emotionless. Which meant their stepfather might not make it through the day.

Megan opened her eyes and gazed at her sister. She brushed a tear away from Marianna's cheek. "We need to get out of here as soon as possible."

Marianna nodded and raced to her bedroom. Megan got ready quickly. She threw on a comfortable pair of capris and a T-shirt then packed an overnight bag. By the time she grabbed a few snacks, Marianna was already waiting at the door.

The ride home was a quiet one. Megan appreciated that her sister didn't want to talk. All she could think about was her stepfather's lack of faith. He'd hurt her. He and her mother. But the thought of him spending eternity separated from God made her sick to her stomach. She wouldn't wish that on anyone. Even Clint.

The realization sparked a notion that maybe she could forgive. Possibly God had been working on her spirit bit by bit over the years to allow her a compassion for her past boyfriend and her parents she hadn't realized was growing.

She couldn't say anything to Clint. Couldn't offer forgiveness. Couldn't share her faith. He was gone. Died before she'd had the chance to emotionally heal from what he'd done to her. But she could talk to her mom and stepdad. The only dad she'd ever known.

Marianna pulled into the hospital parking lot. A fleeting thought that they should have gotten flowers flashed through her mind. No. He didn't need flowers. He needed Jesus. He needed a Savior before he left this life and journeyed into eternity.

Marianna parked the car and then grabbed Megan's hand. "We need to pray."

Megan looked at her sister. The concern etching her brows mimicked what Megan felt. Her sister shared her worry for their dad's salvation. Megan nodded, and Marianna spoke quietly and quickly. Her sister's fervent pleas twisted at Megan's heart, and she knew her sister's burning desire for her parents to know the Lord echoed her own heart's longing. The wrong they'd done to her was nothing compared to an eternity separated from God.

Marianna finished the prayer, and they jumped out of the car and rushed inside. When they reached his room, Marianna walked right in and grabbed his hand. Megan felt glued to the floor in front of the doorway.

She hadn't expected him to look so sick. So frail. Tubes

were hooked up to him everywhere. His skin was yellow. He looked more than gaunt. It was like someone had sucked all the juices from his body and left little more than a barely breathing corpse. How had he gotten so sick so fast?

Megan made eye contact with her mother who sat on the opposite side of the bed. The woman sat like a statue. No visible signs of hurt or worry. She'd stood strong when one man chose to leave her with two small children. Megan could tell she determined to stay just as strong when another left her, even if it wasn't by choice.

Marianna's voice squeaked when she started to talk. "Dad, you've got to listen to me. I've been praying all the way up here. We don't have any time to waste. You need to listen now."

Megan couldn't move. She'd determined to walk confidently in the room, proclaim to her stepfather his need for the Lord. To be bold in her faith. To not take no for an answer from him. To not be concerned with the pain his words had caused in the past. The ugly name he'd called her. The accusation she'd lied.

She couldn't move.

"God loves you, Dad. The Bible says He loved you so much He sent Jesus to die for you. You believe in Jesus, don't you, Dad?"

Marianna's voice grew stronger with each word, and Megan's knees weakened. She needed to be in there beside her sister. Why couldn't she move?

"The Bible says you've sinned. Done wrong. You know that, too. We've all done things we shouldn't have done. All of us."

From the door, Megan watched her father's strained nod. The pain etched across his features ripped at her stomach. Did he hurt from the cancer only or also from the realization of the sins of his life?

She still couldn't believe he looked so sick. It had been only a few weeks since he'd sat beside her in the bridal boutique. He'd tried to talk with her, and she'd been so uncomfortable. Still, he'd said he hoped she'd get the job. She'd gotten it. She should go in and tell him. He'd want to know.

She couldn't move.

Marianna continued. "Just tell Him here." She touched their father's chest. "You don't have to say the words aloud. Just tell Him you're sorry for the sins you've committed. Ask Him to come into your heart. He'll do it, Dad. He promises He will."

Tears filled Megan's eyes. The man who'd raised her since she was just a tiny girl could barely breathe. He didn't even try to speak, but she knew he heard everything Marianna said by the expressions crossing his face. He didn't have much time.

Megan watched him so intently she hadn't noticed her mother stood beside her. "I'm surprised you came."

Megan startled then looked at her mother. "Why?"

Vulnerability flashed across her mother's features. "You hate us."

Megan furrowed her brow. She'd never seen her mother so unsure. "I don't hate you. Either of you."

Her mother didn't respond. A war raged within Megan. She should tell her mother she loved her. It was true her mother hadn't said the words since before the fight that had been etched in concrete in her mind. But God wasn't worried about what her parents did or didn't do. He wanted Megan to forgive. She knew it to the depths of her soul. She couldn't move on until she did.

Her mother straightened her shoulders. She lifted her chin and bore Megan with a look of contempt. "You should have obeyed us. We knew better. And you didn't listen. And nothing has been the same."

Megan sucked in her breath as her mother walked back to the chair beside her husband. No mercy. No compassion. If only Megan could take back that decision to go out with Clint against her parents' wishes. She wished to the core of her being she had listened and obeyed.

But what he did was not her fault. She'd blamed herself for too long. Spent years trying to forgive Clint and her parents.

What about yourself?

Tears spilled down her cheeks. She didn't even try to stop them. Had she ever forgiven herself? She'd been a foolish teenager caught up in the belief that Clint was the boy of her dreams. If she'd listened, that night never would have happened. But she didn't. She'd messed up, and she was sorry.

Closing her eyes, she thought of God's servant David. A man after God's own heart. He'd messed up. Badly. Had sex with Bathsheba. Got her pregnant. Then had her husband killed on the battlefield. His prayer to God after the prophet Nathan confronted him slipped from Megan's lips, "Cleanse me with hyssop, and I will be clean; wash me, and I will be whiter than snow.'"

She opened her eyes and looked at her father lying in the hospital bed dying. Her sister sat at his side, leading him to an everlasting faith in God. Megan looked up at the ceiling and whispered, "Restore the joy of my salvation. Give me a willing spirit. Sustain me."

Forgive herself. She'd spent years trying to forgive others, but she hadn't realized where the forgiveness needed to start. From within.

Her feet moved. She walked to her father's bedside. Marianna still clung to his hand. His eyes were closed. He hadn't spoken the whole time Marianna prayed with him. But despite the labored breathing, his countenance looked at peace.

Megan placed her hand on her sister's shoulder. She looked at her mother whose expression was deader than it had been when Megan and Marianna arrived. The woman needed the Lord. How could she get through this without Him?

Megan looked back at her father. He opened his eyes and saw her. A slight smile spread across his lips. He pressed the back of his head against his pillow and sucked in a deep breath. His words came out just above a whisper. "Forgive me."

Megan gasped as a fresh set of tears washed down her cheeks. She grabbed his hand in hers. She didn't have to think. The words slipped from her lips with a truth that was more than she felt. "I do."

He smiled fully and closed his eyes. Only a few more moments passed before the laboring of his lungs slowed. He took one last gasp of breath. A smile spread his lips, and he was gone.

A sob escaped her mother's lips and Marianna jumped up, rushed to the other side of the bed, and wrapped her arms around their mother. Despite feeling unsure about what her mother might say, Megan followed her sister and hugged her mom.

Words she hadn't said in more than eight years spilled from her mouth. They brought healing hope, and Megan knew she meant them. "I love you, Mom."

Chapter 17

*It is difficult to know at what moment love begins;
it is less difficult to know that it has begun.*
Henry Wadsworth Longfellow

Justin placed the wrapped box on Megan's desk. He fixed the bow once more then inwardly scolded himself for acting like such a whipped pup. What reason would he have for acting that way anyhow? He was simply getting a really good secretary a going-away present. Just because she'd still be there for over a month longer, and just because he talked his father and other colleague into spending more money than either ever would have considered—it meant nothing.

His dad crossed his arms in front of his chest and lifted his left eyebrow. Justin knew that look. He found Justin's actions humorous and ridiculous. Sneaking a peek at Mr. Combs, Justin noted the eldest lawyer of the firm seemed oblivious to everything except the homemade cinnamon bun his wife gave him each morning. One look at the man's expanding waist, and Justin wondered how long it would be before Combs would move into the next size suit. Again.

Justin took his handkerchief from his suit pocket and dabbed at the water that had spilled from the flower vase onto Megan's desk.

"Son, it looks fine." His dad's voice was laced with

humor and a touch of something Justin couldn't quite put his finger on.

"I know." Justin stood to his full height and adjusted his tie.

His father studied him. "Is there something going on between you and Megan?" He lifted his hands. "Not that I mind. It's just that I didn't know."

Justin shook his head. "Absolutely not. Megan is a friend. Her sister is marrying Kirk. We go to Bible study together."

His father harrumphed. He didn't understand Justin's newfound faith. Justin prayed for his dad and that he would be a living example of Christ before his dad. But Justin understood his father all too well. It would take time, and a miracle, for him to see that living a life filled with money and women was no life at all.

And yet living for Christ wasn't easy. The girl from the gym still made advances at Justin. Brandy was gorgeous, and Justin knew how a night out with her would end. He couldn't deny the temptation. But his relationship with Christ had shown him he wanted more. He wasn't willing to compromise for less than God's best in his life.

The front door opened, and Justin found himself smiling at the secretary's surprised expression. Megan's presence stirred something within him. It was a cliché statement—one too often quoted from a popular movie from the nineties, but the truth was Megan made him want to be a better man. He wanted to be more than himself. He wanted to be all that he could be in Christ.

He wanted to be worthy of her.

The thought caught in the back of his brain. His goal had been to work on his relationship with the Lord. To abstain from women who would distract his growth. He needed to stay the course, to find what God wanted from his life.

Megan, he realized, didn't distract his growth in the Lord, but encouraged all those good things in him. He drank in her light blond hair that fell just below her shoulders. Her deep blue eyes spoke of a depth deeper than the ocean.

When had he fallen in love with her?

She smiled as she walked toward them. Justin realized the smile didn't quite reach her eyes. She bent down and sniffed the rose and daisy arrangement then picked up her card. "What's all this?"

Justin's father put his arm around Megan's shoulder and kissed the top of her head. "You're going-away-slash-starting-a-new-career present."

"I haven't even written my resignation."

Mr. Combs swallowed the last bite of his cinnamon bun and wiped his mouth with his fingertips. "Justin told us about your job as a music teacher in the fall. We're very proud of you."

Her eyes glimmered, but Justin noted a small hint of sadness behind them. She hugged his dad and then Mr. Combs. She turned toward him, and Justin sucked in his breath. It was his turn. He would get a hug. Hesitation washed across her features before she halfway wrapped her arms around him and patted his back as if he were a leper whose skin was falling off and who hadn't had a bath in weeks.

His father looked at him, and his left eyebrow rose again. It took every ounce of restraint within him not to tell his father to buzz off. He didn't need his humor-filled, knowing glances.

Justin motioned toward the present. "Open it."

Megan looked at each of them. "You really didn't have to do this."

Justin's dad pointed at the gift. "Open it. Combs and I don't know what we've done."

Justin's face warmed. He didn't want her to know the whole thing had been all his idea. He definitely didn't want her to know that left to his father and Combs, Megan would have quit with little more than her last paycheck.

Megan grinned at him. She unwrapped the gift then gasped when she realized it was a laptop.

Justin opened the box and turned on the machine. "I had the clerk install several different kinds of music software programs. Stuff I thought might help you with your new job."

"Very nice gift." Mr. Combs patted Justin's back. He grabbed Megan's hand in his. "It's been a real pleasure having you with us. We'll miss you when you're gone." He pointed to his office. "But it's time to get to work."

With that, he nodded and walked away.

"I have to agree." His dad grabbed Megan in a bear hug. "You've been the best secretary we've had. I'll miss you." He released her and held both her arms in his grip. "I mean that."

Justin realized he did. Megan had not only been the ideal woman for him, but she was the perfect secretary for his dad as well. He couldn't fathom how they would ever replace her. Again, he realized how much he didn't want to let her go. And not just as a secretary.

Megan looked up at him, her eyes glistening with the threat of tears. "I can't believe you did this. It's more than kind."

With the last words, a lone tear slipped down her cheek, and Justin couldn't stop himself. He wrapped his arms around her and pulled her against his chest. To his surprise, she melted into him, and he had to hold her tighter.

"Thank you, Justin."

The sound of his whispered name from her lips sent trails of delight through him. Feelings he'd tried to hold at bay.

A moment passed, and he felt warm wetness against his chest. The gift shouldn't cause such tears. Something else was going on. He pulled her away from him and studied her expression. "Megan, what's wrong?"

She inhaled a long breath. "My dad died on Saturday."

"I'm so sorry." He pulled her to him again.

"It was hard."

She welcomed his embrace, and he tried not to think about how perfectly she fit against him and how he wanted to always protect her from pain.

She pulled away and grabbed a tissue from her desk. "But he accepted Christ. Just before he died. Thanks to Marianna." She dotted her eyes, and her lower lip quivered. "Our relationship was strained."

"When's the funeral?"

"Not until Friday. His cancer moved so fast the doctors

wanted to look at. . ." She stopped and shook her head.

"I'll go with you."

She looked up at him. "You'd do that?"

Justin swallowed. Never before would he have considered attending a funeral with a woman. Doing anything for a woman that would cause even an inkling of discomfort to him. But everything changed when it came to Megan. "Absolutely."

Megan didn't respond. Instead, she looked at her desk and pointed to the card leaning against the flowers. "I didn't see the card."

She picked it up, and Justin took it from her. "It's probably not a good idea now."

She cocked her head. "What is it?"

With a sigh, he handed it back to her. She opened the card and pulled out the two tickets to the Lexington Opera House. Though it was something he'd never consider doing on his own, he thought she might like to see the Southern quartet that was performing there tonight. He'd bought them on a whim. Now he wished he'd simply stuck with the laptop.

She lifted the tickets. "I've never heard of this group."

Justin shrugged. "Me neither. I just figured you'd like southern music, and when I saw them, I guess. . ." Justin cleared his throat. He couldn't remember the last time he'd fumbled all over himself inviting a woman out for an evening.

She smiled up at him. "I think it will be good for me. I'm assuming the second one is for you?"

Justin nodded. "I'd like to treat you to dinner as well."

Megan bit the inside of her lip, something he realized she did anytime she wasn't sure of a situation. She nodded. "Okay."

Justin sucked in a deep breath. It had been a long time since he'd been so excited about a date.

Justin leaned against his new black sports car. He crossed his arms in front of his chest. "That show was definitely not what I expected."

Megan doubled over and laughed for what seemed the millionth time that night. She stood back up and wiped her eyes with the back of her hand. "Your expressions to their jokes alone were priceless."

"Don't get me wrong. I like Gene Autry and Roy Rogers just fine. I just hadn't expected. . ."

"The quartet was a lot of fun."

Justin nodded. He had to agree with her. Dinner had been terrific, but the show had been an unexpected surprise.

She sobered as she let out a long breath. "I needed those laughs. Thanks, Justin."

She had no idea how much her laughter, her genuineness, drew him. She was like no other woman he'd ever met. He didn't want to take her home for a nightcap and an awkward morning. He wanted to take her home for good. The truth of it scared him.

"I meant it about going with you to the funeral."

Megan shook her head. "That's awfully sweet of you,

but as your secretary, I recall you have court on Friday."

Justin frowned. She was right. He did. "I can see if Dad will cover for me."

She lifted her hand. "I'll be fine."

She looked up at him, and he found himself swallowing hard. He wanted her to kiss him again. Maybe he should kiss her. But what would she think? In his heart, he knew she wasn't ready. He didn't know why, but he could tell it wasn't the time.

He didn't deserve a woman like Megan. She deserved a man who didn't have to apologize to half of the women he'd ever met. He wondered how many years it would be before he'd walk in a restaurant or church building or department store without seeing a woman he'd known in his past. Maybe that day would never come. His sins had been forgiven, but consequences had a way of hanging on.

She picked at her fingernails. "How many more apologies?"

She must have read his mind. He looked up at the heavens. The stars were especially bright. Not a cloud in the sky. A man should be admiring God's natural wonder with his date, not discussing the women he'd wronged.

"Believe it or not, I'm done. Remember, I told you at the café."

"That's right. I forgot."

He stared at her. He was attracted to Megan as he'd never been attracted to another woman in his life. And he wouldn't lie to her. Wouldn't sugarcoat things. She knew what he was. One day maybe she would want to know who he was becoming in Christ. He cleared his throat. "Not everyone was forgiving. Not that I can blame them."

Megan rubbed both of her arms as if brushing away goose bumps, but the air was warmer than usual for June. "Forgiveness is a tough thing."

"This may sound a bit corny, but you like music, so maybe you'll appreciate it."

He pulled his wallet out of his back pocket and opened it. He took out the small folded paper he'd put inside. "I found this old hymn." He cocked his head. "Actually it was by complete accident. Written by this woman, Elizabeth Clephane. It talks about the cross and how it's safety and shelter, and then about the grave just beyond the cross."

He looked at her to see if he was boring her with his nostalgia about some hymn he'd found on the Internet. Her gaze seemed to search him. She wanted to hear the words of the song as much as he'd wanted to know the depths of their meaning. He looked back down at the paper, away from the intensity of her gaze.

He continued, "The song goes on to talk about seeing the form of the One who died there for me." He placed his hand against his chest, feeling the words anew in his heart as he quoted, "'And from my stricken heart with tears two wonders I confess; the wonders of redeeming love and my unworthiness.'"

Emotion threatened to well up and spill out from within him. He cleared his throat and sneaked another peek at Megan. She studied him as if she longed to take a scalpel and pry him open to see if all he said was true. He wanted to be true. To be honest and upright. He didn't want to be the man he once was. He was unworthy. Forever unworthy.

But his unworthiness had been redeemed by God's love.

He wanted to start fresh. Again. The apostle Paul had been the best and most educated among Pharisees. Yet, he met Jesus on the Damascus road and was forever changed. It could be true for Justin. He had to believe God would take the mess he'd made of his life and make him into a man who didn't need to be constantly reminded of his great wealth or need the admiration of the most beautiful of women.

She whispered, "'Beneath the Cross of Jesus.'"

He looked at her questioningly.

She pointed to the paper. "That's the name of the song."

"Oh. Yes. That's right."

He looked at her. She looked as if her mind raced with a million things at one time. When sadness stole over her expression, he clapped his hands. "Enough with the heavy. I had a lot of fun tonight. I thought I'd fall out of my seat when that guy brought out an accordion and they started yodeling."

A smile spread across Megan's face. "I was pretty sure you weren't expecting that. What did you think of the song about learning to yodel?"

Justin shook his head. "I didn't know sounds like that could come out of a man."

Megan laughed. "You wanna try?"

"No!"

Her laughter bubbled out again, gracing him with her inner joy. "You'd better get me home. I gotta work tomorrow." She winked. "Wouldn't want the boss to be mad at me for being tired on the job."

Justin shoved his wallet back into his pocket. He had to do something to keep himself from kissing the wink off her eyelid. And her other eyelid. And her. . . "I suppose you're right."

He opened her car door for her, and she slipped inside. She looked up at him, and Justin wished the evening could last longer. Forever. Her expression grew serious. "I'm really proud of you, Justin. God's really gotten ahold of your life."

He shut the door and walked to the driver's side. He hadn't wanted it to happen. Wasn't even sure when it had. Maybe he started to realize it when she told them she'd gotten the job at the elementary school.

Whenever it was and however it happened, he'd fallen in love with Megan McKinney.

Chapter 18

There never was any heart truly great and generous
that was not also tender and compassionate.
ROBERT FROST

Colt didn't know when or how it happened, but he'd fallen in love with Megan McKinney. He sat perched on the edge of his favorite recliner, elbows planted on his knees, and watched as she held his crying niece in her arms. Megan was the mother Hadley needed and the woman he wanted.

"She was talking all weird." Hadley sniffed. "I mean it's not like I know what she talks like normally, but I could tell she was drunk or something."

Colt leaned back in the chair and squeezed the arms with both hands. Hadley's no-good mother had gotten their phone number and called the house. Colt never would have imagined who was on the other end of the line when Hadley jumped up and raced to the ringing phone. They both assumed it to be one of Hadley's friends. Now that school was over, the girls burned up the cell phone and the land line making plans for one visit or another.

Colt dug his fingers deeper into the chair's arms. *If I'd known it was Tina. . .if I'd known she'd gotten our number, I would have changed it. Better yet, I would have torn out the land line completely.*

Megan shushed Hadley with soft tones and traced her fingers through his niece's hair. "I know that was difficult. I'm sorry it happened to you."

Megan didn't try to defend Tina, nor did she speak ill of Hadley's biological mother. Something Colt couldn't seem to stop himself from doing. She simply acknowledged Hadley's hurt and comforted her. She knew just how to handle Hadley. The right things to say and do. With each stroke of her hand through Hadley's hair, Colt found himself more drawn to the piano teacher.

"Why did she have to call me like that? She never calls me. Never writes. And I get both in a week. And when she calls. . ." Hadley shoved her face back into Megan's chest.

Colt couldn't sit there any longer. He pushed out of the chair and paced the floor. "She won't be calling anymore— I'll tell you that much."

"But I want to talk to her." Hadley looked up at him. Her eyes were red and swollen from crying, but her expression reminded him of the one she'd given him when she was just a little tyke begging him for a new pup.

She'd won him over with that look, and Old Yeller had been a part of the family ever since. But this was different. More was at stake. It wasn't safe or healthy for her to be around Tina. He had to be firm. "Hadley, I believe I know what is best. . . ."

Megan shot him a look of warning and shook her head ever so slightly. Hadley's expression switched from sorrow to confrontation, and she started to hop up from the couch. Megan grabbed her wrist and pulled her back down beside her. "Tell me what she said."

Megan pierced him with another look of warning as Hadley settled back into the couch beside her. Only because he had no idea how to handle the shifting emotions of the twelve-year-old did he turn away, inwardly growling.

"She said she wanted to come see me, but Colt wouldn't let her."

Hadley raised her voice in accusation to him. How could he possibly be the bad guy here? The woman left Hadley. Hadn't even called or sent word of any kind to Hadley in years. She was a druggie and an alcoholic. How could this possibly be his fault? "She has no right. . . ."

Megan shot him another look, this time raising her eyebrows and cocking her head to emphasize she didn't want him to talk. He looked up at the ceiling, willing the good Lord to keep him from lighting into both the women in his living room. The very notion Tina should be able to have anything to do with Hadley was ridiculous. Out of the question.

Not that Megan had suggested he let Tina traipse into Hadley's life. She seemed to simply be trying to get the girl to calm down. Still, he didn't like being told what to do. Even if it was just in glances. And he didn't like that Hadley was acting so foolish as to want to talk with a woman who'd walked out of her life twelve years before.

"She's my mom. I want to know her." Hadley's voice lowered. "But not like she was today."

"It's hard when our parents don't behave as they should." Megan put her arm around Hadley's shoulder again. "I already told you I can't remember ever seeing my dad. And my mom and stepdad hurt me a long time ago. They didn't act like parents should have."

Colt watched Megan as she spoke. Pain etched her brows. He'd been so focused on Hadley before that he hadn't realized Megan's eyes seemed a bit swollen. She still looked adorable, her blond hair framing her face and dancing against her shoulders. But something was bothering her.

She looked down at her lap. "My stepdad died on Saturday."

"Megan, I'm sorry." Colt walked toward her and placed his hand on her shoulder.

New tears filled Hadley's eyes as she stared at Megan.

Megan nodded. "Thank you, Colt." She grabbed Hadley's hand and squeezed it. "I did get the chance to forgive him. Really forgive him. In my heart and by saying the words. Just before he died."

Colt watched Hadley stare at Megan. Was she telling Hadley to have a relationship with Tina? Colt wouldn't allow it. Whatever happened between Megan and her parents was completely different from all that happened between Hadley and his brother and Tina. Her parents weren't drug addicts. They hadn't given her up before she'd been able to chew solid food.

Hadley finally spoke. "When is the funeral?"

"Friday."

"Can I go?"

Colt cleared his throat. He wasn't sure that was the best of ideas. She was still sore at him because he hadn't taken her to his brother's funeral. She was already dealing with all these crazy emotions from her mother's contacts, which he

191

would be sure were stopped. A funeral probably wouldn't be the best place for Hadley.

He watched as Megan looked from Hadley to him. He knew she thought the same as he did.

Hadley looked up at him. She stood and put her hand on Colt's arm. "I want to be there for Megan, Uncle Colt. She's been there for me. For us."

Colt studied his niece. She seemed more grown-up than he'd ever seen her. She needed to do this. To support her piano teacher. The woman she'd grown to love.

He looked at Megan. She was the woman he'd grown to love as well. He wanted to be there for her. To give her someone she could lean on, could glean strength from.

He lowered himself onto the couch beside Megan. It was probably the closest he'd ever been to her. She smelled good, like flowers. She looked wounded, like a hurt pup. He wanted—no, needed—to be there for her. "If you don't mind, I think Hadley and I would like to go with you."

Megan looked away from him. He knew he was acting more intense than he'd ever been before. But his feelings were suddenly so evident. So real. He needed to protect and care for her.

After several moments, she nodded, and he knew he would do anything to make Megan happy.

Maybe going to the funeral wasn't such a good idea. He and Hadley walked into the small foyer of the funeral home. He felt uncomfortable at funerals for people he knew, but to go to one where he didn't know the person who'd passed was a little more than uncomfortable. More like torture.

Around ten people sat in folding chairs waiting for the memorial to begin. Only two stood in front of the casket offering condolences to the family. He watched as Megan welcomed a hug from an elderly woman. Despite the discomfort, he had to be there for her.

Hadley's teacher, Marianna, stood beside Megan. Along with a tall, thin, dark-haired man, whom he assumed to be Marianna's fiancé. At least he thought Megan had mentioned her sister was engaged. Next to them was a very fair woman with short, curly red hair. She must be Megan's mother.

She and Megan didn't stand by each other. Marianna kept her hand around her mother's arm, but Megan stood away from the two of them, on the other side of the man. What had happened between Megan and her parents? She'd mentioned making a bad choice as a teenager. But didn't lots of teenagers make bad choices? And Megan was so upright and wonderful. Whatever she'd done must not have been that bad. Nothing like his brother and girlfriend anyway. It was pretty obvious Megan wasn't doping it up.

He studied her mother more closely. She seemed sad beyond the death with a deep-to-the-core pain. He remembered Megan also mentioned her parents weren't Christians. He'd pray for this woman—for her salvation, and also that she would be able to open her eyes and see how remarkable Megan was.

Hadley pressed her hand against his arm. "Let's go see Megan."

Colt nodded and followed his niece to the front of the room. His cheeks warmed and his collar seemed tighter with each step they took. Funeral homes made him nervous.

He exhaled a long breath. The last one he'd been in had his brother all neatly groomed and inside a brown box. He blinked hard trying not to remember the look of his only sibling in that coffin. His whole family, everyone but Hadley, had been taken off the face of the earth. His church family had always been closer to him than his brother. Still, burying Connor had been like stripping off a piece of his body and shoving it into the ground. Hadley was all he had left, which was why Tina had to stay away from her.

Megan looked up and saw Hadley. A slow smile spread across her lips, and Colt knew they'd done the right thing by coming. She wrapped her arms around his niece. "It's good to see you."

Hadley, who once again seemed more grown-up than he'd ever seen her, folded her arms around Megan. "I'm sorry."

Colt didn't know when Hadley had started growing up. Only yesterday he was teaching her how to mount a horse. Now she was comforting the woman he loved in her time of need. A fleeting thought that Hadley was strong enough to deal with tough issues passed through his mind. He pushed it away. Strong enough or not, it was still his job to protect her.

Megan released a quick sniffle then let go of Hadley. She looked up at Colt, and he didn't wait for her offer. He grabbed Megan up in a deep hug. He wanted her to feel from every ounce of his strength she could count on him to care for and protect her, no matter what the situation.

He felt her quick intake of breath and knew Megan's resolve was crumbling against him. He pressed her tighter against him. She needed to know he could handle her hurts. She was safe with him.

After several moments, she released her hold, and though he didn't want to, he let her slip away. He grabbed Hadley's hand, and they moved to the front row and sat down. A few more visitors offered condolences, then Megan and her family walked toward him and Hadley.

Megan motioned to her mother. "Colt, Hadley, this is my mother, Barbara."

He shook the woman's hand. It was cold, and she never made eye contact. Colt's heart went out to the woman. How hard would it be to lose the person you loved? It was the one blessing he was thankful his parents hadn't had to endure. They passed away together. One didn't have to hurt without the other.

While Hadley shook her mother's hand, Megan motioned to her sister and the man. "You already know my sister. This is her fiancé, Kirk."

The funeral director announced the ceremony would start, and Colt nodded and quickly shook Kirk's hand. The family sat beside them. Megan beside him.

Megan sucked in a deep breath when the man shut the casket. Colt reached over and grabbed her hand. She squeezed his and didn't let go. He tried to focus on the minister's words. The man said Megan's stepfather had accepted Christ on his deathbed with his daughters present. Colt wanted to ask Megan about it. She'd said she had forgiven him. He wondered what had happened. He wished he and Connor had the same type of good-bye. Instead, he'd arrived at the morgue with his brother already dead. Overdosed.

He glanced at Hadley. Her eyes filled with tears, but they didn't spill over her lids. He should have told her about her dad. Deep down, he knew it was pride that kept his lips sealed. He didn't want Hadley to hurt. He wanted to protect her. But he hadn't wanted her to see the man who was her father and his brother. The Baker name was above such ugliness. Such sinfulness.

He studied his niece. She sat beside him, her shoulders back and her chin up. He knew she thought of her dad, of the fact she hadn't been able to say good-bye to him. He'd taken that from her. Couldn't give it back to her now. Or ever.

She was stronger than he'd given her credit for. And he was sorry. On the way home, he'd tell her.

The message finished, and Megan stood up and walked to her family. Feeling a few too many waves of emotion, Colt looked down at Hadley. "You be okay if I step out to the restroom?"

She nodded, and Colt noted once again the strong disposition of his niece. He should keep his eyes open when it came to that girl. The slight lift of her chin was proof she was more like him than her daddy. She was made of strong stuff. And the fact she had an obvious attachment to God made her even stronger.

He swallowed back the knot in his throat. He needed to get out of this room. The stench of death and the reality of his wrong to his niece turned his stomach. He walked out into the foyer and found his way to the restroom.

After splashing cold water on his face and sending up a quick prayer for forgiveness and strength, Colt made his way out of the restroom.

"Colt is the kind of guy I want to see Megan with."

Colt stopped. The hushed voice came from Megan's sister.

"Who's to say she isn't with him? He's here at the funeral, isn't he?"

Colt stepped back closer to the restroom door. It was a man's voice. Probably her fiancé's.

"I'm worried about her liking your friend. That Justin guy she works for. He's wrong for her."

Colt narrowed his eyes. He'd meant to look into that man. Justin Frasure. Megan's boss. He'd had a bad feeling when Megan mentioned him that day at the pond. Her sister evidently didn't approve of the guy.

"Justin has never said one word about liking Megan." It was the man's voice again. "And she hasn't said anything to you either."

"She doesn't have to."

Colt couldn't listen anymore. He stepped back into the restroom and peered at his reflection. He loved Megan McKinney. Justin Frasure would have to move out of the way.

Chapter 19

In three words I can sum up everything
I've learned about life: it goes on.
ROBERT FROST

It was going to be another bad day. The month of June passed in a haze. Megan worked, taught piano lessons, and helped Marianna prepare for the wedding.

She managed through the motions of life. She avoided Justin. He was just entirely too cute, and she simply needed to be away from him. She tried to avoid Colt, though he made it a bit more difficult. After every piano lesson, he had ice cream sundaes ready or the horses groomed to be ridden or a board game spread out on the dining room table. She knew he was trying to help her feel better. Colt had the best of intentions, just like when he kept her father's death from Hadley. But he had a hard time taking the hint when a girl just needed some space. He couldn't fix her, and she'd gotten to the point she wanted to avoid going to his house because she didn't want to *do* anything.

Her mother visited a lot. Preparations for the wedding, she said. But Megan knew it was more than that. She was grieving her husband's death, and she wouldn't allow herself to show it. Or admit it. She'd grown colder with Megan, but Megan didn't have the strength to care. She grieved in ways she hadn't expected. Her father's last plea for her to forgive him played like a broken DVD in her mind. How she wished for the time to start anew with him.

"Get your shoes on. You and I are going out."

Megan shifted on the couch and looked up at her sister. She nodded. It was Saturday. She didn't have anything better to do. Except continue to sulk. "What do we need to pick up for the wedding?"

"Nothing!"

Megan frowned at her sister. "Then what are we. . ."

The front door opened, and their friends Julie and Amber walked inside. Marianna pointed to the girls. "And I've recruited support."

Amber grabbed Megan's hand and pulled her off the couch. "You've been brooding for a month."

Megan stuck out her bottom lip. "I have not."

"Oh yes, you have," said Julie, "and you've had reason to be sad."

"Bill was the only dad we'd ever known," said Marianna, "and I'm thankful he received Jesus as his Lord."

Amber pointed at Megan. "But you need a reason to stop moping."

Megan crossed her arms in front of her chest. "I am not moping."

"You need a haircut." Julie lifted several strands of Megan's hair off her shoulder.

Marianna wrinkled her nose. "Yeah. I don't want you looking like 'The Shaggy D.A.' for my wedding."

Megan giggled at the memory of the old movie she and her sister used to watch when they were little. "My hair is fine." She cocked her eyebrow and pointed at her sister. "I'm taking that as an insult."

"It was an insult," stammered Marianna.

"Actually it's quite thick," said Amber. "You know I've always been jealous."

"But the dead ends kinda stink." Julie waved her hand in front of her nose. "And when was the last time you washed it?"

Megan's mouth fell open. She placed her hands on her hips. "My hair does not smell bad. I'll have you know I just washed it yesterday."

Megan stopped her tirade when she realized Amber, Julie, and Marianna were all trying to hide back chuckles. She felt a smile lift her lips. "You got me."

Marianna wrapped her hand around Megan's elbow. "That's the first smile I've seen in weeks."

Julie opened the front door. "Our appointments are in fifteen minutes. We've got to get out of here."

"We're all going to get our hair cut? Really?" asked Megan.

"We've gotta look good for the wedding," said Julie.

Megan let out a deep sigh and smiled at her friends and sister. "Let me get my shoes."

She went into her bedroom and grabbed a pair of flip-flops off her shoe rack. Dropping them to the floor, she noticed how bad the nail polish looked on her toes. She walked back into the living area. "Maybe we could stop and get our toes done, too?"

Marianna placed her hand over her heart. "My sister is rejoining the land of the living. She's asking for a pedicure."

Julie scratched the top of her head. "Megan loves a pedicure like a dog loves its bone."

"Like a horse adores its carrots," said Amber.

"Like a pig loves its slop," said Julie.

Megan lifted her hand. "Okay. Now, you're just getting gross."

Amber placed the back of her hand against the side of her mouth in a fake whisper to Julie. "But seriously, check out those neglected toenails."

"Hey! They don't look that bad." Megan swatted Amber with the back of her hand.

Julie shook her head. "Honestly, Megan. I've never seen so much peeling paint on your little piggies."

Marianna raised her pointer finger in the air. "Then it's settled. Haircuts then pedis. Maybe a little pizza afterward."

Amber groaned. "No fair. You know I'm trying to lose five pounds so I can fit in my bridesmaid dress."

"I don't have to lose anything." Julie pumped her fist. "Pizza sounds great to me."

Megan laughed as they continued to argue on their way out to the car. She still felt a deep loss in the center of her heart. Part of it probably had to do with her continued near-estranged relationship with her mom. Still it would be good to go out with her sister and friends. She needed this. She hadn't realized how much so until they pointed out her toes.

She looked down at her feet. It was true. She'd never let her nails get so chipped. Even one of the rhinestones on the flower design on her big toe had come off. It had been too long since she'd had a pedicure.

Julie and Amber started to banter over who would sit in the front with Marianna. Megan inwardly chuckled as she slipped into the backseat behind her sister. It was going to be a good day after all.

Megan lifted her shoulders when Justin approached her desk. She had no reason to still feel so anxious around the man. She saw him each day at work, each weekend at church, and on Thursdays at Bible study. It was obvious he'd changed since accepting Christ. Women didn't flock to his office, except those who brought along husbands and sought out adoption help. She had to admit Justin was not the man he'd once been. And she liked the man he'd become. More than liked. Admired.

And that is why her stomach rumbled like a volcano about to erupt each time he did approach her.

He stopped in front of her desk and shoved his fists in his pants pockets—dark charcoal pants that fit him to perfection. The deep-green button-down shirt he wore simply did not do what it should—cover and disguise the muscles bulging from his chest and arms.

Seriously, what was God doing when He formed this man in his mother's womb? Was He experimenting with different physical features to see what combination formed the most beautiful of the entire race? *Gotta give You credit, God. If that's what You were doing, You did good.*

She bit her bottom lip. She would not salivate over her

boss. She would not. And quite frankly, she was getting tired of always having to remind herself not to slobber in his presence.

She looked up at him. His dark brown eyes studied her. And she realized he was nervous. Justin Frasure—nervous? To talk to her? She almost snorted aloud, but the scared puppy dog expression he wore stopped her short. "Can I help you, Justin?"

He swallowed and averted his gaze. Looking back at her, he pulled his fists out of his pockets and wrung his hands together.

What in the world was he doing? He acted as if they didn't see each other practically every day of their lives. He reminded her of a high school boy about to ask a girl on a. . . Uh-oh. Her heart sped up. Surely he wasn't about to. . . She inwardly shook her head. No, it wasn't possible. She was nothing like Justin's type. She wasn't ugly, but she most certainly wasn't flashy or drop-dead gorgeous.

"I was wondering"—his gaze bore into her with an intensity she'd never seen—"if you'd go to a charity ball with me."

Megan lifted her eyebrows and placed her hand against her chest. "Me?"

His expression switched from intensity to amusement. "Yes, you, Megan. I enjoy being around you more than any other woman I've ever known."

Heat washed over Megan's cheeks and neck. He hadn't exactly proclaimed his undying love, and she most certainly didn't want him to do so. She didn't know what to say. She needed to stay away from Justin Frasure. He was her tempting fruit. When she was around him, she thought and felt things she didn't want to think and feel. It was safer to stay away, to say no.

"It's a charity ball to raise funds for overseas adoption. It's formal attire." He reached into his pocket and pulled out several bills. "I wouldn't want it to be a hardship, so. . ."

Megan looked at him with uncertainty. He was giving her money for a dress. It was a nice gesture. Maybe it meant he didn't intend it as a date, simply as a professional outing. She could handle that. She owed it to the company. She'd be training her replacement in the next few weeks. It wouldn't hurt to go with Justin to an event.

"A business date? That would be fine." She took the money from his hand. "Of course I'll go with you."

A glimmer of something passed across his features. Was it regret? Or sadness? She didn't know and didn't want to think about it.

He jutted out his chin. "A business date. Sure. It's short notice. The dinner's this weekend. Is that okay?"

Warmth spread over her cheeks again, as she realized she'd grabbed the money out of his hand without finding out if she could even attend the function. She nodded quickly. "Sure. That's fine. I've got time to look around for a dress tonight."

He opened his mouth then clamped it shut before he turned on his heels and walked back to his office. If she didn't know better, she might have believed he was about to offer to go with her to pick out the dress. She didn't want him to tag along. It would be hard enough to attend a formal dinner without swooning all over the man. And if she could, she'd leave her lips home for the evening. If only that were possible.

She looked at the clock on her computer. Thankfully it was time to leave. She needed out of the office. Needed to clear her head. Going to the mall to shop for a formal gown to go on a "business" date with the most beautiful man God had ever created would be just the thing to help get her mind off Justin. She rolled her eyes as she grabbed her purse out of the cabinet and headed out the door.

Once at the mall, she made her way to one of the nicer department stores. It was one her wallet had never allowed her to venture inside. She hadn't counted the cash Justin gave her until she'd reached the mall. He'd given her more than she made in a week. All for a dress and pair of shoes. Which meant they needed to be nice. Which meant Megan's stomach rolled because she'd never bought anything that nice.

"May I help you, miss?"

Megan turned and saw an adorable, petite brunette. Her hair was cut like Tinker Bell's, her makeup dark, and she wore a diamond in the side of her nose, but her clothes and shoes made her edginess appear even more professional and gorgeous. Maybe this woman would help her think outside of her usual wardrobe choice—though hopefully not too far out. Megan swallowed. "I'm looking for a formal gown, and I need it this weekend."

The woman clapped. "Then we need to get to work. No time for alterations." She extended her hand. "By the way, I'm Avery."

Megan shook her hand then told the saleswoman her

dress size. Avery placed her finger on her cheek and studied Megan's shape. Megan squirmed under the intense scrutiny until Avery grabbed her arm. "Girl, you have a knockout shape. I want to be sure we enhance all the right places."

A thrill raced down her spine. She'd never shopped like this. Never had anyone study her to bring out her best physical qualities. She wanted to be around people who cared about who the person was not what she looked like. Still, it was fun to think of purchasing something special.

Megan gaped at the mounds of dresses Avery pulled off the racks. "I'm going to try on all of those?"

"Maybe." Avery shrugged. "Unless the perfect dress pops out at us before you're through the stack."

Megan went into the dressing room and slipped into the first dress—an aqua strapless gown with sequence beading at the top.

The color was beautiful, but it made her hips look bigger than they were. She stepped outside of the room to show Avery. The saleswoman shook her head and sent her back inside. "Next."

She took off the dress then tried on a deep red that was too dark against her skin, then a black that was too low-cut, then a pink that was too light. It was practically the same color as her skin.

She grew weary of trying on gowns and realized she was happy she wasn't some ritzy guy's wife who had to worry about perfect appearance all the time. Dress shopping was the most exhausting thing she'd done all week.

Avery handed her another dress. It was a smoky blue color, almost the same shade as Megan's eyes. Her heart sped up, and she hoped this dress looked good on her.

Avery winked. "This may be the one."

She bit her bottom lip and smiled. After shutting the door behind her, she slipped on the gown. It had a Grecian look with cut-away shoulders and deep slits in the front and the back. The jersey style gathering made the slits modest yet sensual. A thick band of sequins the same color of blue fit perfectly around her waist. From there the gown flowed like a waterfall all the way to her toes. It was perfect.

She stepped out of the dressing room, and Avery placed her hand on her chest. "Girl, we found it." She looked at Megan. "Don't you think?"

Megan nodded.

Avery snapped her fingers. "And I know just the perfect shoes."

Megan shared her size, and then Avery raced out of the fitting area. She admired the dress. Lifted her hair off her shoulders. She'd wear her hair up. A deep sigh sounded from the back of her throat. She felt like a princess.

Avery arrived with the shoes, and just as she'd said, the silver sequined heels added just the right amount of pop to her feet. Avery shooed her back into the dressing room. "Let's get you out of it before anything happens. You're going to knock your man off his feet."

Megan didn't respond. She could've told Avery it was a business date, that her boss didn't care for her in *that* way. That she didn't want him to. But she felt so beautiful. Though she'd fought against it for years, in this dress, she wanted to impress the man she loved. To see his expression swell with pride that she belonged to him.

She had to get out of the dress and fast. Fanciful, romantic notions were not in her future. As soon as she finished her last weeks at the firm, she would start school in the fall as a music teacher, and she'd be away from Justin. Well, except for church functions and Bible study. But she could try to keep her distance in those settings.

Once dressed in her own clothes, Megan followed Avery to the counter to check out. Avery motioned to a woman in the back then looked back at Megan. "It was a lot of fun dressing you up. I hope you enjoy your date."

"Thank you so much, Avery. You were a huge help."

Megan looked back at the counter and sucked in her breath. The stunning redhead stood behind the register. Justin's old client. What was her name? Sophia. While she rang up the purchase, Megan fumbled through her purse to find the money Justin had given her.

Maybe she won't recognize me. Won't remember me.

"I know who you are." Sophia pointed at her. "You're Justin Frasure's secretary, right?"

Megan shifted her weight from one foot to the other. Shouldn't the woman just ring her up and let her get out of there? Knowing she couldn't be rude, Megan nodded.

Sophia placed the gown in a garment bag and zipped it up. "Awfully fancy dress. It's beautiful. One of our nicest."

Megan nodded again and handed her the cash.

"Going somewhere with Justin?"

Megan bit her bottom lip. Okay, the woman was way out of line. That was none of her business. If her manager walked up on this transaction, Sophia would be reprimanded. She looked at the redhead's name badge, which listed her as a manager. Megan inwardly groaned. *That's just great.*

Lifting her chin, she looked into Sophia's eyes. "As a matter of fact, we are going to a charity ball. It's a business engagement."

Sophia studied her. Megan reached for her purchase. Sophia handed her the garment bag and shoes. A look of regret washed across her face. "I hope he doesn't have to apologize to you later."

The words punched her in the gut. Without a response, Megan walked out of the store. The look of pity on Sophia's face riled her, but it also lifted the guard around her heart that Megan had worked so hard to build. Justin might be the most delicious-looking man ever, but he was only a business date. That was all.

Chapter 20

I like her because she
smiles at me and means it.
UNKNOWN

Justin wiped the sweat from his forehead with a rag then threw it to the floor beside his water bottle. He shifted on the weight bench to face Kirk. "What are you talking about?"

Kirk opened his palms. "Megan. I'm talking about Megan. For some ridiculous reason, Marianna thinks Megan has a secret crush on you or something. She's determined to set her up with this other guy. Colt somebody or other."

Justin tossed the information around in his mind. He'd given in to his feelings for Megan. God had given him the strength to be patient. He hadn't asked Megan on an official date, even though he thought that's what he was doing for the charity ball, and she'd taken his offer a different way. But if Marianna thought Megan had a crush, then maybe he had a chance.

He didn't deserve someone like Megan. He knew that. But she never left his mind. And though he wanted to know her in every way, he had changed. He respected her. He wanted to know her as a person, wanted her to know he cared for every facet of her.

But this Colt guy? Justin looked at his friend. "Who's this Colt person?"

"Megan's giving his niece piano lessons. At the funeral, it was pretty obvious the guy had feelings for Megan. He held her hand while she cried, and. . ."

Justin swallowed back the fury that welled inside him. The man held Megan's hand. *His* Megan's hand. He'd gone to the funeral? Megan never mentioned this guy to him. Was Colt the reason she didn't want him to go with her? Not that they spent time discussing the details of each other's personal lives, but still, if this Colt guy was special to her, wouldn't he have some inkling of a clue? He did see her every day at work and a lot of days at church.

Kirk continued, "I'm really not so sure Megan's interested in the guy. She's always been kinda antiboyfriend."

Justin exhaled a slow breath. Kirk didn't think she liked him. That gave Justin hope. It also meant he was going to have to step up his game if there was another guy vying for the woman he planned to marry.

Kirk took a swig from a water bottle then put it back on the floor. "I told Marianna to just leave Megan alone, that there was no way there was any kind of thing going on between the two of you."

Justin nodded. He looked up at the clock on the wall above the floor-length mirrors. "I've gotta get out of here. That charity ball's tonight." He pulled at the front of his drenched shirt. "And I might just need a shower."

"I forgot about that. Who're you taking?"

Justin cleared his throat and averted his gaze. "Megan."

"What?" Kirk smacked his hand against his thigh.

"What do you mean you're taking Megan?"

He studied the gym floor as he shrugged. "Just a business date."

"I know you better than that. I can tell. . ."

Brandy walked up to the weight bench. "Hey, guys." She waved her hand then traced her fingers through her long, dark ponytail. "How's it going, Justin?"

"Fine." Justin grabbed his water bottle and towel and glanced at his friend. "I've got to go, Kirk."

After grabbing his wallet and keys out of a cubby, he pushed his way out the front door and popped the button on his keychain to unlock the car. Kirk barreled through the door and stood beside him. "I won't let you hurt Marianna's sister."

Pain shot through his heart. His friend had led him to the Lord and watched him grow in his faith, but he still feared he'd hurt Megan. He peered at his friend, his hands itching to form into fists to defend himself as he'd been known to do when they were teens. "I'm not the same man."

"I hope not."

Justin jumped into his car and turned the ignition. "I suppose this means you don't really believe all you've told me about how a man can change once he's found God. If I can't change, then why have I been trying?" He pointed to his chest. "Have you not watched my life these last several months?" He clenched his jaw and spit through gritted teeth. "You of all people should know God's changed me."

A look of regret flashed across Kirk's expression, but Justin jerked the car into REVERSE and skidded out of the parking lot before his friend had a chance to apologize. He thought

Kirk, of all people, would accept him as a new creation.

He didn't deserve Megan. He knew that. His fist pounded the top of the steering wheel. It was selfish of him to even ask her to love him. "God, I just won't do it. I'll keep my feelings for her to myself. No one but You and I know about them."

He pulled into his driveway then headed into the house. "This will be a business date tonight. Nothing more."

Trying not to think about Megan or Kirk or some guy named Colt, he raced through his shower and shave. He put on his tuxedo then headed toward the front door. Out of the corner of his eye, he spied the flowers he'd bought for her. Maybe he shouldn't give them to her. He didn't want her to think he meant them to be a personal gesture. Even though he did.

With a huff, he grabbed the flowers off the table. She had every right to a bouquet of beautiful roses. She had agreed to go with him this evening. He would treat her as a date. A business date.

He made his way to the car then turned up the contemporary Christian music on his radio. He didn't want to think. He needed God's Word through music to penetrate his mind. Anything to keep his mind off Megan.

He pulled into her driveway and sent up a quick prayer of help to feel nothing when he saw her. Maybe she'd have a piece of food stuck in her teeth. Something to keep him from finding her the most adorable woman he'd ever known.

Shaking his head to clear his mind, he walked to the front door and pushed the doorbell. Marianna opened it. Her scowl was evidence enough of her opinion of the dinner date. She didn't speak to him but twisted her head and yelled, "He's here. Remember Mom's coming in the morning to work on the wedding."

She turned back to him, her eyes squinted in disapproval. Her actions were so blatant Justin found them funny. He smiled at her with a grin that usually sent women to swooning. "How are you doing, Marianna? I spent the afternoon with your fiancé."

She barely lifted her head in acknowledgment. He heard footsteps down the hall and looked to see Megan standing several feet behind her. His jaw dropped. His sweet, cute secretary had transformed into a princess.

Her eyes shone to nearly match the color of the long blue dress. Her hair was swept up with rhinestones dotting the sides and top. Wisps fell and kissed her cheeks and neck. Like he wanted to do.

Justin swallowed and willed himself to think pure thoughts. He needed to keep his mind away from his feelings for her. He feared if she took one step closer, he would grab her in his arms and kiss her with the intensity he'd spent many a day wishing he could exhibit.

She smiled, and Justin forced himself to close his mouth. Remembering his manners, he extended the flowers toward her. "Megan, these are for you."

Megan bit her bottom lip, and her face and neck brightened. That was the Megan he was used to, the one he'd fallen in love with. *God, it's just not right that she looks like this all dolled up. How am I supposed to keep my feelings to myself?*

Her hand brushed his when she took the flowers from him. He winced. *God, help me keep my hands to myself, too.*

"They're beautiful, Justin. Thank you." She handed them to her sister. "Will you put them in a vase for me?"

Marianna curled her lip, but she took the roses and headed into the kitchen.

Megan looked back at him and smiled. "Are you ready?"

No food in her teeth as he'd hoped. No lipstick on her pearly whites either. He nodded and extended his arm. She touched the inside of his elbow, and Justin felt his insides shake. He'd never experienced this. He wanted Megan, but in every way. He wanted to be near her, to talk with her, laugh with her. And right now, he couldn't deny he wanted to wrap her in his arms and kiss her with every ounce of energy he could muster.

He didn't know how he was going to make it through this dinner. Pray. He'd have to have constant contact with God to make it through. *You hear that, Lord? You're on double time tonight.*

They walked to the car, and he opened the door. Once she slid inside, he closed it and walked to the other side and got in. Megan arranged her dress to avoid as many creases as possible. "So, do you like it?"

Justin gripped the steering wheel. He hadn't even told her how gorgeous she looked. He'd been so dumbfounded he'd forgotten the most important thing a woman wanted to hear. "It's amazing. You are beautiful, Megan."

She didn't look at him. She focused her attention out the windshield. "Sophia sold it to me."

Justin cringed. He knew exactly who she meant. He hoped the woman didn't ask about him. More importantly, he hoped she hadn't said too many entirely true but ugly things about him either. Judging by the way Megan stared at the windshield, he assumed Sophia said plenty. "Well, she has terrific taste. You're gorgeous."

Megan didn't respond, and Justin realized Sophia may have been a blessing in disguise. If Megan spent the evening cold and collected, he wouldn't fall all over himself trying not to reveal his feelings for her. He couldn't run from the past anyway. There would always be a Sophia somewhere. And Megan shouldn't have to deal with that.

He drove into the garage and parked his car. Megan stepped out before he had time to walk to her side to open the door. He started to grab her hand to escort her inside when she stepped in front of him.

She looked up at him. She'd put some kind of smoky gray color on her eyelids that made the blue in her eyes the most striking color he'd ever seen. Like the darkening of the sky just before a storm.

She took a step toward him and touched his biceps with both hands. His heart pounded in his chest, and his stomach churned. Her gaze moved to his lips, and he thought he might pass out right there in the parking lot. If she kissed him again. . .right there in the parking lot. . .wearing that amazing dress. . .strands of blond hair kissing her shoulders.

He couldn't take it. He wrapped his arms around her waist and pulled her closer. Blocking the protests from his mind, he lowered his lips to hers. She answered his kiss with one of her own, and Justin sucked in his breath, begging God for restraint.

Releasing her mouth, he grabbed her arms and moved her away from him. "Megan, I. . ."

She studied him, waiting for what he would say, what he would do. She wasn't ready for a proclamation of love. He could tell by her expression she needed confirmation his intentions were good.

And they were good. And bad. But they were mostly good. And completely in right standing with God. He had to prove it to her. He didn't deserve her, but he couldn't let her go. He'd move to Africa, if he needed, to get away from his past. But he couldn't give her up. He loved her.

But first he'd have to prove it.

He grabbed her hand in his. "Megan, I'm so glad you came with me."

She seemed confused, but she allowed him to lead her. They walked into the dining hall. As usual, he had the most beautiful date in the room. But this girl was different. She wasn't for the night. She was for life.

Chapter 21

I have held many things in my hands, and I have lost them all;
but whatever I have placed in God's hands, that I still possess.
MARTIN LUTHER

Megan adjusted the fuzzy, pink bride-to-be crown on top of Marianna's head. Megan, Marianna, Amber, and Julie walked into the restaurant. She grinned as several people looked their way. She knew they were a sight with their hot pink T-shirts sporting their positions in the wedding in metallic silver lettering. Megan had designed them herself. They were more ostentatious than anything she'd ever want, but she knew her sister would flip over them.

Amber lifted four fingers to the hostess. "Table for four."

The gray-haired woman winked at Marianna as she grabbed four menus from behind the table. "Looks like someone's getting married."

"That would be me." Marianna touched the silver sash at her chest and laughed.

"When's the big day?" asked the waitress.

"Week from tomorrow," Marianna answered.

Megan shook her head. She still couldn't believe her sister would become a married woman in only eight days. They'd already moved several of her belongings from the apartment, which had sent Megan into a tailspin of emotions. She was happy for her sister, but they'd never lived apart. The thought of it left an ache in her spirit. It would leave a hole in her bank account as well—even if she would make more as a teacher than she had as a secretary at the law firm.

They followed the hostess to the booth, and Megan slid in beside Marianna. The waitress arrived, offering a round of free drinks on the house. They grinned at each other, and Amber asked for four virgin strawberry daiquiris.

Julie tapped the tabletop as she looked at Marianna. "Everything ready for next Saturday?"

Marianna glanced at Megan and inhaled a deep breath. "I think so. Mom's coming in to stay with us this week to help with final preparations."

Megan's stomach tightened. She wasn't looking forward to spending the whole week with their mother. They hadn't quarreled, but the tension was still present between them.

"What about you"—Amber nodded at Megan—"you ready for your sister to move out?"

Marianna looked at her, and Megan knew this was a concern weighing down her sister's heart. The separation would be hard on her twin as well, even though Marianna would have Kirk to keep her company. Megan would have—well, nothing. Maybe she should look into getting a pet. She inwardly shook her head. Nah. Wouldn't have time for one.

"Well, yeah!" Megan wrapped her arm around his sister's shoulder. "I'll get a warm shower for the first time in my life."

Marianna giggled as she shrugged. "If you'd wake up earlier, then maybe. . ."

Megan rolled her eyes, and the group laughed. They all knew Marianna was the last to rise on any overnight outing they'd ever attended.

"Here you go, ladies." The waitress arrived with their beverages, and they ordered nearly every appetizer on the menu.

Marianna peered at them. "You do know we have to fit in our dresses?"

"Tonight is celebration night." Julie swatted the air. "We just won't eat this week."

Megan looked at her sister. Marianna had been fit to be tied for weeks. She probably wouldn't hold down a bite of food after tonight. Kirk had proven his worth in Megan's eyes, though. He'd been patient and understanding, even when Marianna melted into a mess of tears over the napkins being a shade lighter than she'd expected. Though it would be hard, Megan knew she could release her sister to Kirk's able and loving care.

"So, when does school start, Megan?" asked Julie.

"Three weeks. I begin new teacher orientation the Tuesday after Marianna's wedding."

She could hardly believe how fast the summer had gone. Only one more week at Frasure, Frasure, and Combs. The training of the new secretary was going well, and she was secretly thrilled that the new hire was an older, married woman with grown kids and grandchildren.

Her mind ventured to the charity ball two weeks earlier. She'd had the most amazing time with Justin. Dancing. Eating. Socializing. He'd kept her in the crook of his arm the entire night. She'd felt more like his girlfriend than his employee.

And the kiss in the parking lot—their second kiss. This one had been his doing. Her cheeks warmed as she thought of how she'd done nothing to stop the advance. She'd wanted to kiss him more, but he'd stopped it. He'd been the one to grab her hand, lead her into the charity ball, and then treat her like a cherished lady the rest of the evening.

That was how she felt with him. Cherished. It seemed impossible given his past. But the Justin Frasure she knew loved the Lord and lived his life trying to follow Him. She'd promised to spend her life alone, and in her mind she knew it was the safest route. But the man who'd spent much of his life chasing women occupied her thoughts at every moment of the day.

"Are you excited?"

Megan blinked at Amber's question. What had they been talking about? Oh yeah, school.

Megan nodded. "Very excited. I've already picked out several pieces I hope to sing with the different age groups."

Marianna touched Megan's arm. "My sister will be the best music teacher Fayette County has ever seen."

The appetizers arrived, and they each scooped a variety onto their plates.

"I can't wait to see the movie," said Amber.

"Then fro-yo?" piped in Julie.

Marianna groaned at the mention of frozen yogurt as she shoved her third buffalo wing into her mouth. "We're never gonna fit into our dresses."

Megan laughed. "Sure we will."

The waitress returned, and they ordered the steak

dinner the restaurant was known for. Megan already felt busted, but she was enjoying her sister's bachelorette party. Dinner, movie, and dessert were probably a bit tame for today's standards, but it fit them perfectly. And she'd been waiting all week to see the romantic comedy Marianna picked.

"What are you guys doing here?"

Megan turned toward the direction Marianna was speaking. A knot formed in her throat when she saw Kirk, Justin, and Kirk's two groomsmen walking toward them inside the movie theater.

Megan took in their royal blue shirts with black lettering that named Kirk as GROOM-TO-BE, Justin as BEST MAN, and each of the others as GROOMSMAN. She couldn't stop the smile when she noted Justin's look of utter repulsion as he looked down at his shirt then around the room to see if anyone was looking at them. Everyone was.

"Raiding your bachelorette party."

Kirk grabbed Marianna in a big hug and kissed her lips. Megan bit her bottom lip as she sneaked a quick look at Justin. What she wouldn't give to feel his lips against hers like that. Again.

She brushed the thought away and tried to remind herself of her determination to stay single for the rest of her life. Kirk grabbed Marianna's hand in his then lifted it to his lips for a quick kiss. Ugh. The man made her sick. He also made her want that. What a ridiculous combination.

"Man, this ain't cool. The groom and his cronies are not supposed to hang out with us. How are we supposed to flirt with other guys?" Amber nudged one of the groomsmen in the arm. Adam and Amber flirted quite a bit, and Megan wondered if a love match would develop after the wedding.

Adam locked his arm around hers. "Flirt with other guys all you want. You gotta get me out of this lobby. This shirt is ridiculous. I'm losing cool points."

"No kidding," Wayne responded. He fell into step beside Julie.

Megan looked up at Justin. They were the only ones left in the lobby. Taking in the shirt once again, she cupped her hand over her mouth and chuckled.

He spread his arms and grinned. "What?"

"I can't believe you're wearing that."

He turned his body left and then right. "You don't think it compliments my physique?"

Oh, that was so not a fair question. What didn't compliment Justin's physique? The man was a boulder with bumps in all the right places. She knew that for a fact after touching his biceps and feeling their flex the night of the charity ball.

She averted her gaze. "It compliments you just fine."

He cupped her chin, forcing her to look back up at him. His eyes smoldered with a combination of mirth and something else. The frustrating thing was she recognized the something else from the night at the charity ball. He wanted to kiss her. And though that sounded every bit as delicious as a supersized soft drink and a bag of buttered movie popcorn, it was not going to happen. Now was not the time or place.

He grinned, and his eyes gleamed with a tease. The man was insufferable. She knew he could read her thoughts. He sobered and shook his head. "I can't believe they talked me into doing this."

"Gotta admit. I'm a little surprised to see you here."

"It was Kirk's idea." He pointed to her pink top. "I believe you showed those to him, and that's where he got the idea."

Megan twirled from side to side. "You have to admit ours are much cuter."

"Definitely couldn't argue with that."

The gleam returned to his eyes, and Megan found herself shifting her feet. She pointed toward the theaters. "We'd better get in there. Hopefully they saved us a couple of seats."

Justin nodded. Her heart raced when he touched the small of her back to guide her forward. They reached the ticket taker, and she fumbled through her purse trying to find the movie ticket. Her heart pounded against her chest, and her cheeks warmed. She hated that Justin had such an impact on her. He was just a man, for heaven's sake. True, he was gorgeous and a good kisser and a newly committed Christian. Still, the guy didn't have *everything* going for him. Of course, in her addled state, she couldn't think of anything he lacked.

Justin tapped her shoulder, and she halted her rummage through the bag. He pointed to her backside. "The ticket's sticking out of your back pocket."

Heat rushed to her face as she pulled the ticket from the back of her pants. Thankfully she was wearing her favorite jeans, the ones that looked the best on her backside. *Megan McKinney, stop thinking like that.* The thought of Justin noticing her—she shook her head. She needed to get control of her mind.

The teenage guy handed her the stub, and she moved a few steps in front of Justin. Taking several deep breaths, she regained control of herself. Justin moved beside her, and she looked up at him and flashed a mischievous grin.

"Looking forward to the movie?"

He groaned as they walked toward the theater. "About as much as I'd look forward to a root canal."

Megan laughed. She figured the romantic comedy would not be one of Justin's top movie picks. He grabbed her arm and pointed to one of the theaters showing an action film. "We could sneak into this one. No one would ever have to know."

Megan shook her head. "No way. I've been looking forward to this movie all week."

Justin wrinkled his nose, but she could still see the laughter and teasing in his eyes. "Guess I'll have to suffer through."

They walked into the theater, and Megan sat beside Marianna. Her sister scowled at Justin and then at her. Megan didn't understand Marianna. Her sister needed to be encouraging to Justin. He was a new Christian. She knew Marianna didn't want them to date, but she and Justin weren't dating. Nothing close to it.

Marianna placed her hand on Megan's arm. "I forgot

to tell you Colt called and asked me to remind you not to forget the sheet music for Hadley on Tuesday."

Megan's forehead wrinkled in question. "What?"

Colt would have no reason to call and say such a thing. Megan had never forgotten sheet music for Hadley's piano lessons.

Megan watched as Kirk grabbed Marianna and pulled her closer to him. He whispered something in her ear. Something like "Stop it, that's not nice." Megan scrunched her nose. What was that about?

She turned toward Justin and realized he'd stiffened beside her. He stared straight ahead at the commercials on the movie screen. His lips were pursed into a straight, angry line.

"You can't control who she likes. He has good intentions, and he's a good man now."

Megan raised her eyebrows in surprise. Kirk's whisper must have been louder than he'd intended. She knew Marianna didn't like Justin, that she feared Justin would try to hit on her like he had the other women in his past. But she didn't know Marianna thought Justin liked her.

Sure, he was attracted to her, and they'd shared a couple kisses. One was just a moment of crazy insanity, that she still didn't know what had come over her. The other was simply about the moment getting the best of him. They were all dressed up and headed to the charity ball. He'd had a moment of weakness. He'd been a perfect gentleman the rest of the evening. Never once did he make her feel uncomfortable. He'd actually made her feel special being on his arm. But that didn't mean he had feelings for her.

She sneaked another peek at Justin. He sat stiff and rigid. Was that the expression of a man who was jealous? Was he jealous of Colt?

A thread of pleasure weaved through her at the idea that Justin wouldn't want another man to be interested in her. Which Colt definitely wasn't. He was a friend. Nothing more. But Justin? Could she honestly say he was just a friend?

Something in her liked that he might be a bit jealous. The lights dimmed, and the movie started as Megan continued to war within herself about the possibility of Justin having real affection for her. Did she want him to have feelings for her?

She settled back in the chair, determined not to think about it, and enjoy the movie she'd been looking forward to watching. A strong hand reached over and grabbed hers. She sucked in her breath as Justin opened her hand and weeded his fingers through hers.

She looked at him and realized he studied her. His gaze seemed to ask if his touch was wanted. She ignored the warning signals flashing in her mind and gave in to her racing heart. With a blink of affirmation, she squeezed his hand and turned her attention back to the screen.

She felt like a middle schooler on her first date to the movies with her boyfriend. Just because he held her hand in the movie theater didn't mean he really liked her. Take Colt for example. When he held her hand at the funeral, she didn't feel anything. He was just her friend. It was the same with Justin. Even if it didn't feel like it.

Chapter 22

*All truths are easy to understand once they
are discovered; the point is to discover them.*

GALILEO GALILEI

The problem is she thinks I'm just a friend. Colt grabbed
the tea bags out of the pantry and smacked them down
on the countertop. He didn't have to search far into Justin's
life to learn the man was a womanizer. He'd played more
women than Colt had competed in rodeos. Megan deserved
better. She needed someone who was constant and faithful,
someone she could trust and who would love her every day
of his life. *Someone like me.*

The phone rang, and Colt picked up the receiver.
"Hello."

"Hi, Colt."

Colt exhaled a long breath at the sound of Tina's voice
on the line. He looked at the clock. Time had gotten away
from him, but she was right on with the time they'd arranged. Part of him still worried he'd agreed to let Hadley
talk on the phone with her birth mother twice a week. And
he'd only agreed to the phone visits after she'd promised to
start and stay in rehab. Tina had been true to her promise.
He'd checked up on her to make sure.

"How are you doing, Tina?"

"I'm doing pretty good." Her voice sounded happier than he'd ever heard it. Tina had been nice enough, if not overtly shy, when she first started dating his brother, but Colt had never gotten the chance to really get to know her. "I'm enjoying beauty school, and I've gotten two new houses to clean."

Colt smiled into the phone. He really was glad Tina was cleaning up her life. Though he didn't tell Hadley, he'd agreed to pay for Tina to go to beautician school on the condition she kept her grades up and stayed sober. It was her responsibility to find part-time employment. She'd surprised him when she'd started cleaning houses, but she must do a fairly good job, because she was cleaning four houses a week. He'd been checking up with the owners as well.

"That's terrific, Tina. How many days?"

"Thirty-one. I'm still taking one day at a time."

He was proud of Hadley's mother. Everything in him wished it hadn't taken his brother's death for her to realize her need to straighten out her life. And to get to know her daughter. He still worried if he'd made the right decision, but seeing Hadley's expression each time she talked with her mother was proof enough the girl needed to know the woman, if only a little bit.

"I've been watching the clock. Tuesdays and Sundays are the best days of the week."

"Hadley enjoys talking to you also." Colt started to pull the phone away.

"I've started going to church, Colt."

He pulled the receiver back to his ear. "Tina, that is wonderful. That's the best news I've heard."

"Please pray for me." He heard her voice catch, and Colt's heart tightened. The little time he'd spent with Tina on the phone, he'd come to realize he liked her as a person, and he wanted her to come to know Christ.

"I already do."

"Is that Mom?" Hadley raced into the kitchen and swiped the phone from his hand before he had a chance to respond. "Hey Mom."

It surprised Colt that Hadley had been so quick to call Tina "Mom" after having no relationship with her the first twelve years of her life. He listened as Hadley talked about Megan coming over in a bit for piano lessons.

Colt filled a pan full of water and placed it on the burner. He was looking forward to Megan's visit. But he didn't have a clue about how to get her to see he wanted more than friendship from her. Each time he tried to hint at a date, she mentioned some kind of wedding obligation she had with Marianna or the charity ball with Justin.

His cheeks burned at the memory. He'd wanted to insist she tell her boss to take a hike, but he'd bit his tongue. *If I could get her to see how much I like her, then it would be my place.*

He growled to himself. He had no experience with women. Every time he considered simply coming out and being honest with Megan, his hands would clam up, his mouth would go dry, and he'd find himself hiding out in the living room away from her and Hadley.

Tonight he'd talk to her. He and Hadley had made homemade blueberry ice cream. After Hadley's lessons, he planned to ask Megan to go for a walk with him around the property. Her sister's wedding was in a week. After that, she'd be available to go on dates. He hoped she'd agree to go to the upcoming rodeo with him and Hadley. And not just as a friend.

"Uncle Colt! Mom wants to talk with you."

Hadley's voice sounded from the living room. He walked to her and took the phone. "Hi again, Tina."

No one responded, and he looked at the screen to see if Hadley had accidentally hung up. It appeared to still be connected. "Hello?"

"Colt." Tina sounded nervous. "I have something I'd like to ask you."

"Okay."

"Please don't answer today. Just say you'll pray about it. Please."

Colt's gut twisted. He didn't like the sound of her voice. He had a feeling he knew what she was going to ask, and if he was right, the answer was no.

She continued, "I'd like to see Hadley. Maybe next Saturday?"

"We're busy. Going to a friend's wedding."

"What about before or after? Please, Colt."

"No. She's not ready."

"She's not, or you're not?"

Her response pierced him in the heart. Of course he wasn't ready. He didn't want to see the woman who'd run off with his brother, watched him die, and now wanted to slide her way back into his and Hadley's lives. "The answer is no."

"Please just agree to pray about it."

"Fine. I'll pray about it." The water boiled, and Colt

turned off the burner. "Gotta go."

Before she could respond, he hung up. There was no way he or Hadley would be seeing her mother on Saturday.

Colt listened as Hadley played a song he didn't recognize on the piano. Megan said it was some popular song played on one of the children's networks on television. He didn't know the tune, but he could tell Hadley did a good job playing it.

The kid was a natural with the piano. It didn't surprise Colt. His brother had been a whiz on the guitar. Apparently Tina had a good voice. It was how she and his brother met. Connor had been in a high school band, and the drummer invited Tina to sing for them. All too soon, the band became a thing of the past, and Tina and Connor got hooked on drugs.

"That was amazing. I can't believe how well you're doing." Megan's voice floated through the air. "You'll be teaching me before long."

Colt took the break as his cue. He grabbed two glasses of sweet tea off the counter and walked into the music room. "Who needs a drink?"

Megan smiled as she took a glass. Her blue eyes glistened in perfect contrast to the light brown shirt she wore. He could tell she'd been trying to get a little bit of sun before the wedding. Her skin was still fair, but just a hint of a tan touched her nose and cheeks. She shouldn't worry about darker skin. Her ivory color was gorgeous.

"Thanks, Colt. You make the best sweet tea."

Colt opened his mouth to ask if she'd take a walk with him once the lessons were over, but Hadley stopped him. "Megan said she'd help me pick out a dress for the wedding when we're done." She lifted the back of her hair. "And maybe figure out what to do with my mop."

Megan touched Hadley's hair. "You have one of the most beautiful mops of hair I've ever seen."

Colt agreed. Hadley's long brown hair was beautiful. It seemed to have grown thicker over the last few months. He remembered Tina's hair had been like that when she and Connor first started dating. The last time he'd seen her, it was short and thin. Abuse had taken its toll.

Colt wasn't ready to admit defeat. He wanted the opportunity to spend time with Megan. "Remember, Hadley. We made some blueberry ice cream to share with Megan."

Megan raised her eyebrows. "Seriously? That sounds absolutely delicious." She patted Hadley's leg. "Get to practicing, young lady. I want some of that ice cream."

Hadley giggled as she placed her fingers on the keys and started on a new tune. Her practice would be done in less than ten minutes, so Colt walked back into the kitchen and took down three bowls. He filled them with ice cream. "Girls, it's ready when you are."

Hadley stopped playing, and she and Megan filtered into the kitchen. He handed them each a bowl, and they walked to the back porch to eat on the deck.

Colt watched as Megan drank in the expanse of his backyard. He loved that his land rolled out for acres. God's creation rejuvenated him, and he knew Megan felt the same way. She was a perfect match for him. Even in her choice of where to live.

With her spoon, Megan pointed to the bowl. "This is really good."

"You want some more?"

She shook her head. "Oh no. Marianna, the girls, and I had such a big bash for her bachelorette party. We ate just about everything we could get our hands on." She laughed, and Colt smiled at the sound of it. "Marianna is scared to death we all won't fit in our dresses."

"You'll look terrific in your dress."

Megan snorted. "Wait till you see it." She opened her arms. "It's yellow! Yellow!" She pointed to her skin. "This is not a skin tone that goes well with yellow." She smacked her leg. "Pale yellow at that."

Colt laughed at her dramatics. Megan was easy to be around. She made him smile, and Hadley loved her. She was already a good friend, but he wanted more.

Hadley dropped her spoon in the bowl with a clang and looked at Megan. "You ready to pick out my dress?"

Colt wasn't ready to lose her to his niece once again. "Why don't you go ride Fairybelle for a while? You know our rodeo is a couple weeks away."

Megan perked up. "Can I take a ride on Daisy?"

Colt's heart sank. This day was not going at all as he expected. He'd wanted to have some alone time with Megan.

"Well, of course." Hadley responded in her don't-be-silly tone.

Megan looked at Colt for affirmation, her eyebrows raised, and she lowered her lip in a pout. Colt grinned.

How could he resist?

He motioned toward the barn, and Hadley grabbed Megan's hand and guided her away from the house. Colt watched them go. Part of him wanted to follow after them. The other part of him didn't feel like he'd been invited.

He pushed that thought away. They wouldn't care if he tagged along. They were his horses and his barn after all.

He got up and headed toward the barn, shaking off his grumpy feelings. Neither Hadley nor Megan knew of his plans to spend time alone with Megan. He was glad the two of them enjoyed spending time together. It was exactly what he wanted in his wife. Someone who would love Hadley as much as he did.

He'd just get on his horse and take a ride alongside them. He reached the barn and opened the door. To his surprise, Hadley and Megan were already mounted.

"Betcha I'll beat you to the old oak tree," Hadley hollered.

Megan yelled after her. "Of course you'll beat me. I'm riding Daisy." Daisy whinnied, and Megan patted her neck. "I didn't mean that as an insult, girl."

Colt started toward her. Maybe he'd just ride along beside Megan a little ways behind Hadley. They'd get the chance to talk on horseback. Before Colt could say anything, Megan waved as she kicked Daisy's haunches. "See ya later, Colt."

His easygoing filly took off like she was racing for the world's most luscious apple. It seemed every female on the farm didn't want him to have any alone time with Megan. If he didn't know better, he'd think Megan was avoiding him altogether.

Chapter 23

Anger is an acid that can do more harm to the vessel
in which it is stored than to anything on which it is poured.
MARK TWAIN

Megan tied the 137th thick red bow on the back of the white satin-covered fold-up chair. Only sixty-three left to go. Not only was her back stiff, but she felt as if her fingers would fall off. Putting fancy silver napkin rings around two hundred napkins earlier that morning hadn't helped.

Marianna tapped her shoulder. "Megan, the bows look great, but be sure you tie them the same size." She pointed to a table in the back. "Those look a little smaller than the rest."

Megan bit the inside of her lip. It took every ounce of strength not to let her sister have it. She'd stayed up until the wee hours of the night tying extra ribbons to the table centerpieces, had gotten up before the rooster to rush over to the reception venue to start decorating, and had been working ever since. She looked at her watch. It was after three, and she still hadn't eaten lunch.

Marianna continued, "You'll be able to finish these in an hour, right? We have a nail appointment to get to."

Megan exhaled a slow breath. It wasn't possible. She'd

worked all morning and hadn't uttered a single complaint, but it simply wasn't possible to wrap all those chairs in only an hour. She didn't want her sister to go Bridezilla on her, but she had to be honest. "Marianna, I just don't think—"

"I'll help you finish." Her mom grabbed several lengths of red ribbon. "Don't worry, Marianna. The chairs will be ready in time to head over to the nail appointment."

Marianna's features pinched into a stressed-to-the-max expression. "But what about the candy bar? Do you have the dishes ready to be filled tomorrow? And the punch bowls? And what about the silverware?"

Megan's mother placed both hands on Marianna's shoulders. She pressed a kiss to her cheek. "It's all ready. Stop stressing."

Megan watched as her sister closed her eyes and blew out a long breath. She opened them again. "I'm trying to stay calm."

Their mom's voice was tender. "You're doing great."

Marianna nodded and headed off to make sure the kitchen area was stocked with the menu items for tomorrow.

Megan smiled at her mother. "Thanks."

"No problem."

Her mother didn't say anything else, simply got busy wrapping bows around the backs of chairs. Since her step-father's death, Megan had many moments when she wished she and her mom could make amends. She'd even played in her mind with different scenarios of how to broach the subject. Her dad's death had proven life was too short to stay bitter and angry with one another.

But what should she say? How could Megan approach

her mom with the hurt she felt yet still be a witness to her? Christians were supposed to forgive, seven times seventy, as Jesus said. Megan wanted to be a witness, to live, breathe, and walk a life like Christ's. But she needed to be honest with her mother as well. Their relationship would always be false if she didn't express her true feelings.

Maybe she should stop rehearsing what to say in her mind and simply speak from the heart. Allow the Holy Spirit to guide her words. "Mom. . ."

Her mother placed the ribbon she held on the table. "I'll be right back, Megan. Marianna's friends have arrived with the cake."

Megan looked toward the door. Amy and Timmy walked in carrying the wedding cake. Even from a distance, Megan could see that the three-tiered, square, white cake was beautiful. Huge white sugar roses with red tips dotted the first and third tiers. Red ribbon was wrapped around the bottom of each tier.

They disappeared into the kitchen area, and Megan knew they were putting the cake in the refrigerator they'd cleared out to keep the confection fresh. She was thankful Justin had left the decorating party to run a few errands for Marianna. Now that Megan thought of it, maybe her sister sent him off on purpose to avoid any confrontation between him and Timmy.

Megan hadn't seen the couple since the first day Justin visited church. They hadn't been back. Marianna told her they'd been visiting her and Kirk's church. It bothered her they'd stopped going to church, and yet she understood how awkward the situation was. Amy had been a friend to

Megan, not as close as she was to Marianna, but it still hurt that she didn't see Amy at church anymore.

Megan tied another red bow on the back of the chair. She tried not to think of Amy or Sophia or any of the other women who'd been part of Justin's past. She tried not to think of Justin, even though her mind seemed bent on conjuring him up every second of the day.

The irony was the more she thought of Justin, the more time she spent with him, the less she remembered her high school boyfriend. The night at the charity ball, when Justin kissed her then released her and guided her into the dinner, she'd seen the yearning in his eyes. He'd wanted to kiss her more but not overwhelm her. His actions were in direct opposition from Clint's all those years ago. They made her want or at least consider the desire for more than a life of singleness. Maybe she could fall in love. Maybe she could put the past behind her.

"Megan."

She jumped and placed her hand on her chest as she turned to the male voice behind her. "Timmy, you scared the life out of me."

"Sorry 'bout that."

Megan could tell his body was tense, as if he were ready to pummel anyone who went against him. Megan looked at Amy. She'd aged since Megan last saw her. Not in hair color or physical wrinkles or blemishes—she just seemed to carry the weight of something, possibly her marriage, in her eyes.

Megan forced a smile as she hugged Timmy and then Amy. "It's been awhile since I've seen you two."

"Well, we definitely can't go back to church with that

man there." Fury raged in Timmy's voice.

Amy shifted her weight from one foot to the other as she stared at the ground.

Megan felt an urge to defend Justin. Timmy's anger, though Megan understood it, wasn't fair. He and Amy divorced because of his indiscretions. Justin and Amy—the very thought of their relationship made Megan's stomach turn—still, their evening together wasn't until after the divorce was final. Sure, Megan understood not wanting to be around your spouse's past mistakes, but to be so angry and ugly about it when you'd made the same choices didn't make any sense.

Timmy's words slipped through gritted teeth. "You know he forced her."

"What?"

Timmy pointed to Amy. "He forced her."

Megan looked at Amy. Her face reddened as she placed both hands against her mouth. Megan's stomach coiled, and she covered it with her hands to keep from retching. Clint's hands on her arms. His lips pressed hard against her lips. It all came rushing in at rapid speed. She closed her eyes to keep the tears from falling.

"Amy told me about your boyfriend. What he did to you in high school."

Megan opened her eyes. She looked at Amy. Tears fell down the woman's cheeks as she placed one hand against her temple.

How would Amy know? Only one possibility. Marianna must have told her. But why? That didn't sound like her sister. She knew how badly that night hurt her, how it had changed her life.

"We've heard you're his next target," Timmy continued. "You need to know the truth about him. Who he is."

Megan looked at Amy. The woman's whole body shook. Timmy was oblivious to his wife's pain, and he most certainly didn't care about hers.

And her sister told her private business to Amy, and Amy told Timmy. How could Marianna do that to her? Justin forced Amy? He forced her? He was like Clint?

Megan's head started to spin. A chill washed over her, and her stomach churned. With her hand across her mouth, she raced for the bathroom.

"Don't let him do it to you, too!" Timmy's voice yelled across the room.

Embarrassment added itself to her agony as she pushed open the stall and hurled what little bit of breakfast she'd eaten that morning. Her body wouldn't stop trembling, couldn't seem to stop. She grabbed a wad of tissue from the toilet roll and wiped her mouth. She opened the stall door and bumped into someone.

"Excuse me." She looked up and saw her mother. Her heart plummeted.

"I saw what happened." Her mom's voice was low, and Megan knew she couldn't handle any kind of confrontation from her mom. It had been eight years. Eight years. She wanted to be over what Clint did. Wanted to be free. She wanted to love Justin. But he was the same as Clint.

The thought made her head pound, and new tears swelled in her eyes. What kind of warped person continued to fall for evil men? Men who mistreated women for their own selfish designs. She silently begged her mom not to accuse or berate her. At the same time, with what little strength she still had, she lifted her shoulders and pushed out her chin to prepare for her mother's onslaught of words.

Her mom's stoic facade melted, and Megan watched as pain etched her mother's features. She wrapped her arms around Megan and pressed her head against her shoulder. "I'm sorry."

A dam broke inside Megan's heart and spirit, and she cried against her mother's shoulder. She released the pain until there was nothing left in her.

"It's okay, Megan," her mother cooed as she raked her fingers through Megan's hair.

Her mom's tenderness opened the old wound, and she knew God covered it with medicine, cleaning it out, allowing a place for true healing.

Megan sniffed, and her mom held her tighter. Clint had stolen her purity. Her sister betrayed her trust. Justin was not the man her heart wanted him to be. He was the man her head knew he was.

Her heart was shredded.

Megan followed her sister, Julie, Amber, and her mom into the nail salon. It took every ounce of restraint not to lay into her sister for sharing her past with Amy. She didn't want to ruin Marianna's day tomorrow. As her mom told her repeatedly in the bathroom, Marianna loved her and would have shared that information only if she felt it absolutely necessary.

She still didn't understand how telling Amy was absolutely necessary. And Justin. She knew he had been a scoundrel, but what Timmy said made him criminal. She just couldn't imagine Justin doing such a horrible thing. She thought of her parents' disbelief in Clint's actions. They hadn't wanted her to date Clint, but they never expected him to hurt her. She hadn't expected it either. But he had, and her life had never been the same.

"You sit here."

The Cambodian woman's directions to sit in the massage chair snapped her from her thoughts. Megan forced herself to smile and nod at the woman as she settled into the chair. She dipped her feet in the almost-too-hot water and pressed her head against the chair.

Marianna released a loud exhale. "I think everything is ready for tomorrow."

"It looks great. We've done a good job, if I do say so myself," added Julie.

"I don't care if I never see another roll of red ribbon and tiny bottles of bubbles in my life," said Amber.

Megan couldn't help but grin. Amber had spent the entire day tying small red bows around the neck of the bubbles that would be passed out to the attendees to use for sending off Kirk and Marianna.

The group continued to talk, and Megan tried to focus on allowing the chair to loosen her tense muscles. She prayed God would help her understand the afternoon's events and why she felt attracted to Justin, of all people.

Now she felt repulsion for Justin. She didn't want to walk down the aisle with him. Didn't want to see him later that evening at the rehearsal dinner.

God, how am I going to make it through the dinner? God didn't respond, and she felt more frustrated.

"Megan, did I tell you Colt called today?"

Megan opened her eyes and looked at her sister. She hoped her aggravation with her wasn't as obvious on the outside as she felt on the inside. She shook her head. "No. You didn't tell me."

"He wanted to make sure it was all right with me if he brought Hadley's mother to the wedding."

Megan lifted her eyebrows. That was a surprise. She was glad he was allowing Hadley and Tina to get to know one another. Hadley loved talking with her mom, but he was going to let her come for a visit? God must really be working on his heart. *Is that why You're being quiet with me, God? Colt's taking up all Your time?*

Marianna continued, "I think it's terrific he's such a good dad to Hadley. He's so faithful and devoted."

"Definitely the kind of guy a gal would want to end up with," added Amber.

"I wonder if he's interested in anyone," said Julie.

Megan pressed her head against the chair once more. She closed her eyes. Their matchmaking was obvious. But she had news for the lot of them. She and Colt were friends, and that was all. She'd spent years not wanting a man in her life, and after this afternoon, she planned to continue to stay that way. Megan mumbled, "Maybe you should go for him, Julie."

Megan heard her sister's huff, but she didn't respond. If she said much more, Marianna would be hearing an earful for telling Amy about Clint.

"God will bring the right man into Megan's life."

Megan opened her eyes and studied her mother who sat three chairs away from her. Had those words actually come from the woman who gave her birth, who raised her, then accused her of being a foolish liar? The woman who'd never picked up a Bible to Megan's knowledge until she and Marianna bought her one when they were teenagers?

Megan noted Marianna's expression revealed she was just as surprised by their mother's words. Her sister nodded. "You're right, Mom."

The small Asian woman sat in the chair in front of Megan. She tapped Megan's leg, and Megan lifted it out of the water for her to start the pedicure.

Did her mother believe her now? The memory of that night washed through her mind. Clint had died in the car accident. Megan had grown more physically ill with each passing day until Marianna talked her into telling their parents the truth.

"You never should have dated him. If you'd listened to us, this never would have happened," yelled her dad.

"She's lying."

The words had slipped through her mother's lips like a snake slithering through a pasture. They'd contained such vehemence, such vileness. Megan didn't understand it. She'd never gotten over it.

She sneaked a peek in her mother's direction. Her mom watched her. Megan couldn't decipher her expression. She knew a discussion between them was coming. Though she felt disconnected from God, she prayed He'd see her through it.

Chapter 24

*There's nothing like a good cheating song
to make me want to run home to be with my wife.*
STEVEN CURTIS CHAPMAN

Justin straightened the red tie around his neck. He looked past his reflection in the mirror and realized Kirk's face rivaled the primary accent color of the wedding. Justin put his hand on his friend's shoulder and pointed to the couch. "Why don't you have a seat for a second?"

Kirk nodded and pulled at his solid white tie. "Is it hot in here?"

Justin grinned as he reached for the pitcher of water on the table. He poured a glass and handed it to his friend. "No. The temperature is fine. Feeling nervous?"

Kirk took a quick swallow then waved his hand. "Not in the slightest. Why would I be nervous? I love Marianna. I want to marry her. I want to promise to take care of her for the rest of my life, to provide for her, to be responsible for her well-being." He bent forward, placing his elbows on his knees and lowering his head between his legs. "I think I'm gonna be sick."

Justin bit back a laugh. If his friend weren't so serious, he'd rib him for his dramatics. He patted Kirk's shoulder. "Take a deep breath, man. It'll be all right."

Kirk looked up at him. "What if I lose my job? What if I lose my insurance? You know she gets kidney stones. Can you imagine the hospital bill without insurance?"

Justin shuddered. He didn't know she struggled with kidney stones. He'd passed one three years ago. Worst pain he'd ever experienced. Poor woman. He hated that for her. He focused back on his friend. "Marianna is a teacher. I'm sure she can get insurance."

Kirk placed his hand on his chest. "But I'm the man. I'm supposed to provide for her."

Justin grinned. "Sounding a little chauvinistic, aren't we?"

Kirk peered at him. "Justin, I'm serious."

"Man, I know. I'm just kidding with you." He sat on the chair across from Kirk. "I know you want to be sure you can take care of her. But isn't that God's job? And isn't that part of marriage? Taking care of each other in the good and bad times. You've got a job. You're good at it. You can't worry about the future."

Justin thought of Megan. He should be listening to his own advice. He wanted her to be his future. He worried about his past rearing its ugly head. He didn't want her to experience any pain or discomfort by running into women he'd once known. But he had to trust God with all of that. He couldn't let the past dictate the life God had for him now and later.

Kirk sucked in a deep breath and took another drink of water. "You're right, man."

Justin stood and offered his hand. "Come on. We've got a wedding to go to."

Kirk nodded as he took Justin's hand and stood up. He

looked in the mirror and adjusted his tie. "Do you think she'll think I look okay?"

Justin shook his head. "I am not discussing your appearance with you. You're fine."

Kirk grinned as he headed to the door. "I bet she'll look beautiful."

"She looks like Megan. Of course she'll look beautiful," Justin mumbled.

Kirk stopped and turned toward Justin. "Look. We never talked after that night at the gym. I was wrong. You are different. I know you won't hurt Megan. I. . ."

Justin grabbed his shoulder. "I know. But now's not the time to talk about me and Megan. You're about to get hitched."

Kirk blew out a long breath. "Don't say it like that. I think I feel sick again."

Justin nudged him forward. "Get out there. You'll be fine once you see her."

Justin followed Kirk into the sanctuary. They made their way to the front of the church. Marianna, Megan, their mom, and the other girls had done a good job fixing the place up. He liked the red flowers and the little splashes of yellow.

Looking out at the congregation, his legs started to twitch. He enjoyed being the center of attention. Nothing better than walking into a crowded room with a beautiful woman draped on your arm. But weddings were not generally his thing. He couldn't remember the last one he'd attended. Grooms didn't tend to be big chums of his.

Still, he was anxious to see Megan. She'd mentioned the

bridesmaid dress not being a color that suited her skin tone, but the comment had been made in passing. He knew she wanted Marianna to have all that her heart desired for her wedding. Megan's selflessness was one of the qualities he loved about her.

He shifted his weight from one foot to the other. He wanted to see her. Wanted her to walk down the aisle for him. Not to be a part of her sister's wedding. He scratched his neck, wondering if the wedding would ever start.

Sneaking a peek at his friend, he saw the sweat beading on Kirk's brow. If the ceremony didn't start soon, he'd be picking his friend up off the ground. Justin reached into his pocket, pulled out a handkerchief, and handed it to Kirk. Kirk nodded his thanks and wiped his brow.

The music started. The group silenced as one of their friends made her way down the aisle. Another friend followed. Then came Megan.

Justin drank in the pale yellow, strapless dress with the thick red sash around the waist. He took in the length of her neck. The ivory color of her skin. Her hair was pulled up, much the same way as it had been for the charity ball. Though he tried to shake the thought, he wondered how the small of her neck would feel beneath his lips.

She looked at him, and their gazes locked. At first she seemed glad to see him, pleased with his appearance, possibly as eager to be near him as he was her. Then the wall lifted in front of her eyes. She masked her expression then looked away from him.

He had to convince her of his affection. He'd tried to hide his feelings, to spare her of his past long enough. God didn't want him to live in the past. He was going to tell her.

Megan moved to her place across from him. The music changed, and Marianna appeared in the doorway. Justin looked at his friend. Kirk's eyes welled with tears, and his nerves seemed to fade away. Though he never would have believed it possible, jealousy welled inside Justin.

He wanted what Kirk had. He sneaked a peek at Megan. She beamed in her sister's direction. He knew the two of them were close, and he wondered what life would be like for Megan now that her sister would be married. He knew she had to be a bit sad at their soon-to-be separation.

He would be happy to fill Megan's time if she'd let him. Marianna made it to the front of the sanctuary, and out of the corner of Justin's eye, he caught a young girl waving toward them. The girl sat beside an older version of herself and a large, blond cowboy of a man.

Megan partially lifted her hand and grinned then focused back on the ceremony. Justin looked back at the attendees. The preacher spoke of love never failing and always remaining honest and true, and a bunch of other good, wholesome things, but Justin couldn't take his eyes off that family.

Was that the guy Kirk mentioned at the gym? Colt somebody or other? Kirk had said Megan was giving the niece piano lessons, and that the Colt fellow was her uncle whom she lived with. If that was them, then who was the look-alike sitting beside the girl?

Justin looked back at the oversized cowboy. The man scowled at him with a vehemence Justin hadn't seen since the last time he was in the same room with Timmy. He wasn't a betting man, too busy with the girls to worry about games, but Justin felt confident the man was the Colt guy who had his eyes set on Megan.

Well Justin had news for him. He wasn't going to get her. There had never been a woman Justin felt willing to go the distance with, to fight to keep in his life. Megan was different. He wanted her until death did them part. The thought sent a shudder through his body. He never thought he'd feel this way.

One of the tech guys handed Megan a microphone. She glanced his way. Her chest rose and fell as she bit her bottom lip. The music started, and Justin wished he could hold her hand, assure her she'd do a great job.

Megan's gaze shifted to her sister and Kirk as she started to sing of love and commitment. Surely her voice rivaled the angels. Her soft pitch wrapped itself around him. Tears glistened in her eyes as she gazed back at him. His feet itched to go to her, to take her in his arms and promise all the song said.

The song ended, and he turned his attention to Kirk and Marianna as they exchanged their vows. Love and adoration reflected from Marianna's eyes. Though he couldn't see Kirk, he knew his friend felt the same. This was what he wanted. The next wedding he attended would be his own. With Megan.

Justin took Megan's hand in his and guided her to the dance floor. Marianna and Kirk had shared their first dance as man and wife. As planned, the wedding party would join them at the beginning of the next song.

He wrapped his arms around her tiny waist. She averted her gaze, but he stayed focused on her face. He loved the slight smattering of freckles on her cheeks, nose, and fore-head. From a distance, her skin was so clear, so smooth, but up close, the freckles showed. He wanted to trace his lips along the line of those freckles, to kiss each one in turn.

She lifted her gaze to his for the briefest moment, and he noted pain behind her eyes. What had upset her? Maybe it was the wedding. He knew Marianna was moving out, that the two of them had never lived apart. He needed to be a comfort to Megan, to let her know she could count on him, spend time with him whenever she felt lonely or missed her sister.

"Did you bring anyone with you to the wedding?"

Her voice was hesitant, and Justin frowned. "Who? Like my dad?"

"No. I mean a date."

A fist seemed to tighten around Justin's heart and squeeze. Why would she think he'd bring a date to the wed-ding? "Megan, I haven't gone on a date since I became a Christian. Unless you call the charity ball a date."

And he did. He'd had such a wonderful time with Me-gan. They'd laughed through dinner. She'd acted comfort-able, even witty around his colleagues and other so-called prestigious members of Lexington's society. And the kiss. He couldn't look at her lips without replaying their kiss. The one touch wasn't enough. It only whet his appetite for more.

"I don't call the charity ball a date."

Megan sounded angry, but her expression was sad. He didn't know what was going on. They'd had a terrific time yesterday morning putting up chairs at the reception and wrapping ribbons around napkins. He hadn't even seen her since then, so he couldn't fathom what he'd done to upset her.

He tightened his hold around her back. She stiffened, but he didn't care. He loved her, and whatever he'd done to upset her, he needed to make it right. "Megan, you of all people know I'm not the man I was four months ago. I don't want a new woman on my arm every evening. I want—"

"May I cut in?"

Justin turned at the sound of a man standing behind him. The overgrown, blond cowboy looked at Megan with the stupidest smile across his lips. A blush rose on Megan's cheeks, and Justin couldn't tell if it was because she liked the guy or she was surprised he'd ask to interrupt their dance.

Justin inhaled a deep breath. He was a new creation, and part of that was to be civil, even when he didn't feel like it. He couldn't force Megan to love him. She had to do that on her own. The wedding party song had ended. He should let her dance with this guy and then ask her for the next.

Justin forced a smile toward the man and then to Megan. He dipped his head. "Sure."

The man released a throaty sigh when he took Megan's hands. Justin wondered if the guy would drool all over her. He headed toward the punch table and grabbed a filled, dainty glass off it.

He let out a breath. He was behaving as a good Christian man would. He wasn't a Neanderthal. He didn't own Megan. He couldn't force her to stay at his side the entire night.

"The wedding was beautiful, wasn't it?"

Justin turned and nodded to Megan's mom. "It was."

"I'm so proud of Marianna. She picked such a fine gentleman of a husband."

Justin looked at Marianna and his friend. Kirk twirled her around on the dance floor. She laughed as she wrapped her arms around his neck and pulled him close to kiss his lips.

Justin's gut tightened. He wanted that to be him and Megan. He shifted his gaze to Megan and the cowboy.

"Their stepfather was a good man. So kind. Gentle. Wouldn't hurt a fly."

Justin tried to focus on Megan's mother's words, but then Colt lifted his hand to Megan's cheek. Justin's blood burned hot. No one would touch his Megan. He handed the cup to Megan's mother and nodded. "Excuse me."

He bolted onto the dance floor, grabbed Colt's shoulder, turned the man toward him, and said, "Don't even think of touching Megan like that."

The man frowned, and Justin drew back his fist.

"What are you doing?" Megan screamed.

He didn't care what she said as his fist connected with the man's cheek. The guy stumbled a few steps back then lunged toward Justin, knocking him off his feet.

Megan squealed, but he ignored her as he hammered

the guy with a right punch. The man returned the favor with one of his own. He was stronger than Justin thought, but it didn't matter. He'd take whatever the man dished out. By the time this was over, the blond cowboy would know he'd better keep his hands off Justin's girl.

Chapter 25

It's no wonder that truth is stranger than fiction.
Fiction has to make sense.
MARK TWAIN

"Please, Megan. It's your last day in the office. Let me take you to lunch."

Megan looked up at Justin, taking in the deep purple and blue coloring around his left eye, as well as the slit on his bottom lip. She still could not believe he'd hit Colt. For as long as she lived, she'd never be able to fully wipe the vision of the two burly men rolling around on her sister's wedding dance floor. Over her.

She thought Marianna was going to go into cardiac arrest. Even Kirk was punched in the arm trying to break the two of them up.

Eighth grade, Mike Clark and Stan Bowling—that was the last time she'd seen such a ridiculous display of fists.

She didn't want to talk to Justin. She couldn't remember another time she'd felt so humiliated. Hadley cried her eyes out—her mom trying to comfort her. Megan had been glad to see the woman attend the ceremony.

Colt had been just as bad as Justin. He didn't try to stop her boss's insanity but joined in on it. He looked every bit as beaten as Justin with a busted nose and split lip.

She exhaled a long breath and shook her head at her boss. "Justin, I have a lot to do. Tomorrow is my first day of new teacher training."

Justin's dad walked up behind him and patted his son's shoulder. "Come on now, Megan. Go to lunch with the man." He winked, and Justin tensed. "He obviously wants to talk with you."

She found it infuriating the man who had been a lawyer for three decades found his son's skirmish at the wedding humorous. He'd actually congratulated his son for getting in a few good punches. Justin had squirmed under his father's praise. She knew he didn't want that kind of honor, but it served him right. What was he thinking attacking Colt like that? To her knowledge, the two men had never spoken a word to each other.

Justin looked at her with the most ridiculously pitiful puppy dog eyes she'd ever seen. She wanted to stay angry with him. He'd flattered more women than she could probably imagine. He'd forced himself on Amy. He started fights with perfectly innocent men. And yet he still sent butterflies to dancing a rumba in her belly.

She needed her head examined. There was obviously something very wrong with her. Maybe common sense was only delivered to one infant in a mother's womb, and she had missed out.

"Please, Megan. Just lunch."

She snarled her lip. Despite her better judgment, she nodded. "Fine."

The senior Frasure laughed as he walked back to his office. "Have fun, you two."

Megan pinched her lips together as she reached into the drawer and pulled out her purse. The new secretary had already left for lunch. Megan had planned to skip it altogether and make sure she had everything ready for her last day.

She glanced up at Justin. He fidgeted with his office keys. He seemed nervous. He had no reason to act that way. Unless he assumed she might pummel him herself for his behavior at the wedding.

He opened the door, and she walked outside into the warm July air. Normally Kentucky was sweltering this time of the year, but a cold front had cooled the area, and it actually felt nice stepping out into the sun.

Justin cleared his throat. "I thought we'd head over to the café. Eat outside so we can talk."

She nodded, and they walked the two blocks in silence. For someone who wanted to talk with her, he certainly had very little to say. They went into the café, and she ordered a turkey and swiss sandwich on rye bread. He asked for the same, which she found weird, because she'd never known him to eat turkey.

She inwardly shrugged. But what did she really know of the man? They sat together at church, shared scriptures and thoughts at Bible study, worked side-by-side. She thought she'd gotten to know him well. But she never would have guessed him to force himself on a woman or to use his fists instead of his words. He was a lawyer, for heaven's sake—a professional at using words.

There was probably plenty she didn't know about him. Stuff she wouldn't want to know.

He pulled out a chair for her at a table that sat at the far end of the café's grounds. The place was bustling with people enjoying the warm weather, and Megan determined to watch those around her instead of the man she was with. She noted a baby who sat across from his mother. She grinned when the child pulled out or spit out each bite the mom tried to place in his mouth.

"Megan, I've got to be honest with you."

Justin placed his hand on top of hers, and a flash of electricity bolted through her. She hated how her body responded to him. Traitor!

"Okay. What is it?"

She tried to keep her expression blank, her mind on guard, as he looked at her with a sincerity that threatened to make her melt into a pool of foolishness.

"I love you."

"What?" She jerked her hand away from his and frowned. Did her ears need cleaning? Possibly she should make an appointment with her doctor when they went back to the office. Teachers needed good hearing. His gaze was so sincere and sappy that she shook her head. "What are you talking about?"

Justin raked his hand through his hair and tapped the tabletop with his other hand. His leg shook beneath the table. She'd never seen him so uncomfortable. She was beginning to feel a bit unnerved herself.

"I don't know what to say. I've never done this before. Never felt like this before. I want to be with you all the time. To talk with you. To dance with you. To kiss you." He peered into her eyes, and Megan swallowed the knot in her throat. "And when that man tried to touch your face, I just—"

Megan lifted her hand to stop him. "Wait a minute. You hit Colt because he was dancing with me?"

He grabbed her hand again. "You're not listening to me. I love you, Megan. I. . ."

She pulled away again. Her heart pounded in her chest. Her head thumped. "I don't love you."

He leaned closer to her. "But you haven't even given me a chance. Let me win your heart. Let me—"

She raised her hand again to stop him. The words that slipped from her lips had been a lie, and her mouth burned from having said them. Her chest tightened with the urge to take them back, but she wouldn't be a fool a second time. Determined to stay strong, she peered at him. "Do you know why I don't date?"

He clamped his lips shut.

She leaned forward. "Do you?"

He shook his head. She must have looked half crazed, because his brow etched with concern. He needn't be worried. She'd let him know the truth. The ugliness of what Clint had done, and what he, Justin, did to Amy. Maybe he'd never considered Amy's side.

"I went on a date with my boyfriend." The words hissed through her lips, and suddenly she felt ready to say them. To tell him everything. No matter how he reacted or what he thought. He'd hear every disgusting thing she needed to say. "And he took me to our favorite spot to park."

Her mind shifted, and she was there. Up that mountain. Looking over the cliff.

The moon was high. The stars shining. The air clean. Clear. Warm. Clint pulled the blanket from the backseat and laid it out in front of the car. She joined him on the blanket, cuddled up beside him, invited his kisses.

He touched her cheeks with both hands, and she wrapped her hands around his neck. How she loved to kiss Clint. She could kiss him for hours.

Then he pushed her back against the blanket. With all her strength, she tried to push him back to a sitting position. He wouldn't have it. He wanted her to lie back. She'd thought if he only continued to kiss her, it would be all right.

But it wasn't. His hands moved away from her cheeks. She tried to push them away. The look in his eyes shifted, and she knew something had changed. She tried to sit up. Told him no, but he wouldn't listen.

She snapped from the memory and looked at Justin. She wondered how long it had been since she'd spoken. His expression was etched with concern and fury.

"What happened?" His eyes smoldered with a dare for her to speak the truth. He didn't want to hear it, but he would.

"He forced himself on me." She squared her shoulders. It was the first time she'd admitted the truth since the night her parents blasted her for sharing it. She'd been unprepared for their cruel words and disbelief. But she was older now. Wiser. She dared Justin to contradict what had happened.

She bored her gaze into Justin's, ordering him to silence while she finished her confession. "Despite my objections. I told him no. I pushed him away. He continued.

The bruises on my body healed, but the marks he left in my heart remained. I don't want a man. I don't want to love. I refuse to."

Justin lifted his hand as he shifted his gaze to the ground. She sat back, startled by the vehemence of her words. So, he thought her tainted. Found the act disgusting. Good. Maybe he would feel remorse for what he had done to Amy.

He looked up at her, and Megan sucked in her breath at the pain that laced his features. He grabbed her hand in his and rubbed his thumb against her palm. "Megan, I'm sorry."

She jerked her hand away. "Are you sorry for Amy, too?"

He frowned. "You know I wish I could take back my past." He shook his head as he leaned closer to her. His gaze implored her to believe him. "You don't think I forced myself on Amy?"

Her stomach churned. "But Timmy said—"

"Timmy is mad about what happened with me and Amy, but I never forced myself." He moved his chair around the table and closer to her. "I would never do that. Megan, you have to believe me."

Megan looked at the uneaten sandwich on her plate. She hated what Clint had done to her. She hated that she thought of it all too often, especially lately with her heart determined to open up again. She hated Justin's past, what Timmy said, the way she felt for Justin but didn't want to. Her thoughts swirled until she felt she would get sick. She placed her napkin on the table, prepared to run away. Away from her past and present. Away from Justin.

"My past is disgusting," Justin's words interrupted her thoughts. "I wish I could take it back. Say I didn't see women for my own personal wants. I can't. But I never forced a woman. Never."

His firm voice strained against the last word, as if he couldn't comprehend a person behaving in such a vile manner. She wished she couldn't. The memories streamed like a movie in her mind.

His hand cupped her chin, and he tilted her face toward him until she looked at him, their faces mere inches apart. His eyes spoke of earnest sincerity and care. "I'm so sorry that happened to you, Megan. I love you. No matter what happened that night. . .it wasn't your fault."

Megan pushed away from him. Her chest weighed heavy, and she struggled to catch her breath. Standing to her feet, she opened her mouth to speak. Her thoughts escaped her, and she raced away from the café. She didn't want him to be sorry or for him to love her. She didn't want him.

Megan pushed open the front door to her apartment. She couldn't go back to the office. Facing Justin again would be more torture than she could bear. "What are they going to do? Fire me?"

She shut the door and leaned against it. That wasn't the right attitude to have, and she knew it. But it didn't matter. She couldn't talk to Justin. She didn't know if she'd ever be able to look at him again.

She pushed off the door, dropped her purse on the couch, slipped off her shoes, and walked out to the back patio. She could get past him if she never saw him again.

Thursday night Bible studies rushed through her mind, as well as the fact he sat with her at church. She'd just be like Timmy and Amy and switch churches. She had a legitimate excuse. She could say she wanted to spend more time with her sister. That since Marianna and Kirk were married, she didn't get to spend much time with her. It would be the truth.

She thought of her friends at Bible study, and how they'd seen her through some of her darkest moments, even if they didn't know the reason behind those times. And the kids in children's church. How could she give them up? She'd been Meggie to precious six-year-old Hannah since the child's first Sunday in church, at a mere six weeks old.

She leaned against the patio fence. A young mother and her two little boys played some kind of game in the park area behind the apartment. The little boy moved a piece then jumped to his feet and squealed in excitement. Megan couldn't help but smile when the mother offered him a high five.

She'd seen the small family playing in the park area before. Since spring, a year ago. The first time she'd seen them, they passed a bouncy ball to each other. So much had changed since that day.

Megan had been worried and fretted over a good grade in a college class. Now her sister was gone. Her boss had gone over the deep end. And she was embarrassed to go to the piano lesson scheduled for the following evening.

Her cell phone rang. She looked at the screen. Justin. There was no way she was answering the call. She placed the phone on the patio table and looked back at the young family. The phone beeped, and she knew he'd left her a message.

She couldn't talk to him. How could she talk to him? How could he love her? It was ludicrous. First off, she was nothing like the women Justin was attracted to. She knew she wasn't ugly, but she didn't look like she'd just walked off a supermodel's runway. Those were the kind of women Justin liked. She was simply a small-town girl who liked simple things in life. The fact she lived in a city now was just a matter of logistics. It wasn't who she was in her core.

Besides, she didn't want to care about him. She wanted to be single. Too much risk was involved in loving a man. She'd been hurt before. She didn't want to go that route again.

He hadn't forced Amy. She could tell it in his expression. She thought of Amy's reaction to Timmy's words. The woman hadn't known what to do to calm her husband. Megan felt sorry for her.

She looked up at the clear blue sky. It was a perfect day for horseback riding. She longed to take Daisy on a ride, tie the animal to a tree, and lie on a flat rock, basking in the warmth of the day. She wanted to think about when times were simple.

"God, it was supposed to be just You and me. I was always happy with it that way. Why did Justin have to ruin it?"

God was quiet. It frustrated her He always seemed silent. She still completed her Bible studies, still said her prayers, but it was as if she simply walked through the motions. No two-way communication she once felt with God.

But why was He avoiding her? She hadn't changed. Sure, she had feelings for Justin, but she'd done her best to keep them at bay. Aside from the one moment of weakness or whatever it was, when she kissed him at the restaurant, she'd been a rock. Hadn't led him on at all.

Okay, so maybe she did kiss him back at the charity ball, but he'd caught her off guard. And she was all dressed up. It was an easy mistake to get wrapped up in the moment. That's all it was. A mistake.

Her cell phone rang again. She looked at Justin's name once more. She pushed out of her chair, left the phone on the table, and walked back into the apartment. She didn't care about him the way he cared for her. She didn't.

"God, it's me and You against the world."

Peace didn't fill her spirit. No nudging of comfort wrapped her heart. She grabbed a soft drink out of the refrigerator, popped it open, and took a long swig. "God, I start new teacher training tomorrow. I'm going to be a music teacher. It's what I've prayed about. It's what You wanted for me. You've blessed me with the job."

Megan picked up the newspaper she'd left on the kitchen table and threw it away. She placed her morning glass in the sink then moved to the living room and fluffed the throw pillows. She flopped onto the couch and petitioned God again. "Can't we just focus on tomorrow? Get excited about my first day of training?"

Frustrated with the silence, she grabbed the remote off the arm of the chair and turned on the television. It wasn't as if God spoke audibly to her anyway. She shouldn't expect Him to nudge her heart or fill her spirit.

Besides, God was silent with a lot of people a lot of times. She'd just keep reading her Bible and saying her prayers. It wasn't as if she'd done anything wrong. She hadn't forced herself on Clint, hadn't asked her parents to respond as they did, hadn't encouraged Justin to love her. She'd done nothing to warrant God's silence.

In the depth of her heart, she knew that was the problem. She'd done nothing. God was calling her to do something, and it terrified her. She shook her head and turned the television up louder. She didn't want to hear Him.

Chapter 26

*'Tis better to have loved and
lost than never to have loved at all.*
ALFRED, LORD TENNYSON

Colt flipped the thick T-bone steak on the grill.

"Almost ready?" hollered Hadley.

"Won't be much longer." With a pair of tongs, he turned the foil-wrapped corn on the cob. He took two spatulas to flip the foil-wrapped potatoes, onions, peppers, squash, and zucchini. His mouth watered just thinking of filling his belly with the delicious grilled food.

He wiped his mouth with the back of his hand and winced. It had been a week since the wedding, so his nose had healed up pretty much all the way. But he kept hitting the split in his lip, opening it back up, and causing it to take longer to heal.

His blood boiled when he thought of Justin Frasure. He could've pressed charges on the no-good scoundrel. Set him up for a world of chaos as he had to work through all the legalities and still keep his lawyer reputation intact. To Colt he was nothing but a hoity-toity womanizer dressing up in an overpriced monkey suit for a living. The man deserved the inconvenience of a going-nowhere lawsuit.

Colt watched as Hadley tossed a beanbag at the wooden

269

cornhole board. He'd decided not to put his niece through all that. Especially now that her mom was calling her twice a week and visiting whenever he let her.

Besides, he smiled as he turned the steaks again. He'd gotten in a few good punches on Justin Frasure. The lawyer wouldn't soon forget he'd tried to take on Colt Baker.

He grinned at Megan, Tina, Hadley, and her new friend, Valerie. Megan ran to Tina, and they high-fived when Tina threw the last beanbag and it swished straight into the hole. Hadley placed her hand on her hip and stuck out her bottom lip. "I thought adults were supposed to take it easy on kids."

Megan tousled Hadley's hair. "Now what would that teach you?"

Colt chuckled as he took the vegetables off the grill. Supper was finished, but he knew the game was almost over, so he decided to wait to call them.

It was Hadley's and Megan's turns to toss the beanbags toward the board Tina and Valerie stood beside. Hadley tossed first and missed the board completely. She stomped her foot and huffed. Megan tossed and missed as well.

If his count was right, Megan and Tina only needed three points to win. Hadley tossed again, and the bag landed on the board. Valerie whooped, and Hadley grinned. Megan would need four points to beat them.

Megan tossed and hit the board as well. Back to only needing three. Hadley tossed her third bag and hit the board, but Megan tossed and knocked it off. The last throw and Hadley missed. Megan threw and landed it in the hole. Tina squealed and ran to Megan, and they twirled around in a hug.

"You beat a couple of kids. Don't be so happy." Hadley's tone was unkind. She'd always struggled with accepting a loss. Colt started to reprimand her when Megan wrapped her arm around his niece.

"You know, you've gotta be willing to lose sometimes. It was just a game, so lose the 'tude."

Hadley smiled up at Megan, but Colt noted the set in her jaw. She was still angry at the loss, but she wasn't going to say anything disrespectful to Megan.

Colt sucked in a long breath. Only one of the many reasons he'd fallen in the love with the woman. She knew how to handle Hadley. She didn't get all upset about Hadley's outbursts. Didn't make things a bigger deal than they were. However, she still acknowledged and addressed it. Hadley needed a mother like that.

Tina hadn't been sure how to respond. Colt had seen it in her eyes. She was about to apologize for winning or something like that. She wasn't ready for motherhood. He was happy she was trying. He was proud of all she'd done to clean herself up and try to be part of Hadley's life again. But only for visits. She wasn't ready for the real deal. And he couldn't imagine if and when he would ever be ready for Tina to be a real-life mom to Hadley. Probably never.

Colt motioned them to the patio table. "It's ready. Come eat."

Hadley perked up, grabbed Valerie's hand, and raced to the table. "Mom, you want a soft drink?"

Tina nodded and leaned toward Megan. "I love it when she calls me that."

"You're her mom. What else would she call you?"

Colt bit back a response. Well, Tina, for one thing. If he had his say. It seemed weird Hadley had taken to calling the woman who hadn't been in her life for twelve years by a name she hadn't earned.

They sat at the table and passed the food around. Once everyone had their plates filled, they held hands to say grace. He'd hoped to sit beside Megan, but somehow he'd ended up beside Tina and Valerie. Once the amen was uttered, he looked up at Megan sitting across from him. He didn't mind she was his focal point for the meal.

"Can we go riding after we eat, Uncle Colt? Maybe go to the pond and toss rocks and swing?" Hadley's question came with a mouthful of food.

"Don't talk with your mouth full," Megan reminded her, and Colt couldn't hold back the grin at how easy parenthood was for her.

He swallowed his own mouthful and nodded. Wiping his mouth with a napkin, he added, "I think that would be a lot of fun."

Valerie clapped her hands. She was still a bit bashful in front of him. Didn't say much. But it was obvious the idea set well with her.

Tina's shoulder dropped, and she looked down at her plate.

Megan touched her hand. "What's wrong, Tina?"

She shook her head. "I've never ridden a horse." She lifted her gaze and smiled, but Colt could tell she wanted to go with them. "You go without me."

Colt sat back in his chair. That suited him just fine.

While Hadley and Valerie played around, he might get a chance to talk with Megan alone. He itched to spend time with her, but no matter what he planned, something always got in the way.

Megan frowned and looked across the table at Colt. "That's nonsense. Tell her."

Colt lifted his eyebrows. "Well, I. . ."

Megan looked back at Tina. "You can ride out there with Colt. He's got the biggest horse I've ever seen. Thunderbolt won't have a bit of trouble packing the both of you." She glanced back at Colt. "Right?"

"Right." Colt blew out his breath as he put down his fork. All of a sudden, he wasn't hungry.

Colt scooted into the booth beside Megan at the frozen yogurt place. It was the closest he'd been to her all day. Hadley and Valerie had left them alone at the pond, just as he expected. Instead of being able to spend time with Megan, he'd been a third wheel while she and Tina talked about everything from cooking to hair products.

Tina finally left, and he'd offered to take Megan and the girls for a treat.

"I've never been here before," said Valerie. It was the first time she'd spoken to them without using Hadley as a go-between.

Megan pulled her spoon out of her mouth. "It's my favorite. I love getting to pick between the different flavors."

"And all the toppings!" Hadley added. She looked into

Valerie's cup. "What did you get?"

"Cotton candy and birthday cake yogurt topped with M&M's, gummy bears, Snickers, and cherries."

Hadley lifted her eyebrows. "Can I taste it? You can taste mine. I got peanut butter and chocolate yogurt with chocolate syrup, peanuts, and cherries on top."

Colt turned his cup toward Megan. "I feel quite plain with my vanilla and chocolate syrup."

Megan laughed, and her eyes twinkled as she lifted her brows and said, "Can I try it?"

Hadley wrinkled her nose. "Are you making fun of me?"

Colt shook his head. "Absolutely not. You're entirely too cute to make fun of."

Satisfied with the comment, Hadley turned back to Valerie, and the girls took another bite from each other's cups.

Colt tried not to stare at Megan as she took another bite of her frozen yogurt. Her cheeks and nose were burnt from the afternoon in the sun, which made her blue eyes sparkle lighter than the noonday sky. Her hair was messy from the day of riding and cornhole playing. She'd traced her fingers through it and pulled the mass of it back in a clip, but it was still messy, and very cute.

He'd wanted time alone with her all day. For weeks, actually. Though they weren't exactly alone, the girls were so absorbed in each other that this was his chance to talk to her. If only he knew what to say.

"I had a lot of fun today."

She spoke before he had the chance. He nodded and nudged her with his shoulder. "Me, too."

He inwardly berated himself. Why had he just nudged

her? What were they? Ten years old, and she was his neighborhood buddy? It was no wonder he hadn't had girlfriends. He had no idea how to interact with women.

He wanted to tell her she was beautiful, to ask her on a date, to tell her she was the perfect woman for him. She was a country girl with a pure heart. She was good with Hadley and easy to be around. She didn't run around chasing men. He liked that most about her.

"I needed today. To just have fun." She looked at him. The seriousness in her eyes made him squirm. She lifted her hand as if she were patting the air. "You know. No heavy. Just with friends."

He inwardly growled. She thought of him as a friend. That was good. Marriages lasted when the husband and wife were friends. His mom and dad had been the best of friends. But they also looked at each other like they'd hung the moon and stars, too. He wanted that from her as well.

He settled back in the seat. It had been a long week for her. Her sister got married. She quit her job. For which he was thankful. And she started her teacher training. He'd give her a week or two. She probably needed a good friend right now. The fireworks would come later.

"How was your training this week?"

She smiled. "It was amazing. I'm going to love it. I should have gone into education from the very beginning."

"You'll do great."

"I think you're right. It already feels so natural and fulfilling. I've always loved kids. I don't know why I didn't think of it before."

"Hello, Megan."

Megan's face blanched, and Colt turned toward the male voice.

Justin spoke again. "Hanging out with Colt, I see."

Colt jumped to his feet and clenched his fists. If the guy wanted to go another round, then he'd be happy to oblige him.

Megan slid out of the booth and stood between them. He didn't look down at her. He kept his gaze focused on Justin. The man wanted to go another round. The want was plastered all over his face. The skin under his eye was still green. Colt would be sure to find his mark on that spot again.

"Stop it."

Hadley whimpered from across the booth, and for a moment, Colt started to unclench his fists. Justin grinned, as if Colt was too weak to stand his ground, and Colt straightened his shoulders. This time the guy wouldn't get in a single punch.

Megan's hand shoved his gut. "What are you two? Middle schoolers? Stop it, right now. This is ridiculous."

Justin opened his mouth, and Megan turned toward him. Colt winced when she placed her hands on Justin's chest. "I won't have it. I mean it."

Justin looked down at Megan. His expression shifted, and he looked as if she were the dessert he hadn't had the chance to eat. He started to lean toward her, and Colt's muscles flexed.

Before Colt could react, Megan pushed Justin away. "No." She lifted her finger to Justin. "No. I'm here with Colt."

Pain washed across the guy's features, and Colt had never felt such pleasure. Justin didn't look back up at him but turned on his heels and bolted out the door.

Triumph. He was the victor. Megan had said the words herself. She was with him. Not the no-good, womanizing jerk of an ex-boss.

He wanted to wrap his arms around her. Twirl her through the air proclaiming Megan McKinney had chosen him. She'd said it with her own mouth.

He looked at Megan. Tears welled in her eyes as her gaze studied the door. His heart sank. If she was his, then why was she watching the door that Justin bolted out of?

Chapter 27

Lead us not into temptation.
Just tell us where it is; we'll find it.
SAM LEVENSON

Justin's head thumped as he shifted his sports car into gear and raced down the street. "God, I've lost my mind. I was going to get into another fight with that man. I haven't acted like this since high school."

He parked in his driveway and jumped out of the car. He raced into the house and grabbed some gym clothes out of the dryer. He wanted Megan. He wanted her with a passion he had never felt. She was the first woman who'd ever told him no. His mind retraced his life trying to remember a time he'd been rejected. Even in elementary school, he landed the girlfriends he selected. He played the positions he wanted in sports. Went to the schools he wanted. Got the grades he wanted. Clothes, toys, electronics, cars, and anything else his heart desired, he got. No one and nothing rejected him.

Now he wanted Megan. And she wouldn't have him.

He punched the back of the couch as he made his way out the front door. Kirk warned him the Christian life wouldn't be easy. He'd said things about Justin having to surrender his will to God's purposes.

He jumped back into the car, threw his gym bag in the backseat, then pounded the top of the steering wheel. The Christian life hadn't been easy for him. He'd sought out a list of fifteen women to apologize to. Half a year ago, he'd been proud of his little black book. He'd gotten rid of it when he accepted Christ, and truthfully it had hurt.

The wheels of his car squealed when he took a sharp right without braking. "Let's just be honest." He spoke to the windshield. "Some really fun times had been had with the girls in that book."

Things had been simpler for him back then. He got what he wanted when he wanted with no promises of commitment.

He made more money, too. Divorce was a booming business. Lots of people were doing it, and he made a pretty shiny dime off the decimation of marriages. Adoption had proven not quite as popular. He made money but nothing like before. Even cut his bill for a few clients who were slipping into debt trying to finalize their adoptions.

Kirk's words the night of the men's retreat slipped through his mind. "It's going to be harder than you think, Justin. You've belonged to the world all your life, and God isn't of this world. Satan is doing a lot of reigning on earth."

Justin had been in such a euphoric state, excited about his new faith, eager to serve God. He knew the apologies wouldn't be fun, and he expected the dip in his finances when he changed what he represented.

After parking in the gym's lot, he yanked out the keys and grabbed the bag from the backseat. "I've done everything You said," he growled to the Spirit. "Why can't I have

Megan? You know I love her. You know she's different."

Ignoring the Spirit's assurance that God was in control, Justin stormed into the gym. He changed in the men's locker room then made his way to the treadmill. He turned his iPod to one of his old favorites, a song he hadn't listened to in months. Skipping the warm-up, he pressed the treadmill's buttons to a fast pace and ran.

He closed his eyes, trying to rid his mind of Megan's words that she was with Colt. He focused on the rhythm. His blood pumped, and a pinch formed in his side. He ignored it. The pain felt good. Kept his mind off Megan. Off God.

Someone poked his arm. He opened his eyes. Brandy. He pulled out his earphones.

She smiled at him. "Trying to break the machine?"

Justin slowed the treadmill and smiled at her. Brandy was the kind of woman he used to like to take out. Long hair, amazing eyes. Legs that seemed to go on forever. The skimpy blue jean shorts she wore were proof of that. Her strapless top did more than hint at what lay beneath it.

He wiped his forehead with the back of his hand. "Just letting off a little steam."

She shifted her weight to one foot and placed her hand on her hip. "I'm just now getting off. You could shower up, and we could go get a drink." She shrugged. "Maybe let off a little steam without trying to kill yourself."

In the back of Justin's mind, he knew he needed to say no. He'd spent months running away from temptation. Where was Kirk when he needed him?

On a honeymoon with his wife, that's where. He had

what Justin wanted. And Justin was tired of waiting. Tired of trying to fix his life to always have his past thrown back in his face.

Amy had told Timmy he forced himself on her? He knew Timmy had conjured up that story. Still, he'd been hated, accused, and misunderstood more since becoming a Christian than he ever had before. And he was tired of it.

It was time to have a little fun. He looked at Brandy. He could tell she'd be happy to supply it.

He jumped off the machine. "Give me ten minutes to shower and change, and we'll get out of here."

Justin took another gulp of the soft drink. He tried to listen as Brandy talked about the unfairness of her university professor for her summer class. He'd forgotten many nights in his past life had gone this way. He'd sit across the booth from a drop-dead gorgeous gal while she whined about one topic or another. He'd feign interest until dinner was over; then his date would hint at dessert. Never one to turn down a bit of fun, he'd comply.

He frowned. *I really was a jerk.*

"So, did you have Dr. Honeycutt for English 101 when you were at UK?"

Justin blinked. He hadn't caught the last few things she said, but he shook his head. "I don't think so."

"Oh, you'd remember him." She raised her hand level with her neck. "Really short. Comes up to my neck. Bald head. Wire-framed glasses."

He shook his head again. He hadn't had freshmen-level English in ten years. In truth, he hadn't realized Brandy was quite that young. He knew she was a college student, but... He grimaced. Wait a minute, she was taking English 101. Surely she hadn't graduated high school just a couple of months ago. "How old did you say you are?"

"Nineteen." She leaned across the table. "Last year was my first year at UK, but I kinda enjoyed myself a bit much." She reached over and touched the top of his hand. "I'm taking a few classes over so my dad doesn't take away my college money."

His stomach turned. The girl was a baby. Legal. But it was obvious she was not looking for the things Justin now wanted.

Maybe that was a good thing. He'd been playing the Christian card for several months now, and where had it gotten him? A guy lying about him. Several women mad at him. His dad thinking he'd lost all his senses. A dip in his bank account. And it most surely had not gotten him Megan.

He sat up in the booth, determined to pay better attention to Brandy. He'd let the evening play out. Enjoy eating dinner with a woman who wanted to be with him.

"So, where was your gym buddy tonight?"

Justin clenched the napkin in his hand. He didn't want to talk about Kirk. He didn't want to think about his friend while he sat across from Brandy. "On his honeymoon."

Brandy lifted her eyebrows. "The dude got married?"

Justin chuckled. "Yep. Last Saturday. I was his best man."

Brandy smiled as she twirled her fork through her pasta.

"I bet you looked mighty fine in a tux."

She winked, and Justin warmed at the flirtation. He'd missed this—having his ego stroked a bit. The verbal sparring that was sure to set the mood for romance.

He thought of Megan walking down the aisle in her yellow dress. The one she looked beautiful in, even though she'd been concerned about the color. He remembered her voice, clear and perfect, as she sang to her sister and brother-in-law. The love she felt for them reflected in her eyes. He blinked and shook his head. He would not think about her.

He smiled at Brandy. "I suppose I didn't look too shabby."

Brandy placed her elbows on the table then rested her chin in her hands. "Bet it was hard to cage up all those muscles."

He flinched. He was a good-looking guy. Didn't deny it. And he'd always loved being flattered by beautiful women, but Brandy's comment felt wrong. Insincere. Shallow.

He pushed the uneasiness away and grinned at her. "I managed."

He was determined to have a good time tonight. No thinking about Megan. Or God.

"I'm glad your buddy's gone. We've finally got the chance to get to know each other."

He felt her foot rub against his leg. He was pretty sure it wasn't an accident.

"No offense, but your friend kinda gives me the creeps."

Justin frowned. "How so?"

"Just the way he acts and talks." She leaned against the booth and flipped her hair behind her back. "Did you know he gave me a business card inviting me to his church?" She huffed. "A business card, for crying out loud. I mean, who does that?"

Justin bit the inside of his lips. When he'd joined his church, he'd included an invitation to the services on the back of his business cards. He'd received several perplexed looks when passing them out, but he'd been eager to let clients and the world know of his newfound faith.

He pushed his plate away, trying to fight the sickness that warred in his belly. "I'm done eating if you are."

She placed her napkin in her plate. "Absolutely. Let's get out of here."

Justin motioned for the waitress then paid their bill. His heart pounded in his chest as he guided Brandy back to his car. Determining to ignore it, he opened her door then raced over to his side and slipped in.

Brandy placed her hand on his leg. He looked at her, and her grin would have battled the Cheshire cat's for mischief. "Back to your place?"

Justin nodded. "Sure."

He turned on the radio, and contemporary Christian music spilled through the speakers. He growled as he pulled one of his old CDs out of the glove compartment. The last thing he needed to hear was Third Day belting out about God's love.

He started the engine. Brandy hummed along with the tune of one of his past favorite songs. The foul language in the lyrics surprised him. Had those words always been there?

Of course they had always been there. It wasn't like

someone sneaked into his car and changed the words of the CD he had put away in his glove compartment.

He glanced at Brandy. Took in the long, tanned legs. Brown hair spilled down the front of her strapless shirt. She winked as she started to sing the lyrics.

His stomach actually hurt now. Acid welled in his chest. Something he'd eaten had disagreed with him. He pushed back the thought that he knew it was more than that. Stopping at the red light, he realized if he turned left he'd go toward his house. If he turned right, he'd head back to the gym. And Brandy's car.

His spirit warred within him as he stared at the red light. He didn't want Brandy. He wanted Megan.

But Brandy would be a nice diversion from the rejection he felt from Megan.

He wasn't that man anymore. He'd been changed when he accepted Christ.

Didn't he deserve a little fun? He'd lived his faith for months, yet Megan's sister still looked at him as if he were the devil himself. Kirk believed Justin would take advantage of Megan.

Okay, so he apologized for that, but his initial response was not to trust Justin. Was living a life of faith really working for him?

The light changed, and Justin continued to stare at it. His mind and body warred about which turn to make.

Brandy pointed toward the windshield. "It's green."

He sighed and turned. Within moments, he pulled into the gym's parking lot. Confusion covered Brandy's face. "What are you doing? I thought we were going to your place."

Justin pulled his wallet out of his back pocket then handed her a business card. She shook her head. "I don't understand."

"Turn it over."

She rolled her eyes. "You're kidding me, right?"

"I wish my faith had been obvious to you earlier. I'm sorry it wasn't. But I would love for you to join us at worship some time."

Brandy released a disgusted breath as she opened the car door. "Gimme a break."

She slammed it shut, and Justin waited until she'd gotten in her car and driven off before he left. He made his way back to his house then flopped down on his knees, resting his head against the couch's cushion.

"God, You kept me from sin. I was so close. I wanted it, but You kept me strong. Thank You."

He got off his knees, grabbed his Bible from the end table, and settled into his chair. He opened to Philippians. Even though he had memorized chapter 4 in its entirety, he wanted to read it again.

From the world's perspective, Paul had everything going for him before Jesus halted him on that Damascus road. Justin smiled at his Bible, "God, when You stop a guy, You really stop him. You change his whole world."

In the midst of that change, when pain, suffering, trials, and persecutions came along, Paul learned to be content. Justin would do the same.

He looked up at the ceiling. "I still love her, God. I still see her as my future wife."

Peace swallowed him up, and Justin knew God was in

control of all of it. He didn't want Justin going around acting like a teenager, punching men who were smart enough to realize Megan was the most wonderful woman on the planet. He didn't want Justin seeking out other women to fill a void that belonged to his future wife.

God wanted Justin to trust Him, so he would.

Chapter 28

I can forgive, but I cannot forget, is only another way of saying,
I will not forgive. Forgiveness ought to be like a canceled note—
torn in two and burned up, so that it can never be shown against one.
HENRY WARD BEECHER

Having washed down the last chair, Megan sat back and looked around the classroom. Her music room. Kirk and Marianna worked together to put up posters. Her mother set a pile of music workbooks on the table then sat down beside her.

"It's really coming together nicely."

Megan grinned. "Yeah, it is. Two weeks and I'll be teaching twenty to thirty kids at a time in here."

"You ready for it?" her mother asked.

Excitement jump-started the butterflies in her belly. "I'm so excited I could just burst."

"You'll do a good job. You and Marianna were both always so good with kids."

Megan turned and studied her mother. Her red curls lay a little longer on her shoulders than they used to. Her makeup wasn't fixed to perfection as she used to wear it. Even though she'd done remarkably well, Megan knew her mom still grieved their dad's death.

They still hadn't officially hashed out the past, but her

mother had softened toward her. Megan didn't know if it was because of her mother's kindness or because of God's constant hammering, but her heart had become tender toward her mother as well. In time they would deal with the pain from the past. For now she would enjoy the relationship they were building.

The gesture seemed crazy and uncomfortable, but Megan reached her arm around her mother's shoulder. The tension faded, and she warmed as her mom responded to the sideways hug. "I'm really glad you came to help."

"Me, too."

Megan let go, and then her mom tapped her leg. "So, have you heard from either of those boys? Justin or Colt?"

Marianna scoffed. "At least she's done with her job at Frasure, Frasure, and Combs. She'll only have to see Justin at church." She winked. "Unless you start attending with us."

"Justin's a Christian now, Marianna. You need to give him a chance," Kirk reprimanded.

"Are we talking about the same guy? The one who ruined my wedding reception by punching out one of my friends?"

Kirk placed a hand on his hip. "Colt is not one of your friends. You barely know him, and Justin most certainly did not ruin our reception."

"He sure tried. Chasing after my sister. She is not going to be just another one of his conquests."

Megan gritted her teeth at Marianna's words. She still hadn't confronted her sister for telling Amy about Clint.

"Don't involve yourself in my business, Marianna." The words slipped out with more anger than she'd meant to convey.

"What's that supposed to mean?" asked Marianna.

"That means you blabbed about Clint to Amy."

Marianna walked away from Kirk, grabbed Megan's arm, and guided her into the hall. "I did that for you."

"Telling others about my past is not helpful."

"Megan—"

"It embarrassed me. Infuriated me. It hurt." Megan rested her hand against her chest. "I don't want people to know about it."

"I don't want Justin to hurt you."

"*I* have to make that choice."

Megan pursed her lips and stared at her sister. Marianna had to understand she could not tell people about her past without her consent. Her sister blew out a long breath. "You're right. I'm sorry." She wrapped her arms around Megan. "Forgive me?"

"Just stop trying to keep me away from Justin. I'm a big girl. I haven't seen him for days, and when I do, it's all platonic."

Megan remembered Justin's declaration of love, and a shudder washed over her. He'd believed her about Clint. He hadn't blamed her, and she couldn't help but believe Justin that Timmy made up a lie.

"Okay. No more talk about Justin."

They walked back into the classroom, and Marianna picked up and handed the glue gun to Kirk. She sneaked a peek back at Megan and winked. "I still think Colt would make a terrific boyfriend. Surely you saw the way he looks at you."

Megan bit back a growl. Marianna was grating on her last nerve.

"Quit trying to make her like that guy. If she doesn't like him, she doesn't like him," retorted Kirk.

Marianna snarled and swatted her hand at her husband. Megan lifted her eyebrows and pointed toward her new brother-in-law. "I agree with Kirk. Colt and I are just friends."

"But the way he looks at you—"

Megan cut her off. "He does not look at me as you suggest. We are just friends. I think I would know it if he felt anything else for me."

"Then why'd he fight Justin?"

"'Cause Justin hit him first, and boys are weird." She looked at Kirk. "No offense."

Kirk nodded. "None taken. I was a bit surprised by the display myself. Haven't seen Justin physically squabble with anyone since high school. He must really care about you."

Marianna gasped. "Kirk, you take that back." She looked back at Megan. "Besides, it doesn't matter if he likes you. He's the last guy on the planet you'd like, right?"

Megan growled, "Marianna, I thought we just decided in the hall—"

Their mother interrupted, "Megan, honey, why don't you and I go get the supplies you need and maybe grab a bite to eat for all of us. I'm getting hungry."

Megan looked over and spied her mother waving her list of supplies in the air. A break would be good. She needed to clear her mind and get out of the classroom for a few minutes. Even though she appreciated her sister's and Kirk's help, she needed a reprieve from Marianna.

Megan nodded. "That sounds like a good idea."

"Yeah." Marianna walked to Kirk and took the glue gun from his hand. "We'll go, too."

Their mother jiggled the keys in her hand. "Why don't you two stay and fix the broken bookshelf? We'll bring you back something."

Megan bit back a sigh of relief. She loved her sister, but the woman would not stop hammering her about Colt and Justin.

Marianna frowned. "But—"

"That sounds like a great idea." Kirk wrapped his arms around Marianna. "I've never made out in an elementary school."

"Ew!" Marianna punched his arm. "We will do no such thing."

Megan giggled as she walked out of the room. Before opening the bathroom door, she heard Kirk respond, "I was just kidding."

She looked atrocious after spending the morning cleaning and rearranging the classroom. After washing her hands, she splashed water on her makeup-free face to clean off any remnants of dust or grime. She pulled off the University of Kentucky ball cap, ran her fingers through her matted hair, then fixed the ball cap again.

Leaving the bathroom, she took her purse from her mom, then they walked out of the school. She sat in the passenger's side of her mom's car and buckled her seat belt.

Her mom pulled out of the parking lot. "We'll go to the store first."

"Sounds like a plan."

Her mom didn't respond, and the old awkward feeling

she'd known when she'd spent time alone with her mother resurfaced. Megan clasped her hands in her lap. Things hadn't changed as she'd hoped.

"You know, I'm really proud of you. Your dad was, too."

Megan looked at her mom. "I'm glad."

She cleared her throat. God had hounded her for months to talk with her mom, to be honest, to forgive, to restore their relationship. She knew feelings sometimes had to come after obedience. She shifted in the chair. "Mom, I should have listened to you and Dad about Clint. . ."

Her mom shook her head, and Megan was startled to see tears stream down her mother's cheeks. "We were wrong. Bill and I talked about it a ton of times, but we were both so stubborn. Didn't want to admit. . ."

Megan sucked in her breath and pinched her lips together as her mother pulled into the store's lot and parked. Her mom shifted toward her. "You weren't the first teenager to like a boy your parents didn't approve of." She placed her hands against her chest. "I did it myself."

Megan focused on her breathing. She'd never witnessed her mother crying so hard. Years of pain seemed to surface on her mother's body, and Megan's heart began to melt.

Her mom placed her hands on her cheeks. "What he did to you. . .and we couldn't even confront him. I never comforted you."

Her mom's words came fast and short. Megan searched her purse for a tissue and handed one to her mom. She never expected this. Thought she'd have to forgive her mom without an apology, without her belief Megan had been hurt by the boyfriend.

Megan leaned over and hugged her mom the best she could in the front seat of the car. "It's okay. I forgive you."

"It's not okay. The things we said. We hurt you. How could you possibly forgive me?"

Megan thought of the many times she'd said those words to God when she knew He wanted her to forgive her parents. But God's working in a woman's heart was a wondrous thing, because in the depth of her spirit, she knew she did forgive her mom. She shrugged. "Because of God."

Her mom let out a long breath. "Megan, I'm sorry for what I did, but I'm not ready for all that God stuff."

Megan noted her mother's hardened spirit. She'd already backed away from Megan. Deep concern laced its way through Megan. Her mother needed the Lord, but she was still saying no.

Her mom scooped her purse into her hands. "Marianna is constantly harping on me about 'Jesus this' and 'Jesus that.' I'm not ready to believe in a God that would take my wonderful husband from me." She lowered her voice. "Or who would let a man walk out on me when I was trying to care for twin babies."

Megan grabbed her mom's hand before she could open the door and slip out. "Mom, I'm glad we're better."

Her mother's expression softened. She leaned over and kissed the top of Megan's head. "Me, too."

Megan's heart floated as they walked into the store. The two of them laughed as they made their way through the aisles picking up colored folders, hot glue sticks, markers, tape, and a mound of other items.

Her mother pointed to a poster of a kitten playing the

piano. "That is absolutely adorable. It would look so cute on your door."

Megan nodded. She didn't have the heart to tell her mom the only kitten she'd want on her door would be in the form of a UK Wildcat.

She grabbed it out of the case. "I'm going to get it for you."

Megan smiled. Hanging a kitten on her door wouldn't kill her. She'd just tape a UK bumper sticker beneath it.

"Hello, Megan. Mrs. McKinney."

Megan sucked in her breath at the familiar voice. She turned, and her hand went to her ball cap. She didn't want the man to know she cared what she looked like in front of him. Didn't want him to know he sent her heart to pounding and her stomach to gurgling. "Hi, Justin."

Her mother grinned. "I see your face is healed up."

Megan grimaced, but Justin grinned as he touched his eye and then his lip. "The lip took a little longer. Every time I opened my mouth, the thing would split back open."

Her mother's eyebrows knit together, and Megan feared she'd scold him for the behavior at the wedding. Not that he hadn't earned a good scolding; it was just that Megan didn't want it to happen now. At the store. From her mother.

Justin looked at her. His eyes still spoke of the words he'd said a week ago. Words she couldn't believe were true. He said, "I haven't seen you in a week," as he shifted his weight from one foot to the other. Part of her loved that he acted nervous. "I mean. How is the training going?"

Her mother answered. "Actually we've been putting together her classroom this morning. Kirk and Marianna are helping."

He smiled at her mother. "I haven't talked to Kirk since the wedding. Did they have a good honeymoon?"

Megan forced herself to take slow, even breaths as Justin and her mother chatted about palm trees and ocean views. The man's presence sent her heart into a tailspin. It wasn't just his looks. She thought of the conversations they'd had at Bible studies, the way he'd treated her as an employee, the change she'd watched God fashion in him. Though he'd acted like a complete idiot at the wedding reception, she still secretly thrilled he was willing to defend her from possible suitors. Even if Colt was nothing of the sort.

Justin and her mother stopped talking, and he focused on her again. "It's good to see you, Megan. I—I missed you at Bible study on Thursday."

She swallowed. She hadn't been able to go. She wanted to. She needed to. But she wasn't ready to spend an hour with Justin, even with five or six other people there.

She nodded. "It's good to see you, too."

She hated the truth of the statement. For the rest of the day, she'd think about how good he looked in the cream-colored polo and hunter-green shorts. She'd wonder where he was going, since he wasn't dressed for work, and berate herself for hoping it wasn't somewhere with a woman.

Justin walked away, and Megan felt his departure all the way to her toes. She looked at her mother and forced a smile. Her mom was studying her, and it was Megan's turn to shift her weight from one foot to the other in nervousness.

Her mom finally spoke. "That man is crazy about you."

It was on the edge of her tongue to deny it, but Megan

blew out a slow breath and nodded. "I know."

Her mom pressed her elbows against the cart's handle. "Your sister vehemently dislikes him."

Megan giggled. "You can say she hates him."

Her mom cocked her head to the side. "No. Marianna is determined *not* to say she hates him."

Megan averted her gaze. Knowing her mother still watched her, she focused on the different designs of note cards. She leaned down to pick up a cute package.

"What do you think of him?"

Megan grimaced. She knew her mom was going to ask her. She could say she agreed with Marianna, that she didn't care for him in the slightest. She'd tried to force herself to believe that for several months, but it hadn't changed her heart. And she knew God didn't honor her not coming clean with Him on her emotions. "I don't want to, but I think about him all the time."

"Hmm." Her mom pushed the cart away from the note cards and posters aisle. She looked at the list Megan had made. "Did we get everything?"

Megan frowned. That was it? Her mom wasn't going to say anything else? Biting back a growl, Megan nodded. "I think we got it all."

They got into the checkout line, and her mother insisted on paying for the items. Megan thanked her, and they walked to the car. They placed the bags in the trunk then got back in the car.

"Marianna's told me all about him."

Megan did not want to talk about this. She'd spent so much time trying to get Justin out of her mind. She and her mother were finally getting along. The last thing they needed was a guy to talk about. Megan clicked her seat belt. "She's definitely not his number-one fan."

Her mother chuckled. "No. She told me he's known for his womanizing."

Megan nodded. "He definitely was."

"Was?"

Megan swallowed. "He's changed since he's become a Christian."

"Hmm."

Her mother started the car and pulled out of the parking lot. They drove through a fast-food drive-thru then back to the school.

Even though her mother ordered her a meal, Megan wasn't sure she could eat. Just seeing Justin sent her stomach to whirling. And the way he looked, and the sporadic questions of her mother. Megan placed her forehead against the window, hoping the coolness of the glass would ease her pounding head. She wouldn't be able to hold down a single bite.

Her mom parked the car, and Megan reached for the tray holding their soft drinks. Her mother grabbed her hand, and Megan looked at her. "Megan, I don't know about his past. I suppose we all have a past to deal with."

She looked up at the sky, and Megan couldn't decide if her mom was talking about herself or Megan. Probably a little of both.

She gazed back at Megan. "There is one thing I'm pretty certain of. That man is no Clint. After years of seeing the difference between Bill and your biological father, I can tell."

Megan watched dumbstruck as her mom got out of the car and bumped the door shut with her hip. Her mother approved of Justin? She hadn't approved of Clint, even though the only things he'd done prior to dating her was sneak out of the house and skip a few classes, but she liked Justin?

Megan knew Justin was different. He was a new creation in Christ. And probably her parents saw something in Clint her lovestruck teen eyes couldn't grasp. *Well, obviously that was very true.*

She shook her head. Still, she couldn't believe her mom liked Justin. Not being able to help herself, she chuckled aloud. "That man knows how to get a gal on his side."

She opened the car door and slipped outside. She knew it was more than that. She looked to the heavens. "God, when I get home, we're going to sit down alone and have a little talk. And I plan to do most of the listening."

Peace flooded her spirit, and she knew God would be more than happy to share His will with her.

Chapter 29

We must accept finite disappointment
but never lose infinite hope.
MARTIN LUTHER KING JR.

Colt hung up the phone. He'd had a good conversation with Tina. He was proud of how hard she'd been working at beauty school, and she'd kept a grocery store job and her house cleanings for two months. Proof enough she was staying sober. His brother had never lasted at a job longer than two weeks.

Hadley walked into the kitchen and picked up an onion off the counter. "Want some help?"

"Sure." He handed her a paring knife out of the drawer then turned on the stovetop. He poured a bit of olive oil in the pan then placed the marinated steak strips in the skillet. He grabbed another knife out of the drawer and sliced a bell pepper.

Hadley wiped her eyes with the back of her hand. "I love fajitas, but the onions are killer."

He picked up another pepper. "Wanna switch?"

She nodded and gave him the onion. "Did you have a good talk with Mom?"

"I did. How 'bout you?"

Hadley and Tina had been on the phone for at least

an hour before his niece handed over the phone. Hadley begged for him to let Tina visit during the week. He'd been hesitant, seeing how the woman had become more involved quicker than he'd anticipated, but he gave in.

When the woman showed up with a container full of makeup, he'd been sure he'd made the wrong choice allowing her to visit. She picked at Hadley's eyebrows with tweezers and put different creams on her face. He let her slather on the makeup for about as long as he could take it. But when he decided to tell her to stop, she turned Hadley around, and he couldn't believe how good she looked. And still young.

Tina had done a great job. The look of pure excitement beaming from Hadley's face was an added bonus.

Hadley sighed. "I like it when she comes over."

"I know you do."

"But she doesn't know how to be a mom yet."

Colt rested the knife and the onion on the counter and studied his niece.

Hadley continued, "She wants to—I can tell. But right now, she really wants me to like her." She pointed to the skillet. "You'd better flip that meat."

Colt jumped. If he didn't pay better attention, he'd burn their favorite dinner. At least one of their favorites. He flipped the meat and added a bit of salt to the cooked side. "What do you mean?"

"Well, you know how you"—she giggled—"and even Megan will get on to me if I do or say something I shouldn't. I think Mom's afraid to."

She shifted toward him and sighed. "Okay, so I'll just

tell you the truth."

Colt's stomach muscles tightened. What happened between her and Tina? Were they keeping secrets? Was Tina just fooling him? If she was, he'd yank away the phone calls and visits quicker than Old Yeller could gulp down a piece of beef. "What is it?"

The words came out harsh, angry. He cleared his throat to mask his worry. If she didn't think she could tell him what happened, she wouldn't. He'd learned long ago that Hadley was an open book until she felt like he was going to be upset; then she'd clam up, and it would take him days to get to the truth of any given situation.

Hadley must not have noticed, because she got her hands to moving even before she opened her mouth. The girl wouldn't be able to utter a peep if something happened to her hands. "Well, I was telling her about this boy from the rodeo." Her face reddened, and she clasped her hands.

Colt sucked in a deep breath and willed himself to stay calm. He hadn't noticed any boys talking to Hadley at the last rodeo. "Go ahead."

"Well, there was this guy, and he told me I was pretty, which I really liked, because I don't get that too much."

"Hadley, you're a beautiful girl."

She shook her head and waved for him to stop. All the same, he made a mental note to tell Hadley what a pretty young lady she was growing into whenever he got the chance. That was the kind of thing she was missing without a mother. If he had a wife, she'd remind him to say the words when he thought Hadley looked pretty. Like the day Tina fixed her makeup. He should have told her then.

She scrunched her nose. "But I didn't really like the way he told me, because he used a curse word."

Colt's mind raced as to which curse word would be used to tell a girl she was pretty, and in what context. He couldn't think of a single way, unless the kid was being down-right vulgar, and if he was, the boy had better be glad Colt didn't catch him talking to his niece.

The steak sizzled, and Colt turned down the tempera-ture and added the onions and peppers. He mixed them together then looked back at Hadley.

Her hands started moving again. "Anyway, I was telling Mom what he said, and I said the word, too. But just to tell her what he said, not 'cause I talk like that." She ducked her chin and cocked her head. "Well, you would have gotten on to me, told me not to say things like that. That I could get the message across without actually saying the word."

Colt let out a sigh of relief. It was nothing like he feared. Tina wasn't corrupting her. He bit the inside of his lip. "So, are you saying you like it when I get on to you?"

"Yes." Her brow puckered. "I mean no." She shrugged. "Look, don't like go all hog wild on me or anything, but I guess I do like that you won't let me be bad."

From the mouths of babes. Colt bit back a smile. He'd have to remember this little confession the next time he had to ground her for not doing her chores. He remem-bered Tina flinching when Hadley had acted ugly when she and Valerie didn't win the cornhole game. Megan had rep-rimanded his niece but didn't let it ruin the day. Tina didn't know how to do that yet.

"You're probably right about Tina. Right now she's

worried about wanting you to like her. My guess is she feels bad about all the years she hasn't spent with you."

Colt thought of all the things Tina had missed. Hadley's first tooth, first words, first steps, first time to school, first horse ride. There were more "firsts" than he could think of. Not to mention all the seconds and thirds. Every day-in and day-out moment he'd had with Hadley had formed their bond. Tina didn't have that.

A twinge of pain passed through his heart for the woman. She'd chosen her path when Hadley had been born, but she couldn't have realized all she was giving up for drugs and alcohol. Until now.

He wrapped one hand around his niece's shoulder. "I think you and Tina have made a pretty good start."

Hadley grinned. "You've done a good job, too."

He squeezed her shoulder. "You don't need to say curse words to translate what someone else said."

She nodded. "I know."

With his free hand, he lifted her chin. She looked at him with big, innocent eyes. She might be growing up, but she was still his little girl. "And you are beautiful, Hadley Baker."

Red tinged her cheeks, and he let her go. He grabbed a plate out of the cabinet and handed it to her. "Time to eat."

"Megan coming tonight?"

"Far as I know."

"Good. I've been practicing my songs. I can't wait to see her."

Colt smiled. He couldn't wait either. He would ask her out tonight. Even if he had to do it in front of Hadley, the horses, and the dog.

Colt wondered what was wrong with Megan. She smiled when Hadley performed her songs. She went through the motions of guiding his niece through the new material. He could tell Hadley knew something was off as well.

When the lesson ended, Hadley excused herself to call back Valerie, who'd phoned during the lesson.

Colt offered Megan a large glass of sweet tea. She took the glass, drank a sip, then flopped back in a wingback chair. He frowned. "Everything all right?"

She crossed her legs and waved her hand in the air. "Just peachy."

He scratched the top of his head. He didn't have enough experience with women to know where to go from here. Did he ask her another question? Wait for her to talk? It was obvious something was bugging her. He looked around the room. He was pretty sure he hadn't done anything wrong, but one could never be certain.

"My mom and I made up."

He sat on a hardback chair across from her. "That's great. I know that means a lot to you."

He didn't really know the ins and outs of why Megan and her mother had such a stilted relationship. He knew it had been that way for years. From what he gathered, even before she graduated high school.

It didn't make much sense to him. Sure, his parents had been estranged from his brother, Connor, but that was because of drug abuse. Megan didn't have any vice of that sort. In fact, she was an upstanding Christian woman. He'd be thrilled if Hadley grew up to be like her.

The thought brought a smile to his face. He still hoped she would have the chance to see Megan as a daily model for womanhood. Though they hadn't dated, he knew she was the kind of woman he hoped to marry and help him raise Hadley.

She sat up and rested her elbows on her knees. "Colt, we're friends, right?"

He nodded, unsure where the conversation was going.

"Why do you suppose Justin hit you that night at the wedding reception?"

Colt clenched his jaw. He couldn't stand that guy. He knew God didn't want him to hate anyone. Knew God said to pray for one's enemies. But that man made it hard to heed the Lord's words. "Because he likes you."

Megan stood and opened her arms wide. "Wrong. Apparently he loves me."

Colt gripped the arms of the chair on both sides and ground his teeth together.

She smacked her hands against her thighs and started to pace. "Yup. Told me himself. The man went all Neanderthal at the reception because he thought you were flirting with me." Megan threw back her head and snorted. "Like that would ever happen."

Colt wrinkled his nose. Why was it that no matter when he saw Megan and no matter how many times he determined he would ask her out on a date, his plan would get thrown back in his face? Was he really so bad at showing his feelings that Megan had no idea he was attracted to her?

She stopped pacing in front of him then leaned down in front of his face. "Apparently he really"—she lifted up her hands and made quotation mark gestures—"loves me. Like for life. Like now he doesn't want anyone else. Even though he's dated half the state."

Colt stiffened. He did not like the way this was going. He cared for Megan. He was the one believing she was for life. He was better for her. Justin wasn't good enough.

She lifted up her pointer finger and thumb. "Okay, so maybe that's a wee bit of an exaggeration." She smacked her thighs again. "But not much."

He opened his mouth to speak, but she started again. "And apparently my mom approves of him. Of course, Marianna doesn't. She wants me to go after you. Which is ridiculous. I keep telling her we're just friends."

A knife of dawning seemed to twist in his heart. They really were just friends. He wanted more, but Megan didn't see him in that capacity. Maybe if he'd been more vocal earlier on, he'd have had a chance. But it was pretty obvious Justin held her heart. The truth of it sickened his stomach.

Colt leaned back in the chair. He hurt for Hadley the most. Megan would make a terrific mother. He grimaced. He thought he loved her. For himself. Even if Hadley wasn't around. He inwardly nodded. Yes. Of course he loved her. She was a good pick. Christian. Pretty. Talented. Loved the farm.

Irritation swelled within him that she would fall for Justin. He was the better man. A husband a woman could be proud of. His heart twisted. He did hurt, but he needed to cipher through the pain and the humiliation. Which one weighed heavier?

For now, he'd listen to her rant until she realized the truth. And he would start praying for Justin. He'd pray the man would one day be worthy of Megan.

She opened her arms wide. "My mom. That's the biggest joke of all. I've never told you why my mom and I had such a bad relationship. Let's just say it has something to do with the hang-up I have about men."

She raised her eyebrows and pointed to her chest. "And I earned my hang-up. I dated one guy in high school." She lifted her pointer finger in the air. "After him, I swore to never, ever fall for another guy."

She smacked both hands against her knees. "But Justin Frasure. The Justin Frasure. The most gorgeous guy on the planet who could have"—she cocked her head—"and *has* had, any woman on the planet."

She marched back over to the wingback chair and flopped back down in it. She grabbed the iced tea and took a long swig. Placing the empty glass on the table, she leaned back in the chair and looked at him, her expression the most pitiful he'd seen. "Justin Frasure?"

The words hurt, but he had to say them. "You love him."

She shook her head. "But why?"

He shrugged. "Because you do."

Megan closed her eyes, and Colt sucked in a long breath. He would hold his emotions at bay. God would see him through this.

She opened her eyes and stood to her feet. She picked up her purse and walked toward him. "Tell Hadley I said bye." She leaned over and kissed his cheek. "Thanks for being such a good friend, Colt."

Colt didn't move as she walked past him and out the door. He touched his cheek with his hand. He'd finally gotten a kiss from Megan. A kiss of good-bye.

He looked behind him and spied Hadley peeking around the corner. "You care about her, don't you, Uncle Colt?"

He bit his bottom lip. No use trying to hide the truth. She'd know he was lying anyway. What kind of example would that be? He nodded.

"She didn't know."

He shook his head. He knew she didn't.

Hadley walked into the room and knelt beside him. She nestled herself under his arm. "I love you, Uncle Colt."

He kissed the top of her head. "I love you, too."

Things hadn't gone as he planned. His heart felt weak and weary from the hammering it took the last several minutes. He'd been taught that God had a plan in all circumstances, and he'd always believed it. Knew it when his brother and Tina ran off. Knew it when his parents died. Knew it through the daily raising of Hadley. He'd have to know it again.

He looked up at the ceiling and offered a silent plea of help from God to see him through once more.

Chapter 30

What I feel for you seems less of
earth and more of a cloudless heaven.
Victor Hugo

Justin walked into the Bible study room. He knew Megan wouldn't be there. She'd been getting her classroom ready for school to start the following week. Plus, he assumed she was still avoiding him. He missed seeing her. Missed knowing her presence was just outside his office door. Missed hearing her voice when she answered calls or reminded him about meetings. The new secretary was doing a great job, but it wasn't the same.

He nodded at their leader, Kat, as he took a seat beside Brian. He leaned toward Justin, "Ya missing softball yet?"

Justin nodded. "A little."

He didn't want to admit the softball games and practices had been his lifeline. Especially when Kirk married, left on his honeymoon, and was now busy setting up house with a new wife. He'd needed activity to keep his mind off Megan. Unsure how Brandy would respond to him, he'd limited his gym visits. Still hadn't decided if he needed to switch memberships.

Out of the corner of his eye, Justin noticed a familiar form. He shifted and watched as Megan walked in the door.

She glanced at him and offered a slight smile. Justin's heart pounded. He wished she'd sit by him like she used to, but she passed him and sat by one of the women.

Kat opened her Bible. "It's five after. I think we'll go ahead and get started."

Kat rubbed her hands together. "I hope y'all don't mind. I know we've been studying Paul's life for a while, but this week God laid something else on my heart."

Justin sneaked a peek at Megan, her attention centered on Kat.

"And I mean, God just wouldn't let it go." Kat opened her hands. "Have you ever had that happen? You have a plan, an agenda of some sort, and God is just determined you're going to change direction?"

Justin thought of his life before becoming a Christian. He'd been on the fast track to becoming one of the most prominent and wealthy divorce attorneys in Kentucky. Figured he'd settle down and get married one day, but not until he'd sowed all the wild oats a man could handle.

Then God stepped in and changed all that. He wanted to be an attorney, but not for wealth or fame, but to help others who had legal needs—like adoption. He'd started donating to a local counseling group whose sole purpose was to assist struggling couples with the hope of reconciliation. He looked at Megan. And he wanted a wife. Wild oats were a thing of the past.

Kat spoke again. "I want to focus on Jeremiah 29:11, where God tells us He has a plan for us, and that His plan is always for our good."

Megan lifted her hand, and everyone looked at her. She

glanced at Justin, and he had to remind himself to keep breathing. She looked back at Kat. "I had a plan. Thought I'd spend my life doing my agenda." She made a fist and pumped it through the air. "Me and God against the world. I was going to sing contemporary Christian music." She grinned and glanced around the room. "We all know God switched that plan on me."

Kat chuckled. "And those elementary kids will be thankful. You'll be a terrific teacher."

Megan's cheeks brightened, and Justin thought how cute she looked when she was embarrassed. Though he didn't say it aloud, he agreed with Kat. Megan would be the best music teacher.

Megan cleared her throat. "I also thought I'd spend my life single." She glanced at him again and then averted her gaze.

Justin frowned. Was she talking about Colt? He wasn't the right guy for her. Justin couldn't stand the thought of it. And he most certainly wouldn't sit here and listen to her talk about it. Before Megan could say another word, he scooped up his Bible, stood, and walked out of the room.

He strode down the hall to the exit. Part of him felt bad leaving like that, but he wasn't ready to hear Megan talk about Colt. Sure, she deserved a guy like the blond cowboy. A guy who'd been a saint since birth. But that didn't stop Justin from loving her. From praying God would have mercy on his worthless personhood and allow a woman he didn't deserve to love him back.

He pushed through the door, and the hot August air smacked his face. He yanked his keys from his front shorts pocket then wiped his face with his hand. Maybe a dip in his pool would calm his nerves and cool his heart.

He'd promised God the night he saw Colt and Megan together at the frozen yogurt place that no matter what, he would allow God to lead his life. Megan choosing to fall for Colt stung worse than any yellow jacket he'd ever come into contact with, but Justin wouldn't lose his faith.

He heard the door open behind him, but he didn't look back. He didn't want to discuss his feelings with anyone right now. Waving his hand, he said, "Sorry to leave so quick. Got something I need to do."

"What do you need to do?"

Justin stopped at the sound of Megan's voice. He turned on his heels and studied the woman who'd stolen his heart. He felt sure she'd spent most of the day working on her classroom. Her blond hair was pulled up in a ponytail, but some of the shorter strands had escaped and touched the sides of her cheeks and the back of her neck. She didn't have on a drop of makeup, and she sported an old Wildcats T-shirt, navy blue shorts, and flip-flops.

He crossed his arms in front of his chest. He loved this woman. He'd told her as much, but she'd said straight to his face she didn't feel the same. "I need to do stuff."

Great comeback, Frasure. That's telling her.

She squinted at him. "Stuff? You come to Bible study. I start talking about God's plan for my life, and you walk out to do"—she lifted up both hands and made quotation marks—"stuff."

Her sassiness drew him like a magnet, and he took a step toward her. It was none of her business what stuff he needed or didn't need to do. He had every right to walk out of that room. "Yes. That's right."

She thrust out her chin and took a step toward him. "Well, that answer isn't good enough."

"Who isn't it good enough for?"

She pointed at her chest. "For me."

He stepped toward her again. If he reached out his hands, he could take her in his arms. The desire warred within him. He raised his eyebrow. "It's going to have to be good enough."

She pinched her lips. "Justin."

He couldn't take anymore. She was just too close, and she smelled too good. Like some kind of fruity lotion. He grabbed her arms and pulled her to him. Pushing away the knowledge that this may be his last kiss, he pressed his lips to hers.

He took both her cheeks in his hands. He didn't want to let her go. She wrapped her arms around his waist and deepened the kiss. Knowing he had to let her go, he pulled away and searched her eyes for the truth. "I couldn't sit in there and listen to you talk about Colt."

Megan's jaw dropped, and she pushed away from him. "Colt?" She lifted her hands and shook her head. "What is it with everyone thinking there is something going on between me and Colt? We're just friends."

She obviously hasn't taken in the way the guy looks at her.

She punched his arm. "I was talking about you."

"Me?"

"Yes, you." She rolled her eyes and shifted her weight. "Didn't you just tell me last week you loved me?"

He raised his brows. "Yes I did. And you said you didn't love me."

She bit her bottom lip and scrunched up her nose. "Well, maybe that wasn't the complete truth."

"You love me?"

"I do." Her cheeks darkened, and Justin thought his heart would float out of his chest.

He grabbed her arms then wrapped his arms around her, pressing her as close to him as he could get. He looked up at the heavens. "Thank You, God."

She pushed away. "I'm not going to love you if you're going to smother me to death."

He laughed, scooped her into his arms, and twirled her around. "I knew it. I knew you would have to love me back."

She patted his chest. "Seriously, Justin. I'm going to barf on you."

He placed her back on her feet, and his mind traveled to the night he'd taken Brandy to dinner. He had to tell Megan. Had to start off with complete honesty. Especially given his past.

He sobered, fearing she wouldn't believe him. "I've got to tell you something."

Worry etched Megan's face, and he wished he hadn't had that moment of almost weakness. If he told her and she walked away believing he was who he used to be. . . He shook the thought away. He couldn't hide the truth. "Remember the night I saw you and Colt at the frozen yogurt shop?"

Megan frowned, and Justin saw her take in a long breath. "Yeah. Why?"

"I was really upset when I left there. I went to the gym. There was this girl who'd been hitting on me since I started working out there."

Megan took a step away from him. "What happened?"

"Wait a minute." He touched her arm. "Give me a chance to finish."

She crossed her arms in front of her chest. She looked ready to bolt but hadn't done so yet.

"I took her to dinner, and she offered to go back to my place."

Megan lifted her hands and spun on her heels. "Bye, Justin. I won't go there. I have too much in my past. I have to be able to trust you."

Justin reached for her arm and spun her back toward him. "Nothing happened. I took her to her car. I'm not that guy anymore. And I love you."

He watched as Megan stared at him, taking long breaths in and out. He knew her mind churned with what decision to make. It would hurt if she walked away, but he'd been honest. Their relationship had to be based on truth.

Her expression softened. "I believe you."

He took her hand in his. "It's going to be truth all the way for you and me."

"I'd like that."

He grinned and nudged her arm with his elbow. "Unless you're wearing a really ugly outfit and you ask my opinion, and I know if I tell the truth I'm going to get in trouble."

Her jaw dropped, and she punched his arm. "You'd better tell me if an outfit looks ugly."

"Don't worry, I do promise to tell you if you have

something in your teeth."

"Justin Frasure!"

He twirled her in front of him and placed a quick kiss on her lips. "Would you like to go get some frozen yogurt with me?"

She pointed back to the church. "What about Bible study? They'll wonder where we are."

"They'll know we're off making out somewhere."

She punched him again. "We are not."

He rubbed his arm. "You know if you don't stop, you're going to give me a bruise."

Megan grinned. "My purse and Bible are in the room."

"Don't worry. We'll be back before the study is over."

Megan cocked her head. "Well, it is my favorite place."

Justin raised his eyebrows. "Oh honey. We're not going to that one. We're going to the chain store on the other side of town. I'll never go to that one again."

Megan lifted her fist to punch him once more. He stuck out his bottom lip and pointed toward the spot. "Bruise?"

Megan laughed and wrapped her hand around his arm. "Okay. Take me to the chain. I'm sure it's just as good."

"It's even better." He pointed to his chest. "Because you're going with me."

She shook her head. "No. It's because you're going with me."

He sobered as he placed a kiss on the top of her head. "You are right. It's better because of you."

He opened the car door, and she slipped inside. As he walked around to the other side of the car, he offered up a silent prayer of thanksgiving.

Epilogue

Megan's hands grew clammy, and her heart beat with a staccato pattern against her chest. She loved her job as a music teacher and felt the first five months had gone well. There was no reason to be so scared about being asked to see the principal. And yet she felt like one of her fifth-grade students who'd gotten caught doing some punishable activity.

She knocked on Mrs. Carey's office door. The sandy-haired woman motioned her inside. Megan entered then clasped her hands as she stood in front of the massive mahogany desk. "You wanted to see me?"

Mrs. Carey motioned for her to take a seat. Megan sat on the edge, holding her back straight and shoulders up. A smile lit up her boss's face, and Megan let out a breath. "I just wanted to check with you to see how your first semester of school has gone. Christmas break is just around the corner, and you've done such a great job, I haven't had much of a chance to talk to you."

"I love it. It's even more rewarding than I'd hoped." Megan's mind raced with all she'd experienced. The career choice was challenging. She spent more hours in the building than she'd ever anticipated. But the students! How she loved the eagerness and excitement on the faces of the first and second graders whenever she pulled out the instruments to practice playing and singing at the same time. The older students had been eager to learn the historical Kentucky music pieces and were quick to come up with motions to the songs they'd perform for their parents at their concert in a week's time.

She shrugged. "I suppose there have been a few challenges, things I needed to learn."

She thought of the third grader who'd slammed the piano keys cover on his fingers after she'd warned him not to mess with it.

She continued, "But I can honestly say I love this job. Each day I feel more confident that this is where I need to be."

Mrs. Carey looked at her watch then stood up and motioned for Megan to do the same. Megan frowned. She knew her boss was busy, but she'd called her in to talk. Now she acted as if she needed to get her out of the office.

"That's lovely, Megan." She opened the door and guided her out. "I knew when we hired you that you'd be perfect for the students." She motioned for Megan to follow her. "Come on. I'd like to visit your room."

Megan's stomach turned. Her room? She hoped the students in her last class had placed their songbooks back in the cubbies. She normally checked, but she'd been in such a rush about the meeting, she'd let the last class leave without double-checking.

Mrs. Carey smiled. "I haven't been in there for a few weeks. You'll have to show me some of the things the students are doing."

Megan's mind raced. She did have her daily learning targets on the board, right? They were supposed to be posted and current each day so the students knew exactly what they were to be learning that day. Megan's lessons were always planned bell to bell, but for some reason she was always forgetting those targets.

Megan fretted over her desk. She wasn't sure her papers were as neat as she'd like them to be for her principal to visit. They weren't bad, but she wished she'd had time to be sure everything looked as she'd want it. Sucking in a deep breath, she opened the door to the music room.

"Surprise!"

Megan gasped and placed her hand against her chest when she spied all of her fourth- and fifth-grade classes squeezed into the room. Soft music played from her computer. She recognized the song—"Will You Marry Me?" The title swam through her mind, and she sucked in her breath.

She watched as the children lifted up a banner that had been hidden around the bottom of their legs. She looked around the room. Her hands trembled and her legs grew weak. Where was he?

The words "Will you marry me?" spieled from the song and were painted in bright red letters across the banner.

Megan lifted her hand to her mouth as tears formed in

her eyes. She saw movement from the back corner. She bit her bottom lip when Justin appeared wearing a tuxedo and carrying a dozen red roses. She drank in his love-filled yet smug expression. He knew he'd surprised her, and he was proud of himself.

The kids giggled, and she realized several of her colleagues and her principal stood in the door. She could tell by their oohs and aahs that they were as teary-eyed as she.

Justin reached her, and she bit her lip as he bent down and kissed the top of her head. He handed her the flowers then lowered himself to one knee.

Megan wiped her tears with the back of her hand. Her boyfriend was proposing, and she'd be a black-eyed raccoon before she'd have the chance to say yes.

Her heartbeat raced as Justin pulled a black box from the inside of his coat pocket then opened it. She gasped at the large square solitaire on the white gold band. The thing would practically cover her finger.

He took her hand in his and looked up at her. The love in his eyes made her want to melt into his arms. "Megan, I love you. Will you marry me?"

Her body filled with wonder. A year ago she never would have imagined this possible. She wouldn't have wanted to, especially with her then-boss. So much had changed. And she couldn't believe how much she loved him.

"Yes." He pushed the ring on her finger, and she said it again, "Yes."

He stood, and she wrapped her arms around his neck and planted a quick kiss on his lips. The students yelped and whistled, and she let him go. A more fitting kiss would be had later that night.

She laughed as she looked up into his eyes. "You got me good. I had no idea."

Thrill traced his features, and he wiggled his eyebrows. "I know."

She laughed as she looked at the enormous ring on her finger. Then she pressed the roses to her chest. "I don't know how I'm going to make it through the rest of the day."

Mrs. Carey stepped forward. "You don't have to. We got you a sub." She touched Megan's arm. "You don't mind that you took a half day off, do you?"

Megan giggled as she wiped her cheeks with the back of her hand. "I don't mind."

Justin handed her a tissue then offered his arm, and Megan wrapped her hand around it. They headed toward the door, and then she looked back at her students. "Be good for the sub."

Promises of good behavior filled the room, and Megan let her fiancé lead her to his car. She looked at her ring then back up at Justin. "So, where are we going?"

"To our engagement party."

Megan's jaw dropped. "What?"

Justin kissed the tip of her nose. "Don't worry. I've got your dress in the car. We'll stop at your house so you can change. Your mom and sister and Kirk. My dad. Everyone is already there. Lunch will be served when we arrive."

Megan shook her head. "I can't believe you did all this."

"I'm good, aren't I?"

She wrapped her arms around his shoulders and pressed her lips to his. She released him and gazed into his eyes.

How she loved this man. "You're very good."

"Which is why I will stay right here in my car when you go in the house to get ready?"

"What?" she asked.

He winked. "I'll need the distance to stay that way."

Megan laughed as she lowered herself into the passenger seat. She inhaled a deep breath as she looked at the engagement ring, the promise she would belong to Justin legally at a future date. Hopefully soon.

He grabbed her hand in his and kissed the top of her knuckles. He gazed into her eyes, and she thought she would melt into their deep brown depths. "You know being good doesn't come easy to me."

"I know."

He lifted one eyebrow. "Short engagement?"

"Absolutely."

A WEDDING HOMERUN IN LOVELAND, OHIO

by Cathy Liggett

Dedication

To all those in my community who have
inspired this book and blessed my life. . .
I know who you are—and God does, too!

Chapter 1

If this lightning and thunder doesn't stop soon—Megan O'Donnell's entire body stiffened with tension as she tried to see through the quarter-sized raindrops pummeling the windshield of her SUV. She'd had just about enough of the teeming rain and the nerve-shattering booms that shook her mid-sized car.

More than once it crossed her mind to jump right out into the downpour, shake her fists at the dim, menacing evening sky, and make it stop. Make the skies calm again. As if she could. As if she could really control the weather and the heavens.

But. . .she would if she could. She'd do that for Sammy, knowing how frightened the claps of thunder and slashes of lightning made him. She'd do anything for her six-year-old guy. Because that's what moms did, right? Anything and everything they could.

"How are you doing, honey?"

Loosening her death grip on the steering wheel, she reached into the back passenger seat with her right hand, patting his knee where it hung out from under his army-green cargo shorts. "You okay?"

" 'Kay."

Sammy barely had the syllable out of his mouth when another jolting round of thunder surprised them. Megan jumped, her hand flying back to the steering wheel, working to steady the car against the beating rain. But, of course, Sammy didn't jump, didn't react much—not in an overtly physical way. Not in a way that most people would notice.

But then, he didn't have control over his body like most people did. Still. . .that didn't mean he wasn't scared. And she didn't have to turn around and touch him to know his already uncooperative limbs had grown even more rigid with fright. She knew it. She could sense his tension from where she sat in the driver's seat. Could hear the fear in his quivering voice.

"Lau."

"Yes, it was loud, wasn't it, honey?" Gripping the steering wheel tightly, with all her might, she worked to hide her own unease with words that sounded loose and light. "Even louder than Grandpa's snoring." She forced a soft chuckle she wasn't really feeling at the moment.

Flicking on her turn signal, she started to make a right turn off Route 22 onto Columbia, but didn't make it around the corner before a semi flew by in the lane next to her, deluging the left side of her car with sprays of rainwater. She flinched involuntarily as if the water had splashed straight through the window.

"You're being brave, Sammy."

"Bray?"

"Yes, brave. You're my brave guy."

Wishing her car had a rudder or at least four-wheel drive, she cautiously made the turn, making her way through a half-foot-deep puddle. The rain-soaked road grew darker and narrower the farther she drove from the intersection.

Water gushed like miniature rapids in the gullies at the sides of the road. Broken-off twigs lay scattered on the lawns of the ranch-style homes and all over the street, too, resembling a gargantuan game of pick-up sticks. Luckily, the debris couldn't camouflage the winding road she knew so well and had been driving on since she'd first gotten her license as a teenager.

Still, what a night to be out, backtracking all over Loveland.

But promises were promises—and she'd told Sammy days ago that, yes, they could get a bite to eat at Paxton's Grill before her meeting that night. Even though, logistically, it wasn't a sound idea at all. Not when she'd had to leave work in downtown Loveland, go past their house to pick him up at after-school care on Route 22 and then drive back by their house again to go to Paxton's right in the heart of town. After dinner, of course, she'd have to repeat her steps pretty much the same way, driving north from town to drop off Sammy at home so Mrs. Biddle could watch him for the evening, before turning south again to go to the high school where she'd be holding her meeting.

No, none of it made sense. Except for the fact that Paxton's french fries were Sammy's favorite, and she was quite fond of them herself. And honestly, munching on the best fries in town seemed oddly comforting at the moment—no matter how much driving it entailed.

It had been a day and a half at the clinic, with one physical therapy session after another. Record high temperatures the past few days hinted that summer was in the wings, creating as much havoc in the way of twisted ankles, bad knees, and pained shoulders as the first weeks of spring had. And if the day hadn't been challenging enough, she was anxious the evening might be even more so. Never having facilitated a meeting before, she'd been nervous all day long. No, that wasn't true. All week long was more like it.

"Music, Maw-mee?" Sammy's voice, barely audible over the racket from the rain, quavered some as he made his request.

"No problem, honey." She clicked on the radio, already tuned in to his favorite station. Nothing soothed him like country music, and she felt bad she'd been too preoccupied with her own anxieties not to think of it sooner. But there were so many questions—"what-ifs"—plaguing her mind about her All-Stars Sports Day meeting.

As in, what if no one responded to the flyers she'd put up around town? What if the only people at the meeting were the girls she knew from downtown Loveland—like her longtime friend Janey from Sweet Sensations Bakery or Maria from Miss Annabella's Tea Parlor? Or what if, considering the weather, the two of them didn't even show up and it was just—her?

On the other hand, what if the high school cafeteria was buzzing with volunteers? And there were more people there than she'd imagined? Would she really know how to organize more than a dozen volunteers or so?

She'd been so worried about it all she'd barely slept the night before. And she'd brought a change of clothes to work, hoping a more professional look would help ease her jitters. Slipping out of her work uniform—khakis and a black polo—she'd donned a pair of neatly pressed navy capris, a crisp white three-quarter-sleeve blouse with a sash that tied at the side, and a pair of navy heels. The heels were painfully pointy; she'd bought them on sale the season before. But still, standing before the mirror in the clinic's restroom, she felt the look said "take charge." And she would try her best to do just that—for Sammy's sake and for the other kids like him. She'd gut her way through the experience like she did everything else. And no one would be the wiser.

Hopefully.

Good evening, ladies and gentlemen. No. *Good evening, friends.* Or. *It's so good to see everyone here this evening.* Better. *You know. . .* Pause. *For a long time it's been a dream of mine to organize an All-Stars Sports Day event especially for our special-needs kids and—*

"There ye'?" Between the ending of a Blake Shelton song and the first sweet notes of a Carrie Underwood tune, Sammy spoke up from the backseat again.

"Are you hungry?"

"Hun-gey."

"Well, we're almost there. Here we go—down the hill and over the bridge that crosses the water."

Gazing out the window, she looked to see if the river was as high as she imagined it might be. It seemed the closer they got to their destination, the more the rain was actually starting to let up some, now just a slow, steady rhythm. Even so, the river water surged and swirled still turbulent and dangerous looking. "Hey Sammy, you remember the river that cuts through town, don't you? The Little Miami River?"

"Li'l?"

"Yes, little. Not big. Little." She'd gotten used to describing things to Sammy outside the car window. Things that he could've seen for himself if only he could reposition his body to sit up high, or stretch, or lift himself to press his nose against the glass like other kids might.

"Now we're passing the bike rental shop," she added, doing her best to keep her voice upbeat. "No riders on the bike trail tonight though, huh?"

"No bike riders."

"And there's Scoops. We love that place, don't we?"

The mention of the ice cream parlor must've made Sammy's mouth water even more.

"Paxton?"

"Oh yes. There it is. Paxton's Grill. Just a few blocks away. I can see the round yellow-and-red neon sign." Her foot hovered over the brake pedal. "Maybe Allie will be working."

"Like Allie."

"I know. She loves you, too."

"Justin an' Carrie love me?"

"Yes, and Justin and Carrie."

Justin and Carrie, Allie's kids, were like a brother and sister to Sammy—just like Allie had always been to her. She and Allie had practically shared infant seats together. At least, that's the way their moms liked to tell it, and their moms knew all about sister-like friendships. Laura O'Donnell and Pamela Matthews had shared one since they were young girls. And these days, the empty-nest moms were more than friends—they were the owners of one of

Loveland's most successful businesses, the We Do! Wedding Planners. The pair had also garnered a well-deserved reputation for doing a bit of matchmaking on the side.

Turning on her blinker, Megan tapped the brake, creeping the car to a halt, wistfully wishing Allie would be hosting tonight. Allie helped her husband as much as she could since they'd taken over Paxton's Grill from Greg's parents the year before, leaving little time for socializing these days. It would be such a treat to see her even if they only had a moment to catch up.

"Okay, Samster. Here we are. All I have to do is make a left turn so we can park in the community lot and—"

Before she could finish the sentence, an old-model pickup truck swerved toward their SUV, barreling down West Loveland Avenue from the opposite direction. Wasn't it going to stop? Slow down? Wasn't the driver going to notice? Do something?

She froze, trying to think. Turn left? Right?

Her fingers gripped the vinyl-covered steering wheel, and she yanked it hard. Not even sure what she was doing—except for following some unfathomable gut instinct—she veered the car to the right, putting herself at risk while protecting Sammy's side of the car, in case of impact.

Closing her eyes tight, she prayed with all her might, listening to the moaning, groaning, screeching truck brakes. Coming closer. And closer still. Until finally there was silence. The frightening noise stopped.

But her hands were still shaking. Her heart still racing. Anger fueled by fear, she hopped out of the car and began ranting.

MacNeill Hattaway jumped out of the rust-fringed pickup truck, slamming the creaking door behind him.

That was close. Way too close!

He'd decided to drive his uncle's rattletrap thinking it'd be less showy and conspicuous than his red Corvette, but water-slick roads or not, the thing really just wasn't safe. He couldn't—wouldn't—do it again. Not when he couldn't trust the brakes, and not when the questionable steering locked up without a moment's notice.

Of course, it hadn't helped that a deer had lunged across the road in front of him at the same time he'd turned the truck off Route 48 and onto West Loveland. Still, he'd almost gotten himself killed and all because he'd had a craving for a burger from Paxton's before meeting up with a friend later that evening.

Even worse, he'd almost maimed another driver—a woman—who had every right to be standing in the street screaming uncontrollably at him.

Not that he wasn't accustomed to people screaming at him.

Actually he was fairly used to it, being that it was pretty much a part of his job. As a pro pitcher, he'd heard way more than his share of fevered remarks from the Tristate Hawks' fans over the years—both good and bad—all depending on how precisely he could get an orange-sized ball to cross over a seventeen-inch plate from a little over sixty feet away, preferably at a speed of ninety miles an hour or so.

Sometimes he managed to do that handily. Other times, he couldn't do it to save his life, his ego, or his ears from the deafening cries of disgust from the stands.

So, yeah, he was used to people yelling all right.

But he could tell the woman wasn't used to it—or at least she wasn't used to being the one doing the yelling. Instead of flailing arms, hers were crossed over her chest, hugging her petite body. And her voice sort of trembled as it got louder, as if it was usually softer, more controlled, and not used to such extremes.

"What were you thinking? You could have killed us. All of us!"

At least she was kind enough to include him in the mix, he noticed.

"Hey, I'm sorry, miss. I really am. I'm sure I scared you to—"

"To death. Yes! You certainly did scare me to death." She shoved a tendril of dark, wet hair back from her forehead, attempting to tuck it into her ponytail. Letting more of her face show. . .a really nice, pretty face, he could tell that much even through the drizzle. "Do you always drive like that?"

"Do I what? Well, no. I mean, actually there was a deer. A deer that came out of nowhere, leaping across the road. I tried to swerve away, but then"—he pointed to his uncle's truck, ready to explain about the apparently lousy brakes and major lack of steering, but she cut him off.

"Do you know I have a child in my car?"

"A kid? You do? Is he—is she—all right?"

"He. Yes, he's all right. But you frightened him. That's for sure. As if he wasn't already scared enough from the storm."

Oh great! A new infraction to add to his list. Frightening children without even meaning to.

"You scared my Sammy." She suddenly pounced closer, right in his face, as if mentioning her son's name had given her a surge of adrenaline, a boost of courage.

Mac couldn't help but think she reminded him of the geese that had taken up residence around the pond out at his uncle's farm. The mother geese—squawking, hissing, protecting their young at all costs. Ready to chase off an intruder—or go beak-to-toe, if they had to, with anything—or anyone—that got too near.

Of course, unlike the geese, Mac didn't mind the woman getting close. So close he'd caught a whiff of her sweet-smelling perfume. The fragrance wrapped around his head, overriding the competing scents of the rain-cresting river and his running truck engine. And even if her words were harsh, and deservedly so, there was an underlying sweetness about her he detected right away.

"You could've really hurt him." She jabbed a pointed finger in the air, nearly into his shoulder. "You could've killed him, and—and, are you a parent, Mr.—"

"The name's MacNeill."

"Mr. Neil, are you—"

"No, it's MacNeill," he corrected, enunciating slowly. Of course, as soon as he did, he wondered why he even cared.

"That's what I said. Mr. Neil."

"No, my first name is—"

"Whatever!" She planted her hands on her hips. "Are you a parent?"

"A parent?" What was the woman getting at? He scratched his forehead, protected from the drizzling rain by the bill of his baseball cap.

Unbelievably, her voice got shriller. "Yes. Are you?"

"No, but I—I mean. . ." Was not being a parent supposed to make him a total monster? Insensitive to children and their safety? Was that what she was implying?

"Well, Mr. Neil, you should learn to drive like you're one."

"MacNeill." He repeated his name again, this time grinding it out, his jaw tightening. So that *had been* what she was getting at. Which pretty much irritated him to no end. Who was she to make such a jibe? Mother Teresa?

Sure, maybe in the past he'd been reckless in a lot of ways. He'd used his celebrity status inappropriately—for his own good and for illicit pleasures. And yeah, he'd driven many cars many times too fast and too often under the influence. No doubt the tabloids had had plenty to write about him over the years because he'd given them plenty of material. But he could tell she didn't even recognize him as the baseball player most everyone else knew him as. She had no clue as to who he was. . .where he'd been and where he was now in his life.

He hadn't left his custom-built home and taken up residence at his deceased uncle Jake's farm in Loveland on a whim. He'd done it for a reason. It was because he wasn't the same person he used to be. The injury to his elbow had changed him. No, that wasn't altogether accurate. God had changed him. His Creator had given him a second chance. An opportunity to redeem himself and all his bad boy ways.

Couldn't she give him a moment to redeem himself

with her, too?

He drew in a deep breath, attempting to maintain full control of himself as he tried again with the pretty but exasperating woman. "Hey, look—" he started, keeping his voice soft, non-adversarial.

But it was no use. She turned, huffing back to her car without giving him so much as another second to explain himself. Standing there with his mouth half open, he blinked out into the rain. Obviously, protective moms were a lot tougher audience—and a lot less forgiving—than the Almighty Himself.

Chapter 2

W e almost gaw hit," Sammy told Allie as she set down a brimming mound of french fries and a kid-sized burger in front of him.

Megan noted they were definitely getting the royal treatment just as they always did when visiting their friends at Paxton's. Allie even put them at a table at the rear of the restaurant, a cozy nook, where there was more room for Sammy's wheelchair.

"But we didn't get hit, Sammy," Megan countered, disregarding the grilled chicken Caesar salad that Allie had just served her. Instead, she first grabbed for the container of catsup sitting in the center of the wooden table. Shaking it in the air, she reached across the table, squirting a few blobs onto Sammy's plate.

"We're fine," she told him. "Really," she added, bobbing her head in confirmation at her lifelong friend.

Allie slunk down into a black vinyl chair next to Sammy, her eyes narrowing in concern. "But it was a close call, huh?" Biting her lip, she shook her head of loose blond curls. "How scary!" she said, looking both incredulous and pretty at the same time.

Ever since Megan could remember, people always thought she and Allie looked alike when in reality, they didn't one bit. But it must have been some kind of osmosis or best friend thing that kept onlookers saying so. Not that Megan ever minded really. All throughout their growing-up years, she'd always thought Allie was the prettiest girl in their class, inside and out.

"Are you okay, honey?" Allie ruffled Sammy's tufts of toffee-colored hair, shades lighter than Megan's own deep brown. "A little shaken up? Need some more fries?"

"We're fine, Allie," Megan repeated, picking up her fork, stabbing at layers of romaine lettuce. "You know how people get when it rains around here. A little bit of precipitation and everyone turns crazy."

"Cray-hee," Sammy mimicked. Pausing from his munching, he slowly turned his head, looking straight at Allie. "Maw-mee yell at man."

Wasn't it funny how she could never get Sammy to talk when she wanted him to? But now, when it wasn't something she necessarily wanted the whole world to know, or at least something she'd prefer to have the option of sharing with her best friend when and if she felt like it, her child couldn't keep quiet. Of course, she was glad he felt so at home with Allie that he could talk freely with her—but still, it never failed, did it?

"Your mommy yelled at the man? The other driver?" Instantly, Allie's head flew around to face her. *You? Yelled?* She could tell from Allie's shocked expression her friend didn't know whether to be worried or amused. "So, it *was* really, really close."

"Well, it was..." Megan's gaze dropped from her friend's inquisitive eyes down to her plate without really seeing it, playing out the scene in her mind once more. Yes, it had been close. Too close really. Not just Mr. Neil's truck and her car, but at one point she'd actually almost leaped on the man. Had entirely invaded his space, and gotten in his face, and almost poked her finger into his shoulder, and. . . Oh, how her face burned at the memory of her outburst.

And it wasn't just her outburst that was causing her some discomfit, it was the realization that she hadn't been that close to a man since—well, there'd been the time with Aaron Jensen—but that was several months ago. She and Aaron had taken Sammy to a pumpkin patch and they'd been all scrunched into a hay wagon together with a group of strangers. But that was her last sort of contact with the male species that she could remember.

Really, how had she let herself get so out of control with Mr. Neil? She usually wasn't like that. Sure, she'd defend her child to her death, but in a calmer, more dignified manner.

But then was it really her fault? The man was a maniac on wheels! Even if he didn't look like one. . .even if his eyes appeared sympathetic when she mentioned having a child in the car.

But he could've just been faking that, trying to placate her. Trying to smooth over the fact that he was, after all, the one who had been out of control behind the wheel and had gotten her acting so nutty. To the point where she'd jumped out of the car, into the drizzling rain, calling him names that she wouldn't even call her dog—if she owned one.

Feeling suddenly self-conscious and overheated, she laid her fork aside, taking a long sip of her water, not even finishing her reply to Allie. But it didn't matter. Apparently Sammy had a lot more to say, and Allie leaned closer to him, eager to listen.

Smacking his lips, his hand wrapped around several fries, he gave Allie a hint of description regarding "the man." "Man was tall," he told her.

"Oh?" Allie's eyes widened at Sammy's disclosure and Megan's did likewise, astonished by the little tell-all.

It was more information than Megan even realized he knew. Somehow from the way her car had been angled, and the way she and Mr. Neil had been standing in the street, Sammy must've seen far more than she'd imagined from between the front seats and through the windshield. Because, yes, Sammy was right. The man had been at least six feet tall. He'd crossed his arms over his chest, and he'd had to sort of lean down a bit to her, as if listening hard to hear what she had to say.

Or—no, that wasn't it at all, was it? He leaned down as if to taunt her. Yes, that's why she lost her temper and behaved so wildly. Because he was taunting her with those sympathetic eyes of his. Which was confusing and frustrating and—

"Anything else?" Allie wanted to know, quirking a brow at Sammy.

Sammy nodded. "Dark hat."

"Hmm. . .is that right, Meg? Tall, dark hat, and—dangerous?" Allie's eyes twinkled at Megan. "Those are the very best kind." She giggled.

"Please, Allie."

"Did you exchange information?"

"No, of course not. He didn't hit us—he almost hit us. Came really, really close to hitting us." Her mind tried not to linger on the word *close* again. Reaching across her salad, she scooped up a handful of fries from Sammy's plate, downing them before her taste buds barely had time to register what had hit them.

"So you didn't get his name or number?"

"No, I did not get his phone number, silly."

"But you did get his name."

Of course, Allie had noticed her exclusion. "His name was. . .Neil. Mac Neil." Fork in hand again, she pierced the lettuce maybe a tad aggressively, remembering how he'd even been irritable telling her his name. That hadn't been very nice of him, had it? Not nice at all.

"Wait a minute—Mac Neil? Or MacNeill? Are you sure he didn't say—"

But before Allie could finish her question, a blast of Orphan Annie's voice singing "Tomorrow" erupted from Megan's purse, interrupting her friend. Hastily wiping her hands on her napkin, she fished out her cell phone and eyed the incoming number. "Sorry, Al. It's Mrs. Biddle. She might need a ride."

Flipping open her phone, Megan tried to half listen to Allie and Sammy's conversation while Mrs. Biddle prattled on, as she normally did, always taking her time to get to the crux of her call.

But she couldn't make out what Allie and Sammy were talking about. Although she could just imagine as she watched her best friend reach into the pocket of her bib apron and pull out a few after-dinner mints for Sammy. It was Allie's way, her bribe, Megan knew, to get more information about the stranger out of Sammy.

Megan had to smile. Leave it to her happily married friend to continually try to make romantic connections on her behalf. Just because their moms supposedly had a talent for matchmaking, Allie had always thought she'd inherited the trait as well.

"I'm sorry, Mrs. Biddle," Megan apologized into the phone. "I lost you on that last part. You asked if I'd been out in the rain? Yes, I have. And I can come pick you up if that's what you're asking."

Sometimes Mrs. Biddle's husband ran her over to Megan's house and the couple watched Sammy together. Other times Megan provided transportation—which was more than fine with her. A little extra driving was well worth it for her to have the retired schoolteacher to depend on. When Megan counted her blessings, for sure, Mrs. Biddle was someone she always counted twice.

"What?" Megan sat up straight, trying to wrap her head around what Mrs. Biddle was saying. "You're in the emergency room?"

Megan realized she must've said the words a bit loudly because Allie and Sammy ceased their conversation and were both looking straight at her. Meanwhile she listened intently as her usually dependable babysitter told her how she'd slipped in the rain and may have possibly fractured her hip.

Taking in a deep breath, she tried to focus on the other woman, rather than her own concerns about finding another sitter. A replacement sitter she'd need for how many months if Mrs. Biddle needed surgery? Six maybe? At the very least?

Oh, but she shouldn't even be thinking about that right now. How awful of her to even think about her own needs first. Mrs. Biddle was the one who'd been hurt. She could hear the discomfort in her voice.

"Mrs. Biddle, don't worry. We'll be fine. You need to take good care of you. And please have your husband call and let me know how you're doing. Okay?"

"Miss Biddle hurt?" Sammy wanted to know before Megan could even hang up the phone and toss it back into her purse.

"She's at the hospital?" Allie frowned.

Luckily, Allie had served Sammy a mountain's worth of fries because Megan had been eating more than she'd intended to. Anxious about the turn of events, she grabbed another fistful before answering. "She was coming out of the grocery and slipped on the curb in the rain. They're running tests now to see how bad her hip is. She said her husband will call with her prognosis." She bit off the top of several fries all at once. "I don't know. . .maybe I should reschedule the meeting. The problem is, I wouldn't know how to get a hold of anyone. That is, if anyone is coming."

"No way, Meg. You've wanted to do this for so long. Sammy can stay here with Greg and me." Allie pulled his wheelchair closer to the table. "He can help us close up. Right, Sammy?"

"Thanks, Allie, but you guys have work to do and dinners to serve." Megan shook her head. "And I'm sure you'd like to cut out early to get home to Justin and Carrie if the opportunity arises. Besides, I really don't know how long the meeting will last. It could be two minutes or two hours, who knows?" She felt her shoulders slump forward, knowing full well the next call she had to make.

But still, she hesitated. She never did like calling her mom and dad for help. Not that they didn't love seeing their grandson any and every chance they got. But they worked all day long, her mom planning weddings and plotting romances, and her father as a counselor at the high school. Although for Megan, it wasn't just their work schedules that made her hate to call so much. She didn't like to lean on them. It had always made her feel "less than" somehow.

But since she didn't have any other choice. . .

"I'll call Mom and Dad. They'll be happy to see their Sammy."

Retrieving her cell phone once more, after a quick call and a thrilled "yes" from her mother, Megan glanced at her watch. "Sorry, Al." She frowned. "I guess we'll need to-go boxes for our dinners since we'll have to spend extra time running over to their house now."

Her best friend nodded and offered to watch Sammy one more time, before popping up and heading back to the kitchen for boxes.

Sitting at the table waiting for Allie's return, Megan sighed, slogging another several fries through the dabs of catsup left on Sammy's plate. How she hoped the All-Stars Sports Day meeting went well—at least better than the rest of the evening had gone so far anyway. What, with a near car crash and a sitter with a possible broken hip. . .

Could the rainy evening get any worse? she wondered, and then wished she hadn't put that negative thought out into the cosmos.

By the time MacNeill walked back to his uncle's truck, the brunette with some of the more annoying accusations he'd ever heard—and the most interesting eyes he'd ever seen—had already pulled away and was gone from sight.

For a minute, he considered turning around and heading back to his uncle's farm, maybe making some scrambled eggs for supper. It would be a fitting penance since he'd probably shaken up the woman and her child and possibly ruined their dinners. It would also give him a chance to switch out vehicles before meeting up with his old buddy Ted Slater in a couple of hours.

But even through the haze of light rain, Paxton's neon sign beckoned him like it always did. And so did fond memories.

Righting the truck back into the line of traffic, he promised himself he'd retrace his route up the winding country road back to the farm to grab his Corvette after a visit to the local grill.

Driving a short ways up the street, he found an empty parking space and waited for a few cars to go around him before parallel parking there. The truck door creaked again as he shut it behind him, and with a light step, he hopped up onto the paved sidewalk that outlined downtown Loveland. The same sidewalk he used to ride his Stingray bike on.

Back when he was ten, he'd known every crack and bump in the surface. Back and forth, he'd ride his bike to baseball practice, balancing so well that half the time he didn't even bother clasping the handlebars.

When he was a bit older, he and his friends had hung out on the sidewalk for hours at a time, popping wheelies and getting in the way of passersby. All in the hopes of catching some cute girl's attention.

More than once, Mr. Keller had come running out of his hardware store to shoo their group away from the front of his business. And the pharmacist at the drugstore ran them off a few times as well, except when they had enough spare change in their pockets to come into his place to buy pops and candy.

But both of those businesses were long gone now. And as Mac clomped along in the cowboy boots he'd found in the back of his uncle's closet—more comfortable and broken in than the expensive leather loafers he usually wore—he felt as if a part of his past had gone missing, too.

Not that there weren't plenty of new businesses framing Loveland's downtown strip these days. Because there were. Unique, cutesy establishments like the Loveland Music Academy, a tea parlor, a yarn store, and a gift shop—all of which seemed to be more the trend now. In fact, downtown Loveland had become a colorful place since the last time he'd visited, and he figured it had to have been a committee of women who had made it that way.

Who but a woman would think of the window boxes and urns full of plants and flowers spilling out from everywhere? And the American flags and fun-looking flags that poked out of doorways or hung next to awnings? Plus, there were park benches and antique lampposts strewn along the sidewalks in a picturesque style.

No doubt about it, Mac shook his head, the look of West Loveland Avenue had changed considerably since his family had moved away to Florida at the end of his sixth-grade year. Even his beloved Paxton's had undergone a minor makeover, he noted, as he closed in on his destination.

Named after Colonel Thomas Paxton, the first settler to the area, the grill had a foothold on the main corner of downtown and was still the hub of the strip. But it looked slightly more sophisticated than he remembered, with a black wrought-iron fence surrounding it, sandwich board signs announcing specials, and outside—in front of the restaurant—were café tables, vacated at the moment due to the inclement weather.

One thing hadn't changed, though. Mac smiled thankfully as he whiffed the air: the mouth-watering aroma of Paxton's charbroiled burgers. Even after all the places he'd traveled to and all the restaurants and hamburger joints he'd eaten in, nothing compared to the delectable scent of a Paxton burger. It seeped out of the place, drifting toward him temptingly, making his mouth water. The sensation hit him full force as a handful of patrons poured out the door. Mac sidestepped them, letting them pass by before he entered, conditioned to protecting his mending elbow, keeping it out of the way of being bumped.

Stepping inside, he immediately tugged on his cap, pulling it a little lower, hoping no one recognized him. But then he caught himself.

All that was in his past. In the other circles he used to run in. Used to be men would approach him, wanting to buy him a drink. Women used to smile flirtatiously, their eyes full of promises. All had wanted something or had some proposition in mind, but that had been okay with him then. He'd been more than happy to give everything he had to take all they had to offer in return.

It wasn't until after the accident he stopped to realize how empty most of those exchanges had made him feel.

But since he'd been living in Loveland throughout his entire recovery, to date no one had made a big deal about his residing in their midst. For the most part anyway. Sure, every now and then a person here or there would ask for an autograph or come up to chat with him. But mostly everyone acted respectful of him and his privacy.

The hostess station was empty. Still, Mac stood there politely waiting—for a minute or two anyway. Then when a hostess never showed up, he helped himself to a seat, slipping into a red vinyl booth by the front window.

Being in the half-filled establishment always brought back flashes from the past. Like the times he'd come there as a kid after a win at the baseball diamonds just across the bridge. Coaches and teammates along with proud moms and dads would nearly take over the eatery on those summer evenings, all charged up and ready to chow down after a victory.

He even recalled double dates that started out at Paxton's, in particular one on a Fourth of July when he kissed childhood sweetheart Becca Cannon at a table—the third table along the right wall—creating his own kind of fireworks.

Caught up in old memories, he hardly noticed when a

middle-aged waitress showed up at his side out of nowhere.

"Need a menu?" she asked, puffing upward at her bangs, sending them flying off her forehead.

"Not unless you've changed things since I was here two weeks ago," he teased. "You still have the best burgers in town?" He smiled up at her.

"Still do. Haven't changed a thing." The woman reached in her pocket for an order pad, a bemused glint in her eye.

"Good. Then I'll have one with everything on it."

"Everything, huh?" She scribbled the order. "You're a brave one."

He chuckled at her comment, adding, "And some fries."

"You got it."

Mac watched as the waitress made her way to another table, thinking she looked like someone he might've known as a kid. But then a lot of people looked familiar to him. As she started back to the kitchen, he was still trying to figure it out—until his eyes got diverted to another woman. At the back table—a woman he *did* recognize. With a little boy, presumably her son, sitting across from her in a wheelchair. The lady he'd almost run into.

He had to admit, the lady—the mom—biting her lip with a cell phone at her ear, still appeared somewhat flustered, which made him cringe some. Hopefully, he hadn't been the main cause of the stressed look on her face. It didn't make him feel great either to see that her son was obviously handicapped. No wonder she'd been so upset.

Not that he'd nearly hit her on purpose, of course. But still...

He let out a deep breath, berating himself once again

for driving his uncle's truck in the first place. But something about living out at the farm...something about not being in the limelight lately...made him notice how frivolously he'd been living and how materialistic he'd become, making him yearn for simpler things. But he still had to be responsible about it. If he wanted to continue driving the truck, then he needed to pour some money into it and get it fixed. Or start looking around for a safer model.

Well, one thing he could be thankful for, he thought, gazing at the lady and her son, at least he'd been given another opportunity to try to apologize to her. And that's just what he intended to do.

Scooting to the edge of the booth, he was just about to go make amends, when a portly guy in a John Deere cap and a forest green Stihl chainsaw T-shirt blocked his path. "Hey, aren't you Troy Clinger?"

Mac looked up at the stranger towering over the booth. "Nope, sorry. Not me."

"I don't mean Clinger." The man shook a finger close to Mac's face. "I mean, I mean...oh, you know..." The man bent over, placing his fingertips on the table, as if drawing the answer from the Formica tabletop. "Danzer!" He straightened. "Carl Danzer, that's it."

"That's not me either."

"Well, you're someone." The man's eyes narrowed. "I know you are."

"We're all someone." Mac had a ready-made answer, having gone through the same scenario often enough.

"Oh!" The man clicked his fingers in revelation. "Hattaway. MacNeill Hattaway. I knew it all along. My brother went to school with you."

"Oh yeah? Who's your brother?" he asked, then wanted to kick himself for doing so as the man took a trip down memory lane, reciting names, places, and past events that were mainly on the hazy side for Mac.

By the time the guy finally produced a napkin and a pen, and got what he'd initially come over to the booth for—an autograph—Mac looked up and saw that the woman and her son were gone.

It was a shame. Not only would he have liked to apologize, but he could've invited her to the meeting Ted had asked him to attend. It might've been something she'd be interested in.

Oh well. He pushed his cap back from his forehead, remaining positive. It was a small town. More than likely he'd run into her again sometime—though hopefully not literally.

Chapter 3

Megan stood staring at the group of volunteers staring back at her as a drop of rain slid down the back of her neck, paused at the rise of flesh between her shoulders, then tumbled downward like a roller-coaster car, gathering momentum till it hit the gulley at the base of her spine and then disappeared into the waistband of her pressed, polished cotton capris.

Or, at least the capris had been pressed. And dry. And, yes, she'd even thought she looked good and somewhat professional in the navy pants and her once crisp three-quarter-sleeve white blouse. But that had been earlier in the evening before the torrential downpour hit.

Before she'd stood under the lightning-crackling sky getting Sammy into the car and his wheelchair into the trunk.

Before she'd stood out in the drizzling rain, yelling at a maniac driver.

Before she'd dropped Sammy off at his nana and pappy's and had gotten spat on by the gray skies again.

And before some insensitive, careless driver had zoomed by her in the high school parking lot in his Corvette, splashing her, soaking her to the bone.

Oh, this was so not how she'd pictured things going, she

thought, as she braced her shoulders, feeling another drop of rainwater begin its course. Or was it perspiration? Now that she was standing in front of nearly two dozen people—All-Stars Sports Day volunteers—looking at her, waiting for her to say something.

But, no. It definitely couldn't be sweat. The room was freezing. She hadn't remembered the Loveland High School cafeteria being air-conditioned when she'd been in school. But it certainly was now. Her jaw tightened and she could barely feel her hands. Only because she was freezing? Or also because she was anxious from the twenty-plus sets of eyes all directed on her?

"Well, everyone. . .thank you for coming. This is so. . . I just want to say. . ."

What was it she'd planned to say? She'd thought it all out the night before. And she'd practiced every free minute she'd had since. But now—crunch time—nothing would come to her.

She squeezed at her shoulder-length ponytail the way she always did when she was nervous. Big mistake. She'd forgotten it was drenched, sending more water running down her back, along with a chill that followed. She'd been wrong not to have the meeting in Miss Annabella's Tea Parlor when Maria had offered. Spring or not, it was a chilly evening, and it would've been the perfect place to meet on this rainy night.

"I'm sorry there's not something hot to drink." She worked to brace her jaw in an effort to keep her teeth from chattering. "That would sure warm us all up, I know. What a dreary night, huh, for this time of year?"

Only when she looked at the rows of men and women, none of them appeared to be waterlogged like her. Because they hadn't dragged their handicapped child out in the storm? Because they had spouses who could stay at home and watch their kids? Or because they had sitters who had come to their houses, who weren't in the emergency room at the moment?

Suddenly Maria's hand popped up, much to Megan's relief. Maria—her acquaintance from town—who didn't have any offspring but had been kind enough to brave the nasty night along with Janey, a dear friend from grade school whose only "baby" was her bakery. "I could check if there's a coffeemaker in the back kitchen," she offered.

"Would you all like some coffee?" Megan asked the group, but most all of them simply stared at her, mute. How could they all be here for the same cause—a sports day for their special-needs kids—and not be a bit more effusive and friendly?

"I guess we're okay, Maria. But thank you." She nodded before turning her full attention back to the not-so-responsive group. "And thank you, everyone, for coming. And for caring enough to help organize a special day of sporting events for our great kids."

Hugging herself to keep warm in front of the blank eyes that stared at her, she continued, "You know, as a physical therapist, I work with a lot of athletes of all ages. We are continually helping the athletes to heal, and teaching them how to use their bodies properly so they can go out and play a sport, compete safely, and have fun.

"I guess after watching so many kids know the joy of performing at a sport, I've longed to have the same opportunity for my son, Sammy, who was born with cerebral palsy. And I'm sure that's why most of you are here, because you also desire the same sort of fun event for your children."

Seeing a few nods in the audience, she loosened the grip on her arms, feeling encouraged to continue. "Sammy is really excited about the prospect of having this All-Stars Sports Day come together, and I have to tell you, he said the cutest thing the other day when we were talking about it. He said that parents are special and they need a special sports day. Of course, I told him we'd look into that next year after we see how this year's event goes." She smiled at the volunteers, who finally seemed to be responding to her. Talking about kids always was an icebreaker; she felt thankful she'd thought of it.

She spoke for a few more minutes, taking care to touch on several important points, one of them being fund-raising for the event. No one noticeably flinched at the word. Quite the opposite, in fact.

Yes, suddenly the men and women appeared to be tuning in to her. All grinning and sitting up straighter in their metal folding chairs.

"Wow, if you could only see what I'm seeing now. You all look so enthusiastic and eager, ready to forge on with this project. It's exciting."

Only. . .well. . .they did look enthused and animated. But they weren't really looking in her direction, were they? They were looking to the left of her actually. She paused her talk, craning her neck to see—

"This is Cammie Larking, reporting from the cafeteria

of Loveland High School. Tonight we're here to let viewers know about a meeting taking place for a very special cause..."

Megan heard the reporter's voice before she could really take in and grasp the sudden commotion taking place around her. A cameraman with a Channel 4 News emblem plastered on the side of his video camera was walking backward on bent knees, obviously taping the reporter with her mic in hand. While right behind her, Ted Slater, Cincinnati's top homebuilder, waved at the cameraman.

It had crossed her mind earlier that she hadn't noticed Ted in the group of volunteers. She and Sammy had bumped into Ted and his wife and their daughter Hannah, who suffered from cystic fibrosis, at Scoop's ice cream shop a few days earlier. Ted had been adamant he'd be at the meeting to support Megan and the cause.

Of course, she'd never dreamed he meant he'd be bringing a news crew along with him, for goodness' sakes. But she should have guessed. Around town, Ted was known to be as much a promotion man as he was a homebuilder, always landing on the news or in an infomercial for some reason or another. With his ties to the media, having Ted on the committee could really be a help. Except for. . .the cameraman wasn't really angled in on Ted, was he?

No, he zoomed in on the man walking in behind Ted, causing the volunteers to lean forward in their seats to see. Megan leaned closer, too, until finally a man emerged out from behind Ted's shadow. A man taller than Ted and younger. Certainly more fit than the homebuilder, and wearing a baseball cap just like—

Mr. Neil? The maniac who had almost run her down?

What on earth was he doing here? And why did all the volunteers and parents suddenly look so pleased about his presence? And why was Cammie glowing and smiling, standing closer to him than need be with her mic?

"So you've finally come out of hiding?" For some reason, the reporter's voice sounded more coy than professional.

"I've been recouping, not hiding, Cammie," Mr. Neil answered.

"Well, whatever you want to call it, we've missed seeing you out on the field."

"Thanks, Cammie, I appreciate that."

"Ted Slater, Cincinnati's most prominent homebuilder, says your help is what's going to make this first-annual All-Stars Sports Day project a grand slam." Cammie poised the mic at him, waiting for a response.

"A grand slam? Well, I—"

"Come on now. You've never been shy before," Cammie half-cooed, as if she knew that from personal experience. "No reason to be shy now, MacNeill Hattaway."

Megan couldn't believe it. Mr. Neil. Mac Neil. Was really MacNeill Hattaway? Oh, how stupid of her! She'd been so upset at the near-crash, she hadn't put it together.

"I'm planning to do everything I can to help the folks here make it a great event, Cammie," MacNeill was saying.

"I'm sure you will, Mac." Cammie beamed. "I'm sure you will," she added before suddenly swinging the mic around, thrusting it in Megan's face. "And I've been told you're Megan O'Donnell. Megan, all of us women are envious that you'll be working side-by-side with Mac, your new co-chair of the All-Stars Sports Day event—"

Her new co-chair? Of her own brainchild? When had that happened?

Plus, MacNeill Hattaway? She was actually being paired up to work with him? A person who didn't have any children, only plenty of childlike, bad-boy behavior if the tabloids in recent years had been even slightly accurate.

The man had nearly sideswiped her earlier in the evening, and now he'd officially blindsided her, too.

"Do you have anything to add to that?" Cammie moved closer, pressing for an answer.

"Anything to add?" Megan blinked at the news reporter. "Well, I—um. . ." Her cheeks burned and she certainly wasn't chilled any longer. No, she was on fire, beyond steaming. Nothing about this evening had gone as planned from the very beginning. Not one thing.

But then. . .averting her eyes from the ultra-white light of the camera, Megan glanced at the group of parents and volunteers. Their faces had certainly lit up when MacNeill walked in. And their glistening eyes were on her now, at full attention, eager to actually hear what she thought.

And what she thought was—well, what she thought was she had to put her feelings aside, didn't she? Or at least pretend to. Because it really wasn't about her, was it? It was about the kids and the special day that could bring fun, and closeness, and a sense of accomplishment for them. Oh, how she needed to remember that.

She swallowed hard, straining to regain her composure.

"Why, Cammie, I say we're all working together to make this a great event." She forced a bright smile. "Let's play ball!" She raised her fist in the air in a cheer.

"Mac, you're really going to be helping us?"

"Can you sign the back of my T-shirt?"

"Hey, how do you think the Hawks will do this year without you?"

The volunteers swarmed Mac the moment Cammie and her crew departed, everyone apparently delighted he was there.

Well, not everyone. Peering over the group circling him, he searched out Megan O'Donnell across the cafeteria and saw her talking to an older man who was in a wheelchair himself.

If only he could make eye contact with her, mouth out a "sorry," or give her an apologetic smile.

Staring long and hard in her direction, halfway ignoring the hubbub going on around him, in his mind he willed her to look at him. Oh, and she did. For about a split second anyway. She glared at him, and then glanced away, obviously wanting to avoid him.

All he could think was "strike two!"

Yep, he'd done it to the pretty woman again. Caught her totally off guard with the news crew and all. This time, he'd hit her full force without even meaning to—without even having a hand in it.

True, when Ted had asked him to come to the meeting, he'd been thrilled. More than willing to come, excited even to help. He felt like he had so much time to make up for in the "thinking of others" department.

Ted told him he'd be pitching in—no pun intended—like everyone else. Oh, and maybe using his celebrity status to garner a few local sponsors for the event.

But Ted had never mentioned this. Who knew Channel 4 was going to be there? Mac certainly didn't. Although he should've guessed as much, being that Ted was involved. His friend was no stranger to promotion for his homebuilding business, and surely Mac should've realized that where Ted's daughter Hannah was concerned, his friend would undoubtedly use whatever tactics he could to gain support and recognition for the special-needs kids' day.

But the news reporter, the grand entrance—it was all a surprise to him. And so was seeing the mom he'd almost crashed into running the meeting.

And, man. . . She wasn't happy about him being there, news crew or no news crew—he could tell. He'd trained himself to read body language throughout his career, mostly the body language of batters up at the plate and runners on base. It was all part of the game for him and an area where he definitely excelled.

Megan O'Donnell might've fooled the volunteers and the media with her quick cheerleader smile and team-inspired words, but she couldn't fool him. He could tell she hadn't known a thing about Ted's invitation to him, about Cammie's visit, and contrary to the rest of the group, she wasn't happy about it. Her pursed lips and narrowed eyes told him so. Her deadly glare shouted so.

"Hey folks, I appreciate you all giving me such a warm greeting," he said to the volunteers huddled around him. "But, uh, I'll be around for the next few months, and I'll be happy to sign anything. I promise. Right now, though, I think I should properly introduce myself to the woman who started all of this. Can you all excuse me for a minute? I need to shake hands with Mrs. O'Donnell."

"Miss," the lady closest to him said. "*Miss* O'Donnell."

"Miss?" Something inside his chest did a skip.

"I should know. I'm an old friend of hers. My name's Janey. I own Sweet Sensations Bakery."

He dipped his head toward the cute blond. He'd seen her often enough in the bakery, but had never guessed she was the owner. "Greatest bear claws ever. Blueberry muffins are topnotch, too." He nodded the compliment.

"Thanks." She grinned, obviously pleased. "Can I quote you on that?"

"Well, sure. It's true." He grinned. "So. . .*Miss* O'Donnell, huh?"

"Miss. Just like me." She preened.

Mac excused himself then snaked his way through the throng of volunteers toward Megan. Apparently having finished her conversation with the handicapped gentleman, she looked like she was pouring more energy—or was it frustration?—than was necessary into gathering up her papers and purse from the lunch table behind her.

Having already experienced the brunt of her wrath earlier in the evening, he suddenly felt a little apprehensive. Hard to imagine that a pretty, petite thing like her could stop all two hundred pounds of him with one direct glower, but she certainly could and did.

Halting momentarily, he took a deep breath and steeled himself, feeling as young and intimidated as a high school boy asking a girl to the movies. He inched closer. "I, uh, wanted to see if we could try to patch things up."

"Since now we're going to be working together?"

"Exactly." When she continued to glare, he held out a hand. "Look. I really am sorry about earlier. I was completely at fault. I'm glad my stupidity in driving that old truck didn't hurt you or your son."

She looked at his hand like it might bite. "Apology accepted, Mr. *Hattaway*."

Feeling like a fool, he let his hand drop to his side. "I tried to tell you my name. . ."

"Yes, you did. You definitely tried to tell me that you were MacNeill Hattaway, world-famous pitcher."

Now he was getting irritated. "Look, I'm trying to be friends here. And it's Mac. . .just plain old Mac."

"And my new co-chair, to boot."

He could detect the agitation in her tone, and hated hearing it. Still, it wasn't easy keeping the aggravation from his own voice as he answered her.

"Hey, I don't know where Cammie came up with that. I really didn't know about any of the press hoopla. Or some of the things she was saying. Honest. I didn't."

She finally looked at him. Really looked, and he could tell her mind was busy scrutinizing him, weighing what she'd heard in the past and what she'd seen tonight against what he had to say.

Doubt flickered in those big blue eyes of hers. She wasn't buying it.

"You don't believe me, do you? You think I'm here—you think this is all a media stunt for me."

She stared more intently.

"Seriously? That's what you really think?" he prodded.

"Well, you have to admit. . ." She looked away from him, glancing toward the cafeteria door instead. "That was quite an entrance."

"You can be sure that's not what I'm looking for with this experience, Megan O'Donnell. I want this to be all about the kids." That word seemed to bring her focus back on him. "The other thing—the media dwelling on me—I don't need it. I don't want it."

"And that's what I want. This needs to be all about the kids, Mr. Nei—" She caught herself. "Mr. Hattaway."

"Mac," he countered again. "So then. . .that's good, isn't it? We both want the same thing," he said. But even as he was staring into her eyes and saying that, he felt a strange tug. As if maybe—just maybe—with this new co-chairperson there might be something more.

But Megan still wasn't ready to concede. "I guess time will tell." She looped her purse strap over her shoulder and was just about to turn away from him when the Janey girl appeared.

"Hey, can I get a picture of our co-chairs together?" A small digital camera surfaced in Janey's hands. "I'm helping with some of the PR for the event," she informed him as she waved Megan closer to his side. "You need to get a little closer, Meg. Here, let me take your purse for a minute."

Janey grabbed Megan's purse, setting it down by her own feet, and then with a free hand pushed Megan toward him.

He could feel the rigidity in her shoulder next to his.

Could literally feel her reluctance instead of just sensing it. But apparently her friend didn't notice.

"Okay, that's way better." Janey glanced into the camera. "Now, both of you, smile."

Megan's stiffness and aloofness was a bit of an ego bruising to be sure. Certainly, he wasn't used to females not wanting to be around him—reacting to him that way.

But what bothered him even more was the idea that she didn't believe him. Something inside him wanted Megan O'Donnell to take him at his word. The thought that she didn't troubled him, made him start to frown.

Yet. . .he'd had plenty of years of experience putting on a show for the camera. And as Janey snapped a handful of photos of them, Megan wasn't the only one forcing a smile.

Chapter 4

The rain had let up by the time Megan made her way back to her parents' house. Not that it mattered really. Rain or shine, the place she'd called home until she'd moved out on her ill-fated wedding day had always been a warm, cozy haven. That was especially true of the kitchen where her mom's curio cabinets lined the walls, plants and knickknacks adorned the bay window, and where she found her parents and Sammy sitting at the round oak table for four—which could always fit six in a pinch.

"Back so soon, honey?"

Megan honestly thought her mother sounded somewhat disappointed.

In fact, she realized neither of her parents gave her barely so much as a glance when she walked into the room. But then, how could she fault them for that? Both Laura and Kurt O'Donnell had their eyes pinned on Sammy, watching him eat freshly baked cookies—oatmeal cranberry walnut—Megan easily detected from the familiar scent lingering in the air. The grandparents gazed at their grandson adoringly, completely captivated as if they'd never seen such a charming creature eat before.

As much as she didn't want to depend on them for anything, and as much as their love could be stifling at times, she had to admit she was lucky they were doting and devoted. They hadn't been all that thrilled when she announced her engagement to Bryan; they thought it was too quick and their trip to town hall to be married by a justice of the peace even hastier. The doubt was always there in her mom's eyes and forced smiles when Bryan was around. Megan knew he certainly wasn't the match her matchmaking mother would've made for her. And certainly not the kind of stark, non-traditional ceremony her wedding planning mother would have helped her design either.

But after her parents once expressed their concerns about her decision to marry him, the two of them never said anything again. Not even a "we told you so" when Bryan walked out on her and Sammy just a few short months after it was determined Sammy had cerebral palsy.

In a way, it might've been easier if they had said something. If they had clucked their tongues or self-righteously reminded her they'd never thought Bryan was good husband and father material to begin with. It would've given her a chance to say it out loud, how wrong she'd been about him, instead of carrying around feelings of self-loathing about the bad choice she'd made in him—in men—years ago. But conversely, her parents acted like Bryan had never existed. Like marriage vows had never been exchanged.

Instead, through the entire Bryan ordeal, her parents' focus remained steadfast on Sammy. Their eyes always twinkling at the sight of their newborn grandson. And glistening when Megan went to legal lengths to make sure Sammy carried the O'Donnell family name. Her parents thought Sammy was just perfect and poured their love into his heart and life from day one.

Or at least whenever Megan gave them the opportunity.

"It's almost nine," she countered. "The meeting actually lasted longer than I expected." Although it hadn't been all that much of a meeting, had it? With MacNeill Hattaway involved, it'd been more of a media event.

"Have a seat." Her mom nodded to the empty chair at the table. "And some cookies."

Her dad chuckled delightedly. "We were just sitting here watching Sammy chow down."

"So I see." Megan half-smiled at her parents' usual fascination with her son. "This is a big night for you, Sammy O'Donnell. Paxton's fries. And Nana's homemade cookies. What a lot of treats!"

Cookie crumbs dotting his lips, Sammy bounced his head wildly, an over-the-top grin lighting his face. Megan walked around the table, kissing his crown of tousled hair before taking a seat herself.

"We can only stay another minute or so."

"Oh Meggie, you have time for a cookie, don't you?" Her mom scooted the platter toward her. "And a cup of hot tea? You probably need it after running around in the rain and lightning all evening."

Before she could begin to protest, her mother was already on her feet, at the sink, filling the teapot. As if it were a given. As if Megan had all the time in the world to sit and sip a cup of tea. As if she didn't need to drive home, get Sammy bathed and ready for bed, get a sandwich packed for the next day, and get herself ready for bed as well.

That's why it was so much easier to have a sitter. That's why she was going to miss Mrs. Biddle so, so much. The woman was loving, but efficient. She knew how to stick to a schedule. Just thinking about all the chaos and disruptions she might be in for the next few months made Megan want to groan out loud.

"Rain an' lightning?" Sammy interrupted her thoughts, looking up from actively splashing his cookie in his cup of milk. "Bray maw-mee. You my bray maw-mee." He repeated the compliment she'd paid him earlier in the evening.

His good-heartedness quelled her irritation immediately the way it always did. Well, maybe one cookie. . . Maybe they had time for one cookie and one cup of tea.

She picked a cookie from the pile, the largest one she could find, thinking that might prevent her from eating a second or even third one.

"So." Her father leaned forward. "How did the meeting go?"

Something about his posture made him look overly anxious to know. Megan could feel her radar naturally turn onto alert, her words coming out hesitantly when she answered him.

"Good. Good, I think. I mean. . . We have at least twenty volunteers or so."

"Oh honey, that's wonderful." Laura O'Donnell beat her husband to a reply, her voice a little louder than usual as she competed with the simmering teapot. "Did Janey and Maria come? They're such nice girls. I love working down the street from their shops. I stop in to visit every chance I get."

"They were both there." Megan nodded. "And of course, lots of parents." She broke her warm cookie in half, taking small savory bites.

"Great, great," her dad replied, though he eagerly brushed off the information. "Was there anything else? Anything else happen?"

"Happen?"

A feeling of déjà vu crept into her bones. Oh, how many times had she sat at this same table in her younger days, lured by a plateful of cookies and lulled into such a complacent confidence that she'd said more than she'd meant to about a certain boy she liked or had given away secrets about the things she and her friends were up to.

Well, that wasn't about to happen now. She was older and in control. Her parents weren't about to get her going on and on about what was on her mind. Like Mac and his grand entrance. And his self-appointed co-chair position. And about his—her heart stopped for a moment thinking of his eyes, of all things. The way he stared at her so intently when he'd come over to give her his made-up story about how he didn't know anything about the news reporter or cameraman.

An involuntary shiver coursed its way up her back, shimmying her shoulders.

"See, you're shivering." Her mother set a steaming mug down in front of her. "A cup of tea is exactly what you need."

Before she could mumble a thank-you, her dad kept prodding. "Yeah, happen. Did anyone else show up? You know, besides those girls you and your mom know. And the parent volunteers. Anyone else?"

Her lightbulb might've been dim, but it didn't take too long for it to go off.

"Oh, this town." She shook her head. "This small, small

town. Did you run into Ted or something, Dad?"

Her father nodded. "Sure did." His grin was slightly comparable to Sammy's ecstatic one moments earlier.

"And you didn't warn me?"

"Warn you?" His head jerked back.

"What's there to warn about, honey?" Her mother chirped in, a bit too quickly. "Hattaway—he's—well, he's very nice looking. And he's—"

"You knew, too?" She'd been set up to be run over and no one had bothered to tell her? Stomach churning, Megan set the cookie aside.

"Oh yes!" Her mom settled back down in the chair next to her. "Can you believe it? Your wonderful idea—it's going to be bigger than ever now! With celebrity backing. It's so, so exciting."

"What exciting, Na-naw?"

"MacNeill Hattaway, Sammy." The look on her dad's face as he answered his grandson shone with pride as if just being in on Ted's secret meant he'd had a hand in things where Hattaway was concerned. "That all-star pitcher is going to help your mom with your special sports day event."

"MaaNil?" Sammy's eyes grew as round as the cookies he chomped on.

"That's right, MacNeill." Her dad turned to Sammy with his hand in the air. It took a struggled few moments before Sammy managed to lift his right hand and high-five her father.

Oh great. MacNeill Hattaway was a name Sammy was familiar with. She should've known.

Even when Sammy didn't have the chance to watch

sports with his pappy, he wanted the television tuned in to the sports channels at home. And even though he couldn't participate in the community's organized sports, sports were his all-time favorite thing—even ahead of country music, Paxton's fries, and his nana's cookies. Hadn't that been the reason she'd thought of the All-Stars Sports Day event in the first place?

"But Hattaway doesn't even have kids." Megan grimaced at the beaming faces surrounding her. "Why should he care?"

"Why wouldn't he care?" her dad retorted. "You don't need to father a child to care about one."

"Besides, Meggie," her mom added, "perhaps Mr. Hattaway wants to redeem himself." She didn't have to say why the pro ballplayer might be in need of redemption. Everyone at the table—well, excepting Sammy—had read or heard plenty about the questionable life and times of MacNeill Hattaway.

"Redeem himself?" Megan rolled her eyes. "You mean get good publicity is probably more like it."

"Don't you think you're being a little harsh, honey?" Her mom put a hand over hers. "People do deserve second chances, don't you think?"

For a moment Megan wondered if her mom would think Bryan deserved a second chance, too. Not that Megan would've given him one anyway. But then she realized her mom hadn't thought Bryan worthy of a first chance. Once again, Megan wished she'd listened to her mother's warnings back then.

"I just don't want the focus to be all on MacNeill

Hattaway and not on the kids." She frowned at her parents.

But even as Megan said the words out loud, she knew there was something more she wasn't saying. Thoughts she was keeping all to herself.

No, she didn't want the spotlight off the special-needs kids. But she also didn't want a man coming along to "save the day" like some Disney prince. Because not only was that such a non-reality in her non-fairytale world, but really and truly, she didn't need some male doing that.

She could manage just fine, like she always had. All by herself.

As Mac made a slow turn onto his uncle's property, the low, wide tires on the Corvette clawed at the nuggets of gravel lining the driveway, tossing them aside in every direction, threatening to nick the red glossy paint.

He let up on the gas pedal a little more. Even though the car wasn't his, even though he was only driving it to be helpful since a friend of a friend had a father-in-law with a waning car dealership who wanted his endorsement, he still felt compelled to take good care of the vehicle.

Luckily he hadn't been driving the sporty classic last November, though. November sixth to be exact. The night of his near-fatal crash.

Inching up the drive, the fullness of the opal moon shed a forgiving light on the weather-worn boards of his uncle's oak barn, making it appear almost unblemished under the redemptive glow. For more years than he cared to remember, he'd forgotten how awesome moonlight could be.

Instead, living in his high-rise condo in the city, he'd always been charmed by the sight of urban lights—the flickers of neon, the lit-up billboards. They always lured him. Jazzed him up. Made him want to prowl the streets, many, many times when he would've been better off home alone.

As he pulled the Corvette up close to the side of the barn, Bitty, the stray cat making its home there, froze and stared into the headlights before jumping off a bale of hay and skittering away into the night. Mac got out, and leaning against the car, felt like he wouldn't mind disappearing into the night, too. The rain had stopped hours before, leaving the acres of grass and wildflowers smelling cleansed and fresh. The moon included him in its light, giving off a feeling of comfort that the city's tempting glitter never held for him. Everything around him had a feel and smell of healing. He felt grateful for that.

Yeah. . .if he'd been driving the Corvette the night of the accident—the night he'd been under the influence, totally inebriated, he wouldn't be standing in the moonlight now. He would've been a dead man for sure. But the Corvette had been in the repair shop that week, ironically. The loner car he'd been given was an SUV that protected him a bit more than the sports car ever would've when he lost control and ran into a brick building at top speed. Not that the SUV spared him injuries. Not by a long shot. From what he learned later, he was thrown from the crumpled vehicle and lay on the side of the road, unconscious, bleeding, and broken. He woke up in the hospital days later clueless as to when or how he got there.

But if I had to go there to get here. . .Lord, it's a good thing, I guess.

Turning toward the house, boots scraping the skillet-sized earth-sunken stones that formed the sidewalk, Mac wished the same thing he always did as he made his way up the wooden steps and across the width of the wraparound porch to the front screen door.

He wished that his uncle would be waiting for him inside.

A few inches shorter than Mac, but with a heart at least twice the size, Jake Lochen, his mother's brother, was a man he enjoyed immensely. Truly a man to be admired, though not for his worldly status necessarily.

Years ago, in fact, when his parents confided that his uncle was ill and having trouble keeping up with payments on the farm, Mac had stepped in and paid off the mortgage. He couldn't stand the idea of his uncle losing the property and not living out his final days there, finding whatever joy he could in his "piece of heaven on earth" as he fondly called it.

Of course, Mac couldn't handle the thought of losing the farm either. Jake had taught him an awful lot on those ten acres when he was a young boy. He had many good memories of his visits there, and of his uncle, who never ceased giving him lessons on pitching. Lessons about life. And teaching him about God.

Mac had gone on to perfect his pitching just as his uncle had trained him, and was lucky enough to play in the major leagues, in his former hometown, no less. Problem was, as his pitching led him to more and more success and fame, he'd pretty much turned his back on everything else.

Making his way into the old farmhouse, he turned on the floor lamp sidled up against his uncle's favorite worn leather chair. Mac hadn't yet sat in that chair. He still had too clear a vision of his uncle sitting there, reading his Bible on summer mornings before they went out to toss. Or visions of Jake bent forward over a newspaper on the floor, whittling some knickknack or another on evenings when it was too brisk to be outside on the porch doing the same thing.

Instead Mac walked past it, shucking his spring jacket and removing his baseball cap, tossing them onto an antique church pew on the opposite wall. The pew had always been a catch-all for everything. Jackets, hats, baseball mitts. It was also the spot where his uncle parked his walking stick.

Uncle Jake had used a walking stick daily—long, long before he'd ever become ill. As a young boy, Mac had never understood since he couldn't detect any problem with his uncle's legs or gait.

"It's a reminder," his uncle told him when Mac, at about eight years of age, finally got up the nerve to ask.

"Reminder?" Mac had been totally confused. "Like of how to walk?"

"In a way." His uncle chuckled. "It's a reminder for me to depend on God. Not to try to make the walk alone."

Mac picked up the walking stick, rubbing the smoothness of the carved pine, marveling not for the first time at his uncle's talent. Jake had made many a walking stick and handed them out to friends and visitors alike. Some had intricately carved knobs and handles; others were awesome combinations of wood, braided and glazed like some fancy bakery bread. Just holding the walking stick in his hand also forced Mac to recall the essence of his uncle's faith.

And to reflect on his own.

If only Uncle Jake were still around to see the changes in him since the accident! Not that the man had ever criticized him for his scandalous behavior—he never had. Jake Lochen never judged and rarely lectured. Instead, the very few occasions they'd spent any time together in the past years, Uncle Jake had only promised to pray for Mac.

"I'm trying, Uncle Jake," Mac whispered into the silence. "God knows I'm trying."

As he used his uncle's walking stick to make his way upstairs to the bedroom, he thought about all the handicapped kids who were in need of assistance just to eat, walk, and barely play. Hopefully, his volunteering for the All-Stars Sports Day really could make a difference.

Hopefully, too, someday the Megan O'Donnell lady would look at him with a smile in those pretty blue eyes of hers. Instead of gazing at him in a distant way. . .unable to connect or trust.

Chapter 5

"Oh Megan, I'm so glad you stopped in."

Megan watched Janey slide a tray of Morning Glory muffins into the bakery case, making her decision even more difficult. Without fail, Sammy always asked for jelly doughnuts from her friend's Sweet Sensations Bakery. But Megan couldn't help eyeing all of the yummy choices and considering them. What should she get this time? A freshly baked muffin? Or her usual cinnamon twist?

"It's Saturday. Why wouldn't I stop in?"

A visit to Janey's bakery was part of her and Sammy's Saturday morning routine. If the weather conditions were even so much as passable, she'd come in, chat with Janey, and gather up their order. Meanwhile Sammy waited outside right where he wanted to be, with his wheelchair parked on the edge of the community basketball court on the opposite side of the bike path. That put him in prime position to watch the groups of kids who gathered there to shoot hoops and play pickup games on their day off school. Generally kids who were used to him and the other way around.

Sammy enjoyed that time immensely and the bit of freedom that came with it. But so many times as Megan glanced out the bakery window and saw him sitting across the bike path in his wheelchair, on the sideline, unable to be a part of the action, an all-too familiar pang tugged at her heart. This morning was no exception.

"I just e-mailed you." Janey pulled her from her thoughts. "I have pictures to show you."

"Pictures?" Megan's eyes darted between the muffins and doughnuts. "Pictures of what?"

"From the other night. At the meeting." Her friend's voice turned slightly accusing. "Megan, why didn't you tell me MacNeill Hattaway was going to be there?"

Megan looked up to see Janey pull her hands to her hips. "I would've at least redone my makeup. Or brought cupcakes or something," she prattled on. "Did I tell you he complimented my bear claws?" A proud smile erupted on her face.

Megan stared at her friend, blankly, mostly not understanding one wee bit why everyone seemed to care so much about what MacNeill Hattaway thought. Did everyone really need to hang on to his every last word?

"Janey, I don't have time to look at pictures. Sammy's over there at the basketball court, and—"

"It'll only take a minute, I promise. Cindy Duncan wants a photo to accompany the press release she's written for the *Loveland Herald* and the *Cincinnati Enquirer.* I thought you'd want to decide which photo it should be."

"I'm sure you can choose, Janey. I trust your artistic eye."

Truly, Megan wasn't trying to heap undue flattery on her friend. Janey had always had a creative streak in everything she did. It was even obvious in the way she'd decorated her bakery. The shop was surprisingly unique, with an art deco style that was both striking and homey at the same time.

Plus, Megan flat-out didn't need to see pictures of

MacNeill Hattaway. His face was already imprinted on her mind, thank you very much. And she would be seeing him at their next All-Stars meeting on Wednesday night. Wasn't that soon enough?

But before she could protest any further, Janey dusted off her hands, pulling a digital camera out of her apron pocket.

"Seriously, Janey. Sammy's out there. I really don't have time. If I could just get my latte and our doughnuts?"

Glancing into the sunshine that poured in the bakery window, Janey waved toward the basketball court. "You worry about him too much, Meg. Sammy is less than ten yards away. He looks perfectly content. Perfectly comfortable."

She followed Janey's line of vision and knew it was true. Sammy did look fine. But the fact of the matter was, she wasn't.

Even after nights and days of stewing, she still wasn't comfortable at all with the entire Hattaway hubbub. And she really, truly didn't care to see photos of her and him, standing side-by-side.

"I'm not making this decision on my own," Janey said firmly, coming from behind the bakery cases. "Besides," she said with a giggle, "you should look at these pictures, for real. Hattaway's so gorgeous and hunky. Maybe you'll want to blow one up. Poster-sized."

Right. Megan could barely refrain from rolling her eyes.

"Did I tell you Mac also likes my blueberry muffins?" Janey preened.

Megan wanted to groan. A few fast-flung compliments here and there, a couple of appearances at fund-raisers, and soon MacNeill Hattaway would be up for sainthood, all of his past forgiven.

"He should. Your sweets are incredible, Janey. I've told you that a zillion times." But somehow her compliments didn't carry much weight. Not like Hattaway's anyway.

In fact, Janey dismissed what she'd said with a wave of her hand and started up about the photos all over again. "Here. You have to look." She thrust the camera's screen in Megan's face. "Don't you two look great together? I'd thought of nabbing him for myself, but after I saw that picture of you two. . .well, guess I'll have to find my own baseball star."

Forced to look at the photos of Mac and her, Megan could readily see what Janey was talking about. They did look good together. Aesthetically speaking of course. And why wouldn't they? Her dark hair contrasted perfectly with his sun-streaked blond. And his athletic look and build complemented the girl-next-door persona everyone always told her she exuded. Yes, they went together "picture perfectly" like two people in a car advertisement or something. Only, unfortunately, she wasn't a model getting paid to smile. She'd forced that on her own.

"So which one?" Janey clicked through the series of pictures she'd taken.

"How about the first shot you showed me?" *Did it matter?*

"Oh great. I like that one best." Janey nodded with approval, sliding the camera back into her pocket. "I like the way Mac's kind of looking at you in that picture. I'll copy you on it when we send it to the newspaper so you can have a record."

"Really, Janey, don't worry about it. It's not a big deal."

"Are you kidding? MacNeill Hattaway not a big deal?"

Megan couldn't stand to hear it any longer. "Hey Janey, I hate to be a nudge, but I should be getting back to Sammy. Do you mind getting my latte and his doughnuts together? And I'll take a cinnamon twist. I really hate leaving him alone for so long, you know?"

It was the perfect excuse, one she didn't mind dredging up. Anything to remove herself from any more talk of the local baseball hero. But as soon as the words left her mouth and she glanced out the window again at her son, the excuse had turned to reality.

"Oh my—" Words froze in her mouth. Her heart lurched in her chest.

In the short time she and Janey had been looking at photos, the younger kids had disappeared from the basketball court. Apparently, they'd been shooed off by a gang of teenaged boys who had taken over the area. That might have been more normal than frightening, except for the fact that the boys weren't shooting hoops. In fact, she noticed the ball had rolled off past the edge of the court. And Sammy's eyes were wide as the boys turned their focus on him and his wheelchair. In fact one of them stood behind the chair, rocking it back and forth, hoisting it up and down.

She wasn't sure what was going on. But that was all she had to see. Heart pounding, her maternal instincts at full throttle, she bolted out the door.

Hands at his waist, Mac gazed up into the sunlight flickering through the branches of the birch trees lining the running path, trying to catch his breath.

Jogging three miles had never been so hard in his life! How he'd ever been as stupid as to get behind the wheel drunk all those months ago was certainly beyond him.

For at least the thousandth time he inwardly chided himself for ever being so irresponsible. For ever being so negligent as to cause the accident that left him with pins everywhere in his body—his ankles, his knee. . .and though his pitching elbow was healing, there was still the question if it would ever be completely right again.

These days it was hard to believe he'd ever been that dumb. But obviously he had been. *Really dumb.*

Shaking his head at himself, he glanced around at the serene setting, squinting at the glistening strip of river that ran along the jogging path.

Many a time, he'd heard his uncle talk about having a heart of gratitude. How a man needed to humble himself and realize where all good things came from. He finally knew what Uncle Jake had meant. Feelings of thankfulness came easy nowadays. Such as, he was thankful that he hadn't hurt anyone else the night of the accident. Of course, he was also thankful that his life had been spared despite his recklessness. He'd really needed the chance he'd been given to reacquaint himself with the things that mattered in life. God being at the top of the list.

Claiming one of the iron benches off to the side of the path, he closed his eyes. Raising his face to the sun, he soaked in the warm, healing rays. But all too quickly the peacefulness of the moment was interrupted by jeering voices. Most likely coming from teenaged boys, he guessed.

Slowly opening one eye, he glanced in the direction

of the disruptive sound. Yeah, there was a tribe of them, all right, all huddled together on the basketball court that flanked the jogging path.

Only. . .whatever they were up to didn't look like anything good.

His other eye shot open.

Not a one of them was dribbling the ball. Actually not a one of them had a basketball in their hands. In fact, the only ball in sight had rolled over onto the grass. And there was a wheelchair he could see, right in the middle of the noisy bunch.

Could it be—? He peered more closely.

It was! Megan's son sat in the wheelchair, in the center of the group. And it looked like the boys were moving in on him, on—what did Megan say his name was again?

Sammy. She had called her son Sammy the night the two of them had stood out in the pouring rain together, her finger nearly jabbing his chest.

Instinctively, Mac's jaws tightened. So did his fists. Whether it was Sammy or not, the idea of a bunch of boys ganging up on a defenseless kid made him crazy. Hustling toward the court in long, quick strides, he struggled to keep his temper in check. But it wasn't easy—especially when the kid behind the wheelchair kept jostling the thing, acting like he was going to dump Sammy out of it.

The name MacNeill Hattaway might've been synonymous with a lot of rotten things in the past—but "bully" wasn't one of them. It was also something he had never tolerated very well. Not since he'd been friends with a neighbor kid Robbie, who had Coke-bottle glasses and had always been picked last in gym.

"Hey guys." He stepped onto the court and crossed his arms over his chest, tucking his closed fists under his armpits. "What's going on here?"

"Who wants to know?" The tall, lanky kid standing behind Sammy's wheelchair didn't even bother looking up from under the oversized cap, sunk down over his eyes and face.

Even so, Mac leveled his eyes at the kid, felt his teeth clench. "I do," he ground out.

But the kid didn't flinch. Kept his eyes downward. "Don't worry, dude. He likes it. He's my kid brother." He nodded toward Sammy.

"Brother, huh?"

"Yeah." The kid shrugged. "Brother."

Mac eyed the other boys, who for the most part, couldn't keep from smirking. He shot the kid another stone-cold expression, but again the kid wasn't looking anyway. "So what's your last name, *dude*?" he repeated the boy's own word emphatically.

"Smith." The kid didn't skip a beat.

"Yeah? Smith, huh? That's interesting."

"Yeah, why?"

"Because that's not his name."

"Oh right. Like you know his name? Who are you, the bike path police or something?" The teenager snorted at his own not-so-clever joke, and then glanced around in search of his friends' knowing grins. Mac figured him to be the ringleader of the group since most of the boys chuckled along with him.

"His name is Sammy O'Donnell."

"Wha?" Sammy, who had been sitting stiffly, not

moving an inch, slowly turned his head toward Mac's voice, coming face-to-face with him. "You know my name?"

"Yes, I do, Sammy."

"Hey." Sammy's face lit up suddenly. "I know you name, too."

"He talks weird," Mac heard one of the boys in the group say.

"Probably because he is weird." Another smart-aleck boy answered back.

But Sammy didn't appear to hear the jibes from the boys. "You MaaNil. MaaNil Haa-away." His tense face broke into a smile.

"What?" Unable to contain his surprise, the boy behind the chair finally looked straight up at Mac. "It's you."

Mac recognized the teen right away and snatched the concealing hat off his head. "Reese? Reese Calvin. Are you serious? What do you think you're doing?"

What's going on now?

Megan stopped and froze just yards from the basketball court, her heart still pounding. It was all she could do to stand back for a moment and not run the rest of the way to Sammy's defense. But it looked like MacNeill Hattaway, of all people, had already done that.

When she'd sprinted down the bakery steps and across the bike path, she'd seen a man jogging up to her son. Fit looking, in running shorts and a sweatshirt. Tall, and towering over the teenagers and Sammy's wheelchair. The man had looked familiar from a distance. But she'd never dreamed it would be Hattaway.

Yet there he was, surprising her again. He seemed to be everywhere these days.

Unbelievably, he also apparently knew the teen who had a grip on Sammy's wheelchair.

"I thought you liked sports, Reese," she overheard him saying. "That's what you told me at the baseball clinic."

"Who says I don't?" The boy shrugged.

"Well, hmm. . ." She noticed Mac uncross his arms and rub at his chin as if pondering the question. "You have a basketball court here. And a basketball. Yet instead of playing a game, what you choose to do is taunt Sammy here in his wheelchair. That's not cool, Reese. And it makes me think you like bullying a whole lot more than sports."

"What do you mean *taunt*?"

She thought Mac might lose his temper a bit when the kid asked that. But Mac remained patient, unfettered.

"I think you know what it means. If you don't, somebody can look it up on their iPhone."

She didn't know if it was the derisive tone in Mac's voice that caused the Reese boy to drop his hands from the wheelchair grips or not. But he did and was quiet about it.

"Now, what do you think your next move is?" Mac asked him, to which Reese gave a dull, "Huh?"

Mac repeated the question, nodding his head toward Sammy. "What do you think your next move should be?"

Reese shifted from foot to foot.

"He wants you to apologize," one of the boys at the helm of the group, about the same size as Reese, shouted out.

"I know that, doofus," Reese sputtered back at him.

"Actually"—Mac looked around—"I think a group apology would be real nice," he said with a sardonic smile.

Murmurs of "sorry" filled the air. Some of the boys, Megan noticed, even went so far as to pat Sammy on his shoulder or hand. All the while, Sammy smiled, not a begrudging bone in his body, just looking happy to be sitting in the midst of the action.

That taken care of, Mac addressed the group again. "Now it looks like to me, there's a basketball over in the grass. Somebody needs to go get it."

"I will!" The least virile-looking boy in the bunch suddenly appeared empowered by Mac's command. He ran as fast as he could to retrieve the ball.

"So what do I do with it?" the boy asked as he dribbled the ball awkwardly back onto the court.

Megan was just as curious, wondering what Mac could possibly be up to. He may have been wondering himself because he paused, taking a moment to scratch at his head.

"Uh, okay. Here's the deal," Mac told the boys. "How about we do something constructive? How about you ten guys divide yourselves into teams? An 'A' team and a 'B' team. Make it fair. Because if the teams aren't even, Sammy and I are going to make them that way. Aren't we, Sammy?"

She watched Sammy's grin grow to cover his face.

"Then you're going to play a quick game of b-ball—let's say twenty minutes. I'll time it. Whichever team has the most points when time's up wins doughnuts from Sweet Sensations."

A mingling of cheers erupted then dissipated quickly. The boys got down to business, forming their two ragtag teams.

Chapter 6

B eing a mom had its rights. Walking onto the basketball court where there was a group of ten males or so who had been teasing her son was one of them.

But. . .

Even though Megan still had emotions coursing through her, wanting to knock some heads together for the way the boys had been treating Sammy—and scaring the wits out of her—and wanting to let MacNeill Hattaway know that she could handle matters with her son on her own, thank you very much, she bit her tongue. She kept her cool. At least this time anyway.

Mostly because Janey was right, at least to a certain small degree. Though Sammy might be six years old and handicapped, he really wasn't exactly a baby anymore or oblivious to the world around him. He was becoming more impressionable, beginning to notice things she wasn't even aware he was noticing. Just like how he'd sat at Paxton's the other night and told Allie all about the near crash with Mac and how she had "yell at man."

Six-year-old perspective or not, she had to realize how her reactions and emotions affected him. Though she'd protect him to her last dying breath—which she hoped wasn't any time soon since she was his only guardian—better to do it in a more controlled way, for sure.

So as the teen boys sized up their teams and began to play, she settled herself on the opposite side of Sammy's wheelchair, where she could easily witness Mac's zeal for the game. Like the true competitor he was, he was taking the rivalry between the boys very seriously. She completely startled when he apparently sensed her presence, immediately turning his attention from the action on the court to greet her.

"Hey," he said quietly, with warmth in his voice.

Or was she imagining it? The intense expression on his face smoothed for an instant at the sight of her. He even smiled. And for a reason she couldn't fathom, it didn't look to be a strained smile, like the ones they both wore in the picture Janey had shown her minutes earlier.

Nonetheless, it was a quick, confusing greeting, and before she knew it he was back to business again, shouting out coaching tips to the boys and calling fouls on them.

In contrast, Sammy sang out her name. "Maw-mee!" he shrilled, unable to contain himself with all the excitement going on around him.

Truly, her son's face couldn't have been any brighter or his smile any wider, making her realize even more that she'd been right not to run over and fuss at the boys or Mac and ruin things. Though he looked happy to see her, she could tell he was nowhere near ready to be ripped from Mac's presence.

And certainly, she had no trouble understanding that.

He probably felt more like a part of the game than he ever had before. It wasn't every day a kid got to hang side-by-side with a baseball superstar or any superstar for that matter. And for Sammy, a true fan, it had to be even more special.

"Who's winning?" she asked, since she hadn't been paying all that much attention to the game.

"The Tees," Mac told her. "But the Skins are going to clinch it."

So MacNeill Hattaway was psychic, too? *Of course!* She should've known.

"Why do you say that?"

He offered a knowing, sideways grin. "They want it more."

"They're big doughnut fans? I overheard what you told them. They're vying for doughnuts, right?"

"It's about the doughnuts to the Tees. It's about winning to the Skins. They want to win more."

"Ahh."

She squinted, trying to see the game through Mac's eyes. As the minutes ticked off Mac's game watch, she really did begin to discern what he meant. The players on the Skins kept looking to him for approval when they made a basket or defended well. It was obvious they shared something with him—the love of the game? The sport of it all? Who knew? His watching them, his approving nods, apparently meant a lot, though.

Whether she wanted to admit it or not, there was a sort of magnetism about the legendary MacNeill Hattaway. She could see it, even more, she could feel it—now that she experienced him in his element. His love for the game, apparently any game, unmistakably overflowed and seeped into most everyone around him. And he was right. The Skins caught up with the Tees and surpassed them in the last minutes.

"Cover your ears," he warned her as he bent down slightly to cover Sammy's ears with his hands.

"What?" She barely had time to comprehend what he was up to. Before she knew it, he pursed his lips and with some freaky skill he possessed, let loose with the loudest whistle she'd ever heard come from anyone's lips. A definite and nearly deafening signal that the basketball game was over.

"Time's up!" he shouted. "Way to go, Skins! Nice work, Tees."

Sweating and cheering, the Skins picked up their T-shirts from the side of the court, twirling them in the air, before high-fiving Mac and making a run for it across the jogging path over to Sweet Sensations.

"Can udder boys come?" Megan heard Sammy ask Mac, his voice nearly being drowned out by the hoopla.

Mac's forehead wrinkled as he studied her son's face. "You really want the Tees to come, Sammy?"

Sammy nodded. "He, too." Her son made a wobbly attempt to point at Reese, the boy who'd teased him most.

"Okay." At Sammy's request, Mac invited the rest of the boys, and more cheering resulted.

Meanwhile Reese rushed over to offer his services. "I'll push Sammy over to the bakery." He grabbed the wheelchair handles.

Mac raised a brow. "Gently?"

"Of course, gently."

Ironically, Megan noticed, Reese almost appeared offended by Mac's question. She had to smile at that, but didn't mind Reese's change of heart, especially since she was close by and could keep an eye on how he treated, or mistreated, her Sammy.

"So how should we do this?" Mac asked her after the boys took off ahead of them.

"Well, we can't let all these kids go into Janey's shop." She glanced at the group whose all-out exuberance could be mistaken for plain old rowdiness. "How about we go in and grab a few dozen doughnuts and some drinks and let them wait outside at the café tables? Or better yet. . ." Her thoughts suddenly turned to Janey who she knew would make a fuss of her and Mac being together. "You stay with the boys. Let me go in alone."

"Alone? Don't be silly." Mac splayed out his hand, inviting her to go up the wooden bakery steps ahead of him. "My treat, remember?"

Only, after Megan had tolerated Janey's uncontrollable gushing over Mac, and after dozens of doughnuts were boxed up and ready to be paid for, Mac patted his hips for his wallet.

"Oh, no way." He groaned. "Forgot I had on running shorts. I don't have a dime on me."

"No problem!" Janey exclaimed. "They're on the house, you two."

"You are not giving us the doughnuts for free, Janey." *Or turning this into a "we two" situation.* Megan reached into her purse for her wallet.

"But this is exciting! Having you both here, you know, at the same time," her friend chattered, over-splashing coffee into their to-go cups.

"Exciting or not, I'm paying. So you may as well tell me

how much. Unless you want me to overpay."

After squaring up with Janey and getting back outside, Megan noticed Reese had already pulled Sammy's chair up to a table and was sitting next to him. All the other boys filled the remaining seats. Distributing doughnuts all around, Megan pointed to the only place left for her and Mac to sit—a waist-high rock ledge that also served as a flower bed in spots. They hoisted themselves up on it.

"That was pretty lame," Mac confided. "I invite the guys for doughnuts. And you end up buying."

He bit into his bear claw, and Megan was suddenly aware—almost mesmerized—by the size of his hands. No wonder he could handle a baseball so deftly. Although. . . at the moment he didn't look like the poster boy for a tall, handsome pro athlete the way he typically did. Unshaven, his hair disheveled, with a slight tear in an old college T-shirt. In a way, he actually looked more interesting to her than he usually had. More human. More. . .likeable really. Well, maybe that was going a bit far too fast.

Working to take her eyes from him, she tried to focus on what he was saying instead. He was still embarrassed about not having his wallet.

At first, she had to admit, she had been put-off back in the bakery, wondering if he was trying to pull the Hattaway charm thing. Get something for nothing. But even if he was, did it matter? In a way, she'd been glad to pay.

This was probably the best Saturday morning Sammy had ever had at the basketball court, what with the "high stakes" game and the camaraderie of the other boys. Even now she knew he was soaking in as much as he could.

Maybe he couldn't entirely follow all of the boys' banter about sports and whatever else they were saying. But he was glowing, sitting in the middle of it all, with a few of the guys asking if he needed any help with his milk and doughnuts from time to time.

And it had all started with MacNeill Hattaway coming to Sammy's defense.

Maybe she needed to let down her defense as well. At least just a bit.

"These kids will probably never forget this," she told him. "The Saturday morning MacNeill Hattaway bought them doughnuts."

"*Almost* bought them doughnuts." He corrected her with the same easy smile he'd given her earlier.

"Ha! True."

"And, trust me, they went crazier at the mention of free doughnuts than they did at the mention of my name."

"Maybe that saying is true? You know, the one about 'the way to a man's heart is through his stomach.'"

"Could be." He grinned and she sensed he was enjoying himself, or at least enjoying their repartee. Which maybe was a good thing after all, she supposed. They would be working together. A lot. For the next several months.

"I really will get the money back to you, Megan."

"Do I look like I'm worried?"

It was rhetorical of course, so she didn't expect an answer. She also didn't expect the way Mac looked at her. Really took a minute to look at her as if appraising her expression. As if seeing something more than she wanted to share.

Yes, they'd been talking easily, making some of the strain

from a few nights prior begin to fade away. Even so, it was only talk. And his looking at her felt like more than that.

Turning away from his gaze, totally aware of her burning cheeks, she busied herself, dusting off the sugar from her hands. Wiping them with a napkin. Placing the napkin in her empty white doughnut bag. Crumpling the bag into a small ball.

"Finished with that?" Mac hopped down from the ledge, reaching out for the bag. As he walked over toward the trash can, she tried to not watch him, tried not to notice the way he moved with such agility.

Instead, she glanced over at Sammy and once again saw him beaming. She felt her heart relax and warm, and if it could speak it would've surely cooed "aahhh" at that moment. It was a feeling, a deep contentment she didn't experience often. No, not often enough.

Once again, whether she liked it or not, a small voice niggled inside her, reminding how they'd gotten to this place, this moment.

MacNeill Hattaway.

He was rubbing his right elbow as he walked back to their spot along the wall. Second nature to her, she couldn't help but ask, "Is it bothering you? Your elbow?"

"Not so much anymore, honestly. Just acts up once in a while."

"Have you been seeing a physical therapist?"

"Not really. I'm past that phase. It's been a lot of months since the accident. I still do some exercises on my own to continue to strengthen it though."

"Did you do something to make it act up?"

"Yeah." He laughed. "You might say that. I fell the other night."

"Dare I ask?"

"Probably not." He half-chuckled, shaking his head. "Not one of my brightest moves. Why? Are you a doctor or something?"

"I'm an 'or something,'" she told him. "A physical therapist."

"Really? That's great. Everyone needs a physical therapist from time to time. Actually," he harrumphed, "I seem to need one almost all the time. Where do you work?"

"See that? Right over there?" She pointed to the building where she spent at least forty hours of each week.

"With the green roof?"

"That's the place. I could. . . I can give you a quick ultrasound treatment if you want. It may help ease the discomfort."

As soon as the words were out of her mouth, she wished she could retract them. Is this what MacNeill Hattaway did to people? How he got them to react to him? By being charming? Humble? And smiling a lot?

Make a person forget about his past. . .

Maybe even make me forget mine, too?

Well, she wasn't going to get caught up in him like everyone else always seemed to do. She couldn't afford to. If he took her up on her offer, that was fine. In the clinic she'd be on her own turf. In a place where she was in command. Where she felt comfortable. Even if she was alone with MacNeill Hattaway, it would be absolutely no problem. She could handle the situation without a doubt.

"The clinic's not open on Saturdays?" Mac asked as Megan pulled out her keys, unlocking the wooden door to LPTC, the Loveland Physical Therapy Clinic.

"Every other," she told him. "But I'm lucky enough that I don't have to work on Saturdays so I can spend the time with Sammy. Plus, going to Janey's on Saturday mornings is a family tradition of ours. We'd both go through withdrawal if we had to stop."

She laughed, and to Mac, the sound filled the place, causing the rows of metal exam tables and exercise equipment to instantly feel less sterile, homier. He watched as she moved around the room in her jeans and flip-flops, set down her purse, washed her hands. She started to flick on some lights, but then changed her mind, which was fine. There was so much sunshine pouring in the arched windows, making her dark, shiny hair even shinier, that lights were unnecessary. Plus they were only going to be there fifteen minutes or so. Her friend Janey had said she'd be more than happy to keep an eye on Sammy, who was still content to be sitting with the other kids, listening to them talk sports.

"So this is your home away from home?" Mac asked her.

"Monday through Friday." She nodded to the exam table closest to him. "Want to hop up there?"

Pushing a small portable cart in front of her, she made her way over to him. As she pulled the cart up close to the table, he was familiar enough with the ultrasound equipment it housed not to have any questions.

Except for one or two about her.

"How long have you been doing this?"

"Why?" Her eyes smiled into his, taunting. "Are you nervous?"

"Uh-uh. Not at all. I'm sure I'm in capable hands."

At least her hands felt good anyway as she squirted cold gel on his bare arm then proceeded to warm the substance and his skin with her soothing, expert touch.

"I've been here eight years now." She lifted the handpiece and began rubbing it in a circular motion around his elbow area. "Now I have a question for you. . ." she hedged.

"Okay."

"How did you hurt your elbow?"

"You mean the first time? Or the other night?"

"Let's start with the most recent incident," she suggested.

"Fair enough. . ." Plus, he imagined she'd already heard about his prior car accident. Hadn't everyone? A person had to be living in a cave not to.

"You said you fell?"

He nodded. "I couldn't sleep the other night. So I got up, grabbed a flashlight, and went outside looking for something and fell into a ditch. Pretty much hit elbow-first."

Megan stopped rubbing. "Excuse me, say that again. You were doing what?"

He sighed. Apparently, vague wasn't going to cut it with her. "I've been living out at my uncle's farm for the past few months. He passed away last year, but I'd already bought— well, that doesn't matter. The fact is, my uncle used to whittle. He whittled canes mostly, dozens of them. Like I said, I couldn't sleep. I started thinking about my uncle Jake and his whittling. So I got up." He shrugged. "And I went searching for a good piece of wood I could use."

"To whittle?" She sounded shocked, still holding the handpiece upright. "You whittle?"

"I, uh, I'm just getting started," he admitted.

Her forehead crinkled slightly. "Was your uncle crippled?" She cued in on the fact about the canes.

"No, he wasn't. Not physically. He just thought most everyone was spiritually."

He thought for sure she'd press him for clarification about that statement, but instead as she went back to work on his arm, her questions turned back to whittling, as if she just couldn't get over the fact he was attempting to try it.

"I like to do stuff with my hands," he explained. "Especially now that I'm not pitching."

"You're probably used to working out a lot, I imagine."

"Yeah. It's been quite a change all around. My body misses the practices, the workouts. I can't do everything to the degree I did prior to the accident, but it's getting better. I'm getting there." He paused. "It's all good. Good it happened. I guess that sounds a little crazy to you?"

"Honestly, I've heard it before."

He chuckled, feeling a little chagrined he'd exposed himself like that only to hear such a nonchalant response. "So I'm kind of like 'same old, same old'?"

"I'm sorry." She paused, looking up at him in a way that made her eyes collaborate with the words coming from her lips. "I apologize if I made it sound like that. I'm just saying I've had a lot of mangled people come in the door saying they think their accidents were good things. That they were out of control, and the accident saved their lives."

"It not only saved my life. It saved my soul."

He didn't know why he was telling her all this. Except for the fact he'd asked God for a chance to see her again, to makes amends with her, and here was that chance. It wasn't like he was trying to win her over—Megan O'Donnell wasn't a game to him. Not like so many other women had been in the past. It wasn't the way he wanted to operate anymore. But she didn't know that. And somehow he wanted her to. Which was crazy. They were only going to be working together on a sports day event, and then beyond that. . .

Why did his mind keep going there?

"So what are you doing tonight?" The question slipped out of his mouth just as she placed the handpiece back in its spot and grabbed for a cloth to wipe the goo from his arm. It surprised him almost as much as he could see it surprised her.

"What?" Her hands stilled. Her eyes grew wide. "Tonight?"

"What I meant to say is, I need to repay you for the doughnuts. Do you and Sammy have dinner plans?"

"No. . ." She swiped his arm quickly, deftly, tossing the cloth in a receptacle on the cart. "No," she repeated.

"Do you want some? Plans, I mean?"

He watched her body almost twitch in response to the question. Standing there, biting her lip, he wondered what all was going through her mind.

Or did he really want to know?

All he knew for sure is that hesitation was rarely a good sign. At least on the field it never had been. He doubted it was in this case either.

"I should say no," she said finally.

"Should?" He stuck his neck forward. "Or are you saying no?" He wasn't sure how much to push. This was definitely unfamiliar territory to him. When had a woman ever said anything but yes to him?

"I guess. . .yes."

Yes? Dear Lord in heaven, she was killing him with her ambiguity. "Yes, dinner? You and Sammy?"

She shook her head. "I mean yes—I'm saying no."

"Oh." His head lolled back on his shoulders as if he'd deflected an imaginary blow. "Yeah, okay. That's okay." He gathered his bearings and nodded.

He thought he'd been tired after his run! But asking a simple question and getting a not-so-simple answer had taken another kind of toll on him. One he wasn't accustomed to.

"But thank you anyway," she added politely.

"Sure." He shrugged, trying hard to sound indifferent. "No problem." He slid down from the table. "Thank you for the treatment. I'm sure my elbow will be feeling a whole lot better." He started to make his way toward the door. "Really appreciate it. Hey, and tell that son of yours—tell Sammy, I said good-bye, okay?"

"Sure." She nodded. "Unless, if you're going past the bakery, you could tell him yourself."

"Naw, I'm sure he's doing fine. Plus, it's about time I get home and shower." He glanced down at his sweatshirt. "You know, get the day started."

"Yeah, me, too." To his ears, she sounded almost relieved.

"Thank you for helping out Sammy today. That was nice of you."

"Not a problem." He grabbed the doorknob to let himself out before they could politely thank each other for one more thing one more time. "I guess I'll be seeing you around. . ."

"At the meeting on Wednesday."

"Right. Wednesday. Meeting. Wouldn't want to miss it," he said easily, tipping his hand good-bye.

Closing the door behind him, he walked down the sidewalk through Loveland, making his way toward his car. Until a thought stopped him in his tracks. A startling realization. One he couldn't totally grasp.

He really had meant it, hadn't he? What he'd said back there?

He really didn't want to miss the meeting on Wednesday. More than that, he didn't want to miss the chance to see Megan O'Donnell again.

Chapter 7

"Na-naw! You pretty!"

Sammy spotted his nana's reflection across the shop the moment Megan pushed his wheelchair through the handicap entrance of We Do! Wedding Planners.

As Laura O'Donnell turned from an oval antique wall mirror, the pearl-trimmed, shoulder-length wedding veil donning her head turned with her, its rustle as hushed as a whisper.

Megan had to agree with Sammy. Her mom did look pretty, almost glowing in fact.

But then everything in the We Do! Wedding Planners shop always seemed to have an ethereal quality about it. Almost as elusive and otherworldly as love itself, Megan had always thought—and still did, as she glanced around the establishment.

The evening sun shone through the storefront windows, its shimmering beams bringing out the lively amber luster in the giant oak armoire that stood behind the petite Louis XIV reception desk. Nearly tall enough for castle decor, the armoire's doors were flung wide open like welcoming arms, white satin and lace spilling out from the formidable piece of furniture from sample wedding dresses stuffed inside.

Two overstuffed upholstered love seats the same color as pink candy hearts sat in a room to the right of the entry, cozily arced around a diminutive coffee table. On top of the table sat a delicately painted floral china tea setting that looked fit for a princess, no less, with photo albums of exquisite We Do! brides who had already taken their walk down the aisle. And on this late spring day, instead of burning logs, the fireplace was filled with a huge pot of late-blooming tulips in a variety of corals, pinks, and yellows.

To the left of that sitting area, a staircase with a banister wrapped in eucalyptus garland accented with baby-cheek pink bows led to the upstairs workroom and computers. But as a young girl, Megan imagined more than once it looked like winding steps that just might lead to heaven.

In the middle of all that fluffiness, Sammy had a practical question. "You getting married, Na-naw?" He frowned.

Megan unzipped his light Windbreaker and removed the baseball cap from his head. Ruffling his smooshed-down hair, she noted the confused look on his face. She would've been baffled as well if she hadn't caught her mom on numerous occasions doing the very same thing—trying on wedding veils.

The "veil thing" was, after all, how her mom and best friend, Pam, had gotten their start as wedding planners. Once upon a time, many summers ago as little girls, the two of them had organized pretend weddings in their backyards, attended by all their favorite stuffed animals of course. The bride's main prop for those special occasions had been a lacy half-slip—size 6X—that they'd used as a wedding veil. Tattered from many summers of use, and yellowed from time, that same half-slip hung in a shadowbox frame on the wall at We Do! Wedding Planners, displayed like a well-earned diploma.

"Getting married?" Her mom giggled at Sammy's inquiry. "I'm already married, Sammy, you know that. To the most wonderful man in the world."

"Pap-ee?"

"Yes, your pappy. But"—she slid the veil from her head—"I think there's someone else I know who may be getting married soon." She smiled broadly in Megan's direction.

"Why—why are you looking at me like that?" Megan suddenly felt her shoulders stiffen. But then maybe it was the surroundings. For the past several years, she hadn't been all that comfortable in her mom's shop. The place was so different from Megan's work environment. And her mom so different from her, she realized.

Every hour of her mother's workday appeared to be wrapped in love and romance and frills. While Megan, well, she just didn't have time or energy or even the interest to fuss with those sorts of things.

"I'm not looking at you like anything, honey. I'm thinking about Sylvia Pruitt."

"Sylvia Pruitt? The old maid who lived in the Victorian on the riverbanks?"

"She still lives there, and she isn't an old maid, Meg. She's been unlucky in love, that's all. But that's behind her now. Thanks to Pam."

"A little Pamela Matthews matchmaking, huh?"

Her mom nodded. "Both of us were involved to some degree, but I suppose most of the credit goes to Pam." She reached for a hanger. "I was just trying on veils thinking about which one might suit Sylvia best if she—"

"Decides to marry?" Megan stuffed Sammy's baseball hat in his backpack.

"Oh no. If she decides to buy her veil and gown through us. No doubt, she'll be getting married. And soon."

"To whom?" Megan knew her voice sounded incredulous, and she didn't mean to be mean, but she couldn't fathom it. *Sylvia Pruitt? Getting married?* As kids they used to dare each other to run across Old Maid Pruitt's yard, hoping not to get caught in case she really had gone crazy without love and might cast some sort of weird spell on them.

"Martin Chandler." Her mom's eyes flashed bright. "Sylvia and Martin, together at last. Isn't it perfect?"

Megan would've never thought of pairing up the spinster and funeral home director together. But now that her mom mentioned it, in an odd way the two did conjure up a likely match. "I guess it could work." She shrugged.

Watching as her mom tucked the veils she'd been trying on back into the armoire, Megan noted how gently she nudged the satiny puffs of pristine white dresses into their places before shutting the cabinet doors for the day. Once again she couldn't help thinking how farfetched it was that her mom, along with her We Do! business partner, spent their days—their lives actually—in such a way. Treating love like it was something palpable.

"So!" Her mom turned to Sammy. "Are you ready to have some fun with me and your pappy tonight while your mommy's at her meeting?" She bent over and gave Sammy a kiss on the top of his head.

He nodded excitedly. "You an' Pap-ee wach me?"

"We sure are."

"Miss Biddle can't. She hurt. She like her flowers, though."

"You took flowers to Mrs. Biddle? That's sweet."

Sammy nodded again while Megan filled in the blanks. "We went to see her last night after work. She's still at the assisted living facility recovering from the surgery and doing rehab."

"Miss Biddle give me a kiss, too," Sammy spoke up.

"Well, how could she resist?" Her mom chuckled softly. "You're such a handsome guy, you," she said, giving Sammy reason to beam. "So it sounds like poor Mrs. Biddle has a ways to go yet in her recovery."

"I'm looking for another sitter, though. I have a few leads," Megan stressed. Of course, she didn't know how successful any of them would be. It wasn't easy finding someone reliable and trustworthy who was also comfortable with a special-needs child. "I'll find someone soon. You don't have to worry."

"Worry?" Her mom looked more crushed by Megan's words than fretful.

"I mean if you have other things you have to—"

"Nothing is more important than our Sammy." She shot Megan a stern look.

Oh, they'd covered this ground before. Round and round so many times. And it didn't matter what her mother said, or what her father said either, Megan simply hated to ask them for help. Point blank.

"You try to do too much yourself." They'd pleaded. *"We're*

not meant to do life alone." They'd lecture. Which just wasn't true in the first place. She wasn't doing life alone. She was doing it with Sammy. And there were plenty of single moms out there doing even more than she was. All by themselves.

"I hear what you're saying, Mom," she appeased, not having time to rehash it all again. "I just meant—well, you and Dad work all day and—"

"Speaking of which," her mom interrupted, turning her attention to Sammy, "your pappy is so excited that you'll be there tonight to watch the baseball game with him."

"Baseball game?" Sammy's eyes grew wide. Her mom was definitely speaking his language. "To-nigh?"

"Oh yes." Megan's mom nodded. "The Hawks are playing the Cubs."

"MaaNil buy me doughnuts."

"What did you say?" Her mom gave a little chuckle. "Doughnuts? MacNeill? MacNeill Hattaway bought you doughnuts? Did I just hear that right?" She glanced back and forth between Sammy and Megan, the smile on her face growing so wide Megan thought her face might crack in two.

"Well, Hattaway didn't really—" Megan started to explain the entire story, but she couldn't burst Sammy's bubble that way. "Well, he didn't really have to," she repeated, switching gears. "But yes, it was his idea to buy doughnuts for some of the boys."

Her mom shook her head. "I don't get it. Where? When?"

"Saturday morning, down on the bike path." Megan checked her watch. "But really, Mom, I don't have time to go into it."

Yet that didn't stop Laura O'Donnell, matchmaker extraordinaire—and curious mom.

"You mean you're *seeing* MacNeill? Besides when you're at the meetings?"

And that's when her mom got that funny look on her face. The one with the slightly raised eyebrows, the faint smile, and dreamy eyes. The one that spoke of romantic possibilities and happily-ever-afters.

Oh, thank goodness she hadn't accepted Mac's dinner invitation. Neither her son nor her mother would've ever gotten their heads out of the clouds again!

As it was, Sammy hadn't stopped talking about Mac and the doughnuts for a second over the past five days, telling everyone they ran into all about his special morning at the bike path. Not only did he repeat the tale to whoever would listen, but he woke up talking about it and went to sleep with MacNeill Hattaway's name on his lips, too.

No wonder it had been so hard for her to get her mind off Mac since Saturday. The scene on the basketball court . . .eating doughnuts outside Janey's shop. . .the time they'd spent alone at the clinic together. If Sammy hadn't kept mentioning his name, surely she wouldn't still be thinking about Mac. Stewing over all he had confided to her. Wondering who he really was—what he was all about. Remembering how he'd looked at her while they were sharing time on the rock ledge together. A look that had definitely unnerved her. And surprised her. Although she shouldn't have been surprised at all since. . .hadn't he had as much practice with women as he had with pitching a baseball?

Suddenly her cheeks warmed again as they'd been doing the past several days. Spring allergies possibly? Hopefully her mom wouldn't notice. Knowing her, she'd read more into it than was true.

"No, Mom, I'm not seeing MacNeill," Megan answered flatly. "Not besides the meetings," she added, emphatically.

"But Sammy just said—"

"Well, yeah. I mean, we bumped into him on Saturday but—"

"Maw-mee and MaaNil go 'way together," Sammy piped up. Unfortunately.

"Ya'll went away together?" her mom asked breathily.

Now her mom's eyes didn't just look dreamy, they were wide with amazement. Approval and amazement. No doubt her mother could twist her and Mac's trip to the clinic into a romantic rendezvous. Which it wasn't. At all.

She let go of a sigh. She was so tired of all the Mac-Neill Hattaway jibber-jabber. And it sure didn't help quell the uneasiness she felt thinking about seeing him again in just a matter of minutes.

"Mom, really, please."

"Please, what?"

"Please don't look at me like that."

"But Sammy just said—"

"Mom, Sammy is the best son in the world, but he's an impressionable six-year-old. An impressionable six-year-old with a very big mouth." She arched her brows at Sammy, hoping to reprimand him with her best evil-eye look. But his grin grew all the wider.

Exasperated, she shook her head. "Look, really Mom, I

need to run. I'm going to be late for my own meeting."

"You mean the meeting with you and MacNeill?"

"I mean the meeting that I'm facilitating with Hattaway where there will be dozens of other volunteers in attendance." She handed over Sammy's backpack. "Sammy has a little bit of homework in his folder. A paper on shapes, right, Sammy?"

"Yes," he answered, before retelling his encounter with Mac for the hundredth or so time. "Doughnuts good. MaaNil nice!" he told his nana, who of course, looked delighted, savoring every tidbit of information.

"I bet they were very good, Sammy," she cooed at her grandson. "And I bet MacNeill is very, very nice."

Oh. My. Goodness!

Megan felt as if her blood pressure was rising sky-high. If she didn't make a quick exit, she was afraid she'd let out a scream. Or a very loud groan. Or who knew? "Okay, I've really got to run, Mom. Really." She pecked her mom on the cheek. "Thanks."

"You're welcome, sweetie. And don't worry. Stay out as late as you want. We'll get Sammy's work finished. Your dad can help him while I make dinner. But first"—she squatted down alongside the wheelchair—"I think we should visit the garden, Sammy, don't you? We'll cut some flowers to take home to Pappy."

Sammy nodded eagerly, and as Megan watched her mom push the wheelchair to the back door of the shop, her heart conflicted in a million ways.

She felt inadequate, needing to lean on her mother, but glad Sammy had a grandmother who loved him so.

She wished she could linger more often with Sammy just like her mom was getting the chance to, but it seemed she always had to rush to the next thing and the next, or their world would surely fall apart.

And while she felt happy that her mom was teaching her son about flowers, she wondered why she wasn't a flower person.

Unlike her mom, she didn't know the first practical thing about growing and nurturing a garden. Why she hadn't absorbed some of that knowledge long ago, she didn't know. All she remembered as a young girl was marveling at her mom's springtime peonies that grew to be nearly as tall as she was. And in the summer, there would be daisies lining the white fence, armloads of them, plentiful enough to pick. Back then, while she'd wait for her mom to finish up work for the day, she'd sit on the back porch of We Do! Wedding Planners pulling at the daisy petals.

He loves me, he loves me not, she'd repeat over and over in her head, with little regard for the plucked petals falling to the ground. She said it just the way her mom had taught her. She said it all the while dreaming of love and marriage and never-ending bliss.

But that was only because that's what little girls do...

Chapter 8

Mac caught a whiff of something sweet—the same scent he recognized from his night out in the rain a week earlier—and knew Megan had arrived early for the meeting.

Looking up from an article he'd been reading in the *Loveland Herald*, he watched as she set her purse and meeting notebook on the cafeteria table and then switched her cell phone from the cream-colored jacket into the front pocket of her jeans, keeping it handy for emergency purposes he supposed. He'd never seen her hair down before. It waved around her face before falling to her shoulders, its ebony darkness making her clear blue eyes shine even bluer.

He thought he'd just sit tight and let her come to him for a change, not wanting to appear overly eager, especially after his awkward exit from her clinic the other day. But somehow that thought didn't hang in his head very long. The metal folding chair squeaked as he set down the paper and got up to greet her. "Hey."

"Hey." She glanced up at him, and then over his shoulders at the clock above the exit. "You're early, aren't you?"

He gave a slight smile. "It's another Uncle Jake-ism. He always said, 'If you're not early, you're late.'"

"I had a grandmother who shared the same maxim." She returned a polite smile before grabbing up her notebook.

"Well, since we're both here ahead of time, I guess we could sit and organize our thoughts some."

"How about over there?" He pointed to the same row of chairs he'd just been sitting in, chairs that faced the lone cafeteria table and were already lined up with other rows for the volunteers who were due to arrive in the next few minutes. All the other tables had been folded upright and were pushed against a side wall.

"So, let me guess," he said as they settled in their seats. "You were a cheerleader, right? When you went to high school here?"

She tilted her head and stared at him. A reaction he realized he deserved. After all, the question did sound odd—even to him. But truth was, when he'd been sitting earlier, his mind had wandered from the newspaper he'd been reading. Looking around the cafeteria, he'd imagined Megan O'Donnell there years ago, eating lunch with her high school friends. Talking. Laughing.

"Uh, no," she answered. "Actually, I was a bandie. Played the french horn."

"A bandie, huh?" Somehow that didn't jibe with his image of her. With her petite figure, pretty face, and go-get-'em personality, he pictured her more with a pair of pompoms in her hands. "Really? Well, I always thought the french horn would be a great instrument to play."

"You're kidding, right?"

"More like faking it." He relaxed, letting go of a grin. "I'm not sure I even know what a french horn is."

"It's kind of like an Italian horn, but different."

"An Italian horn? I don't think I. . ." He caught the

glimmer in her bright eyes and laughed. "Okay. Guess I had that coming," he conceded. "So where did you bandies sit for lunch? Over there?" He pointed to the south side of the cafeteria where some residual glow from the setting sun illuminated the red maples outside an oblong picture window.

"Nope. The more popular kids sat there. Bandies sat over there." She raised her arm in the opposite direction, to a darker corner of the cafeteria.

"Oh." He frowned.

"Don't worry." She laughed—he sensed more at his expression than anything else. "It didn't scar me for life or anything, not being one of the more popular kids."

"No, it's not that. It's just, I thought—" Chagrined, he scratched at his clean-shaven cheek. "Hmm. . .guess I'm not so smart after all."

She raised a brow as if astonished by his admission, but kindly kept any smart retorts she might've had to herself. "You were in Florida for high school, weren't you?"

As she spoke, he tried to keep his mind off those glossy pink lips of hers. But it wasn't easy. Blinking, he nodded. "Uh, yeah. But being back here. . .well, you know, sometimes I wonder what things would've been like if my family had stayed." No, that wasn't true. He'd only started musing over thoughts like that since he'd met her. Wasn't that right? Not letting that realization sink in any deeper, he switched gears. "So, what's on the agenda for this evening?"

She flipped open her notebook, clearly more than ready to get down to business as she scribbled some notes. "Well, I thought we'd talk about how we're going to divide the volunteers into groups to—"

"You know. . ." he drawled, interrupting her—not because he wanted to, but because he couldn't hold off any longer. "I, uh, there's something I need to talk to you about before we get started."

"Uh-huh." She kept writing.

"The head of the school board called me."

The pen stopped, her hand hovering over the page. The heavy lashes that shadowed her cheeks suddenly flew up. "Phil Ellis? Really? I didn't realize you knew Phil."

"I don't. But he called the other night. Said he graduated a couple of years ahead of you, right? In the class of—"

"He called to tell you we went to high school together?" Her eyes narrowed warily and those pretty, full lips of hers went thin. So much for the smiles he'd won from her just minutes earlier.

"Ahh, not exactly. He wanted to get some autographed photos from me."

"Autographed photos? And you're telling me this because. . ." She squinted, obviously puzzled and rightfully so. He was even confusing himself with his cryptic account of the conversation. He needed to man up and tell her the main reason for Phil's call. Even though he dreaded doing it. He had to give it to her straight.

Taking a deep breath, he spat out the bad news. "Aw, it wasn't just about autographs. Phil called to let us know the school's going to have to renege on their promise. We're not going to be able to use the stadium for our All-Stars Sports Day."

Her mouth fell open at first, but then she apparently

recovered quickly, jotting notes in her book. Her reaction surprised him until she shook her head and replied, "That's not funny, Mac."

"Funny?" Putting his hand on the back of her chair, he leaned in close, able to keep his voice soft but unable to hide the irritation he suddenly felt. "You really think I'd joke about something like that?"

Her face was only inches from his when she looked up, searching his eyes. Obviously she found the truth there. "Oh no. You *are* serious." He watched her face crumple. "But I don't get it—why?"

"There're some problems with the field. They're going to have to tear it up and redo it and the track this summer. So the stadium's out of the picture."

Volunteers started to trickle in, and she put up a good front, feigning smiles and friendly waves in between his explanation, but he knew inside she had to be in turmoil.

"And they didn't know that before they gave us the go-ahead?"

"Initially they'd planned to wait and put in the new field next summer. But now they're afraid if they don't take the money from the state this summer to make the improvements, they might risk losing the funds altogether."

He hated to hear the heavy sigh that came out of her. Hated to see the way her face and body went slack. It was a look of defeat so unlike her that it about did him in. Making him want to comfort her. To take her in his arms and let her know it'd all be okay as he knew it would be.

But before he could do more than blink, her body language changed.

"Well. . ." She shifted, tilting her chin upward, raising herself in the chair. "We just have to think of someplace else, that's all. I'm not putting this event off until next year. I'm just not," she added, a defiant tone in her voice. "The kids are so excited. And people are here, wanting to help." She glanced over her shoulder at the chairs filling up behind them. "We just have to figure out—wait a minute, I know—Ted! He'll have some ideas. We can talk to him about it tonight." A sparkle regenerated in her eyes.

"I don't think he's going to make it tonight."

"He's not? How do you know?"

"He called me the other day. After he heard the news."

"Ted called you, too? You both knew and I—I didn't?"

"Well, I—"

One of the dads stopped him mid-thought with a clasp on the back of his shoulder. "Hey, Mac. Sorry to interrupt, Megan." Shane Dugan leaned down between the two of them. "Mind if I get that autographed baseball hat from you tonight? Hate to push, but Chase's birthday is this Friday and—"

"It's in my car, Shane. How about I grab it after the meeting?"

"Great." Shane clapped him on the shoulder again. "Really appreciate it, man."

Megan gave a warm smile in Shane's direction, but the moment he walked away, her mouth tightened again. "I don't get it. I wish— You should've called me, Mac."

"Yes, I should've. But there's only one problem. You've never given me your number."

Her cheeks reddened at that, making him believe it was

intentional and not just an oversight that she hadn't shared her number with him. A low blow to his pride for sure. But his pride was what had been getting him into trouble over the years, and he was trying—hard as it was—to put it aside most of the time now. Haggling about should'ves and could'ves wasn't going to make things any better for either of them at this point.

"Look. That's the bad news, but there's some good news," he told her.

She looked up at him tentatively, biting her lip.

"I ran into some of the guys—some of the volunteers— at the gym, and they all agreed. We can have the All-Stars Sports Day at my place. Out at the farm. It's perfect. Plenty of fields in those ten acres where we can set up the activities. Plenty of space for parking."

He had hoped by offering the farm for the event, and getting some preliminary okays from several of the dads, that it would be a help to her. Make it one less thing on her list to stress over. Something to make her life easier. After all, she did have a job. And a child. A handicapped child at that. The woman definitely had her hands full and seemed happy to be doing it all, something he truly admired about her.

Still, he wasn't sure his suggestion met with her approval. Not until she scribbled something else in her notebook and then ripped out the page, handing it to him.

"No need for a thank-you note," he teased. "Not necessary."

"It's my cell number."

"Ah."

Folding the paper into squares, he started to tell her not to fret, that he'd only call for their event planning purposes not for pleasure. But then he wasn't sure he wanted to make a statement that he might want to retract someday. All he knew as he tucked the paper into his shirt pocket was that he'd never, ever, had such a hard time getting a girl's phone number before. In fact, in the past, he'd rarely had to ask. Numbers just appeared everywhere—in his pockets, in his gym bag, on his windshield. Wherever. But not so with Megan.

He'd learned a long, long time ago, however, that nothing worth having ever came easy. And crazily, there was something about Megan that made him think and feel she might be worth the irritation and degradation she put him through.

As they both rose from the chairs to greet the volunteers, she paused and laid a hand on his arm. "Thank you, Mac," she said softly, a fervent sheen of appreciation glimmering in her eyes.

Oh yeah, he thought, as his heart did an involuntary flip. Megan O'Donnell definitely had his number, too.

Chapter 9

"Notice anything different?"

Megan gave Janey the once-over as her friend handed her the to-go cup of coffee she'd ordered. Taking the lid off the cup, she blew into the steaming brew, appraising Janey's appearance at the same time.

"You just got your hair highlighted, right? It looks good. I like the caramel color running through it."

"No, silly. Not me." Janey waved a hand in the air. "The bakery. Notice anything different about the bakery?"

Megan had noticed a lot of "different" things about the bakery—mainly the signs. Everywhere. Signs that looked tacky and out of place. Signs that she wanted to ask Janey about, but didn't for fear she'd say something that might hurt her friend's feelings. But since Janey brought it up...

"You mean, that maybe?" Megan pointed to just one sign, the closest one on the glass bakery case right in front of her. A neon-green rectangular thing that looked shoddy and out of context in light of Janey's usual good taste. "That's, um, different."

"Exactly! Since MacNeill Hattaway said my bear claws are his all-time favorites, I thought a little sign saying so would entice my customers."

A *little* sign? Megan didn't reply, but instead continued to blow, blow, and blow some more, pretending to fixate on her too-hot coffee.

"So what do you think?" Janey asked.

"Well, I. . ." Megan stalled, replacing the lid on her cup, searching her mind frantically for something constructive to say. But she didn't have to come up with anything. Unknowing to him, Sammy came to her rescue.

"Where my jelly doughnuts go?" He pointed at the same bakery case from his wheelchair right beside her.

"Right where they always are, little guy," Janey answered him. "They're right next to"—she scuttled around to the front of the case to have a look for herself—"the bear claws." Her shoulders slumped. "Oh, I guess the sign is kind of big, isn't it? You can't see the jelly doughnuts at all and only a part of the glazed tray. Hmm. . ." She bit her lip, frustration clouding her face. "Well, what do you think of those signs?" She pointed to a trio of white shelves lining the wall, all stacked with a variety of breads. "Do you think they're oversized?"

"I certainly don't have a problem seeing them," Megan replied as diplomatically as she could. She read the two closest to her. " 'Mayor Goodwin's Favorite Sensation: Pumpernickel Rye.' 'Librarian Martha's Favorite Sensation: Cinnamon Raisin Bread.'"

"Sammy's favorite is—"

"Jelly doughnuts. I know, honey, that's why I have a couple right here." Megan waved the doughnut-filled bag in her hand at him before turning back to Janey. "I guess I don't understand why you're doing this, Janey. Sweet Sensations is so cute and warm and inviting—and you do a great business. With the signs, well, do you think they might detract just a bit from the homey atmosphere you've got going here?"

Janey shook her head, bringing a defensive hand to her hip. "You don't understand, Megan."

Isn't that what she'd just said?

"Remember Sean Shaffer?" her friend continued.

"Your almost-prom-date-senior-year-of-high-school Sean Shaffer?"

"Exactly. Hard to forget, isn't he? The way he dumped me and went to prom with Amanda Richter?"

It certainly had been easy for Megan to forget Sean. She'd never thought of him again after graduation when everyone had gone their separate ways to college. Apparently, Janey had never gotten over him or past their senior prom fiasco. However, Janey's side of the story had never quite jibed with Sean's. He'd always claimed it was her who dumped him first and that's why he'd asked Amanda.

"What does Sean have to do with Sweet Sensations?"

"Everything!" Janey blurted out. "Everything!" she repeated.

Megan shifted on her feet, and even Sammy sensed Janey's explanation was going to take more than just a minute.

"Maw-mee, doughnut please?" he asked.

She'd just heard his little stomach growl and didn't want to put him off any longer. Her plan had been to take their time and eat their doughnuts outside. But they'd already gotten to Janey's later than she'd hoped to, and she sure hadn't planned on a lengthy conversation with her friend, voyaging into past loves, dumpers and dumpees.

"Sure, honey." She set her coffee cup on the counter, plucked some napkins from the dispenser there and laid them across Sammy's lap. "Go ahead and eat your jelly doughnut here." She pulled one from the bag. "Then we have to get going. We don't want to be late."

"Late?" Janey's ears perked up as she moved back behind the counter and started making a fresh pot of coffee. "Late to where?" She poured out what little residual coffee was still in the pot and began to refill it with fresh water.

"Oh, you know, we're, uh, taking a ride."

"See Mac farm," Sammy sputtered between chomps of doughnut and spurts of jelly.

Janey immediately set the carafe down. "You're going out to MacNeill's?" Her eyes widenend.

"Just to check out the place for the event." Megan nodded. "Allie and her kids were going to come along, but Carrie has a bad cold and Allie didn't want Sammy to catch it."

She'd asked Mac if it'd be okay for Allie and her kids to come out to the farm along with her, making it sound like his place would be something fun for all of them to experience. But that was only half the truth.

In reality, she was just plain nervous to be alone with him. He confused her. He didn't make sense. No, MacNeill Hattaway didn't make sense at all. Not in the way he looked at her. Not the way he was so nice to her. Not the way he acted interested in her. Not when he could have his pick of almost any woman on the planet.

Was it because they were using his farm for the event? Was he thinking that meant there was something more going on between them? Something he expected? Although honestly, he had even been acting nice and interested long before the farm situation came up.

And the worst of it was, when she was around him lately, she confused herself, too. Why did she have such a hard time looking into his eyes? Was she afraid of who she might see there? Maybe a man so different from the one she first believed him to be? Not that it mattered. It really, really didn't. She'd vowed long ago not to let a man—especially not a man like MacNeill Hattaway—into her and Sammy's life again. But then, oh—she had to be crazy to even be thinking thoughts along those lines.

"Take a lot of notes." Janey's voice interrupted her thoughts.

"Notes?" She shook her head, trying to clear it of one MacNeill Hattaway. "Oh, I will. For sure. We have to figure out where to set up the parking area. Then we need to know where all the booths and events will be situated around the property."

"No. I mean, take lots of notes so you can tell me everything about the place."

"Janey, it's the old Lochen farm out on Route 48. You know the place well."

"I know, but it can't be the same old farm anymore. Not with MacNeill living there now. That's different. . .oh, hold on. Can I help you, sir?"

Saved by one of Janey's customers, Megan swiped at Sammy's gooey mouth then gathered up the used napkins and threw them away along with her half-empty coffee cup. Tugging her purse onto her shoulder, she was ready to push his wheelchair toward the door where she could call out a good-bye to Janey, when her friend returned, stopping her short with another guy matter.

"So, I never finished my story about Sean Shaffer."

"Oh right. What's going on with him?"

In a millisecond, Janey's pretty hazel eyes narrowed, making her look atypically malicious. "He's back in town; that's what's going on with him," she practically hissed. "He's back in town, and he's doing it to me all over again."

Megan tried to make the connection. Was there a community dance coming up she didn't know about? Had Sean tried to invite Janey or something? "Sorry, Janey, I'm not getting it."

"The Donut Emporium? The one in the gas station right across the bridge?" Megan noted that Janey refrained from saying "duh," even though her tone implied she wanted to. "That's his, Megan. That's Sean's place."

"The Donut Emporium?" She knew of the small doughnut shop of course, but had never considered stopping there. After all, her allegiance was to Janey, and besides that, she and Sammy had enjoyed their routine at Sweet Sensations for forever.

"But Janey, your place is totally different. It's not a little shop; it's more like a haven. A really comfortable one. And you have breads and coffeecakes and birthday cakes, all in addition to your doughnuts. Plus a variety of great coffee drinks, did I mention that? And—"

But Janey wasn't listening. "I just can't believe him. It's like the guy has it out for me or something, always ruining my life."

"Oh Janey. People change, don't you think? I doubt if

he's the same old Sean you remember him to be." Not that Megan remembered him as the sneaky, conniving guy Janey thought him to be anyway. "Besides, hasn't the Donut Emporium always been there?" she asked her friend. "Like ever since we can remember?"

"Well, yeah, but now Sean's running specials. And he's sponsoring a girl's softball team. And he's sending out those coupon mailers. I got one in my mailbox yesterday. My heart about sank to my knees."

"Oh." Megan could just imagine what that must've felt like. She was almost afraid to ask her friend the next question. "Have you—have you noticed a decrease in your store traffic?"

"Yes. Not a lot," Janey said somberly. "But some."

"And that's why you made all the signs?"

Janey nodded.

Her friend had always had the ability to create quality bakery products and had a great sense about what it took to create a charming atmosphere for Sweet Sensations. But Janey's strong suit had never included marketing. Of course, in the past that had never been an issue. Sweet Sensations never required much advertising and pretty much sold itself on its own merits.

But if Sean was going to keep chipping away, trying to attain a bigger piece of the pie, so to speak, Janey probably did need to take some action.

"Well, what if you did this? What if you made the signs a tad smaller for starters?" Megan suggested. "You know, get some of those starburst things you can buy at a craft store. You want them to be visible of course—just not in the way, you know? And then, maybe you could turn it into a promotion so it all makes sense."

"Meaning?"

"Meaning, uh, a contest." She tried to think fast. "A contest where all your customers have to do to enter is to write down their favorite Sweet Sensation. They can enter each time they visit your bakery. Whoever's name you draw wins a Sweet Sensations gift card or free baked goods for a week. Or whatever you decide."

"That's a great idea." Janey's eyes lit up as she brainstormed. "I can run it in conjunction with the upcoming Amazing Race. Maybe I'll even get some new customers that way."

"Who knows if it'll work?" Megan shrugged. "But you can try it."

"I just don't know why Sean Shaffer is doing this to me, Megan." Janey finally picked up the carafe again and poured water into the coffeemaker. "First the prom, and then this." She pushed the BREW button.

"Janey. . ." Once again Megan started to tell her she suspected that wasn't Sean's primary intention. He was probably just trying to make a life for himself back in Loveland. But doubting her friend would care to hear that, she gave Janey a reassuring smile instead. "It'll all be okay. Don't worry."

Janey nodded and gave Megan a smile, too, though a wan one at best. Her friend taken care of for the time being, Megan bent down to Sammy who had been patient beyond belief. Removing his ball cap, she kissed him on the forehead. "Ready, Samster?"

"Reh-hee," he replied, taking his cap from her hand and clumsily fitting it back on his head.

"Oh! I packed up some bear claws for MacNeill." Janey came from behind the counter with a bakery box. "And there're extras for you guys." She settled the box into Sammy's lap. "Don't eat them all up on the way to the farm."

"Not to worry," Megan promised.

Just hearing Mac's name—or even thinking about him—created an instant quiver in her stomach. She hadn't been able to eat anything all morning and didn't plan to anytime soon.

Mac was just pulling a navy T-shirt over his head when he heard the crunch of Megan's SUV on the gravel drive. He'd cut the time close, but everything had taken him longer to get ready than he thought it would.

Though he'd been getting better at cooking for himself the past few months, and even forced himself to settle in and watch a cooking show every now and then, it wasn't like he was a whiz in the kitchen by any means.

Pizzas might look easy with a little sauce and cheese and what-not on top, but when you were trying to make one from scratch—crust and all—there was more preparation involved than he would've thought. And the worst part was definitely the clean-up. Somehow he'd managed to have more sauce on the counters, floor, and wall than on the pizzas themselves.

He wasn't sure how the end result would taste, but he

thought the house sure smelled good when he took the pizzas from the oven. Wrapping them in foil, he packed them with three drinks, a salad, and some plates and plastic utensils in a broken-down but still usable picnic basket he'd found in his uncle's hall closet.

Setting the lunch on the island, he noticed his phone vibrating alongside it on the counter. Picking it up, he checked the display. Hal Halvorsen, his agent. Well, Hal's weekly check-in call would have to wait, Mac decided. Because he had something—actually a pair of someones—more important to attend to.

Sliding into a pair of Reefs by the front door, he sent a word of thanks heavenward for the sunshine as he sauntered outside to the driveway. Of course, the prettiness of the day wasn't even a contender where Megan was concerned. Already out of the car and opening up the trunk door, her hair was piled on top of her head and she had on some kind of yellowish dress that hit just above her knees, showing off the curve of her calves. She peeked at him over her sunglasses as he shuffled down the stone walkway toward her.

"Hey! Glad you made it. Let me help you with Sammy's wheelchair." He sidled up next to her.

"Hi." She seemed unusually shy to see him, and he had to admit as much as he was looking forward to her coming, he also felt a sudden twinge of awkwardness.

"Oh no—it's okay. I can get it. I'm used to it."

"I'm sure you are," he said, as he stepped closer and grabbed at the metal frame, his hands just inches from hers. "Got it." He lifted the chair out of the car, over her head, and onto the ground, suddenly aware of how many times a day—a week—a year—that Megan went through the same motions. Unfolding the chair, he took it upon himself to push it over to the rear passenger door where Sammy was buckled in.

"Mac. It you," Sammy chirped as Mac opened the car door.

"Yes, it's me, Sammy. How you doing, bud?" He unclipped the seat belt and lifted Sammy out of the car and into the wheelchair.

"Do good," Sammy answered him.

"He's always doing good, isn't he?" Mac smiled at Megan.

"Most of the time he is." She smiled back.

Mac pushed the chair out of the gravel and into a grassy area to the side of the driveway, feeling somewhat silly about how happy he was about the news he had to share. "So, Sammy. . .do you like surprises?"

Sammy gave a vigorous nod.

"Great, because I have a surprise for you."

"Suprise? For me?" Sammy grinned up at him before turning to his mom. "Buh it not my birt-day, is it, Maw-mee?"

"No." She laughed. "You've got a ways to go yet. Your birthday isn't until the week after All-Stars Sports Day."

"This is an everyday sort of surprise," Mac told them. "Actually it's just something I've been fiddling with."

"More whittling?" She lifted her sunglasses from her eyes, settling them on top of her head, exposing every pretty feature of her face to him.

So she'd remembered, had she? The thought made him smile.

"No, I've been doing some of that off and on. But this is something I made that's a lot different and a whole lot bigger. Something for Sammy and the other kids for the All-Stars Sports Day. I figured he could be the first one to test it out today before we get started on our work. If that's okay with you, that is."

He could see the curiosity in Megan's eyes—how she squinted at him even though the sun wasn't shining in her eyes in the least. Looking at him as if she was trying to figure it all out. Figure out why he was going to such ends. Couldn't she just believe he was doing things simply because he wanted to? Wasn't that reason enough?

She glanced at her son whose face glowed with excitement then back at Mac. Mac figured his excitement probably showed on his face as well. She shook her head, smiling as if she'd been outnumbered. "It's fine with me, Mac."

"Where surprise?" Sammy asked.

Mac motioned toward the clearing to the left of the house and barn. "It's right over there. Ready to see?"

Again, Sammy nodded with earnest, and having Megan's permission, Mac pushed on through the grass.

"Did you have a hard time finding the farm?" he asked as Megan walked by his side.

"Oh no. I'm somewhat familiar with these back roads. The only hard thing was getting away from Janey's bakery."

"Bring you bear claws," Sammy spurted out.

"Bear claws?" Mac chuckled. "My favorite."

"Oh, believe me, we know. Janey has signs all over Sweet Sensations."

"Signs?" He couldn't imagine what she was talking about.

"It's a long story, trust me, and. . ."

He'd been enjoying the first easy flow of conversation they'd had since she got there. It had taken Megan some time to even look his way when she spoke to him. But her chatter came to a halt when she spotted the wooden structure he'd created. She paused in her tracks. "What's that?"

"That's the surprise."

"Surprise for me," Sammy stated, growing more excited at the sight of the mass of wood.

"Yes, for you."

"I like it," Sammy said brightly, his enthusiasm never lacking. "I like it, Mac."

Mac laughed from his belly. "Like it? You don't even know what it is, do you?"

"No. Buh, I like it," Sammy answered him. "It from you."

Sammy's words caught Mac off guard, jarring his heart in an unexpected, touching way. Megan had raised one sweet kid. No wonder she wanted to protect him fiercely from all there was out there that could harm him or his spirit in any way. Mac could certainly understand and appreciate that. Why, just the way Sammy looked at him—with no judgment, no expectation—just pure joy and trust, like the world rose and set in him, made Mac want to make that happen.

"I hope you like bowling," he told Sammy.

"Like it on TV."

"Now you can do it yourself," he informed Sammy, pushing the wheelchair up against the wooden ramp. "At least I think it'll work," he told Megan. "I sort of did a test-drive myself. But we'll see how Sammy does. The ramp might need a little tweaking."

He grabbed a light bowling ball from a plastic container sitting next to the ramp and pulled out ten bowling pins from the bin.

"You're serious." Megan's lips crinkled into a mystified smile. "Aren't you?"

"Very." He set up the pins in a triangle a ways from the base of Sammy's chair. "I made the ramp adjustable. Sammy's chair looks like a good height for it the way it stands right now. But I figured not all kids would have chairs the same height. Or some kids might have longer torsos or whatever. Bottom line is, they need to be able to sit high enough to throw the ball down the ramp." He picked up the lightweight ball and handed it to Sammy, who didn't waste any time hurling the ball down the ramp, knocking over a majority of the pins.

"I good bowler," Sammy stated, pride in every word.

"Really good," Mac said, picking up the pins and ball, getting them all in position again. "Of course, we'll need several volunteers to help set up the pins and so on. And I do plan to paint the ramp and make it look decent. I also just put this wood down as a platform." He stomped on the sheets of plywood beneath their feet. "I figured I'd see Sammy in action first, make sure everything works before I get a cement guy out here to pour a slab and so on."

"I can't believe— I can't fathom you did all of this, Mac."

"It wasn't that big of a deal. I have time. And a barn where I set up a work table. Just did some measuring, hooked up a saw, and—"

"Didn't it hurt your elbow?"

He shrugged. "Not really."

"Do again?" Sammy asked.

Mac didn't know how many times he retrieved the ball and set up the pins for Sammy. Sammy's delight made it easy to keep at it, not noticing the minutes clipping by at all.

"My turn," Megan finally said. "You take a rest."

"No, it's okay. I can do it."

"Got it," she said firmly, grabbing the bowling ball from his hands. Then she smiled, letting him know she was only mimicking the way he'd taken over, grabbing up Sammy's wheelchair earlier.

She kept smiling, too. Every time Sammy knocked down the pins, she clapped for her son, and then looked back at Mac, thanking him with her smile before she set up the pins all over again. And as Sammy and Megan's laughter rang out across the fields, Mac couldn't think of anywhere he'd rather be. Somehow it all felt so much better than other days he'd spent in the sun, even the days with thousands of fans cheering his name.

Chapter 10

M egan couldn't believe how nervous she'd been on the drive out to Mac's place. Now she couldn't believe how relaxed she felt, sitting on a patchwork quilt on his lawn, the length of his long, lean body stretched out beside her.

Mild rays of sunshine dripped languidly from the sky like rich golden honey, sweetening their spot on the grass below. A gentle June afternoon breeze ruffled the leafy limbs of the maple tree overhead, partially shading the faded blanket that looked like it'd seen many a picnic in its day. Letting her head fall back on her shoulders, Megan marveled at how peaceful she felt soaking in both the warmth of the sun and the caress of the breeze.

"It's wonderful here, Mac." She sighed.

"It's a perfect day, isn't it?" He looked around the grounds appreciatively before nodding down at Sammy who was sleeping soundly, his head nestled in her lap. "I think the bowling wore him out." His mouth curved with surprising tenderness at the sight of her sleeping child.

"Yes, the bowling and Bitty." With a gentle touch, not wanting to wake him, she brushed aside the hair from Sammy's forehead. "He really enjoyed playing with Bitty."

Her eyes settled on the gray-and-white barn cat that had wrapped itself into a curlicue and lay napping by

Sammy's side. Such a sweet sight, Megan didn't bother to mention how excited Sammy had been the night before— so excited he hadn't gotten to sleep until late.

Of course, she didn't dare say that she hadn't slept well either, worrisome thoughts about spending time alone in Mac's company busying her mind into the wee hours of the night as well.

"I don't think I've ever seen him eat so much pizza. I haven't either, come to think of it." She laughed. "It was delicious, Mac. You really made it all by yourself?"

"Would this face lie to you?"

Her gaze shifted to his smooth-shaven jawline, still uncomfortable with the way her cheeks involuntarily warmed every time she looked at him. Though she knew his question was rhetorical, inwardly she automatically responded anyway, calculating all she'd seen—and felt—in the past couple of hours.

After all, as much as she wanted to believe it was only the tranquil setting responsible for their special outing, looking at Mac, she knew it wasn't true. There was no denying he had gone to a lot of trouble to make her and Sammy feel welcome and at ease—starting with his insistence on getting Sammy's wheelchair out of her car. Then there was the surprise of the bowling ramp he'd built. Along with the pizza he'd made from scratch. And the quilt and picnic basket? Somehow he'd managed to find them somewhere or another.

Plus, there were no news cameras around to record his hospitality. No reporters taking notes. Was it foolish of her to believe there was no deception in his motives?

"What made you think of the bowling ramp?"

"I'm not sure." His broad shoulder crooked upward. "About a week ago, I woke up around three a.m. and couldn't get the idea out of my head."

"Do you always wake up in the middle of the night with things on your mind?"

"Yeah." His brow tilted. "Yeah, actually I do."

She'd been referring to the after-midnight whittling incident Mac had told her about, but the way he steadied his eyes on hers. . .well, it made her think he was referring to something quite different. Something that might have to do with her. Causing her breath to hitch as she struggled to look away from him, out onto the acres of sun-soaked fields and woods. Exactly where they needed to get going to, she reminded herself. That *is* why she'd driven all the way out to the farm in the first place.

"I think we should go have a look around your property now, don't you?"

"I can carry Sammy into the house if you want," Mac offered. "He can nap on the couch or in my bed."

"Oh." She straightened. "I think he'll be okay here. Can we just keep a watch on him?"

"We'll make sure not to walk out of eye range."

Sammy barely stirred when she lifted his head from her lap and settled him gently on the quilt, making sure the shady limbs covered him. Mac held out his hand to help her up, and though she was reluctant to grasp it at first, not wanting to think about his fingers closing around hers for even an instant, she did anyway.

He pulled her to her feet and she was acutely

conscious of his tall, athletic physique—taller than what she usually felt comfortable around. Even still, she noticed that his powerful, well-muscled body moved with easy grace through the grassy field. All around them was land as far as the eye could see, and on the outskirts of that, copses of trees that hemmed in the property on all sides. A small pond broke up all that green with a glittering blue where a few ducks lazily glided across the water.

Wildflowers grew in clumps every so often, dotting the earth with golden yellows and royal purples. But even though he had ownership of all that land and beauty, Megan noticed Mac seemed more excited by it rather than proprietary.

"Your uncle lived here all of his life, didn't he?"

"Most of his adult life. It was great for me, coming out here to visit him."

"Did he ever get lonely? I mean when you weren't around?"

"I don't think so. Uncle Jake had a lot going on, and he was married for a while, you know."

"Oh? There was a Mrs. Lochen?"

Mac nodded. "She passed when she was fairly young, and they hadn't had any children. I don't remember her very well; I was so young at the time. All I know is there was no other woman Uncle Jake ever talked about after Aunt Emily died."

She let the information sink in. Funny, how she'd known there was a Lochen Farm owned by Jake Lochen and had passed the place more times than she could count, but she hadn't known Mac's mother's brother or realized his ties to Mac. She also had no clue as to how pretty the Lochen property was beyond what she could see from the road.

"Are you sure you want to host the event here? I mean, aren't you concerned it might make a mess of your land?"

"It's nothing that can't be cleaned up." Mac shrugged. "And it's for a good cause, Megan. Of course I want to host it."

"What about parking? Where do you see the cars going? You don't want them to damage any of the grass and all."

"They won't," he said easily before turning to look back from where they'd come. "I'm thinking the area up where Sammy's napping would be best for the parking—in the lawn that lays in the front of the house and to the sides. That's a few acres and can easily fit hundreds of cars."

"You've actually been thinking about this. I'm surprised." The realization caught her off guard and so did her words, blurted out with no filter.

"Of course I've been thinking about it. Why wouldn't I be?" His brow furrowed quizzically, but only for a split second before he continued, "There are eight events, right?"

"Maria is chairing the Events Committee, but yes." She nodded. "I think at last count there were eight. Oh, and now the bowling ramp makes nine."

"Nine events, which can be spread over this expanse of fields."

He waved his arms wide, visibly excited to be offering his property to her. She felt her excitement growing along with his as they scanned the acreage together.

"We need to make room for bleachers at each event," she noted.

"Bleachers, definitely. I'll get out the tractor and get this place mowed. I'm also planning to have a temporary fence put up around the pond. I don't want anyone to fall in. Or try to jump in."

"We'll find the money in the budget for that, Mac," she assured him. "You shouldn't have to pay for it."

"Not necessary. It's on me."

"Thanks, Mac, that's really nice of you, but. . ."

"You know. . ." He picked up a clump of dirt from the ground with his left hand, flinging it off into the distance. Turning to her, his words slowed to a lazy drawl, making each sound more emphatic. "You were doing really well till you got to that 'but' part. How about just saying, 'Thanks, Mac, that's really nice of you?'"

He gazed into her eyes, and she caught a flicker of humor twinkling there. But even more, she sensed an invitation. An invitation for them to come to terms with one another. To be friends.

Or more?

She wasn't sure as his lips curved in that irresistible MacNeill Hattaway grin, causing her heart to flutter against her will. Causing her to concede to his wishes, even though she didn't want "something for nothing" from him or anyone else.

But for the sake of moving ahead without contention and just to get out from under that smile of his that could blind more than the June sun, she swallowed hard and answered him.

"Mac, thanks. That's, um, really nice of you."

"You're welcome, Megan."

Grateful for an excuse to tear her eyes from his, she glanced over her shoulder to check on Sammy. He and Bitty were still cuddled up together, fast asleep.

"Looks like they're down for the count." Mac chuckled. "Want to walk some more?"

She nodded, and both mindful not to stray out of eyesight, they surveyed more of the farmland, discussing which event would fit which part of the property best. Again, Megan felt mildly shocked at how much thought Mac had put into the planning already and felt even more ashamed than she had earlier. Had she really misjudged him so badly?

"You—you really do want to help, don't you?" Her thoughts tumbled out loud again, and though she hoped they sounded complimentary, especially compared to what she had been thinking about Mac just weeks...actually only hours before, evidently it didn't sound the same to him.

Suddenly his jaw clenched noticeably, and she'd never heard his voice so harsh as he replied, "I wouldn't have signed up for the job if I didn't want to, Megan."

So much for the peaceful, unspoken truce they'd established just minutes before. "Well, I mean—" He stopped her before she could blurt out an explanation.

"I can tell you exactly what you mean." He paused for a moment, and when he spoke again his voice took on a calmer tone. "You think I'm doing this for myself, don't you? You think that I'm trying to get back into the good graces of the public again. That I figure they'll forgive me, and then I can turn around and do the same irresponsible things all over again. Right?"

"Well, I. . ." She bowed her head. It was true, everything

he said was true. She'd judged him for his past and would barely let his present actions count for anything. But, oh, how she was sorry for that now. If there's anything she remembered from her Christian upbringing it was not to judge others—and she usually wasn't hard on anyone—but herself.

"Mac, I'm sorry. I really, truly am. I've been unfair."

With the crook of his index finger, he gently lifted her chin. "Don't be sorry, Megan. Really. It's all right."

But it wasn't all right. She'd sat in judgment of Mac because it had been so easy. After all, the newspapers and tabloids had already done the work for her. She'd rolled her eyes when most of the locals stood behind him, even with her parents and the volunteers. Most of them had gotten past his former indiscretions. They were thrilled to be working with him and giving him a second chance.

But not her. Oh no. She couldn't let it go, could she? She couldn't because—

She gasped at the realization. It was because she was afraid. Afraid ever since that rainy night when she'd jumped out of her car shaking her finger at the tall, good-looking guy whose concern showed all over his handsome face. Ever since then she'd felt the need to protect her feelings. To protect her heart.

Oh yes, she'd made up a whole list of reasons in her mind why MacNeill Hattaway was so awful. Why he couldn't be trusted. But at the core of that was her heart, and in her heart she hadn't been feeling that way about him at all.

The truth was, the more she was around him, the more she couldn't stop thinking about him. She couldn't stop blushing when he looked at her. And she hadn't wanted him to help chair the event partly because just the thought of standing next to him made her stomach go all jittery and. . .

"Mac, I—"

Ever so softly he pressed a finger to her lips. "Megan, listen, it's okay. You're right. You are," he repeated. "I am helping out with the All-Stars Sports Day event for me. I am doing it for myself."

She felt her eyes grow wide as she gazed into his narrow ones, his admission sending her emotions into a jumble all over again.

He could feel his temper rising at Megan's question, but it wasn't because of her or what she asked. It was because of him. He just wanted to be with her. To share the perfect day in the present. But it wasn't that easy—not with his past dragging everything down again. Not that he didn't deserve it of course.

Still, he hated seeing the way the distrust appeared so quickly again in her eyes. But then, he did set her up for that, didn't he? He needed to explain exactly what he meant, once and for all. Then maybe she'd believe him. Then maybe her eyes would reflect the trust and appreciation he'd caught a glimpse of earlier.

"Look, I don't blame you for your speculations. But what I'm saying is, it's not in the way you think, Megan." His voice softened. "Yes, I'm doing this for myself. I am. But only because I don't want to be the same insensitive, self-involved guy I was before."

He paused, looking away from her, watching a blue jay flit from one tree to the next while working to gather his thoughts before he spoke. "I felt honored, blessed, when Ted asked me to help with the special-needs kids. Honestly, I felt lucky he'd even talk to me again."

She crooked her head upward. "You and Ted? I got the impression you two were friends."

"Yeah, well, Ted and I played knothole as kids. He was the only person I stayed in touch with from Loveland all through my growing-up years. But that was mostly because our moms stayed friends after our move."

He searched for the blue jay again, wanting to look anywhere but at Megan, hating to admit what he was about to. "I was never that great of a friend to Ted, though. I missed out on his wedding. Our team was playing out in L.A. at the time and of course, I was scheduled to pitch."

"It's not like you could help that, Mac."

"No, but I didn't even acknowledge his big day with a present and. . ." He shrugged, not in a big rush to tell the worst of it, the part he felt most guilty about. "The thing is, the Hawks were in town years later when I got news that Ted and Wendy had a little girl with cystic fibrosis. Yes, I was here, and I could've easily made a phone call or gone to the hospital for a show of support. But it seemed too hard. Too hard for me. That's all I thought about. Myself. It was easier to go out and party after our series than to think about what was going on in Ted's life. I didn't feel like I had any words of wisdom to share with him and Wendy, so I took the easy way out. I just didn't show up."

The light, consoling touch of Megan's hand on his arm

made him turn to face her.

"I'm sure it was an awkward time for them as well, Mac. It can be unbearably difficult at first—when you find out the precious baby you've come to love so completely for nine months—or in Sammy's case, seven months—is born physically or mentally challenged."

He started to ask her questions, but then thought better of it. Maybe, like him, she just needed to explain herself.

She slid her hand away and continued rubbing the material of her dress between her fingers like she might a worry stone. "Your emotions are totally jarred. There's so much you can't comprehend. All the while you're carrying your darling little baby, all you can think about is them and their future. And then the baby is born and all of that isn't a reality anymore. You're so unsure of everything, so worried about any possibility of a future your child might ever have."

"So, you didn't know about Sammy until he was born?"

"Not at all. His development was proceeding just fine. My pregnancy was textbook perfect. And then, seven months into it I began having problems that forced Sammy to be born prematurely. The cerebral palsy is a result of that."

He couldn't imagine how hard that must've been, to think everything's fine, and then suddenly not turn out like that at all. Obviously, the only thing he had to compare it to was being ahead in runs going into the bottom of the ninth and then having the last batter up hit a grand slam. But how banal was that? Having a life—your baby's life and livelihood at stake—was something he honestly couldn't fathom.

"I was a mess. I didn't want to see anyone. I was ugly, blaming myself. Blaming God. And blaming myself again when my husband, Sammy's daddy, walked out on us months later, thinking how I should've never married him in the first place."

Megan shook her head and fingered the wisps of hair around her face and at the back of her neck, tucking them all back into place. Almost like she had said too much and was trying to pull herself together again.

"That sounds like a normal reaction," he offered, wishing he'd been there with her. But then that was a dumb thing to think. Six years ago, he'd been a mess, for a whole other set of reasons.

"It wasn't pretty. But, oh, what a handsome little guy my Sammy was!" She brightened at the mention of his name. "When I'd see him sleeping or lying in his crib it was so hard to believe there was anything less than perfect about him."

"And that's probably all you see in him now. Perfection."

"You're right." Her smile warmed him, a reward for his insight. Not that he'd had to think very hard about it. Pride for her son was written all over Megan's face.

"So I guess what I'm saying is that in the beginning—I mean, even if Ted knew about Hannah's condition—it may not have been a good time to visit him and Wendy anyway."

"I could say that if I'd even tried, Megan. But fact is, I didn't. Thanks for your absolution, though."

All that being said, it felt like time to move on, now that they'd put some remnants of their pasts to rest. Walking in comfortable silence, they came to shorter patches of grass, where a white oak tree that appeared to be as old as the settlement of Loveland itself stood with its branches stretching out in every direction like points on a compass.

"What a great tree." Megan stopped to admire the oak before moving closer to lean against the massive, solid trunk.

"I climbed it more than a few times back in the day." Mac rubbed his hand over the lowest branch, noting how the bark had smoothed over time.

"What's that over there?" She pointed to the corner of the field where he'd spent a considerable amount of time as a kid. "It looks like there's a fence or— Oh, is that a baseball diamond or something?"

He laughed. "A little hard to detect it's so overgrown. But yeah, that's where my uncle taught me all about baseball. Well, baseball and life—and all about God, too. That's why I couldn't ever let anyone else buy this place when Uncle Jake passed. I had to have it for myself. There are too many memories here. A lot of good memories."

"Better memories than your World Series win?"

"Different for sure. Richer in a way."

"So. . .did you always like baseball?" Megan squinted into the sunlight that flickered through the limbs of the tree, looking so pretty with her face turned up at him that it took him a second to process her question.

"Like it? Uh, no. I loved it. Always did. Loved everything about it, even the history and trivia of baseball. For example, did you know before the first catcher's mask was developed in the late eighteen hundreds, catchers wore rubber bands around their teeth to try to protect them?"

"Really?" She smiled. "I've never even thought about anything like that."

"Yeah, well, I probably did because I burned to know about every aspect of the game. I loved the tools of the trade.

Always cleaned off my bats, and I'll never forget how good it felt when my parents bought my first real baseball mitt for me." He shook his head remembering. "I really loved the smell of that thing."

She giggled at that, the sound drawing a smile to his face. "The smell of your mitt?"

"Oh yeah." He chuckled with her. "The smell of a leather mitt always got to me."

"That's funny."

"Not really. You're the same way."

"The same way? Uh, I don't think so. I do not go around sniffing baseball mitts." She laughed.

"No, but you take in the aroma of what you love."

She scrunched her face at him.

"It's true. I've seen you smell an apple before you bite into it. And many times I've seen you sift your fingers through Sammy's hair, and then take a whiff of it before you kiss him on the head."

"Ha! That makes me sound like some kind of mother dog or something."

"You do have sort of floppy ears now that I'm noticing."

"Floppy ears?" She gave a playful shove to his shoulder. "I don't have floppy ears."

"I'm kidding. You actually have very cute ears." He watched as she fingered one of her tiny pearl earrings. *And a cute nose. And sweet lips. And. . .* "I'm just saying you can't get enough of your little guy you love him so much. Even the scent of him."

Her expression sobered instantly. Suddenly she looked at him as if she was seeing him for the first time. "And that's—that's how much you love baseball?"

"That's how much I loved baseball." He nodded. "I'd fall asleep with my mitt covering my face at night, and I'd have it sitting on the table near my cereal bowl each morning. I read everything about the game I could. Played every day, even if I'd have to toss the ball up against the side of the house by myself. There was nothing, not one thing, I wanted to do more. Not one thing I loved better."

"You keep—you keep saying loved. As in past tense. . ." She hesitated before she asked, "Are you afraid you won't play again?"

He smiled. "No, it's not that. I can feel my elbow is improving all the time, and God willing, it will heal completely. I still love baseball, trust me. It's still deep in my blood."

He could tell she wasn't about to press him, yet he continued anyway. "But I've learned success can take something that you love—something simple and pure like throwing a ball over a plate—and make it all complicated and twisted if you let it. And of course, over time, I let it. I let everything get to me. The ups. The downs. The money. The fame. The simple thing I loved got tainted in the process. If I get the chance to play again, I hope I'm smarter than that this time around. I hope I've learned my lesson."

"I bet your uncle enjoyed sharing that success with you, though. I bet he was really proud."

"He was. But, knowing Uncle Jake, I think he'd be even more proud of me today. Now that I'm trying to get back to the basics he taught me. Especially back to the kid-like faith I used to have."

He couldn't believe how much he'd said. Things he'd never told anyone else before. Things he'd never felt comfortable sharing. But it seemed in the short walk around the property, they'd come a long way.

And suddenly he realized there was another scent he was falling in love with. The scent of Megan. Sweet as the blossoms on the purple bush that blossomed outside his bedroom window all through the month of May. Fresh as the sunshine warming the back of his neck as he stood facing her. Megan, so wholesome and pure, like no other woman he'd ever known. Megan, with eyes he wanted to get lost in, who went through every day not seeing how beautiful she was inside and out.

Like the young boy who wanted to know everything about the sport he loved, he was a grown man who wanted to know everything about the woman in front of him. He wanted so badly to touch her face, her hair—to know what those lips that drove him beyond crazy would feel like pressed against his.

Placing his hand on the trunk of the mighty oak tree, next to her shoulder, he started to lean toward her.

He'd never asked permission to kiss a girl before. Women had always given themselves up willingly to him. But Megan wasn't just any woman. With her, it felt only right to ask for such a perfect gift.

Her lips seemed to part in expectation as he stepped closer still. Her hands came up, covering his chest.

In every way she appeared as ready as he was. Still, he wanted to be sure. He wanted to ask.

"Megan, may I . . ."

But before he could get the rest of the words from his mouth, she screamed. She pushed hard at his chest, shoving him away.

Chapter 11

"What do you think, Meg?"

Later the next afternoon, Megan gazed at her mom who stood outside the dressing room in a glittery, pearl-white gown, balancing herself on her tiptoes.

"This dress? Or did you like the blue one better?" Her mom worried her lip, but even as she did so, she couldn't contain the excitement bubbling up inside her. "Oh, I can't even remember the last time your dad and I had a black-tie affair to go to," she said, sounding as giddy as one of the high school girls Megan imagined her father counseling. "Whose idea was it anyway? To have a black-tie fund-raiser for your sports day event? Wendy Slater's? I've told you the story, haven't I, how we gals at We Do! got Wendy and Ted together?"

Megan could not only see her mother clearly from where she sat in the mauve retro-round accent chair in Sophisticates Boutique, she could hear her plainly, too. But focusing on her mom's words was a whole other matter. And trying to decipher which of her mother's questions to answer first, even more challenging. Her mind was still far away, high up in the clouds. Still trying to wrap itself around the fact that she'd almost kissed MacNeill Hattaway.

Almost. Kissed. Mac.

Her mind wouldn't stop repeating the news to her heart—as if her heart needed any more reminding. As it was, it felt like it'd been positively beating out of her chest all day long.

"Megan, are you feeling okay?" Her mom came down on the balls of her feet, the gown swishing as she leaned forward. "Your cheeks look so flushed, honey, and you don't seem to be very 'with it' today. Have you been taking your vitamins? How's your sleep been lately?"

"I'm fine. Really, no worries, Mom. I'm good."

Even though, no, she hadn't gotten much sleep. Again. But there was no way she was going to mention that to her mom, who would only ask why. And what would Megan tell her? That she'd been awake most of the night, wondering about Mac once more? This time, imagining what it might have been like to actually kiss him?

Her mom would be so thrilled she'd want to throw a party for all of Loveland—or assemble a parade, complete with a marching band to traipse down the main street of town.

So, no, the almost-kiss with Mac had to remain a secret for now. One she could barely believe herself.

"Well, if you're sure you're okay. . ." Her mom tilted her head.

"I'm sure," Megan replied as convincingly as she could, not wanting to cause any worry. After all, her mom was so excited for them to be spending an afternoon together. Her dad had taken Sammy for the day, giving her and her mom time to have a leisurely salad at Paxton's and to visit with Allie before wandering into Sophisticates a few blocks over.

Even though the fund-raiser dance was still many weeks away, Mom was determined to make the most of their excursion.

"Well then, which dress works best?" Her mom poised a forefinger thoughtfully to her cheek. "Your dad really likes me in blue. But I don't know. The blue dress was more elegant. This dress is more glitzy."

"Can you try on the blue one again so I can make a better comparison?"

If truth be known, Megan had been daydreaming so much, she hadn't really zeroed in on the blue formal the first time around. Luckily, her mom hadn't noticed and looked more than happy to oblige. "Good idea!" She headed back into the dressing room.

Good idea. . . . Megan settled back against the throw pillows once more. *Really, had it been a good idea?* To let Mac get so close to her?

But then. . .it had all happened so quickly. One minute she was leaning up against the tree and they were talking, and the next minute he was moving closer and closer.

And she didn't do anything to try to stop him because— well, because during the hours they'd spent together he'd been so tender and sensitive. So much so, she found herself crazily wondering if his lips would feel that way, too. And then, when he started to ask permission to kiss her, it was so sweet. A side of Mac she never knew existed. In response, she couldn't help but tilt her head up toward his. As she did, that's when she heard the rustling in a patch of trees just off to the side of where they were standing.

That's when she spotted a man through the trees

holding a camera, aimed in their direction.

That's when instead of kissing Mac's lips, she screamed bloody murder right into his ears.

She cringed at the very thought, then straightened abruptly as her mom slipped out of the dressing room.

"Here I am in blue again." She rose up on her tiptoes once more. "I'm just not sure." She smoothed the front of the satin gown. "Are you?"

Sure? Megan wasn't sure about anything these days. So confused that she'd actually prayed the night before—for herself. Something rare for her. But she needed some kind of clarity. Badly. She wasn't sure what to think at all about the feelings washing over her heart lately. Where was it all coming from?

After Mac's attempt at kissing her was interrupted, he went chasing after the intruder, and she went running to make sure Sammy was all right. She really wanted to believe it when Mac came back out of breath, apologizing for her having been frightened. She really wanted to trust him when he told her he'd had the same thing happen a couple of times since he'd lived there, but he hadn't done anything because he didn't like the idea of putting barbed wire around the property. Deep down, she really wanted it to be true that he hadn't hired someone to take a picture of them together—that it wasn't a part of some crazy publicity stunt.

Yes, she wanted to believe him, and the weirdest part was, she wasn't even sure why. The only thing she knew for certain is that after the awkward incident she doubted Mac would ever want to try to kiss her again. He probably thought she was some kind of excitable nut case. And who could blame him?

On a simpler note, the other thing she could be sure of—now that she was forcing herself to concentrate—was the best dress for her mother.

"Dad's right, Mom. Blue is definitely your color. That gown makes your eyes pop, and it's a great style for you. You're such a young-looking nana."

"Wow! Do you really think so? I guess it's worth every penny then."

Her mom beamed as she headed back to the dressing room, but before she slid back the curtain, she turned. "Are you sure you don't want to try on a few dresses while we're here?"

"No, I'm fine."

"Oh, come on. We have time. How often do you and I get to shop like this?"

Megan knew her mom was right and didn't want to disappoint her. Especially not on their rare mother-daughter day. Plus, she had spied a few dresses she wouldn't mind trying on.

While her mom changed back into her street clothes and a sales associate took the blue gown they'd decided on up to the counter, Megan sifted through the racks, studying the dresses and price tags. After selecting several possibilities that matched both her criteria, she headed to the dressing room while her mom switched places with her, settling into the mauve chair.

It reminded her of the past, of shopping for homecoming dresses and sorority formals the way her mom oohed and aahed over each selection. But when she tried on a one-shoulder, red satin gown, the look that came over her mom's face confirmed what she thought. The dress was definitely the one.

"It's really pretty, isn't it?" She ran her hand over the expensive-feeling material.

"*You're* really pretty. I love how striking it looks with your dark hair. That dress looks like it was made for you, Meg." Her mom got up from the chair only to crouch down and smooth out the slightly flared hemline. Then she stepped back, her arms crossed over her chest, her eyes skimming Megan up and down, up and down, appraisingly.

Megan was sure her mom was considering what shoes would look best with the gown. So it stood to reason her tuna melt lunch did a flip in her stomach when out of nowhere her mom asked, "What about Mac?"

"Mac?" Her cheeks tingled just saying his name. "What about Mac?"

"Is he wearing a white tux or a black one?"

A tux? She almost gulped aloud. Nearly the last thing she wanted to think about was Mac. And the *very* last thing she wanted to think about was Mac in a tux, and how handsome he'd look in one. "I have no clue, Mom."

"You mean you're not going together?"

"Going together? I don't know. The dance isn't for weeks."

"Well, I just assumed you might, being you're both the co-chairs."

"Yes, but. . ."

"I'm just thinking the press and everyone will be taking pictures of the two of you together. But black or white, either color of tux will work well with the red."

Black or white? Megan wished it was all as simple as that. But just thinking that Mac could be taking someone else to the dance suddenly made her stomach drop, leaving her feeling all topsy-turvy like a silly young schoolgirl with a crush. That was exactly why she didn't want to get all caught up in feelings for him or anyone else. She had enough things in her life that she needed to keep under control. Her son and his happiness and welfare. Her job. Her standing in the community. Who had room for anything else? For things like crushes. And kisses. And—she shivered. . .

"Whatever. I love the dress. I'm getting it."

"Good. While you get changed, I'm going to check out the evening bags. I haven't had a new one in eons." Her mom nodded toward the display of purses by the window. "Wait a minute. Is that—?"

"What?" Megan stepped down from the mirrored platform, peering in the same general direction.

"Is that Janey?" Her mom pointed toward the window.

Instantly, Megan spotted the person her mom was talking about and just as quickly she understood the reason her mom had such a puzzled look on her face.

"It does look like her, doesn't it?" Megan stuck out her neck to get a better view as the Janey look-alike, pausing to put on a pair of sunglasses, resumed her brisk pace down the sidewalk.

"Exactly like her."

"But with long red hair. Hmm. That's weird."

"Yes. . .weird."

She and her mom turned to each other and shrugged, neither able to put the pieces together. Clearly, nothing really was as simple as black and white.

Mac cut the power on the riding lawn mower the moment he caught sight of Bill Helmsley standing in the driveway. Evidently Bill had finished putting together the estimates Mac had asked for.

Sliding off the mower, he brushed some dry blades of grass from his faded jeans as he walked toward Bill, already having a fairly good idea of what the man was about to say before he said it.

"How's it look?" Mac tipped his baseball cap back on his head.

"Well, I went through the whole house, and I tried to make the estimates as reasonable as I could. But…" Bill sucked in some air and slid several papers from a clipboard, handing them to Mac. He shook his head as he continued. "There's just not much way around most of the improvements you want to make. It's an old house, you know? Narrow halls and steep stairways. It's going to take some money and creativity to make your house wheelchair friendly. That's all there is to it. But I guess you already knew that, didn't you?"

"I figured as much." Mac took the papers and without looking at them, folded the estimates in quarters before tucking them into his back pocket. He liked the remodeling contractor Ted had hooked him up with the minute he'd met him, sensing he was honest and straightforward, so he didn't hesitate to ask, "When's the soonest your crew can get to work?"

"Yesterday."

Mac crooked a smile. "That sounds good. Just give me a day to look over the estimates to see if I have any questions. Then I'll give you a call and you can get started."

"Sounds great, Mr. Hattaway."

"Mac." He held out his right hand.

"Yeah, Mac. Thanks." Bill shook his hand. "I'll look forward to hearing from you."

As Bill's pickup backed out the driveway, Mac turned to look out into the fields. He'd walked the grounds earlier in the day with a sales rep from a local company who said they could supply materials for a rubberized walkway. Luckily, it wouldn't be any problem to put the rubber pathway over the grasses to construct a temporary sidewalk for the wheelchair participants and their families on event day.

But just like hours earlier, his eyes veered from the grassy meadows and caught sight of the oak tree where he'd nearly kissed Megan. And for the second time that day, he didn't know whether to laugh or frown about his near-kiss miss.

It was just his bad luck, wasn't it, that a stranger would be lurking on his property at the very moment he was about to become acquainted with Megan's sweet lips? Scaring her half to death. At least scaring her enough that she just about busted his eardrum with her scream.

Or maybe. . .

He squinted at the formidable oak and could almost see Megan leaning up against it in her pretty yellow dress again.

Could almost hear the brave tremor in her voice as she recounted the circumstances surrounding Sammy's birth, including the way her husband walked out on their family. That must've hurt to the quick, he imagined. But Megan squared her shoulders as she spoke about it, and her courageous front only made him respect and care for her even more.

So, yeah. . .

Maybe it had been a good thing that they hadn't kissed after all.

Not that he liked dwelling on that. Not that he didn't still want to kiss her in the worst way. In fact, kissing Megan was pretty much at the top of his mind every time he saw her. And he hated to admit it—couldn't even believe he was thinking it—but there it was: Kissing Megan was on his mind all the time he wasn't near her, too.

Even so, maybe it would be better to slow things down. *Let her know I'm sincere. Not try to push her into something she might not be ready for.*

Ah, man. . . He groaned inwardly, his insides protesting at the thought. *Do I really want to do that?*

Watching long shadows blanket and retreat from the fields over and over again as the sun drifted in and out of the clouds, he stood weighing his options.

Yeah. . .I'll take it slow, he finally resolved to himself. *Take my time,* he vowed. *And be sure not to look at that big old oak tree anymore, reminding me what I missed out on.*

It sure wouldn't be easy. He shook his head. But if he won Megan's heart as a result then his restraint would be worth it.

In the meantime, he was still going to go forward with his plans to make his house wheelchair accessible. He had to do something to make himself feel hopeful, like he was moving ahead in a relationship with Megan. He had to do something that would hold some kind of promise that she and Sammy would stay a part of his life.

What else was there to do? Except maybe have another talk with God.

Oh Lord, this isn't easy. Putting my pride aside and being patient where Megan is concerned. Not even knowing where it's all leading. Or if it will lead anywhere. But, as uncomfortable as it is, Lord, I'll try because Megan and Sammy are the best things that have ever happened to me. I have these deep feelings for them. Feelings like I've never had before—and, well, I thank You for this chance, Lord, I do. And if it ends up Megan and I are just friends, I guess I'll have to put up with that. But I hope that's not what You want, Lord. He looked up at the wisps of clouds stretched across the sky.

I don't think that's what You want. Do You?

Chapter 12

A nd these are my parents, Laura and Kurt O'Donnell."
Mac extended his hand as Megan introduced him
to the couple sitting in the matching lawn chairs on the
Nisbet Park ground. Wearing bright neon runners' gear,
they fit right in with the sportive backdrop of the park,
which was decked out with colorful balloons and banners
for Loveland's Amazing Race festival.

"It's nice to meet you both," he said sincerely.

"It's *really* nice to meet you, MacNeill." Megan's father
hopped up from the chair, pumping his hand.

"Excuse us if we're a bit sweaty and disheveled from the
race," her mother added, her blue eyes and welcoming smile
reminding him a lot of Megan.

"Are you kidding? I think it's great you both signed up
for the Amazing Race," Mac told them.

"They've been participating since the initial event years
ago," Megan chimed in.

"Yeah well, it's a fun event." Kurt chuckled. "Even if I
will be sore tomorrow."

"I know I'd be," Mac agreed. "It sounds like a grueling
triathlon."

"Ah, it's not so grueling. And it's not really a triathlon
either." Kurt shook his head. "Even though you are on foot,
traipsing through downtown Loveland. And then, you're on

a bicycle on the bike trail. And you even do some tubing on the Little Miami River. But what's different is all along the way, they have these challenge stations set up. Kind of loosely based on that TV show."

"Very loosely," Laura added.

"That's what I said, honey." Kurt raised a brow. "Isn't that what I said?" He glanced at Mac who then glanced at Megan who only shrugged and smiled.

"Yeah well, I'm sure it's a good time," Mac replied. "I wasn't even aware Loveland had an event like this until Sammy mentioned it."

He had hoped maybe Megan had put Sammy up to inviting him to the after-race festival when the two had been out to visit his farm the week before. But when all was said and done, he doubted it. Sammy had probably done it all on his own. But, whatever. He wasn't going to be picky about where the invitation had come from. He was just glad to be there. After all, it felt like a month of Sundays since he'd spent any time with Megan and Sammy, even though it'd been closer to seven days.

He'd been glad, too, that Sammy had noticed his new truck by the side of the barn the week before and asked for a ride in it. Megan had reprimanded Sammy for being so forward. But for Mac, it wasn't an inconvenience at all. It gave him the perfect excuse to pick up Sammy and Megan for the festival.

"Well, I'd say you were probably busy with more important things in past summers than our Amazing Race. Like traveling around the country striking out batters, right?" Kurt asked, a wide grin spanning his face.

"I don't know how important that was..." Mac shrugged. "But yeah, that was the objective."

He felt Megan lay her hand on his forearm, trying to direct his attention to the other folks seated around them. "And this is Allie and her husband, Greg. But I'm guessing you may already know them from Paxton's."

"I do." He nodded at the couple spread out on a blanket with their daughter and son. "I can't stay away from the place."

"And we're glad." Allie smiled.

"Definitely." Greg nodded. "Thanks again, Mac, for all your help with our Major League night at the grill a few weeks ago."

"Not a big deal. Just signed some autographs."

"You helped out at the grill?" Megan turned to him, her face registering surprise. "Where was I that night?"

"I don't know. But Mac's being humble. It *absolutely* was a big deal," Greg replied. "Your being there that night brought in a slew of people, Mac," he reconfirmed. "We made a lot of money for the community peewee teams, which we wouldn't have done without you."

"Ahh-hem. Ahh-hem."

The woman, sitting in a lawn chair next to a man close to her age, audibly cleared her throat. Donning a lavender visor over her blond-highlighted hair, she also wore a teasing smile.

Megan laughed and reached out to pat the woman's shoulder. "And, Mac, last but certainly not least in my heart, these are Allie's parents and my second parents, Pam and Jim Matthews. They always sign up for the race with Mom and Dad."

"Nice to meet you, Mac." Pam reached out. "I work with Megan's mom."

"Oh yeah?" Mac shook her hand. "What do you all do?"

"You don't want to go there," Greg called out.

Mac turned to Megan who only blinked, suddenly seeming slightly uncomfortable. He held out his hands, not understanding. "What?"

"Oh, Greg's just being silly." Pam waved a playful hand in her son-in-law's direction. "Megan's mom and I plan weddings. We've been friends forever and so have our girls. Allie and Megan practically shared the same pumpkin seat."

"Pumpkin what?" Again, Mac was having a hard time understanding.

Jim laughed as he stood up to shake Mac's hand. "Pumpkin seats. Don't worry. We've heard it a thousand times, Mac. The girls have been together since they were wee little and cute as pumpkins sitting in their pumpkin seats."

"Ah—well. I believe it," he said, still wondering if they were actually talking about a pumpkin-shaped seat.

"So, how's the pitching arm doing?" Mac got the sense Jim was trying to segue to more manly topics.

"It's uh. . ." He started to say he was due back to the team doctor soon to see about clearance to play again. But he really didn't want to get into all of that. Not right now at least. Instead he shrugged. "It's doing pretty good, I think."

"Megan is a physical therapist, you know," Kurt piped up.

Before he could answer, Megan gave him a look that said please-excuse-my-parents then tilted her head at her father, her lips curling into a sweet, patient smile. "Trust me, Dad. He does know that."

"Just thought I'd mention it." Her dad shrugged.

"So, it was a good race then?" Mac seized the opportunity to steer the conversation away from the topic of his elbow. "For the four of you?"

"It gets bigger and better every year," Laura exclaimed.

"Oh, you like it because you get through the challenges so easily." Her husband pretended to sneer.

"I do like puzzles and matching things, what can I say?" Laura grinned.

"I'd think running, biking, and tubing on the river would be challenging enough," Mac quipped.

"You would think so, wouldn't you?" Allie tuned in, while re-tying her daughter's gym shoe. "But supposedly the challenge stations make it even more fun. At least that's what these guys have to say about it." She stopped what she was doing for a moment to point in either direction at both sets of parents.

"I plan to sign up for it one of these years," Megan chirped. "It sounds like fun to me."

"It's nothing awfully strenuous," Kurt explained to Mac. "Or I wouldn't be able to do it. Like at the Loveland Stage Company—that was Challenge Seven, I think, you had to 'dance a bit or spell a hit.' And I still know a few disco moves, so. . ." He flung his arm up and down John Travolta style, making everyone laugh, including the kids.

"Hey, I don't mind admitting it's nice to sit down and rest at some of the challenges," Jim added.

"No kidding." Pam laughed. "I didn't think I'd ever get you back on your feet after the challenge in the parking lot of the Loveland Massage Center."

"The one where we got to sit and feed each other water from baby bottles?" Jim chuckled. "What can I say? I was really thirsty."

Everyone laughed again, and as their merriment died down, Sammy spoke up and filled the void.

"Pap-ee, Mac bring us in new truck."

"Is that right?" Kurt turned from his grandson to Mac. "I thought I spotted you driving around town in a shiny new Ford."

Mac nodded. "I loved my uncle's old truck—a '77. But it wasn't safe anymore. In fact, the brakes were so bad on the thing, I almost ran into Megan and Sammy the night of the initial All-Stars Sports meeting. That's how we first met actually, down on West Loveland near Paxton's."

"Really? Did you tell me that, Megan?" Mac noticed Laura trying to make eye contact with her daughter. "That's quite a coincidence, isn't it? And really very ro—"

"Mom!" Megan cut her mother short. "Aren't you going to be too tired to cook out tonight after you've been in this race all day?"

"Definitely," Pam spoke up. "Which is why we decided that you kids are going to do the barbecuing. Your mom and I made all the side dishes yesterday. The brats and burgers are at your mom's house just waiting to be cooked."

"That sounds more than fair," Megan answered before turning to him once more. "I sure hope you like brats and burgers, Mac."

Everyone turned their eyes on him.

"Of course I do. Burgers. Baseball. A Ford pickup. It all goes together, doesn't it?"

"And Ize," Sammy chimed in.

"Ize?" Mac looked at Megan.

"Oh, that's right. Ice. I promised the kids shaved ices," Megan explained. "But I also promised to hand out these cards for Janey." She pulled a pack of postcards from her backpack. "To announce the contest she's running."

She bit her lip, looking apologetic and of course, Mac felt an instant desire to make everything right for her. But it was Greg who jumped up from the blanket and began to take charge.

"Well, if it's okay with everyone. . . Allie and Megan, you two go ahead, feel free to pass out the cards," he suggested. "Meanwhile, Mac and I will take the kids for ices. That'll give the parents a chance to relax and bask in the glory of having another Amazing Race under their belts." He smiled at their elders. "Then later we'll head to the O'Donnells' to barbecue."

"Sounds good to me." Kurt settled deeper into the lap of his chair, closing his eyes.

Eyes drooping, Jim didn't look far behind him. "Me, too," he agreed.

"How about you, Mac?" Greg asked. "That okay with you?"

"I'm in." Mac nodded, shuffling behind Sammy's wheelchair. "Sounds like a plan."

"Are you sure, Mac?" Megan leaned close, laying a hand on his forearm again. "You don't mind taking Sammy? And being with my family all evening?"

"Mind it?" She really had no clue, did she? "I'm all over it," he said, feeling warmed he could make her grin. "Ready, kids?"

While Megan and Allie headed in one direction, he and Greg started off in the other. As he pushed Sammy's chair and Justin and Carrie held their dad's hands, their group made their way through the crowd of race participants and curious observers. It reminded him of a time when he and his family belonged to this town. Making him feel like he belonged to a place—this place—again.

I should give Mom and Dad a call down in Florida tomorrow, he thought as they strolled across the bike path to the Hawaiian Ice Hut. *Wonder how they're doing? It's been awhile...*

Megan watched the full moon play hide-and-seek, flickering in and out of sight between the trees, as Mac eased his truck over the winding road leading to his farm. The breeze coming in the window felt slightly cool on her face after being out in the sun the entire day, but not enough to have to put her sweatshirt on. Or to worry about Sammy being chilled.

It was way past his bedtime, as a matter of fact, and she couldn't believe she'd said yes to yet one more activity before Mac dropped her and Sammy off at home. The three of them had already packed so much into the day, spending the afternoon at the Amazing Race festival, and then all evening at her parents' house, barbecuing and visiting while the kids played. But she was as intrigued as her son was when Mac mentioned he could bring the moon to Sammy.

Oh please! Who was she kidding? Truth was, she was

more than intrigued with Mac, too.

Even now, she couldn't help from turning to look at him, his angular profile lit up by the bluish glow of the dashboard lights. He appeared so serious and purposeful as he gripped the steering wheel, intent on getting them to the place he'd promised. And he looked so handsome...making her suddenly conscious of what a mess she must look like after spending an entire day outdoors.

Her white shorts and gauzy white top had been a mistake to wear, no doubt. Clearly neither was spotless or fresh at this point. Plus her hair! She didn't even want to imagine what it looked like. It'd gotten wavy and out of control in the first hour in the sun. She'd pulled it back into a ponytail without even looking, and it'd stayed that way the rest of the day.

But not so with Mac. The outdoor activities and sunshine had only made his complexion more golden. His mussed hair and day-old whiskers only made him more rugged-looking and attractive—and hard not to look at.

To her embarrassment, he must've felt her staring because he turned, and even though it was only for a moment, he gazed at her in a way that made her think he hadn't noticed that her shorts were less than white and her hair more than messy

"What a great day, huh?"

"Yeah, it was, wasn't it?" Her cheeks flushed in the wake of his attention.

"You've got a really nice family," he said, his eyes turned back to the windshield. "And good friends. Really easy to be around."

"They're keepers, for sure. Sometimes they try to help a bit too much, but—"

"That's better than having it the other way, don't you think?"

She nodded in the dark, not really wanting to explain at that exact moment that though his logic was sound, it wasn't that easy for her to accept all the help. Or any of it actually. "Sometimes. Probably. Yes," she answered, indecisively and was glad when he changed the subject.

"You look a lot like your mom."

"You really think so? People always say that, but neither of us sees it that way."

"You're kidding. There's a strong resemblance in the shape of your eyes. The way you smile. You have a great smile," he complimented. "It's so. . .bright."

"It's our family secret."

"Yeah, what's that?"

"Teeth-whitening strips," she told him honestly, and he chuckled at that.

"No, seriously. I don't mean just white. I mean bright. As in happy."

Oh, that was how she had been feeling lately. Happy. At least she felt that way when she wasn't also feeling confused and scared about the way she was feeling.

"I'm sure you hear that a lot, though, don't you?" he asked, refocusing his eyes on the road. "About your smile?"

"Actually I do. Usually once a week."

"Yeah?" He did a double take. "That often, huh?"

"Uh-huh. When I see Dan. Dan always tells me that." Did she actually see him flinch? *Seriously?* She was only being playful, teasing. She didn't mean anything by it.

His hands tightened around the steering wheel. "Do I know Dan?"

She nodded in the dimness. "Actually, yes you do. He's really a great guy and very mature."

"Mature? I'm not sure how to take that."

"Mature, meaning he'll be seventy-two in August."

That news seemed to ease Mac's shoulders. "Hmm, I think I like this Dan guy already."

"You do like him." She smiled. "Dan Hoffman? He's one of the volunteers?"

"Oh yeah. Dan. He told me he's one of your patients. He was also a good friend of my uncle Jake's." He paused and shook his head. "You really had me going there for a minute."

They both laughed, and she couldn't believe he'd reacted so possessively. *Really? MacNeill Hattaway? Who could have his pick of about any woman in the universe? Jealous?* She had to wonder if it was because he really did have feelings for her. Or was it just because he didn't like to lose—at baseball or anything else?

She found herself hoping it was for the former reason, not the latter.

"What funny?" Sammy asked from the bench seat behind them.

"Your mom's funny, that's what," Mac told him.

"Funny? Maw-mee?" Sammy's voice registered disbelief.

"I know. Hard to believe, isn't it, sweetie?" Megan glimpsed at her son in the backseat. "Mommy's not always so funny, am I?"

Sammy shook his head vehemently, making them laugh, which only made him shake it all over again.

"You nice, Maw-mee. Buh not funny."

"Yes, she is nice," Mac agreed, his comment causing her to look his way. "Pretty, too."

Mac gave her a sideways glance, and she didn't know how he managed to do it, but his grin widened in approval at the same time his eyes narrowed in seriousness, causing her heart to race in her chest.

Thankfully she managed to escape his gaze when they came around the bend to his farm, and he had to divert his attention to turning his new truck ever so gently onto the gravel driveway.

Slowly pulling all the way to the end of the drive, Mac turned off the engine. Before she could find the door handle in the dark, he was out of the truck and around to the passenger side of the vehicle. It wasn't like she needed any help, but there he was anyway opening her door, helping her descend gracefully. Then he grabbed the wheelchair from the bed of the Ford before hoisting Sammy down from the back cabin.

"You take me to moo-n, Mac?" Sammy asked while Mac settled him into the chair.

"No, I said I'll bring the moon to you."

"Oh."

Either way, Megan knew it didn't matter to Sammy. As long as he could be with Mac, his idol and new pal, her son didn't have a care in the world. The thought suddenly niggled at her that the day the three of them had shared felt too perfect. Too wonderful. A day with MacNeill Hattaway that she would've never believed could be true. So, why was she thinking it was for real? A tingle of warning prickled at her cheeks.

What if she and Sammy were just something to keep Mac amused while he was healing? What if he didn't care for Sammy as much as she thought he appeared to? Or maybe not for her either? Or what if—

Oh stop it! she commanded her mind. *Just stop with the "what-ifs,"* a voice inside her pleaded. *Things have been great today. So easy and natural. With just the three of us. And with family and friends. Mac even said so. Don't ruin it all. Not now. . .*

She tried to look beyond the thoughts in her head to the sky far beyond her reach. "The moon does look pretty big out here."

In the wide open space, far from town, with no competition from streetlights or house lights, the huge moon looked as white as ever and so did the stars, abundant against the purplish night sky.

"You haven't seen anything yet," Mac promised from behind the wheelchair.

"Where are we headed?"

He pointed to the left. "To the barn."

"Barn?" A hint of glee permeated Sammy's voice. "I like barns."

Megan didn't bother to remind her zealous and easy-to-please son that he'd never been in a barn. Instead she let Mac push him along and lead the way, much like he'd been doing all day.

She noticed Sammy didn't say a word but rather sat in

awe as Mac unlatched the barn doors and slid them to each side.

"This is a nice barn," Megan said, following behind them. "Not that I've been in a lot of barns. But this one's so clean, really nice."

"I had it redone when Uncle Jake was still alive. He had a few horses for a while until he got too sick to take care of them and had to put them up for adoption. He liked to spend a lot of time out here whittling in their company."

Mac stepped to the side and turned on what looked to be a small battery-powered lantern before pushing the wheelchair deeper into the barn. "I don't want to turn on a bunch of lights. It'll ruin what I want to show you."

"Smell funny in here," Sammy remarked.

"It smells like a barn, honey." Megan chuckled.

At the sound of the voices, Bitty sauntered out of no-where, meowing her way toward them.

"Bitty!" Sammy extended his arm over his chair.

"How about you let your mom hold Bitty for a minute until we get to where we're going?" Mac suggested.

Megan scooped up the cat in her arms and followed along behind Mac and Sammy until they reached the middle of the barn. She was still puzzled about what Mac was up to even as she watched him pull at a dangling rope, and a makeshift staircase descended from the rafters.

"Ladies first." He motioned for her and Bitty to head up the steps in front of him and Sammy.

The air grew warmer and the lantern's light dimmer as Megan made her way up the ladder to the loft, Bitty nestled against her chest. Settling down onto a bed of hay, it was only seconds later when Mac and Sammy's heads popped through the opening.

"Hey guys."

"Mac carry me," Sammy stated the obvious as Mac deposited him onto her lap and Bitty hopped off, finding a place to curl up near her feet. "He nice. And strong," Sammy added.

"I think I should hire you to do my PR work, Sammy." Mac chuckled before moving closer to the barn wall. "Now. . ." he paused. "Are you two ready?"

They both nodded, Megan for one wondering what they should be ready for. But then they couldn't have imagined it anyway. Because as Mac opened the large wooden window that ran most of the length of the loft area, so much light flooded in that she and Sammy both gasped.

The moon that had seemed a galaxy away when viewed from the ground now suddenly looked so close. Close enough to reach out and touch, just as Mac had promised. And surrounding it were so many stars, glimmering and twinkling before their eyes, Megan thought it'd surely take till dawn to count them all.

Mac settled in next to them then, and all at once she was totally aware of how close he was. The scent of him, musk and soap blended together, was familiar to her now. So was the pleasant feeling it awakened in her. His shoulder leaned against hers in the dark, connecting them in an unspoken way, feeling easy. Comfortable.

Cuddled together, they all sat in awed silence looking out into the vast sky until Sammy rasped his thoughts out loud.

"God is big!" he said, his voice full of amazed wonder. "He very big!"

"And good," Mac said, low and reverent. "God is good."

Then, as if he hadn't surprised her enough that day with all his tender ways, he surprised her again by reaching for her hand. Gently. Softly. He covered his large, strong hand over her smaller one, making it feel like a perfect fit. His clasp warmed her. His touch assured her. And the words he spoke never felt so true as they reverberated through her. Because suddenly in the veil of night there seemed to be so much light in her life. So much to be thankful for, that tears sprang to her eyes.

There was family. . .and friends they'd spent the sunny day with. There was the welcome weight and warmth of Sammy's body leaning against her chest. Sammy—her son—who could not walk through the world, but who could send her heart on trips of bliss. There was Mac—oh, sweet, heartthrob Mac—wanting to share time with them, becoming a part of them, making her feel things she hadn't felt in a very long time.

And there was God. God who Sammy talked about as if he knew Him, as if He was his friend. God, who really did feel like He was everywhere these days. So, so close.

Oh yes, it all felt right. So right that she couldn't help but squeeze Mac's hand in reply. So good that she couldn't stop the unseen tear of joy, escaping down her cheek.

Chapter 13

I'm Jason. I'll be your server today." The waiter wiped his brow then steadied a pen over his ordering pad all in one motion. "Did you want to order lunch now? Or wait for your friend to get here?"

"I think I'll wait." Megan squinted up at him, shading her eyes from the sun. "He should be here any minute."

"Take your time." Jason slipped the pad back into his pocket. "I'd sit out here all day if I could. I'll stop back when I see him."

"Thanks."

Megan already knew Tano Bistro's menu by heart, so there was no need to look it over one more time. Instead, she settled back into the rattan chair and checked out the scenery along the sidewalks of downtown Loveland, wishing she, too, could sit outside forever on such a gorgeous day.

The humidity was almost nonexistent after the rain the day before. Quite a rarity for summer in southwestern Ohio. Even so, she couldn't sit and enjoy the outdoors for all that long. Her next patient was due to arrive in an hour and fifteen minutes, and she needed to be back at the clinic a few minutes prior to that.

Still, it was nice Mac had suggested they meet for lunch in the middle of the week to discuss event details. Such a different change of pace, it almost made the obligations of the day fall away for just awhile. Making her feel like she was on a mini-getaway. To somewhere other than Loveland, Ohio. To some faraway place. Where she'd be having lunch at an outdoor café. *With Mac.*

She couldn't believe the way the crazy image danced around in her head, instantly making her stomach feel all fluttery. And make her heart feel the same way. Even a drink of her ice water didn't help at all to cool her flushed cheeks. Or to distract her thoughts from the image of the two of them that kept coming to mind.

But then. . .she wasn't used to thinking about lunches with men. Or thinking about men in any kind of romantic way at all. For years, the only males she'd longed for in her day-to-day thoughts included Mr. Clean and a grocery deliveryman. Both of whom she'd hoped would come along and make her everyday life a bit easier.

But hard as she tried, she couldn't conjure up those imaginary characters now. Those mundane daydreams had disappeared into thin air like the fuzzy white flowers of a dandelion blowing in the wind. Leaving only more thoughts. . .more daydreams of Mac. And her. Together. Sitting under an umbrella at an open air café in—hmm. . . maybe Paris? Rome? She tilted her head trying to envision it all. But she'd never been abroad. And even for a daydream those places felt far too extravagant.

But what about, say, Hilton Head Island?

Sliding her elbows on the table, she cupped her chin in her hands, gazing out at the passersby ambling up and down the sidewalk. Letting her mind drift for a change.

Yes. . .she really could see the two of them in South Carolina. She really could imagine them in Harbortown, to be exact. With Sammy safely stowed at his grandparents' house in Loveland. Or no. Better yet, Sammy would be in Hilton Head with them, and her mom and dad would be there—one big, happy family. They'd all stay together in a four-bedroom condo. A really plush one with three bathrooms and a terrace off her bedroom. Why not, since she was daydreaming anyway?

After a day at the beach, her parents wouldn't have any qualms about watching Sammy while she and Mac slipped out for a few hours in the evening.

The two of them would head over to South Beach, walking through the shops there, holding hands—just like he'd held her hand the night before. Not really buying anything—oh, well, except for maybe a Hilton Head T-shirt for Sammy. And then, they'd stop for ice cream on the pier at an outdoor café. They'd sit and talk some. Laugh a lot. People-watch a little. Marvel at God's exquisite sunset . . .and hold hands some more.

Mac's nose would be pink from the sun and his hair even blonder than when they'd left Loveland after just a couple of days on the beach. He'd be wearing a yellow T-shirt that would bring out the amber in his brown eyes and accentuate his tan. So relaxed in his khaki shorts and Reefs, his long muscular legs would be stretched out languidly and crossed at the ankles.

She'd have on a sundress of course. Or no, she'd be in her white ruffled skirt and a tank top actually. A fun and feminine summery outfit very similar to the one the girl strolling down the sidewalk toward her was wearing. And she'd throw on some breezy, brightly colored bangle bracelets like the girl wore. Which looked very cute along with the straw hat over the girl's very red hair, and—

"Janey?" Megan blinked. She sat up straight.

Her incognito friend stopped dead in her high cork-heeled sandals, sliding dark, trendy Ray-Bans down her nose.

"Megan?" Janey leaned over the bistro's wrought-iron railing. "How did you know it was me?"

"Um, well, because you look like you."

"I do?"

"Only with red hair."

"It's a wig," Janey entrusted.

"So I gathered," Megan answered, not letting her friend know it was the second time she'd laid eyes on her that way.

"Do you think most people would know who I am?" Janey leaned over even more, lowering her voice. A lock of red synthetic hair fell to her cheek. "I mean, with the wig on?"

Megan could tell her friend wasn't searching for the most honest answer, so she tap-danced around the question. "I've known you for forever, Janey. So, of course, *I'd* know you no matter what color hair you have."

Standing up straight, Janey appeared to be considering her answer. "Yeah, I guess that's true," she finally said. "You're probably right."

Removing her sunglasses, Janey dangled them from the rounded neck of her tank top. It pained Megan to see the frustration clouding Janey's usually bright eyes. "Is everything okay, Janey?"

"Okay? You mean as in, why am I wearing a wig?"

"Well, I mean. . ." Megan shrugged. "Your hair's been looking so good lately with all those pretty highlights you've been getting. Are you experimenting with a new look or something?"

Janey nodded. "Yeah, I just thought. . ." At first her friend's body stilled as if she were ready to deliver a sound explanation. But then her face crumpled and her voice faltered as she blurted out the truth. "Oh Megan, I can't lie to you. I can't. And it's so good I bumped into you because I need to tell someone. I do. And who else would I tell, but you?"

Breaking through the bistro's metal enclosure, Janey apparently was so wrapped up in her own issues that she didn't even notice the gate closing with a crash behind her. But several diners did. They looked up from their plates at the intrusive noise as she plopped down into a matching rattan chair across from Megan. "I can't keep carrying this secret around inside of me, Megan. It's starting to drive me crazy!"

"You have a secret?" Megan pushed the glass of ice water meant for Mac across the table suddenly aware—and feeling slightly guilty—that her friend wasn't the only one who hadn't been disclosing things lately. Certainly she hadn't been very forthcoming with Janey about all the feelings she'd been having for Mac recently.

Janey's bracelets clanked on her arm as she took her time sipping at the water. "Yes. Yes, I do." She nodded, like she was unable to stall any longer. "It's—I've—well. . ." Janey's shoulders slouched. She let out a long, defeated-sounding breath. "Megan, the truth is, I've been spying."

"Spying?" Megan could feel her brows knit together instantly as if someone had pulled a loose string, tugging them tight. "Seriously? On who?"

Nibbling her lip, Janey answered meekly, "On Sean. Sean Shaffer."

"Ohhhh." Megan's eyes widened involuntarily as Janey's confession sank in. "Ohhhh," she repeated.

"No, not 'ohhhh' like that. It's not like some guy thing." Janey shook her head, her fake wavy red locks swaying. "I'm not really spying on him. On Sean. It's more like I'm spying on his doughnut shop, the Emporium."

"Seriously?"

Eyes downcast, Janey nodded, looking dismayed. "And do you know I actually saw some of my regular customers there? At least I thought they were *my* regular customers— *not Sean's*. They come to Sweet Sensations for lattes and a cheese Danish, and then they turn around the next day and go see him for black coffee and jelly doughnuts. I mean, it might sound silly to you—but it kind of hurt to see that." A pouting frown pulled at her lips. "You know what I mean?"

"It doesn't sound silly," Megan replied. Whether she wanted to admit it or not, she'd probably feel the same way if some of the families she'd come to know over the years decided to go to another clinic for their therapy treatments.

"I just don't know what I'm doing wrong."

"Doing wrong?" She leaned over the table, closer to her friend. "Janey, you're not doing anything wrong. You have great product." She tried to assure her. "It's just sometimes people get a taste for something a little less than perfect, I guess."

"A *little* less? You're saying Sean's cookie-cutter right-next-to-the-gas-station doughnuts are just a *little less* tasty than mine?"

Janey's eyes narrowed like darts of accusation, penetrating Megan's resolve. Feeling like she was suddenly on the witness stand, she fumbled to come up with the perfect answer. "No, no, of course not. I'm sure we're talking *a lot* less. Way less. I'm just saying—well, like, do you always want steak? No. Sometimes you just want a regular hamburger, you know?"

"I'm a vegan, remember?"

"Well, you know what I mean, Janey. The same thinking applies to your situation."

Megan tried to hide the frustration in her voice. But attempting to comfort her friend was never an easy task, and Janey's doughnut problem had certainly spoiled the wistful daydreams she'd been enjoying about Mac.

"There's always going to be competition. That's just the way it is," she said, hoping to end the conversation, knowing Mac would be there—in real life and not just a daydream—any minute.

"I know—I know. . ." And instead of the usual spark Janey got at the mention of the word *competition*, she uncharacteristically sank deeper into the chair, perplexing Megan even more. Surely Janey wouldn't stay and sulk when Mac arrived, would she?

"So how's the contest been going?" Megan tried to steer Janey's thoughts toward something concrete, and hopefully, positive. "Did you get some interest last weekend? I saw a lot of people coming and going from your place."

"I did get a lot of the Amazing Race traffic." Janey nodded. "I hope you and Allie got my e-mail thanking you guys for handing out the postcards. The cookie jar is almost filled to the top with entries."

"Well see, that's a good thing, isn't it? And proof that a whole slew of your customers have a Sweet Sensations favorite." She paused, still thinking about Janey's trips to the Donut Emporium. She hoped Sean hadn't recognized her. It'd be so embarrassing if he had. "Did Sean know it was you?"

"Sean?" Janey shook her head. "Oh no."

"Really?"

"No, not at all."

"How do you know?"

"I just know."

"But how?"

"Because if you must know, he flirts with me when I visit his shop. Would he ever do that if he knew it was me?"

Megan wasn't sure how to answer that question, so she ducked it with an indirect response. "Well, regardless, he must think you're pretty if he's flirting with you. Right? How's Sean looking these days, by the way? Still have that baby face of his?"

Before Janey could answer, the waiter was back at the table again.

"So what do you think? You ladies ready to order?" he asked, pad in hand once more.

"Oh," Megan spoke up. "This isn't my friend."

Janey blinked at her, baffled. Megan noticed Jason react the same way. "Well, I mean she's my friend. But she was just passing by. She's not the friend I was expecting," she explained.

"Oh yeah, That's right. You said your friend is a 'he.'" Jason slid the pad into his pocket again. "No problem. I'll be back."

"He?" Janey quizzed as Jason walked away.

"Mac."

"Ohhhh," Janey replied in the same singsong way Megan had a few minutes earlier. "A sweet little lunch at Tano's with Mac. Nice!"

"Actually, we're just reviewing some things for the Sports Day event."

"Uh-huh. You really need to catch me up on things, Meg."

"I have been keeping everyone up-to-date. I sent out an e-mail just last week, talking about Volunteer Day and how we need volunteers to head out to Mac's farm to do some preliminary setup work. But it'll be on a Saturday, so I figure you'll be working, right?"

"No, I mean you need to catch me up about you and Mac."

"Well, we—he's—I'm—" Megan stammered, not sure where to begin and what it would all mean in the end anyway.

"Hold that thought," Janey teased, and then laughed when Megan couldn't manage to put together a sentence. "I can't wait to hear everything. But I'll give you some time to gather your thoughts. I have to get back to the bakery anyway. Lucy loves baking but she's not fond of waiting on customers, and I've been gone longer than I said I'd be."

Her bracelets jangled again as she took one last sip of

water. "I can't believe the dance is coming up so quickly!" Standing up, she slung her cloth tote over her shoulder. "Megan. . ." She paused, removing her sunglasses from her tank top then settling them into her mane of fake hair. "Can I ask you a favor?"

"Sure. But I hope it doesn't involve borrowing dressy shoes for the dance. Most of mine are dated. I don't even know which shoes *I'm* wearing yet."

"Oh no, not that. Your shoes wouldn't fit my big old feet anyway." Janey waved a hand at her. "No. . .I just—I'm wondering if you'll stop in."

"To Sweet Sensations? Of course I will. I always do, don't I?"

"No, I mean to Sean's. To the Donut Emporium. Will you stop in and do a little looking around?"

"You want me to spy?" Megan could barely believe her ears. "And wear a red wig like you?"

"Of course not. You don't have the coloring for a redhead at all." Janey looked at her blithely. "No, just be yourself. Stop in and check out things for me. I need your perspective. Will you? Please?"

Megan moaned. "Really, Janey?"

She loved her friend, but loathed the thought of getting involved in her spying drama. Actually she tried to refrain from getting involved in most of her dramas. Though the two of them had been close for forever, listening to Janey was as far as she usually liked to go.

"You know Sammy loves jelly doughnuts. You know I won't get out of there without buying him one or two." Megan tried to discourage the idea, playing on Janey's typically competitive nature.

"As long as Sammy doesn't start liking Sean's better than mine, it's okay. I can deal with it." Her friend's voice softened. "Please, Megan," she begged, her brow furrowing. "It would really help me to know what you think."

"I already told you what I think, Janey. Remember, my steak and hamburger theory?"

She tried not to look directly into Janey's pathetic, pleading eyes. Without a doubt, her friend was going to the extreme to come up with the poorest, most pitiful expression ever. But even if Megan didn't get all the way sucked in by Janey's pouting face, there was no escaping her incessant, imploring voice.

"Puh-lease? Pretty, pretty please?" she repeated.

"Oh Janey!" Megan sighed at her relentless friend. "Okay." She finally gave in. "Okay. I'll *try* to get over to the Donut Emporium."

"Promise you'll try hard?"

Megan couldn't make herself say yes. But she couldn't force herself to say no either. Not with the way a glimmer of light began to shine in her friend's eyes. Not with the way a smile tugged at Janey's lips for the first time since she'd sat down. Instead, Megan simply smiled back and gave her red-haired friend a little wave good-bye.

"Yeah, sounds good." Mac stood on the downtown side-walk, holding his cell phone to his ear, trying to wind up his weekly chat with his agent. "Of course you'll be the first to know what Dr. Kline says, Hal. But my appointment's not for weeks."

"I know I'll be first." Hal half-chuckled and half-harrumphed in Mac's ear. "Because I'll be calling you the minute you leave Kline's office," he promised. "And be careful with your elbow in the meantime, will you? None of that heave-ho, manly manual labor stuff you can't seem to get enough of on that farm of yours."

"No worry." Mac glanced up at the We Do! Wedding Planners sign. "Not tackling anything too manly and physical today, Hal," he said, as they exchanged good-byes and he opened the door of the shop.

Besides the sound of soft chimes that greeted him, the first thing Mac noticed about the inside of We Do! was that it was very, very pink. The direct antithesis of any stadium locker room he'd ever been in.

The second thing he noticed is that all of the women there grew quiet the moment he walked through the door.

Lord, I need Your help here, he prayed as he stepped farther into the establishment, which somehow instantly reminded him of colored Easter eggs and Pepto-Bismol all rolled into one.

He hadn't thought it through at all when he'd decided to pay a visit to Megan's mom at her place of business. From the overall reaction he was getting, it was obvious males didn't typically drop in to the shop. Except for maybe a UPS man now and then. Or, other than that, maybe when an intended groom accompanied his bride-to-be for a scheduled appointment. But beyond that, he could pretty much tell a male's presence was a rarity.

Luckily though, Laura O'Donnell seemed to be the type who could smooth over any uneasy situation easily. Handing her client a photo album to browse through, she excused herself and came sailing over to him.

"Mac!" She glided around the reception desk, a warm smile gracing her face. "It's good to see you." She laid a welcoming hand on his arm and, leaning in closer, lowered her voice. "Please excuse all the gaping mouths. It's not often a baseball superstar comes wandering into We Do!"

Already feeling awkward enough, he brushed off the compliment. "Or any man, I imagine. Sorry I just showed up like this. I should've called first. Or made an appointment." He scratched his forehead, chiding himself. "I was just going to meet up with Megan over at the bistro and thought I'd stop in here on my way to ask you a question. But I can always give you a call later. . .when you're not busy."

"Oh no, it's fine. I can take a moment. Ask away." She leaned against the reception desk, crossing her hands, as if she had all the time in the world.

"Well, I've been wondering. Can Sammy keep a secret?"

"Sammy? Hmm. . ." Laura's face contorted. "Well, he certainly kept a secret about his pappy's new fishing rod at Christmas last year. For several months actually. So, I think I'd have to say yes."

"And how about you?" Mac tilted his head. "Can you keep a secret?"

She laughed, her eyes twinkling. "Most of the time." She nodded. "It depends on what it is, I suppose. Care to tell me what you have in mind?"

"Well, I know Sammy is in day care this summer while you and Megan are working. But I also know in the evenings, if Megan has to go out, she depends on you and Kurt to watch Sammy."

"Reluctantly she relies on us, yes. But only because Mrs. Biddle, her regular sitter, still isn't up to watching him."

"I've heard." Mac nodded. "Well, what I was thinking is that Sammy really liked the bowling ramp I built for him. I'm in the process of making a few more in case it's popular with the kids on event day. Right now, one of the ramps is sitting over at a warehouse that Ted's brother owns. Anyway"—he shifted on his feet—"I thought it'd be fun for Sammy to get some practice on it. Then on Event Day he could surprise his mom with how good he's gotten."

"Oh Mac!" Laura clapped her hands together. "That sounds like fun—and like a secret I can keep." She laughed. "So you'd pick up Sammy at our house when we're watching him and take him over to practice?"

"Well yeah, on nights when I know I have enough time to get back and forth without bumping into Megan."

"I love it! Count me in!" Her eyes sparkled with gratitude. "Thanks so much for thinking of this, Mac. Sammy will be so excited. Oh, and Kurt may even want to join you and Sammy sometime."

"The more the merrier," he said, realizing how much he meant it. After all, having Kurt's help with Sammy would make things go quicker and smoother. Plus, he had enjoyed talking to Megan's dad the night of the barbecue. They'd talked about a lot of the baseball greats and even baseball history. Few men knew the sport like Kurt did.

"Let me give you my cell number." Laura was already looking for her readers. Finding them, she slid a business card from a holder on top of her desk and took her time writing out the seven-digit phone number. "Do you know if you all have sold many tickets for the fund-raising formal?"

Mac blinked at the change of subject. "Uh, I think last I heard Wendy said we're about sold out."

"That's wonderful!" Laura turned from the desk, holding the card in her hand. "It should be a great night. I can't believe it's coming up so soon."

"Yeah, you're right. The summer is flying by." Mac held his hand out for the card. But Laura acted as if she didn't see his hand there at all. Instead, she smiled, tilting her head thoughtfully.

"It is, isn't it? And such a nice thing to do this summer. The dance. Are you asking a certain someone?" She finally relinquished the card to him.

"Asking?" He took out his wallet and slipped the business card inside. "Uh, I assumed Megan and I would be going together."

Laura didn't say anything. But she didn't have to. The way she peered over her glasses at him, eyebrows arched, said it all. He'd have to be blind not to pick up on what she was getting at.

"But I shouldn't assume that," he said slowly. "I should ask her at lunch today."

Her slight smile instantly blossomed into something even more special and genuine. "The bistro has great food, don't they? You two will enjoy your lunch, I'm sure," she said, ushering him to the front door. "Oh, and Mac—about Sammy. I'll talk to him. Mum's the word." She put a finger to her lips.

Mac had to grin to himself as he left the wedding planners' shop, suddenly aware of what had just transpired. Megan's mom must be really good at her job with soon-to-be-married couples. Easygoing, but somehow direct, she undoubtedly had an uncanny ability for organizing people and guiding them toward the right decisions without them really realizing it—until afterward.

As the noon traffic stopped for him at the crosswalk, Mac caught a glimpse of Megan already seated at the bistro. Even in her red work polo, she still looked so pretty, a sight that could make his heart hum. But that wasn't the only thing that added an extra lift to his step as he crossed the street. It was the realization that in Laura O'Donnell's own subtle yet effective way she'd just given him her stamp of approval.

Well, that's one lady in the O'Donnell family, he thought. Although from the way things had been going with Megan, he got the sense her feelings for him were growing, too. At least it certainly seemed that way.

But I can sure use Your help to fan the flame, Lord! He appealed to his Father in heaven just as Megan spotted him. And with a smile he'd grown to love, she waved.

Chapter 14

Megan wasn't quite sure what made Mac ask her to the dance when they'd had lunch at the bistro over a week ago. All she knew was that she was glad he did. Or at least she *had been* glad, until she started getting ready for the special night. That's when reality struck and the idea of being on a date with Mac—a formal date—made her so nervous that her hands began to shake.

Which didn't help a bit as she attempted to put on her makeup. And didn't help either when she was trying to do such a meticulous job of it, especially when applying makeup wasn't something she felt very adept at to begin with.

Oh, just calm down. She tried to comfort the reflection staring back at her in the bathroom mirror. *Calm. Down. He's just a man.* She brushed eye shadow on her lids. *Just a—*

Okay, maybe Mac's maleness wasn't such a good topic to dwell on, she decided as her stomach began to flutter. Better, instead, not to think about him at all. *Best to think about the details of the dance,* she thought as she fished through her makeup bag for her mascara.

But drawing the mascara wand from its tube, she swiped at her lashes realizing that there wasn't much to think about in that department at all. Once she had helped Wendy pick out the spot for their dance at the Oasis Golf Club and Conference Center, Wendy's four-person fund-raising committee had taken care of most of the details for the evening. So no issues there to contemplate.

Sammy. She forced her thoughts to switch gears. She could always think about him, she thought, putting the mascara back in its place and digging out her berry blush.

But, actually, everything was also fine in the Sammy department. Lucinda, a cousin of Allie's husband, happened to be in town and offered to watch Sammy along with Carrie and Justin for the night. She was someone Megan had met before, and she had no reservations about leaving Sammy with her, so. . .

That left her mind drifting back to Mac again, and—
Oh, could it be any hotter in here?

Cheeks reddening under the rosy blush, she hurriedly applied the finishing touch, covering her lips with a soft, creamy cherry color. She couldn't wait to get out from under the globe bulbs burning bright above the bathroom mirror.

Thankful to exit the master bath, she stood in her bedroom fanning herself and glimpsed at the clock on her nightstand.

Eight minutes! Eight minutes until Mac was due to arrive! In an instant her heart was racing in her chest, partly because she needed to hurry. And partly because that meant she'd be seeing him soon.

Or is it "mostly" because I'll be seeing him soon?

The thought teased at her as she swooped up her gown from the bed and then made herself slow down to delicately step into it. Thankfully, the red satin material felt smooth and cool, non-clingy against her skin. Zipping it up the side, she plucked her new silver strappy heels from their box and slipped them on. Then she stopped for a moment to have a look at herself in the mirror, and decided—not bad.

Not bad at all.

The jeweled silver ring on her one-shoulder gown worked perfectly with her shoes, and she swayed her hips just slightly, loving how gracefully the skirt of the dress fell from the four-inch-wide inset waistband that hugged her snuggly.

Surprisingly, she'd done her hair herself and it actually turned out looking good. Not wanting to hide the gown's one-shoulder feature by wearing her hair down, she'd gone online and taught herself how to make an elegant ponytail— far unlike the haphazard way she usually pulled back her hair into a rubber band without even consulting a mirror.

I think I'll be using this new technique again. She turned her head left to right and left again, checking out the result, still shocked she'd managed such a feat.

She'd also had another nice surprise—well, actually three of them—when she was trying to figure out accessories for the evening. Hoping not to have to spend more money, she'd gotten her jewelry box out of the closet and dusted it off. Inside, she rediscovered a diamond bracelet and matching earrings that her parents had given her when she graduated college. Neither had been worn for forever— or at least long before Sammy had been born.

Yes, overall, assessing herself from head to toe, she'd done a good job of pulling her look together for the eventful evening. Smiling at her reflection, she was feeling pleased and confident. That is, until she heard the unmistakable rumble of Mac's Corvette pulling into her driveway.

Her breath hitched as she tiptoed over to her bedroom window quietly, as if he could hear her heels creeping over the carpet. Barely pulling the dusty-blue curtain aside, she peeked out surreptitiously and watched as Mac's tall muscular body unfolded from the small car, making the vehicle almost appear toy-like. So handsome-looking in his black tux, he paused, as if he'd remembered something. Then he reached back into the car, bringing out a bouquet of ivory roses. It made her smile to see the way he stopped and straightened his jacket and tie with his free hand before he proceeded up her walk and rang the doorbell.

Even though she knew it was coming, the sound still gave her a jolt, causing her fragile heart to beat in unison with the click of her heels as she crossed the hardwood entryway to open the door.

"Hey." She smiled up at him. "Come on in. It's still hot out there, isn't it?"

"Sure is." He ducked in the door, and right away his slow grin melted her the same way the evening sun caused beads of perspiration to dot his hairline. "These, um, these are for you."

"You didn't have to bring me flowers, Mac. But thank you." She sniffed at the flowers, taking the bouquet he held out to her. "They're—"

"Beautiful," he said.

But the way his eyes shone as he gazed at her, she knew he wasn't talking about the flowers at all.

As the band played another familiar-sounding song, and she and Mac slow danced across the ballroom floor, Megan couldn't help but think back to a Fourth of July when she was ten years old. That particular summer her dad had bought packages of sparklers and handed them out to every kid on their street.

She'd always thought the houses up and down their block were somewhat special, and she never tired of looking down the lane at the eclectic group of homes. Some residences had sprawling yards surrounding their low, lengthy ranches. Other lots featured Victorian two-stories or cottage-style homes with postage stamp–sized yards and wildflower gardens on each side of the house.

But that night—with kids waving dozens of wands of crackling yellow and gold. . .with fireflies twinkling across all the lawns. . .and bursts of color shooting into the sky— their street transcended its everyday kind of special. Instead, it was transformed into an enchanting, magical kingdom. A place right out of a fairy tale.

And being in the ballroom at the Oasis again, Megan couldn't help but feel that same way again.

When she'd made the trip with Wendy to check out the center for their fund-raiser dance months earlier, the room had appeared fine for their purposes. Clean. Doable.

But now, glancing around its perimeters, her eyes caught every glimmer and sparkle here, there, and everywhere. The shimmering light from the gold wall sconces. The twinkling crystal centerpiece vases filled with orchids. The glittery gowns that draped the women as they glided across the dance floor. Even the sheen from the men's ebony tuxedos seemed to capture the light and shine.

All of it blended, illuminated so breathtakingly, transforming the ordinary rectangular room into a magical setting.

Or maybe. . .it wasn't any of that at all.

Maybe. . .it was just the feel of dancing in Mac's arms that had her thinking that way.

He felt so tall and solid against her, yet he moved so easily. Effortlessly, actually, he glided them across the dance floor until finally she had to look up at him. She had to look up to make sure he was real, and not some Prince Charming. To make sure the moment was real because she wasn't used to that kind of fairy-tale feeling in her life.

"What is it?" He gazed down at her, his smile as smooth as the lines of the tux that fit every part of his body. . .perfectly. So perfectly across his broad shoulders. And down the strong arms that held her close.

"What's what?"

"What are you thinking?"

"How can you tell I'm thinking?"

"Oh, I can just tell."

Probably because she wasn't jabbering a mile a minute, she figured, like she had been during their first dances. But she hadn't been able to help herself. She'd been nervous. Being so close to Mac sent tremors through her that were both delightful and disturbing at the same time. It didn't matter that she was a mom of an almost seven-year-old and that she was too old to be acting semi-giddy, she had been anyway. Unlike her usually reserved self.

"I'm thinking about the Fourth of July."

"Ah. Fireworks, huh?" His brows arched with interest. "I like how you're thinking. You are feeling fireworks? Yes?" he teased, adding the last part with a slight Italian or French or whatever kind of accent. A very bad, but funny, imitation of an accent.

She laughed. "Not those kinds of fireworks. That's not what I was thinking about."

"No?" He looked disappointed, or if he wasn't, he was doing a fine job of acting that way. Better than his accent. "Really?"

"Well, yes. But, no."

He chuckled. "Ah well, a guy has to try, doesn't he?"

But no, Mac didn't have to. Not really.

Because you're gorgeous and every woman in this room can't keep their eyes off you, she thought, but before she could come up with some cute response, she felt the pressure of his hand on the small of her back. Felt the way it intensified as he added, "And I'll keep trying."

His words, like his touch, warmed her, and as he held her closer, she finally laid her head on his shoulder and let her eyes close. Let his strength and grace lead her. Let a wave of calm wash over her. Let go. So rare and trusting. Aware of nothing but the feel of her cheek against his solidness. Wishing she could stay that way forever, and she did, until her eyes fluttered open at the sound of his voice.

"Hmm. . .that's not good."

"What's not good?" She looked up from his shoulder.

"Wendy's waving to us." He paused. "But. . .I have an idea. I'll act like I didn't see her." He suddenly swung their bodies halfway around, sped up their tempo, leading them away from where Wendy was standing by the tables, beckoning them.

"Mac!" She giggled, trying to catch her breath from that and their dart across the dance floor. "We can't just ignore her. It's probably time for us to introduce the volunteers and everyone."

"Aw. . .can we not be the co-chairs for one night?"

She laughed at the pouting little boy face he pulled. "Hey, I was going to chair the event all on my own, remember? But then you had to push your way in and save the day." She needled him with a smile.

"Well, of course I had to. But you're glad I did, aren't you?" His lips suddenly went from a frown to the lopsided Hattaway grin no woman could resist.

But, unfortunately, she had to try to at the moment. Because now Wendy was waving her arms, not just her hand, attempting to get their attention. "We really need to go see what Wendy needs."

"I know," he grumbled. "But we need to finish this dance, Ms. O'Donnell."

"That's not a problem, Mr. Hattaway."

That promise made, he released her from his arms and took her hand, leading them off the dance floor.

Not a problem at all, her heart sang out.

Truly, if anyone would've told her six years ago, even six months ago, that she'd be dancing in MacNeill Hattaway's arms all night long, laughing with him, teasing him, not wanting to be anywhere else except with him, she wouldn't have believed it.

And yet there she was. There he was. It was happening. *Oh Lord, is this really You doing all of this? Is it? Because it seems too unreal to be true.*

Oh, how she wanted to trust in a plan for her heart designed by God. How she wanted to believe there was something between her and Mac—something more than one magical, fairy-tale night.

And just as much as all that, she wanted to trust in love again. Because in that instant she realized that was exactly what she was feeling.

Mac turned left out of the Oasis parking lot, veering the 'Vette toward Megan's place, trying to remember the last time he'd driven a date home and had to go through the whole say-goodnight-on-the-doorstep sort of thing. In high school maybe? After some big dance perhaps?

Of course, he also couldn't recall the last time he didn't want an evening to end.

It wasn't lost on him how right and good it felt being with Megan. And how different his feelings were for her from any woman he'd ever known. In his former life she would've been the girl he shied away from. Big baseball star that he was, he still wouldn't have felt "worthy enough" to be with her. Not someone like Megan whose values were so on target. Someone who was a loving mom, a dedicated physical therapist, and also a member of the community everyone admired. A woman who he felt he might taint with just the touch of his hand.

But things had changed now. He had changed.

"I will repay you the years the locust hath eaten." The verse echoed in his head.

When he'd first been hospitalized after his accident, a nurse named Chantel had prayed over his life as he lay there in those first hours wishing for an end. Wishing he were dead.

No doubt, the angel of a woman had heard about his off-the-field antics as most people had. But instead of judging him, she prayed to God for him, repeating that verse from the book of Joel, petitioning for restoration of his body and soul, over and over again.

At the time, he didn't quite know or care what the words she mumbled over him about locusts and all that meant. But little by little, as he started healing, and mostly as he began to seek God on his own, he began to realize more and more how Chantel's prayers had been answered. And how his prayers were being answered, too.

The hollowness he'd felt for so long—the shame that always burdened him—those feelings all began to fall away. And in their place was God's love and grace, filling an emptiness in him—a void—he'd attempted to satiate in so many other ways for so many years.

And then, he met Megan. And in his heart he couldn't help but sense that Megan was a part of his renewal as well. Another gift that God had given to bring him to fullness and victory over his past.

He was thinking about it, mulling it over on the way

to her place. So much so that he barely knew how they got there, and was almost surprised when the 'Vette puttered up her driveway nearly on its own.

Helping Megan out of the car, together they took the short yet long walk up to the door. *Her* front door. Lord, help him! After an evening of being the suave date in a tux, he suddenly felt unprepared and self-conscious about what to do or say next.

He scratched at his chin. "I, uh…right this minute I feel like such a—"

"I know. A schoolgirl." She finished the sentence for him.

He chuckled at her sincerity. "I was going to say a rookie." He smiled. "Pretty much the same thing, though. You, too, huh?"

"Uh-huh."

His palms suddenly felt sweaty. Like bases were loaded, and it was a full count. Only before, he could rub his clammy palms on the legs of his baseball uniform. Now he rubbed them together in midair.

"Awkward," he admitted, his MacNeill Hattaway womanizer persona nowhere to be found.

"Somewhat." She nodded.

"Yeah, well…"

He gazed into her eyes then silence fell between them. The glow from the porch light lit her face, and the way she looked back at him had his heart thumping in his ears, blocking out the sounds of the summer evening he'd been aware of just moments before, the crickets chirping in her yard, barking dogs echoing down the block, cars whooshing down the street with open windows leaving trails of voices, laughter in the air.

For him, there was only her...and of course, his desire—wanting to kiss her so much. But he bit down on the inside of his mouth instead, that pain not even close in comparison to the way he ached from wanting to kiss her. But he'd promised himself he'd hold back. Promised.

A June bug flitted from the porch light, buzzed around his face, seemingly trying to remind him of the same thing. He whisked it away, and with that wave of his hand the moment he and Megan shared seemed to fly off to somewhere, too.

"So..." He finally spoke. "It was a really good dance."

Megan glanced down at her silver shoes, just barely sticking out from her red dress. She sighed. At least he thought he heard her sigh. Because the moment between them had passed?

"Really good." She looked up at him, nodding agreeably. "People were very generous with their bidding and donations. Wendy and her group make a great team."

"Yeah. We make a pretty good team, too. You think? You and me."

"Yes. We do, Mac." She blinked, new warmth entering her eyes. "We do."

"Megan, I—"

You were going to take things slow, remember? A voice reminded him, once again cutting him off from sharing what was on his heart.

"Yeah?" She sounded expectant.

"I, uh..." He practically winced out loud, trying so hard to tamp down the urges he was feeling, wanting to reach out and take her in his arms. Instead, he took her hand, but afraid he'd pull her into his arms, he held it loosely. "Can I give you a call tomorrow?"

"A call?" For a moment she looked like she couldn't decide. The thought that she might say no caused his jaw to tighten. "Sure," she finally said, much to his relief. "Sure."

She slid her hand from his, crossing her arms over her chest.

"Okay. I'll do that," he promised, backing down the porch steps onto the sidewalk. "I'll call you," he said, but she'd already turned and had taken her key from her little silver purse and was starting to unlock her front door.

Another few seconds and she'd be gone. Gone from him, except for in his thoughts where he was sure she'd be all night, and he'd be kicking himself for letting the evening end without her in his arms. And for not spending every last minute he possibly could with her.

Halting in his tracks, he spun around. "Megan?"

She turned, tilted her head.

"I was just thinking."

"Yeah?"

"You owe me the rest of that dance."

"What?"

"We didn't finish our dance. We got interrupted, remember?"

Finally. . .a smile. The smile he'd become accustomed to. The smile that made him feel lighter. That made him smile, too.

"I do remember. But—"

Before she could say anything more, he strode across the

walk to the bottom of the porch steps. He held out his arm, reaching up to the top step where she stood.

"You want to dance here? Now?" She giggled like she thought he was crazy. But he could tell she was pleased.

"Is that okay?"

She didn't answer. Instead she took his hand, descending the two steps as poised and graceful as a princess descending a winding staircase leading to some mansion's grand ballroom.

Only she wasn't icy or pretentious or aloof as some royalty might be. No, God—King of kings—had made His princess Megan warm and caring, and had crowned her with a beauty that was far more than skin-deep. And then, He'd done another thing, Mac realized as Megan stood before him and he pulled her close. God had also made her a woman—the woman—who fit perfectly into his arms. Like no other woman ever had in his life.

Holding her in the circle of his embrace, he started to take a step to dance, but his feet would barely move. Instead, immersed in the moonlight, they swayed to the melody of their beating hearts, his yearning for her growing with each moment. Until finally, he couldn't stand it any longer.

Lifting her chin with his hand, he brushed a gentle kiss across her forehead. A feathery kiss to her cheek. But, of course, it wasn't enough for him. And not for Megan either it seemed. He felt her yield to his touch, and so he claimed her lips. At last. Pressing his lips against hers, he covered her mouth and devoured the softness there. And felt a rush of pleasure when, thankfully, she returned his affection with a passion that matched his own.

Chapter 15

Megan placed the gas nozzle back into its slot and tightened the gas cap before glancing at her watch.

Nine forty-five. Still plenty of time before her eleven o'clock patient. She'd thought Sammy's dentist appointment would run much longer than it did so she hadn't scheduled her first patient until later in the morning. But, in a way that was good. At least now she'd have some free time to spend with him before running him to day care on Route 22 before her workday started.

Scooting back into her SUV, she turned around to Sammy, who was staring out the rear window. "Hey kiddo, what do you think about a jelly doughnut this morning?"

The mention of his favorite sweet pulled her son's attention from the shiny silver and red motorcycle in the gas line opposite them.

"You kidding, Maw-mee?" Surprise widened his sweet eyes.

"No, I'm not kidding." He always had a way of making her laugh. "Is that a yes?"

"Yeh! Buh don tell Doctor Bell. He get mad."

No doubt, it was slightly crazy to be indulging in a serious amount of sugar only minutes after Dr. Bell's hygienist had finished cleaning Sammy's teeth. But Sammy's report had been good—great actually. No cavities and double stars for pink gums and proper brushing, something Megan helped him with each morning and night.

And besides, with the Donut Emporium right there at the gas station, she was thinking she could kill two proverbial birds with one stone. She could also visit Sean's place for Janey and tell her friend all about it when they met up for dinner later that evening.

"Don't worry, Sammy. I won't tell," Megan promised, as she started the engine and drove all of twenty feet or so across the parking lot that the station and doughnut shop shared. "And we'll brush your teeth with the new brush Dr. Bell gave you once we get to day care, okay?"

"Yeah, brush 'em," he agreed.

Luckily there was a handicapped space open, giving Megan plenty of room to get Sammy out of the car and into his wheelchair. The space happened to be closer to the gas station than the Emporium, but that was okay. The sun felt pleasant as she pushed Sammy's chair along the sidewalk the two businesses shared—not unbearable the way it'd be feeling in another couple of hours. Its early morning glint bounced off the cars and the storefronts where she happened to catch her reflection in one of the windows.

At first it startled her to see herself. Sometimes lately she didn't recognize the woman smiling back at her. In the past, she'd made a point of smiling, always wanting to put on a happy front. She didn't want anyone to think for a minute that she didn't feel blessed to have Sammy as her son—that she didn't feel honored to be his mom.

But truth was, the incredible fatigue that came from caring for a special-needs child could really zap the life out of her. Often that smile was over-the-top and forced.

Yet since Mac. . .

She felt her cheeks heating thinking about their first kiss. And how it felt to dance in his arms. Thinking about the way he often looked at her. How his smile would go all the way to his eyes, which made her smile more. Yes. . . sometimes she'd catch a glimpse of herself in a mirror or window, and it would absolutely surprise her. She looked so happy. Genuinely happy. Scarily so! Because of Mac, things in life were so much lighter for a change.

"Here we are, Sams. Our first visit to the Donut Emporium." She started to grab for the door, planning to prop it open with her foot while she wheeled Sammy inside. But the door opened on its own accord.

Well, that wasn't exactly true.

"Welcome. My name is Rachel." A nine-or-so-year-old blond wearing a beaded headband, jean shorts, and a lavender T-shirt with sparkles, held the door for them. "We're glad you're here."

Hmm. A four-foot greeter! Now that's something Janey doesn't have at Sweet Sensations.

"Thank you, Rachel." Megan grinned, pushing the chair over the threshold into the bakery where a heavy smell of sugar hung in the air like a cloud of fog.

"We glad we here, too!" Sammy said a bit loudly, causing several customers hovered around the bakery case to turn to look at him. But if Rachel noticed, she wasn't embarrassed. Instead, she nodded at Megan's hands clenched around the wheelchair's handles.

"I can do that for you."

"Yeah?"

Rachel nodded.

Megan sized her up quickly and decided she looked strong and capable enough. She leaned down to get her son's permission. "Sammy? Would you like Rachel to push your chair?"

Sammy nodded vigorously, as she thought he would, his eyes twinkling, already entranced by his new acquaintance.

After getting in line, it was only a matter of minutes until the customers in front of them had cleared out. And there was Sean Shaffer staring at her from behind the glass case.

She really didn't know how Janey could act so nonchalant about seeing Sean again. He was even better looking than he had been in high school. His baby face had matured into easy-on-the-eyes, all-grown-up, good-looking features. It was a warm and friendly face, and his body wasn't so bad either. He was average height, shorter than Mac. But still, even with an apron on, you could tell he had a good physique. Obviously he wasn't much tempted by all the doughnuts he was around every day.

Tilting his head, he squinted. "I feel like I know you, but I'm really bad with remembering names. Sorry."

"Megan." And when he still didn't recognize her, she added, "O'Donnell."

"Right! Your dad was my guidance counselor."

"Probably. He had that last part of the alphabet. *P* through *Z*."

"And this is your little guy?" He nodded to Sammy.

"He sure is. And Rachel is your—"

"Niece. I'm just helping my sister Tammy out. I told her Rach could come and hang out at the shop on days that she works. Helps her save on babysitting money."

Something Megan could relate to. "That's really nice of you."

"It's just until school starts. And she's really been a help. Haven't you, Rachel?"

But Rachel was more interested in Sammy than the adult conversation.

She squatted down to get even with Sammy's face. "What's your name?"

"Sammy."

"Sammy, cool." She spoke to him as if they were equals in age and every other way. "I like your chair. A chair on wheels is a good idea. I could use a chair on wheels when I get tired of standing at the front door."

Megan noticed Sean frown. "Rachel honey, I told you. You don't have to stand at the front door all day."

"That's okay. I don't mind," she answered her uncle.

"Women in my family. . ." Sean shrugged. "They're a hardworking bunch." His lips slid into a proprietor's friendly grin. "So what can I get you, Megan?"

"Actually we just need one jelly doughnut."

"Coming right up." He grabbed a sheet of waxed paper from the dispenser. "That's all?"

"Oh, and I could stand a cup of coffee."

"No problem." He moved in swift motions behind the counter, retrieving the order. But after she'd handed Sammy his doughnut and got her wallet out to pay, Sean paused.

"Wait a minute." He clicked his fingers. "You were good

friends with Janey Saunders, weren't you?"

Megan's hands stilled like she'd been caught stealing a handful of doughnut holes. "Uh, yeah. Yes," she admitted.

Sean harrumphed and rolled his eyes. "I still never got why she told everyone I dumped her at prom senior year. What an imagination! But. . .whatever." He shook his head. "A buddy told me she's the owner of Sweet Sensations bakery."

"Uh, yeah," Megan repeated herself. "Yes, she is. She's had the place for a couple of years."

"Good for her. That's great." Megan noticed his obvious sincerity. "Hopefully she doesn't twist things around and think I'm after her business or anything. Truth is, I finished college with a business degree but then wasn't happy with that, so I went on to culinary school before I moved back here. I'd love to own my own restaurant someday and not just be a doughnut man. But it's all a process. . . ." He grabbed a rag and swiped at the glass counter. "But anyway, back to Janey. Hopefully, she's cool with everything. She still can't be as delusional as back in high school."

"Janey? Ha!" Megan groped for a few dollars from her wallet. "She's uh—Janey's fine. So how much do I owe you?"

"Two dollars."

She couldn't wait to get out of there, her cheeks burning, but Sean took the money and asked, "Anyone else you run into from school?"

"Not really. But you know, I mean, plenty of people are still around. It's just I'm busy with Sammy and work and. . .stuff."

Like sneaking around to doughnut shops for my friend who

really still is a bit delusional. She dropped her wallet into her purse and zipped it up, hoping to hurry out of the shop. But Sean had more things on his mind.

"Hey, come to think of it. Do you remember a redhead in our class? There's a woman who's been coming in here, and well, she reminds me of someone. I just can't put my finger on who. I've gotten to talk to her some, but just when I'm on the verge of asking her name, she scoots out of here before I can find out."

"A redhead?" Megan could feel her face going into a full-fledged burn. "Um, the only *real* redhead I can remember from school was Melanie Ellis." Well, that was a version of the truth.

"No, definitely not her. This woman is taller. Usually has on a sunhat and sunglasses. Really great sense of style and, I don't know. Just something about her."

He had a misty look in his eyes that made Megan want to die on the spot. No doubt he was taken by the mysterious redhead and maybe even wanted to ask her out.

It was the same starry-eyed expression her almost-seven-year-old had on his face, she noticed, as he stared at Rachel. Sammy, her special-needs son, who was pretending to be especially needy and intentionally messier than usual, getting jelly all over his shirt so Rachel would continue to wipe it off.

I'll never get those stains out! Megan sighed.

Oh, did she have a lot to say to Janey tonight. An entire earful. Or two.

The morning hadn't been going anything like Megan had planned, and the trend continued when she arrived at the clinic.

"Your eleven o'clock just called and had to reschedule." The receptionist worried her lip. "I tried to reach you."

"Oh." Megan moaned. "I had my phone on silent and didn't even think to look at it. But thanks for trying, Ellen," she tried to say brightly even though she felt her shoulders slump in disappointment. If only she'd known she had more time, she and Sammy could've visited Mrs. Biddle, whose recovery had been going remarkably well. Or she could've taken Sammy to nearby Montgomery for a really nice breakfast at First Watch or the Pancake House. Instead of ending up at Donut Emporium where she'd evaded the truth, and was still feeling bad about it even though she only did it to protect her "redheaded" friend.

"It looks like your next patient isn't due for another thirty minutes or so."

"Well, in that case I think I'll try to get caught up on some paperwork," Megan said. But as soon as the words were out of her mouth, she remembered that Mac had a radio interview. His first radio interview to promote their All-Stars Sports Day event. And, glancing at her watch, she figured he might be in the midst of it right at that moment.

Bypassing her office, she walked down the hall to the employee lounge where a portable radio sat on the kitchen counter. One of the other therapists had brought it in at the beginning of baseball season so they could tune in to games in between patients. Turning it on, Megan switched it to the correct station, feeling an instant gush of warmth when she heard Mac's voice.

"Yes, Trista, that's true," he was saying as Megan settled into a cushioned chair. "A lot of people in Loveland and many local businesses have been working together to ensure All-Stars Sports Day will be a true success."

"And now, tell us, what kind of activities will be on hand for the participants?" the interviewer—Trista—asked.

"All sorts of things," Mac told her. "Whether a child is wheelchair-bound or not, we'll have outdoor bowling, croquet, basketball, and all kinds of fun races just to name a few activities. Also, luckily, some of my baseball buddies from the Hawks will be there that day to play ball along with a handful of volunteers. Whoever wants to challenge them should go online and sign up. We plan to rotate players if we get overloaded."

"You're obviously pumped about this, huh, MacNeill?"

"I am. It's one of the most exciting things I've ever been involved with in my entire career."

"And speaking of your career, some people may wonder how you got from there to here—to heading up an event like this."

"I don't think it's much of a stretch really. I've always loved sports, especially baseball. This event gives me the opportunity to help disabled kids play, or even discover some sport that they might enjoy."

The interviewer giggled in a way that sounded out of context, causing Megan to frown. Why did she have the feeling the woman was fishing for something?

"Uh-huh. Oh sure, I get that part, Mac." Trista's voice suddenly sounded sweeter than Sammy's jelly doughnut. Plus, she'd gone from MacNeill to a friendly "Mac" fairly quickly in Megan's opinion.

"The bottom line is, you like games, right?" the interviewer cooed.

"Well, sure. Sure I do."

"And it seems you've played your share of them. On the field. And off the field."

What on earth? Megan shot up straight in the chair, stunned. Staring at the little silver box, she willed Mac to come back with some brilliant response. Something to defend himself. Or a segue to change the subject entirely. But he stammered and hemmed and hawed, sounding as caught off guard as she was.

"I—excuse me?" is all he managed to get out.

Trista, however, didn't skip a beat.

"Is that why you've never been able to settle down with one person and take a relationship seriously?"

"Hello!" Megan jumped out of the chair. "Is this an interview or an inquisition?" She shouted at the inanimate radio, wishing so much she could come to Mac's aid. Luckily, for the sake of their All-Stars Sports event, Mac was doing a better job of keeping his composure than she was. He simply laughed. It was a forced sort of laugh, she knew, but at least he maintained his cool.

"You know, Trista—" he started slowly, his voice even.

Ever the expert, Trista cut him off deftly before he could fully recover. "On another note, sounds as if you have some news you may want to tell us about."

"Some news?" Mac asked.

Some news? Megan repeated in her head.

"About the rumors."

Megan blinked once at the radio, and then once again, waiting to hear Mac's reply. *Rumors? Really?* Was there something he'd failed to tell her? Something everyone else knew?

"I'm not sure what you're referring to," he finally said, allowing Megan to let go of a pent-up breath she didn't even realize she'd been holding.

Trista prodded on. "Isn't your agent talking to other teams?"

"Agents are always talking. That's what they're good at."

"Oh, you sure are the coy one, MacNeill Hattaway, aren't you?" Trista's tone had gone all gooey again. "Well, if you won't tell our listeners then I will. Rumor has it that once you get that elbow of yours healed you could be playing for the Mariners or the Miners."

The Mariners or Miners? Seattle or Sacramento? Megan felt her heart sink all the way to her toes. *Thousands of miles from Loveland, Ohio? Really, Mac?*

"Like I said, agents are always talking. I can't comment about that, Trista."

"But it is a possibility then?"

Megan crossed her arms over her chest, feeling like she was about to get hit with some unsettling news. But Mac's answer was vague.

"In major league sports, anything's a possibility, Trista."

"Of course." Trista sighed at the ambiguous answer, and

Megan did, too, for a whole other reason. "So, MacNeill, since we're running out of time here," Trista began to wrap up the interview, "is there anything you *would* like to comment on?"

"Sure. I just want to remind folks that they can go on-line to get all the details about the All-Stars Sports Day games at. . ."

Megan didn't need to hear any more. In fact, as she edged up to the counter to turn off the radio, she almost wished she'd never turned the thing on in the first place.

It had been hard enough to be reminded about Mac's past dealings with women. To have it publicly restated that the man she'd fallen for had never, ever been involved in a lasting relationship before.

But then the other issue—the news that he might be traded! Just the idea of it caused her knees to go weak. Grabbing on to the counter for support, she stared at the white tiles behind the sink, Mac's words playing over and over in her head.

"*. . .anything's a possibility. . .*"

That definitely left a lot of doors open. And was it true that he couldn't comment? Or that he wouldn't?

She wished so much she could've seen Mac's face to gauge his expression because she certainly couldn't read anything into his voice.

Oh dear Lord, what have I done? She buried her head in her hands. *What have I been thinking?*

Somehow she'd let down her guard because of Mac's attentiveness to her and Sammy. She'd succumbed to all of his sweetness. . .his charm. . .and ultimately—his kiss.

Somehow, yes somehow before she knew it, she'd come to love the man!

But the guy she loved was the Mac she'd seen riding his tractor through the fields when she pulled up to his driveway. It was Mac, the co-chair she'd been so reluctant about at first, whose fervor to create a special day for the disabled kids was unrelenting. The man who knuckle-bumped the volunteers and kept them charged up and smiling.

And then. . .when the time was right, it was the man who could make the world go away when he held her in his arms and drew her close to his chest. And who used those same strong arms to lift Sammy up time and time again. Who would swing her son in the air till Sammy giggled in a way—so free, so gleefully—that she had to swallow back the lump of gratitude in her throat and blink away the tears from the corner of her eyes.

That was the Mac she knew. That was the Mac she loved. She didn't even know the baseball-playing Mac. Wasn't acquainted with the World Series–winning pitcher. She'd only read about that Mac in newspapers and tabloids.

And if Mac started playing ball again, traveling, having women falling at his feet—what then? Even if he could handle that, could she? Could she really handle having a relationship with a celebrity? Someone who could possibly get uprooted, moving from team to team, year to year? Is that the kind of life she wanted for herself? More than anything, is that the kind of life she wanted for Sammy?

And what about Mac? Could she ask him to give it up?

"You okay?" Ellen breezed into the lounge and grabbed a bottled water from the refrigerator.

"Stomach's just a little queasy," Megan answered truthfully. Probably because she felt like she'd just fallen from the cloud she'd happily been drifting along on for the past few weeks.

But it's all my fault. All my fault. Sammy and I were just fine. For so many years we've kept it together. I've kept it together, all under control. And then I did what I said I'd never do. I had to let a man into our lives. And not just any man—but a pro athlete for goodness' sakes!

"I probably just drank a lot of coffee without enough food." She shrugged an excuse to her concerned-looking coworker.

"There's a box of Saltines in the cabinet." Ellen pointed over Megan's head. "Or I have some yogurt in the fridge. I hope you're not getting a summer bug or anything. Those are the worst." Ellen scrunched her nose sympathetically.

Megan sucked in a deep breath. "No, no bug. I'll be fine." She drew herself up straight.

She had to be fine. No matter what, for Sammy, she had to be. But, oh, how her chest ached! Everything in her heart wanted Mac. . .wanted to be close and stay close to the Mac she knew. But doubts and fears weighed in heavily, warning just the opposite. Cautioning her to take a step back. Before it was too late.

Chapter 16

Even hours after the interview, while driving to the team doc's office for his appointment, Mac was still berating himself for the turn his talk with Ms. Newmark had taken. He sure was out of practice, he thought, as he guided his truck up Columbia Road.

He'd never been that crazy about interviews to begin with. Had never cared for the spotlight much—which he figured most people would probably find hard to believe, considering how much media attention he attracted. But even so, he used to be more adept at steering an interview in the direction he wanted it to go.

Typically, with most female interviewers, he could use his swagger and any number of compliments to get off a sore topic and onto a more palatable one. And with guys, it was generally easy to buddy up and banter about games and statistics till time ran out.

Plus, a lot of interviews were done over the phone now and not at the stations, which didn't help. It was always better to see who you were facing. Who you were dealing with. Like this Trista Newmark woman.

He stopped at the next intersection and turned the air-conditioning down to low, mulling over the woman's name in his head.

Trista. Trista. Newmark. The name sounded more than

vaguely familiar, but he couldn't fathom why.

Aw well, maybe it's good I didn't lay eyes on her. Maybe the woman would've turned me to stone. Undoubtedly, she wanted to make things uncomfortable for him for some reason. And she had!

He pushed on the accelerator and at the same moment his cell phone vibrated in the drink holder of the console. He picked it up, glancing at the screen. Hal. He clicked on the phone and didn't even bother with a hello.

"You were listening, huh?"

"Yeah, obviously Ms. Newmark isn't a fan of yours."

"Uh, that's putting it mildly." Mac chuckled. "It's okay, though. I'm a little rusty fending off touchy subjects. But I'll get my chops back. Plus it didn't help that she caught me off guard the second time around with that business about getting traded. Wonder where that came from?" he asked—as if he didn't know.

"It never hurts to leak a rumor here and there, Mac."

"Rumors. Aren't those sort of like lies, Hal?"

"No. Look it up in the dictionary. A rumor is an unverified story, and stories are fiction. It's the nature of the game. Keeps your name in the news."

Good old Hal. He never gave it a rest. "You could've warned me."

"Yeah, well, even so, you pulled it off. You were getting your act together by the end there. . ." Hal's voice drifted momentarily. "You on your way to Kline's office?"

"I'm pulling in as we speak."

Making a right turn into Dr. Kline's lot, Mac parked his truck in the reserved section alongside the red brick medical building.

"Let me know how it goes," Hal requested. "Actually, I'll call you back in an hour to hear what I'm already programming to be fantastic news, okay?"

Mac half smiled. "Sounds good," he assured him before clicking off the phone and cutting the ignition. Sliding out of the truck, he scuffed over the pavement in his sandals, realizing for the first time that morning that his stomach felt nervous.

Who knew what news Dr. Kline would have for him? He thought his elbow was feeling better. Feeling fine actually. But it really wasn't up to him whether he'd be okayed to play ball again. And that's what the appointment was all about.

It is what it is, right, Lord?

He had all the faith in the world that God would see him through any answer the doc gave him. Still, he paused on the sidewalk a moment, rolled his shoulders back, and inhaled deeply before he slipped into the side entrance of the facility designated for Hawks players and other pro athletes.

Immediately, a receptionist welcomed him and ushered him into an examination room reserved for pro athletes under Dr. Kline's care. It was only minutes before the orthopedic surgeon bustled into the room.

"What's up with those Hawks?" the doctor asked, by way of a greeting. He extended his right hand, and Mac reached out to shake it, always appreciative of how the busy Dr. Kline made sure to make eye contact.

"They're doing fairly decent."

"Yeah, decent is the word for it. But not great."

"Ah. There're some new guys on the team. Young ones. But they'll get it together."

"Let's hope." The doctor rolled his eyes. "So how's the elbow?"

"That's what I'm here to find out."

Mac extended his arm again, and this time the doctor took a few minutes to examine it thoroughly.

"Everything feels good. And looks good. How does it feel to you?"

Mac shrugged. "I've been whittling and doing some work at the farm. I feel like the physical labor has been building it up lately, not breaking it down."

"Farm work, huh?" The doctor smiled, clearly amused but also looking at Mac more respectfully than Mac had ever noticed before. "Think you might want to leave the cow pasture behind and get back out on the mound again?"

"Are you asking me, Doc? Or telling me?"

"I'm telling you, Mac. Considering all that arm of yours went through in the accident, I didn't know if I'd ever be able to say this—but you're cleared to pitch again." Dr. Kline patted him on the back. "You're good to go, number sixty-one."

"Thanks, Doc. I mean it. Really, thanks," he kept repeating, stunned. Excited. And relieved.

In fact, all the way out to his truck, it didn't feel like his feet touched the ground. He couldn't believe that in less time than it had taken for Trista Newmark to drag him through his past, Dr. Kline had given him hope for his future. A chance to play ball again.

He hadn't bothered to tell Megan about his appointment, not even knowing if anything would come of his visit to Dr. Kline, figuring he'd deal with it on his own. But now, hopping into his Ford, he reached into the console for his phone and started to call her, wanting to share the good news with her. And her alone.

But then he stopped himself.

She'd be working and most likely wouldn't pick up her phone anyway. And besides that, he decided, getting his elbow cleared was big news. Really big. The kind of news you tell in person. To a person you care about.

He'd try to keep quiet about it until he saw her the next time, although he wasn't sure when that would be. She'd be busy having dinner with Janey later and he'd be busy, sneaking Sammy out to practice bowling.

Still and all, there was another someone he needed to talk to, wasn't there? A conversation that couldn't wait. So he drove to the nearest church he could find and luckily found its doors unlocked. He wanted to get down on his knees and give thanks and praise. He wanted to ask for forgiveness once again, too.

Because while sitting in Dr. Kline's office he'd finally remembered why Trista's name sounded so familiar. And why she probably had been harsh with him. Trista had a younger sister named Trina whose heart he *had* played games with years ago. But those weren't the kinds of games he wanted to play again. No, not anymore.

Megan eyed the row of blue umbrellas topping Paxton's outdoor café tables. "Do you want to eat dinner inside or out?" she asked Janey.

"Oh, let's try outside. I've been inside all day. Or, no." Janey changed her mind. As usual. "It's still kind of hot out here. Why don't we go in?"

"In is good," Megan agreed wholeheartedly, pulling open the old-style wood door of the grill.

She was more than glad to escape the oppressive heat of the evening. Her head had been pounding for hours as if Colonel Thomas Paxton's entire eighteenth-century militia had been marching across it. After the day she'd had, to say she was plain worn out emotionally and physically was an understatement. She was more than ready for any creature comforts and could feel her body relax a bit and go "ah" at the cool feel of the restaurant's air-conditioning. The cushioned booth she and Janey settled into felt heavenly to her tired limbs.

More feelings of well-being spread through her when silver-haired Geneva, who'd been serving at Paxton's since Megan was a teenager, came to the table bearing two icy cold glasses of water with lemon. "Hot out there, isn't it, girls?"

"I hope the weather lady is right." Janey nodded. "I hope we get some of the cooler weather she's been promising."

"It's getting closer to back-to-school time." Geneva slipped two straws from the hip pocket of her khaki capris and laid them on the table. "Things should be getting cooler soon," she said as her eyes lit on Megan. "So...do you know what you want, hon?"

"I—I. . ." Megan could feel her mind still reeling from the events of the day. For a moment she almost forgot

Geneva was asking about food and not something more philosophical as in what she wanted out of life and love in her pursuit of happiness. But then the question clicked. "I'll just have the usual," she finally replied.

"One grilled chicken Caesar salad coming right up." Geneva nodded before turning to Janey. "And are you trying another wrap tonight?" She winked knowingly.

"Why not? I'm almost through the list. How about the Big Veggie Wrap? That sounds good."

"They are good." Geneva's eyes widened reassuringly.

"Is Allie working tonight?" Megan asked before Geneva could slip away. No doubt she needed some ibuprofen for her headache. But a dose of Allie's company could always work wonders.

"Yeah, she's in the back." Geneva pointed toward the kitchen. "Covering for our dishwasher who has the flu." She rolled her eyes as if she might not believe that excuse. "I'll tell her you gals are here. I'm sure she'd like an excuse to take off her rubber gloves and say hi."

As Geneva walked away, Megan pulled her purse onto her lap and reached into the deep pocketbook, feeling around for her container of ibuprofen.

"Are you trying to tell me something?" Janey asked when she pulled out the plastic bottle. "I know I can be a real pain."

"Oh no, it's not you." Megan gave a soft smile at her friend's self-deprecating humor. "It's just—it's been a day."

Not only had she endured Mac's interview, but an hour later, Dan Hoffman had come in singing Mac's praises throughout his entire therapy session. Everything he'd had to say was true, but she'd been trying to get Mac off her mind by working instead of being reminded of him every second of work.

But that hadn't happened. Not even when Dan's session was up. Someone else tuned in to the Hawks' afternoon game, which led to more chatter about baseball and their fellow Loveland-ite Mac. By the time she'd seen more patients, picked up Sammy from day care, and driven to her parents' house, all she wanted to do was take a few minutes to put her feet up on the couch before meeting up with Janey. But her mom had rushed her out of the house as if she couldn't wait to get rid of her.

She sighed, opened the ibuprofen, and shook out a pill. It wasn't until then that she remembered how the entire day had started—with her crazy trip to Donut Emporium. How could she have forgotten that?

"By the way, I did it," she told her friend.

"Did what?"

"I dropped into Donut Emporium for you."

"You did?" Janey's eyes darted from side to side as if someone nearby might hear what they were talking about. Of course, Megan could've told her that no one did hear, and no one cared to hear either. "What did you think?" her friend leaned forward, looking overly conspiratorial.

"About the place?" Megan lifted a shoulder. "It's, you know, it's a doughnut shop. I mean, it's super clean and he had his cute little niece Rachel greeting people. And I suppose it's in a good location. I mean, if a person needs to stop and get gas, too. But again, Janey, when it comes to your bakery, it's like I told you before—they're two different things."

"Was *he* there? Did you see him?"

"He, Sean? Oh yes, my dear friend, *he* was there."

Thinking back on the conversation with Sean and how she'd evaded the truth made her head hurt even more. She shook out another pill. Placing the tablets on her tongue, she gulped them down with some icy water.

Meanwhile, Janey's lips pursed together tightly. A look of ill ease contorted her face.

"Janey, I really can't imagine that you don't think Sean's cute."

"Cute?" Her friend's eyes grew wide. "How can I think he's cute? He's the competition, Megan. And that's the only way I need to see him—as the competition."

Megan shook her head. "He's not really, you know. He's not actually trying to compete."

"How can you say that?"

"He's just a guy with dreams." Megan shrugged, recalling her conversation with Sean. "Just a guy who would like to open a restaurant but had to settle for a doughnut shop for the time being. It's really not that complicated."

"You're siding with *him*?" A pouting lip immediately erupted on Janey's face.

"Of course not. If I were, I certainly wouldn't have evaded his questions this morning."

"You told a lie?"

"Well, I didn't tell the whole truth, that's for sure. He asked me if I knew a redhead who'd been coming into his shop. And then he described you." Taking a packet of crackers from the condiment basket, Megan tore at the wrapper. "I have to warn you, he had that funny look in his eyes. Like he'll probably ask you out if you ever go in there again, Red. So you'd better be careful about traipsing into the Emporium. Or be prepared with a reason why you can't date him."

Megan bit into a cracker, brushed away some crumbs that had fallen on the table, and then looked up at Janey—whose cheeks were unusually flushed. More like on fire. "Oh my gosh!" The realization hit her. "That's your plan?" She sputtered cracker crumbs into the air. "You *want* him to ask you out? So then you can stand him up the way you think he stood you up at prom?"

Instantly her friend scooted back from the table, looking sheepish. But it took a few moments and some direct staring into her eyes before Janey came clean. "Okay, yes. Yes, it had crossed my mind to pay him back. But then I realized that's just silly and petty, and that it's about more than that. It's about business. It's about Sweet Sensations."

"Hmm. All about business, huh?"

Even that didn't ring true to Megan. She knew her friend would never intentionally harm anyone, but she also knew the girl had a penchant for winning. Janey Saunders hated to lose at anything—whether it was a game of tennis, making muffins, or having the upper hand in a relationship.

If Janey wasn't deliberately trying to even an old score with Sean then it could only mean one other thing. Something Megan should've recognized in her friend much sooner. Especially considering she'd done pretty much the same thing with Mac, protesting wildly about him to anyone who mentioned his name when he'd first come into her life.

"And you're sure it's not about any other 'sensations'?"

She stressed the word long and clear. "Maybe some you're feeling for Sean?" Megan cracked a smile at her friend.

But Janey only frowned. And groaned. "Oh Megan. . . what have I done? Even if I had some, well, interest in Sean—I mean what do I do at this point? Whip off my red wig and say, 'Surprise! It's me, Janey!' He'd think I was crazy."

"He already thinks you're—" Hurriedly, she stuffed the uneaten half of the cracker in her mouth to stop from saying more.

"Already thinks what?"

Megan worked to swallow the dry thing. "That you're— c–cute."

"You mean he thinks the redheaded girl is cute."

"Oh. Yeah. Yeah, you're right."

With that sad epiphany and the rest of the day still weighing on her, Megan slumped back in the booth. Rubbing at her temples, she wished the ibuprofen would kick in quickly. "Oh Janey. . .this guy stuff isn't easy, is it? How did we get ourselves into these situations?" She let go of a deep sigh.

"Situations? What situations?" Allie suddenly appeared with their tray of food and a bright smile.

"Allie! It's so good to see you!" Megan knew she sounded over the top. But she couldn't help it. Seeing Allie, her spirits lifted immediately, like the cavalry had suddenly arrived.

"Sit and we'll tell you everything." Janey scooted over to make room.

"Wish I could, but it's one of those nights around here." Without having to ask, Allie correctly set their plates down in front of them. "I'm filling in for the fill-ins."

"How are the kids?" Megan asked, ignoring her salad for the moment. "Everyone good?"

"Great. They're coming with me to help with the Volunteer Day out at Mac's farm." She paused, scanning the table. "You all need anything else? Extra honey mustard or anything?" Allie glanced between the two of them.

Megan shook her head along with Janey. "We're fine." She unrolled her napkin in her lap. "I'm so glad you're bringing the kids out."

"Yeah." Allie nodded. "I think it'll be good for them, although they probably won't last very long."

"That's okay. It'll just be fun to have you guys there for however long."

"So. . .how's everything going with Mac?" Allie plopped her hands on her hips, looking bent on cutting to the chase. "He's not one of your 'situations,' is he?"

Megan should've known her intuitive and inquisitive friend wouldn't let her earlier question go unanswered. Glancing from Allie to Janey and back to Allie again, she finally found her voice and 'fessed up. "It's—it's a long story. I just think maybe— I don't know, I'm thinking I should take a step back."

"Back?" Janey jumped in. "Like back to under a rock?" She looked at Megan like she'd gone crazy.

"Excuse me, *Red*? You should talk."

Allie leaned over the table, spreading her hands referee-style between them. "You two are beginning to sound like sisters. I don't know what you all are talking about, and I wish I had time for the details. But the thing that I've found

works best with Greg is honesty. Pure and simple honesty."
She paused thoughtfully. "And well, peanut butter cookies.
Those work great. Oh—and foot rubs. He really likes—"

Allie must've realized that she and Janey were staring at
her because she stopped there. "Well, maybe you just want
to start with honesty."

Straightforward and sensible. No wonder she and Allie
had always been the best of friends. "Sure you can't sit? For
just a minute?" Megan asked again, hoping more chatting
with Allie would help clear her head. But Greg was waving to his wife from the kitchen, and after a round of hugs,
Allie went back to work. Meanwhile, she and Janey let the
subjects of Sean and Mac rest while they ate dinner, which
was probably better for their digestive systems anyway.

Once they finished and the table was cleared, Janey got
out her publicity folder and started going through the papers inside.

"This is the press release Mary Duncan wrote up. I'll
be sending it to the *Enquirer* and the *Loveland Herald*. It's
an update, giving more details about the activities now that
we have that information. Oh, and this"—she pulled a mint
green paper from her stack—"is another flyer advertising
the event. It'll probably be the last one to go out."

"I love the All-Stars Sports logo you came up with,
Janey. It looks great in print and I can't wait to see it on the
T-shirts."

"Thanks. It did turn out good, didn't it?" Her friend
preened. "Mary and Beth Hermann have offered to take the
flyers to Maineville, Montgomery, and Milford and put them
up on bulletin boards in Starbucks and places like that."

"That'll be great."

"Oh, and thanks for sending this to me also." Janey slid a photo from the folder. "Do you have the disc for it? I'm not sure just yet where or how we might use it. But I'm glad you had someone take it. It's a darling picture of you and Mac and Sammy."

"Me and Mac and Sammy? From Amazing Race day? Or what?" She couldn't imagine what Janey was talking about. "Can I see?"

Janey handed her the photo and Megan's heart stopped still in her chest. "I—I didn't send this to you."

"You didn't? It came without a name. That's why I assumed it was from you. Honestly, I was wondering why you didn't just drop it off to me at the bakery."

"Oh, this is. . .this is creepy." A new pain shot between her eyes.

"You didn't know anything about it?"

"No, not at all. Well, I mean that day Sammy and I went out to Mac's farm for the first time, there was a man there with a camera. He ran off as soon as we noticed him. Mac went chasing after him, but never caught up. And. . .well, I guess I didn't realize he'd taken pictures of us." She sighed. "Or at least I'd hoped he hadn't."

She stared at the photo in her hand. It would've been a great picture of the three of them on the blanket enjoying each other and the sunshine, if it hadn't been taken by some person lurking in the shrubs. It would've been a nice way to remember the day, if it hadn't been taken by someone who'd been stalking them. "I don't understand why someone would do this. It's not like they're making money from it."

"Yeah, not true paparazzi, I suppose." Janey reached for

the photo and folded it in half and in half again as if she clearly meant to discard it later. "I'm sorry I upset you." She shoved the bent-up photo back in the folder.

"You didn't do anything. I just don't understand. . .who?"

"I don't know. You and Sammy were in Sweet Sensations before you went out to Mac's that day. Someone could've overheard us talking about it." Janey bit her lip. "Maybe?"

"But why?"

Janey shrugged. "Probably because Mac's a celebrity. I mean, it's just like that Trista lady this morning during the radio interview. Who knows why she went after him?"

"You heard that, too?"

"Yeah." Janey sounded solemn for a change. "That's why you said what you did earlier? About backing off? Is it true you think he'll get traded from the Hawks?"

"I don't know what to think. Or what I think." She looked into her friend's sympathetic eyes. "But I know I need to stop wondering and go ask Mac."

And that was the honest truth.

Chapter 17

Mac had barely gotten home from his bowling practice with Sammy, locked up his truck, unlocked the front door of the house, and flicked on the outdoor lights when he heard a set of tires hit the gravel driveway.

Seeing Megan's white SUV wind its way up the drive by the light of the half moon, he hustled out onto the wraparound porch, quickly grabbed the whittling knife he kept in an antique milk case by the front door and a birch limb he'd been working on resting up against the case. Plopping himself down into one of the weatherworn wicker chairs, he leaned back and propped his feet up on the wide wooden railing that ran the length of the porch.

As if on cue, Bitty came meowing out of the evening darkness and curled up by his feet, making it look like the pair of them had been sitting there together for hours that way. Which happened to be a good thing, since he'd implied to Megan that he'd be hanging out at the farm all night while she was out to dinner with Janey.

Knife and tree limb in hands, he pretended to be engrossed in his whittling. But, of course, his mind was a hundred miles from that, happily focused on Megan instead.

He was surprised that she was dropping by instead of heading over to her parents' to pick up Sammy, but glad, too. His time practicing bowling with Sammy had been really special, and now the chance to spend a few hours with Megan would be even more so. Altogether, both activities made him feel privileged, like he'd won the lottery or something. And the other good thing—he wouldn't have to wait any longer to tell her the big news about his elbow.

But after he heard her cut the engine, noticed the headlights go off after a bit, and then watched her amble slowly up the sidewalk with her head bent down, he sensed something wasn't right.

Immediately his legs dropped from the rail with a thud. He laid the whittling paraphernalia aside and got up from the chair, wanting to go toward her. But the way she wouldn't even look up at him paralyzed him. He froze in step as Megan paused on the second porch step and wouldn't come any closer. Felt his stomach instinctively twist when she didn't bother to reach out and pet Bitty like she usually did.

"Did I interrupt anything?" Megan finally looked his way, but managed to avoid his eyes.

"Are you kidding? I'm glad you stopped over. Want to sit?" He pointed over his shoulder at the pair of once-white chairs.

"No. I have to go pick up Sammy. Just thought I'd drop by on my way."

He knew her parents' house was in the complete opposite direction, but didn't mention it.

"How was dinner?" he asked instead.

"Good."

"Paxton's is always good."

"True. It always is."

And there it was—an awkward silence. They rarely had

those anymore, not since they'd first met. But they sure were having one now. Mac felt pressed to fill the void.

"Sure you don't want to sit down?" Maybe if he could just keep her near him, close in his camp, he could unravel whatever was suddenly tangling up things between them.

"No." She fidgeted with the keys in her hand, barely looking at him. "I just— Well, I needed to talk to you is all."

"Okay. No problem."

But it wasn't okay, and the way she was acting was a problem. He tried to soften his expression, making it easier for her to speak. But his jaw clenched instinctively, as if preparing to get struck by who knew what. "I'm all ears."

"Well, I—I was thinking. . ." She rubbed at her forehead as if it was paining her to do so. "Tomorrow all the volunteers will be out here, and well, next week is the big event and—"

"Oh yeah—and don't forget Thursday they'll be announcing the event at the Hawks' home game. We're still on for that, right? I wanted you to meet some of the guys. They're characters. But underneath it all, they're okay guys." He forced a chuckle, despite the unease he felt between them. "You'll like them."

"Yeah. . .that's one of the things I wanted to talk about." Megan paused, bit her lip. "I—I don't think I can go with you."

"Yeah? You have to work? Need a sitter?" She really hadn't planned ahead for the game? That stung a bit.

"No, I. . ." She shifted on her feet, causing the shadows around her face to shift as well. The light caught her features, and he had a clearer sight of the gripping consternation there. How had that happened when the last time he saw her she only had smiles for him—and what he thought was love shining in her eyes?

"That's—that's what I was going to talk to you about, Mac. I mean in a week this'll all be over, you know? Sports Day will be over. And well, when it is, we won't exactly be tied together anymore."

Not tied together anymore?

"What?"

"Well, if it wasn't for the All-Stars Sports Day event we would've never met. Even you said that at one point."

"Yeah, but I just meant—"

She talked over him, noticeably intent on cutting him off. "And you're right, we wouldn't have met. So now that the sports day is almost over—well, next week—there's no reason you—we—need to keep seeing one another."

"No reason?" In a millisecond, his chin hardened. Anger surged up into his head, making it feel as if his brain could explode instantaneously. Despite that, he worked to control his voice. "You really think there's no reason?"

"I'm just trying to be honest with you, Mac. I mean, it just makes sense that we'd back off. You know, now that we're not going to have anything to connect us together anymore."

What was she talking about? Where was all of this coming from?

Nothing to connect them? That was like a bullet to the heart.

He clenched his teeth. Okay. Well. If she couldn't see all the things they had in common to connect them, he sure wasn't going to stand there and enumerate them all.

And if she truly didn't feel connected to him in all the ways he felt attached to her, what was he going to do? Beg her to feel differently?

He couldn't believe the humiliation, the hurt. He'd never had to beg a woman for anything before. His pulse pounded in his temples as he tried to contain his temper. His fists clenched at his side.

"I don't know why you're suddenly acting this way," he ground out. "Aren't you even going to tell me why you changed your mind?"

He lifted his jaw, prepared to take whatever comments she dished out. His insides in turmoil, he tried to make eye contact, ready to see the truth for himself in her eyes.

But she turned her face away, looking out past the glow of the porch light, into the dark night instead. When she didn't answer him at first, a trickle of hope seeped in. Tempting him to reach out to her. But it was obvious she'd made a decision not to stand within his reach. He shoved his hands into the pockets of his jeans instead.

"Megan? Aren't you going to answer me?" So frustrated, his words came out in a bark. "Is this really what you want?"

She turned at the sound of his voice, and he thought he saw tears coming from her eyes. But she backed down the steps into the blackness before he could be sure of what he was seeing. There was no denying what he heard though.

"Yes, it's—it's okay with me," her voice hitched on the words.

He stood stunned as she fled down the sidewalk to her car.

Megan could barely see through her tears well enough to make the turn-around by Mac's barn and to head out of his driveway onto Route 48. Luckily the dark, winding part of the country road had become more familiar to her over the past several months. She'd driven it often lately, easily sailing over the once-foreign curves on her way to the farm. And every time she did, the drive and just thinking of where she was headed gave her that warm, excited feeling of coming home.

Just like Mac had.

Oh, what have I done? She sobbed into the darkness.

"What have I done?" The words echoed back at her. So did her remorse. The talk with Mac hadn't gone anything like she'd wanted it to. It hadn't gone at all the way she'd planned it would.

On her drive over to see him, she'd decided she'd do exactly what Allie had suggested. That she'd be honest and open and tell him everything that was on her mind. How she really wasn't sure she could handle being involved with a professional baseball player. How she liked control and didn't do topsy-turvy all that well and didn't know if she could take being in a relationship with someone who would always be traveling. Or who could get traded to a city across the country.

And the whole celebrity thing. She'd really wanted to talk with him about that. Sure, there were countless women out there who might find Mac's star factor attractive and alluring. But it didn't hold much appeal for her. In fact, it frightened her more than anything.

Especially where Sammy was concerned. And especially after Janey showed her that photo of the three of them. To think that being in a relationship with Mac could put her and Sammy in the limelight—make them targets for gossip and subjects for sneaky thrill-seekers who wanted to get a picture of them all—scared her. Point blank.

She was going to say all of that. Get it all off her chest. And from there, she'd imagined they could sit and talk, sort things out. Truly, in her heart of hearts, she thought just seeing Mac would ease much of the fear she'd been feeling about the two of them being together.

But then she'd pulled into his driveway.

And right before she turned off her headlights, she looked across the field and saw it—the practice diamond where Mac and his uncle had spent so much time together.

Baseball. It truly was Mac's first love. He'd told her that. And the thing was, he didn't even have to tell her. She could see it in his eyes. In his whole being. He came to life just talking about it.

She'd felt so much closer to him the day he'd shared that with her—all about his love of baseball.

Funny though, how now the realization of how important the sport was to him made her feel so distant from him.

Baseball was what Mac was meant to do. He was great at it. It was his calling. Others might still be wondering if he'd ever play again. But from all she'd seen and all she knew about elbows, she didn't know any reason why he wouldn't be out on the mound next season.

Which was nothing short of a miracle.

But then miracles do happen when they're supposed to.

"And Mac is supposed to play ball," she whispered to herself.

The reality of it felt like a stab to her gut, making her crumple in the car seat. It hurt so much, realizing she shouldn't get in the way of that with all her reservations. Her hang-ups. And fears.

She loved him. Yes, she loved him too much for that to happen.

And, no, he shouldn't have to give up his first love. Shouldn't have to compromise or choose. And by backing out on their relationship the way she had, she'd made it easy for him. He wouldn't have to make choices or concessions.

Of course, he hadn't looked happy about it. But once he started playing ball again, he'd be fine. Everything would be okay again. For him.

A block from her parents' house, she paused her car at a stop sign, sitting there awhile wishing in some small way that knowing that gave her some sort of solace. At the moment though, her heart ached intensely. And it seemed impossible and improbable that it would ever stop.

Finally pulling into her folks' driveway, she grabbed a tissue from her purse and blotted at her eyes. Took a few final sniffles, tried to pinch some pink into her cheeks, and put on a fresh dab of lipstick.

Hopefully, her mom wouldn't notice she'd been crying. The last thing she needed was to listen to her mother right now. But...as she shut the car door and walked up the drive, she wondered if she should've listened to Allie.

True, in the end she'd done what she thought was right—what first came to her heart. But oh, how it hurt. Oh, how it felt so wrong!

Chapter 18

Even with all the people swarming around his farm for Volunteer Day, and even though he was bent over a makeshift worktable involved in making a wooden booth from scratch, Mac could still sense exactly where Megan was at all moments.

They'd barely said a polite hello to one another when she'd first arrived with Sammy and her parents. Quick as they could manage, they'd gone their separate ways busying themselves with all there was to do with All-Stars Sports Day just a week away. The problem was, even hours later, he could still feel her presence as if she were tethered to him.

Unfortunately, where Megan was concerned, he had a natural sixth sense about her. Similar to the sixth sense he'd had on the pitcher's mound where he could easily pick off runners who were trying to steal bases behind his back.

Only with Megan, it was far worse. There was no reprieve. No three strikes and batter's out, with a time to rest during the next half inning. Instead, the feelings didn't stop. Making it super difficult to concentrate on all the pieces of wood strewn around him while he could perceive her traipsing across his property, helping out the groups of volunteers. And making it much harder than it needed to be to construct a simple, last-minute balloon stand, especially when all he really wanted to do was reach out for her—which apparently was exactly what she didn't want from him.

Much as he couldn't stand it, as he bent over his work his mind was totally focused on her and clearly not on the task at—

Hand!

"Ah, for the love of Pete!" He shot up straight, flicking his hand in the air, trying to shake the pain from his thumb.

"It works a lot better when you hit *the nail* with your hammer. Not your thumb," a male voice came up from behind, razzing him.

Mac craned his neck around to see. "Thanks, Dan," he grumbled, too irritated to greet the older man any other way. "I'll have to remember that."

"Hurt much?"

It hurts something awful, he wanted to say. But, of course, Dan was talking about his thumb and not everything else that was aching inside of him.

"Only when you keep talking about it." He slung back a gruff retort. Too gruff. But Dan let it slide. He only chuckled.

"Place is crawling with volunteers, Mac."

"It is at that," Mac agreed. He rubbed his sore thumb on the leg of his jeans before bending back over his project. "Lots of them here today." And he was particularly glad there was assigned staff to coordinate the entire group so he could be off working on his own projects, on his own time, and in his own space. As it was, he wasn't in any mood to have to act diplomatic and pleasant with the rest of the world.

"You and Megan have done a great job organizing this

event. I can already see it's going to be tip-top," Dan complimented. "Next Saturday is going to be unforgettable for a lot of kids and their parents. Yeah. . ." Mac glanced up from his hammering for a moment to see Dan looking around, sizing up the surroundings where many of the booths and activities were already in place. "You and Megan make a good team for sure."

Good team. Yeah, right. . . He'd said the same thing to her the night they'd first kissed. So much for that kind of thinking.

"Whatever." He shrugged and turned back to something far simpler for his mind to figure out—the two-by-fours and nails. But Dan wouldn't let it go.

"Well, you do," he insisted. "You two are a perfect pair togeth—"

"Oh jumpinjehoshaphat!" Mac yelped, dropping the hammer, grabbing onto his throbbing thumb once again.

Dan sniggered. "Lucky for me, I was just about to offer to hold the board for you. You're kind of dangerous today. You okay?"

"Of course I'm okay. It's just a hammer."

"I mean you and Megan. Are you and Megan O'Donnell okay?"

"Me and Megan?" Shaking his head, Mac bent over to pick up the hammer he'd thrown on the grass. "Don't know what you're talking about."

"Really? Because I saw Megan the other day at the clinic, and she was doing the same thing. Trying to avoid talking about you the same way you're trying to avoid talking about her. So, what did I do?" Dan cocked his head, tucking his thumbs into the brown belt holding up his baggy blue jeans. "I put one and one together."

"You mean you put two and two together."

"No. I mean, one and one. Making two. You two. You and Megan. I've seen the way you act around each other at the meetings. First there was this rivalry between you both." He chuckled. "That was amusing to watch. But for a long time now, things have been different. I definitely think there's something going on between you and Megan. In fact, I know there is. After all, I might be growing old and senile—but I'm not an idiot."

Mac felt his insides uncoil a bit at Dan's self-deprecating comment. "Nothing senile about you, Dan. You're one of the smartest men I know."

"Yeah. I know, I know." Dan laughed. "I was only saying that to try to get you to smile. But. . .since that didn't work, maybe I can get you to talk. Would you rather talk some?"

"Trust me, Dan. There's nothing to talk about, and I've got to get this booth built pronto. There's a crew of volunteers waiting to paint it."

"Okay, you don't want to talk? Fine. I'm here. I volunteered. I can risk my life and stand and hold the boards for you. We don't need to talk."

But that promise didn't last long. As soon as Dan shuffled around to the end of the boards Mac was nailing together, he started up again.

"What do you think about the Hawks?" he asked over Mac's pounding. "They're doing pretty good in this series with the Sox."

"Haven't been following it."

"Haven't been following the Hawks?" Mac detected amazement in Dan's voice even over the noisy clash of the hammer.

"Nope. Not really."

"Why do you think that is? Because you still have a bum elbow? Because you don't think you'll be playing again?"

"No. My elbow is perfect. No pain while I'm hammering. See." Mac stopped long enough to stretch his arm, twisting it every which way. "It's fine."

"Well, now." Dan's chest inflated and a genuine, broad smile filled his face as if he had something to do with Mac's recovery. "That's something to celebrate!"

"Yeah. Yeah, I thought about celebrating," he said, his mind trying hard to block out thoughts of Megan again. As if it was possible.

"But then?"

"But then. . ." He puffed out a disgusted sigh. "Okay. You're right about Megan. Yeah, we've been, well, together. Really together. I've never met anyone like her. I've never felt this way, and. . ." He stopped, suddenly wondering why he was telling the old man so much. Wondering why, too, it felt good to be doing it. "Bottom line, I was going to tell Megan. She was the only person I really wanted to tell."

"And then. . ." Dan urged him on.

"Nothing 'and then.' She came by last night and pretty much said we were over. Just like that."

"Hmmph." Dan's white-tipped, wiry eyebrows narrowed into one long stripe. "She threw you a curveball, huh?"

"Seriously, Dan? A baseball pun? Not really in the mood for baseball puns right now."

Dan's shoulders scrunched upward in apology. "I didn't mean for it to be a pun, Mac. It's more of a saying than a pun, I think. A colloquialism." He paused, as if to consider that fact before he pried more. "Did you try to call her and ask her why?"

"Are you kidding?" Mac grabbed the joined boards, laying them aside. Reaching for the next pair of boards to be nailed, he could feel the anger—and well, hurt—surging through his veins again. "Look, I've done everything to show her I care. Everything. For her and for Sammy. And if she can't see it or feel it—or whatever—I don't know what else to do."

"Oh, I get it." Dan nodded. "It's the pride thing."

Mac ground his teeth. "No, not the pride thing," he objected, even though everything inside him was working to tamp down the idea that it might be 100 percent true. "It's the right thing," he argued instead. "She wants me to leave her alone? Fine, I'll obey her wishes. Even took her number out of my phone so I wouldn't be tempted to call her."

"So after you got mad, and deleted her number from your phone, then what did you do?"

"What did I do?" Mac felt his jaw drop a foot. "Dan, are you not hearing me? I did nothing. That's what she wants. That's what I did. Nothing. If she wants to talk to me, she'll have to call."

What else could he do? He'd woken up two mornings ago like he'd been waking up for months now, thinking of Megan. And of Sammy. Thinking the three of them were—a team—a pact—a *something*. Thinking they were on their way to becoming a unit. A family, hopefully. And then to find out Megan wasn't feeling the same way. . .it left a hole in his heart, far bigger than the entire Hawks' baseball stadium.

Oh great. He shook his head at himself. Now he was conjuring up stupid baseball references. Lame! He dug into his work apron for a half dozen nails.

"Well, you could've at least prayed," Dan piped up. "Have you done that? Have you prayed about it?"

"Pray about it? Of course I've—" Mac stopped mid-sentence, his thoughts churning while a new kind of heat flamed his neck, his cheeks. Embarrassment.

He hadn't prayed, had he? He'd only kept asking why. That really wasn't much of a prayer, was it? It was more like a theme for a pity party.

"You know, your uncle Jake, God rest his soul, had a saying."

"I think I know what you're going to say, Dan."

"The one about—if your problem is big enough for you to be troubled by, it's big enough to pray about. But if it's not big enough to pray about, you shouldn't be troubled by it."

"Yeah, I remember. And, well, believe me, I'm very troubled."

Mac suddenly sensed Megan's presence even more, as if she were so close, right behind him. Looking up toward the house, he saw her there, her form outlined behind the curtain as she stood by the kitchen window. "Of course, praying. . . I mean, it still doesn't mean she'll change her mind, does it?"

Dan shook his head sympathetically. "I don't have all the

answers, my friend. I can only suggest you go to the One who does."

Megan was glad when Wendy asked her to help retrieve the sandwiches the sub shop had donated for the volunteers' lunches from inside Mac's house. Quickly depositing Sammy with her mom, she was happy to escape the great outdoors and head in. Mostly because no matter which field she found herself in or which booth she helped with, she couldn't get far enough away from Mac and the feelings for him that kept welling up inside her.

But then, what was she thinking? Because standing at Mac's kitchen sink, washing her hands, didn't offer any relief from thoughts of him either. She had to force herself not to pull back the thin cotton curtain to glimpse at him while he hammered away at his project. Had to mindfully tell herself "no, no—and no" since everything inside her felt so drawn to him.

And, why hadn't it occurred to her how vulnerable she'd feel being in his house again, anyway? Especially in the kitchen surrounded by his familiar everyday things— his oversized olive green coffee mug, his baseball cap lying on the oak kitchen table alongside a folded morning newspaper.

And then, there were the more than ordinary things that permeated the area like lingering, taunting ghosts— the memories of being there with him sharing an evening. A meal. Laughing with him and Sammy over something silly. Not to mention how she could almost feel the way it used to feel when he'd come up behind her as she stood at the sink and he'd place playful kisses at the nape of her neck, sending shivers and tingles all the way up to her—

"The guys from the sub shop put the drinks for the volunteers over there." Wendy's slight Kentucky accent snapped her out of her reverie. Thankfully!

Megan turned from the window to see her pointing to a row of Styrofoam coolers lining one side of the kitchen wall.

"And I'm crossin' my fingers all fifty sandwiches are in the fridge just like the sub shop guys promised me they'd be." The door squeaked as Wendy opened the refrigerator and peered inside. "Yes ma'am. They're here, all right," she said. "Plenty of room for them, too. Doesn't that poor Mac ever do any grocery shopping? Or know how to cook a supper or two?" She peered over the refrigerator door. Clearly amused, her eyes twinkled at Megan. "You need to teach that boy his way around the kitchen."

Megan was surprised the refrigerator could be as empty as Wendy was saying. It'd always been stocked when she and Sammy used to come over. "He makes a really good pizza from scratch. . . ." she murmured, wondering why she felt a sudden urge to defend him.

But Wendy barely heard her. She was already back to business, as usual. "Now I'm thinkin' all we need are some baskets. Or a couple of trays to carry the subs outside to the picnic tables."

Wordlessly, Megan moved over to the island and bent down, pulling open the cabinet doors. She sifted through the items stored there, pots and pans clanging together, making a racket until she finally retrieved two metal cookie sheets.

"How about these?" She rose up with the pair in her hands.

"Great. You want to hold 'em while I load 'em up?"

"Sure," she said lightly, even though she felt an instant heaviness come over her.

It wasn't that it was hard to stand and hold cookie sheets, by any means. It was just that it weighed on her sadly, recalling how she'd put the cookie sheets to use one rainy night. Mac had pulled Sammy's wheelchair up to the kitchen table and the two of them sat there, working on a model car together. Meanwhile, she had happily busied herself making chocolate chip cookies. It felt so right, the three of them together like that.

Luckily though, Wendy's chatting distracted her from memories again. "Is Mac doing some major renovations in here? It sure appears that way," she commented. Looking up from her task of mechanically placing subs on the tray, she nodded at the huge sheets of plastic draped through different parts of the living room. "What all is he doing?"

"He's making some of the rooms bigger and hallways wider and. . ." Megan shrugged, her eyes downcast, watching the pyramid of sub sandwiches grow on the sheet. "Just doing some general remodeling, I guess."

She and Mac had never talked in any great detail about the renovations. He'd always been somewhat vague, like he simply planned to give the place an overhaul—a facelift. She'd never really thought to question him beyond that. It wasn't her place to as far as she was concerned, and honestly, she wasn't that interested. They'd always had so many other things to talk about.

"His uncle Jake lived here for a long time," she explained to Wendy. "So I think he wanted to make a few improvements here and there. Which is good, I guess, especially if Mac ever needs to move out of state and put the house up for sale."

The thought had come to her just as she said the words out loud. Had that been in the back of Mac's mind all along? The truth of the possibility jolted her full force, jerking her head back on her shoulders. Evidently Wendy had the same sort of reaction. Her head shot up out of the cold cavern.

"Move? Sell? Why would he do that? Now that his elbow has been cleared, he'll be back playing with the Hawks next season, won't he?"

Mac's elbow was cleared? The cookie sheet suddenly dipped from Megan's grasp, causing the stack of subs to skitter across—and almost off—the metal tray.

"Whoa. Is that thing getting heavy?" Wendy reached out to upright the sheet.

"No. It's—it's fine."

And Mac's elbow was fine. He'd been cleared. Something she'd never doubted would happen. In fact, it was exactly what was supposed to happen—Mac getting back to playing ball again. Still, the news—hearing that it was for real—threw her insides totally off-kilter.

"That's twenty-five sandwiches anyway," Wendy was saying. "I'd say we're ready for the second cookie sheet."

In a haze, Megan walked over to the island and slid the

full cookie sheet off the top of the other one and onto the counter. Keeping the remaining empty sheet in her hands, she moved back over to the refrigerator, standing like a sentry once more.

"How did you find out?" she asked Wendy. "About Mac's elbow, I mean."

"Oh, he mentioned it to Ted this morning," Wendy told her, leaning into the refrigerator, pulling out handfuls of subs. "When we first got here. He also invited Ted to go to the Hawks' game with him this Thursday night. Guess he'd planned to go with someone else," she chatted, hands moving the whole time. "But the plans fell through, and— okay—" She stood up to her full height. "That's it for the subs. That's the last twenty-five." She shut the refrigerator door then paused. "Hey, wait a minute. Weren't you supposed to go with Mac? Didn't ya'll mention that at one of the meetings? They're announcing the event at the game, right?"

"Yeah, but I just—can't." Megan tried to avert her eyes from Wendy's. "I'm glad Ted gets to go, though."

She didn't want to share the reason why, and Wendy was kind enough not to press her.

"Oh, Ted is thrilled. He gets to meet all the players and everything. I'm so sure I'll be hearing about it all for days and days."

For a moment, it filled her mind—the hurt look in Mac's eyes when she told him she couldn't go with him. And then, when she told him. . . Well, she didn't even want to think about it. Didn't want to remember the way he looked at her. Confused. Hurt. Disgusted. She couldn't blame him for any of it. But now he'd be playing ball again. Now it would be all good for him again. She knew it would. . . .

"Okay." Wendy clapped her hands together. "All we need are napkins. Do you think Mac would mind us using some of his?"

"I sincerely doubt it." He was only the most generous man Megan had ever met. The thought caused a cramping around her heart. She set the second full cookie sheet on the island momentarily and rubbed at her chest as she walked over to the pantry.

In the meantime, Wendy lingered by the pantry door, reading the framed embroidered message hanging on the wall there. Megan had always assumed Mac's Aunt Emily must've enjoyed doing cross-stitch because her work was all throughout the house. More than once, just like Wendy, she'd stopped to read the colorfully stitched quotes.

"'Prayer changes things,'" Wendy read out loud. "What a great reminder! So simple yet so true. Don't you think?"

"Uh-huh." Megan nodded. But even as she stepped into the pantry, retrieved a package of napkins, and closed the pantry door behind her, her insides ached, wishing she could believe to the core of her being that those words really did hold true.

Evidently never-stop-moving Wendy believed because she'd ceased movement for a moment and actually stood staring almost reverently at the cross-stitch. And Mac. . .he believed the same thing. So many others she knew did, too.

Sighing, she wedged the napkins under her arm and grabbed one of the sandwich trays. "I can get this tray if you can get the other one," she said to Wendy. "And we can have some of the guys come in and get the coolers, right? They're probably pretty heavy."

"No way we're breaking our backs over those," Wendy agreed.

And as the two of them got on with the business of feeding the volunteers, and she and Mac stayed busy trying to avoid one another, Megan still felt those words gnawing at her.

Prayer apparently did change things where other people's lives were concerned. But for her, things—even falling in love—seemed to be so complicated. Something always blocking her happiness. She wasn't sure why that was true.

Chapter 19

"How many days till All-'tar Day, Maw-mee?"

Megan guided her SUV through downtown Loveland, feeling her shoulders droop when she had to stop at a crosswalk for an older couple holding hands. Everyone seemed to be holding hands these days, didn't they? Young and old folks alike?

"This is Thursday, Samster. So two more days. It's this Saturday," she answered automatically, her mind not completely tuned in to him. She was too busy trying not to let her eyes—and heart—stray to the bistro where she and Mac had shared lunch weeks earlier. Or the shady bike trail where they'd pushed Sammy along some evenings. Or Paxton's. Or the ice cream shop, or. . .

She pulled her wraparound sunglasses from the visor and put them on, hoping to at least dim some of the memories of Mac somewhat. Besides, she'd taken a couple of days off work so she could concentrate on other things that needed attention in her life. Things like Sammy's birthday invitations, getting her oil changed, some last-minute details for the sports event, and just to make herself feel better—a trip to the hair salon later that evening for a trim she needed desperately.

"We see Mac then? This Saturday?"

"Sure. You'll see Mac then." She sighed involuntarily,

already hoping Event Day wouldn't be as awkward as Volunteer Day the weekend before. Not that she and Mac hadn't been completely civil with each other then. They were totally polite when they needed to be. All day long. And into the evening.

And it had felt just awful!

"An' how many days to my birt-day, Maw-mee?"

"Nine more days. It's the Saturday after this one."

"We see Mac next Saturday for my birt-day," Sammy said. Only it wasn't a question this time. It was matter-of-fact. Expected.

Megan hadn't mentioned anything to him of course, about what was going on between her and Mac. She'd hoped by only seeing Mac on the weekends at the different events, Sammy would slowly get weaned from his presence in their lives overall.

And it was so much better for that to be happening now—just the way that it was—she convinced herself. So much better than if she and Mac had kept going on the way they had been and after a year or so, he dropped out of her and Sammy's lives. That would've been twice as hard, wouldn't it?

After all, Mac could be living someplace else by then. Or be so wrapped up in playing ball and traveling with the team, he wouldn't even remember them back in Loveland. Who knows? He could even backslide, slip into old habits, turn into MacNeill Hattaway, the womanizer, again.

There were so many reasons why it was better she cut the cord now, not just for Mac and his career, but for Sammy and her, too.

So many reasons. . .

Except there was no way she could explain all that to Sammy, was there? When Mac wasn't around, Sammy was still obsessed with him, forever talking and asking about him.

But then, why wouldn't he? Mac had always treated him incredibly well.

"I don't know if Mac will be there or not, Sammy. We mailed his invitation earlier, remember? But sometimes people are busy," she told her son, being realistic.

Sometimes they don't want to see certain people because of certain things.

But of course she couldn't say that. Instead she opted for, "And sometimes they have other reasons why they can't—"

Her son cut her off. "We not mail Rachel's invitation. We take to her?"

"That's right. Because we don't have Rachel's address."

And they didn't even know her last name actually.

"We take to her now?"

"Yes, indeed. Right now." She crossed over the Little Miami Bridge, flicked her left blinker, then came to stop at the red light at the intersection. "Are you excited?"

"I like Rachel a lot."

"I know you do, honey."

Sammy had a short list of the people he'd wanted to invite to his birthday party. Obviously, there were his grandparents. Then Allie and Greg and their kids, Justin and Carrie. But he also wanted to ask Mr. and Mrs. Biddle, whom Megan learned was improving much each day and would probably be ready to watch Sammy again in January or so. As well, he wanted to invite the Slater family. Janey was next on his list, and he hoped she would bring him a dozen jelly doughnuts. But, definitely at the top of his list were Mac and Rachel. And the more he talked about Rachel, the more she realized how much of a crush he had on the girl.

"My hair look okay?" he asked from the backseat.

"Your hair?" Megan glanced in the rearview mirror. Was he serious? When had he started thinking about his hair? Or even noticed he had any?

"Mac pat my hair down sometimes. He say, 'You a handsome dude, Sammy.'" For a moment his voice didn't sound like her son's. It took on an older, more confident tone, mimicking Mac.

More than that, it sounded full of all the loving conviction Mac had always lavished on her Sammy.

A lump rose in her throat.

"Mac—Mac says that?" She'd seen and heard Mac do and say a lot of things to Sammy. But that was a new one.

"Yeah. He says, 'Girls like handsome dudes like you, Sammy.'" He gave a half giggle. "Then he goes, 'High five.' And we smack hans. Sometimes we smack hans, though, and then Mac, he take my han and he holds it. Tight."

Tears sprang to the corners of her eyes. *Oh Mac. Oh Mac.* In a million years, would she ever be over him?

The car honked behind her, and with tear-blurred vision, she glanced up to see a green arrow. She rounded the corner, Sammy unaware of the emotions that welled up inside her.

"We almost there, Maw-mee?"

"Al—" She cleared her throat. "Almost, honey."

Megan glanced back at him and couldn't believe the huge smile that lit his face. In eager anticipation of seeing Rachel again, she was sure. As if she didn't have enough to be emotional about, how it tugged on her heart that a girl was tugging on his!

By the time she pulled into the Donut Emporium lot and parked, his nearly seven-year-old body trembled with excitement. But once Megan got him out of the car, into his wheelchair, and handed him Rachel's invitation, they made their way up to the doughnut shop door, and all of that changed.

"Where Rachel?" he asked when the door didn't open automatically with his new friend on the other side.

"I don't know, Sams."

Megan held the door open with her leg as they inched inside. But the shop was empty and she could see Sammy's instant disappointment. His shoulders sagged immediately; his hand holding the invitation fell limply into his lap.

Until Sean and Rachel came bounding out from the back room.

"Sammy!" Rachel ran to Sammy's side while Megan whispered a thanks to the heavens.

"You can't imagine how much he's been looking forward to coming here," she confided to Sean.

"You mean seeing Rachel, I suspect." He smiled. "We were just in the back finishing up lunch. How are you guys doing? Can I get you anything?" he asked pleasantly.

"We'll have two jelly doughnuts to go. And Sammy has an invitation to give to—"

But before she could get the words out, Rachel was

squealing. Sammy hunched his shoulders at the sound, but couldn't quit grinning, reveling in her excitement.

"Uncle Sean! Can I go? It's for Sammy's birthday. See?" She waved the invitation in the air.

After figuring out that Rachel's mom would be working the day of the party, but that Sean could bring Rachel, Megan gave him directions to her house. She also encouraged him to stay instead of just dropping Rachel off, telling him about some of the other guests he might know.

"Will Janey be there?" he asked in particular.

"Uh, you mean Janey Saunders?"

"Do you have any other good friends named Janey?"

"Not a one actually. Janey will— You know she actually hasn't gotten back to me yet."

Which was absolutely true. But it was also true that her two dearest friends, Janey and Allie, had never missed one of Sammy's birthdays no matter what. Still. . .she wasn't exactly sure why Sean was asking. Just in case Janey's being there might keep him away, and subsequently Rachel, was there any reason to mention that?

"I can't wait to come to your party, Sammy," Rachel cooed. "It'll be so much fun!" She took hold of Sammy's hands and clapped them together. Megan had to smile at the two of them, both laughing like it was the funniest thing ever.

"Mac right, Maw-mee," Sammy told Megan ten minutes later when they'd left the doughnut shop with their bag of treats.

"Mac?" Her heart leaped involuntarily. If only he knew he was killing her, bringing up Mac's name all the time.

"Uh-huh." Sammy beamed. "Girl do like handsome dudes like me."

"You right, Mac."

Mac pushed Sammy's wheelchair through the warehouse, over to the spot where he had the practice bowling ramp all set up. Fortunately it was cool inside, but he always brought a couple of water bottles for him and Sammy anyway.

"What am I right about, buddy?" he asked while glancing at his watch to see exactly what time it was. Laura said Megan would be back from her hair appointment by around seven thirty, so Kurt would return to pick up Sammy at seven fifteen. That meant they had about thirty-five minutes to practice and rest in between. Plenty of time—

"Girls like me."

Mac erupted with a laugh. "Of course girls like you. What's not to like? Is this a certain girl you're talking about?"

He pushed the wheelchair up to the bowling ramp and came around to face Sammy. He saw the telltale glint of infatuation in Sammy's eyes when he said, "Rachel."

"Rachel. The girl at the doughnut shop, huh? Your mom talked about you two meeting each other a few weeks ago."

Mac had never known—and figured he would never know—the privilege or joy of being married to Megan. But he sure felt the pain of being divorced from her, even outside of marriage. It didn't feel good mentioning conversations they'd had in the past, knowing their interactions in the future would be slim to none. Sometimes it didn't even feel good being around Sammy and being reminded of every good time, every quiet time, and even every in-between time the three of them had shared together.

Bittersweet. Maybe that was the word for it. He wasn't sure. He only knew that he wasn't about to give up being around Sammy. Not if he could help it. Simply put, the boy meant the world to him. He didn't want to give up on that relationship as well.

"Rachel pretty."

"I'll bet she is."

"You like pretty girls, Mac?"

"Sure." Mac shrugged. "Pretty. Nice. Smart. Fun."

"My mom pretty and nice. You like her, right?"

"Yeah, I do, buddy. She's— You have a good mom," he said, unzipping the bowling bag, trying not to dwell on that too much. "Hey, you remember what we said, right?" He handed Sammy the orange lightweight bowling ball. "We're practicing because it's fun to work at something you love. It's fun to get better at it."

Sammy hugged the ball in his lap. "An' we want to surprise Maw-mee."

"And, yes, we want to surprise your mommy." Mac unscrewed the cap on one of the waters, offering Sammy a drink first. Sammy shook his head, so Mac took a long swallow.

Well, that had been his first thought when he'd come up with this practice bowling scheme. He thought it'd be fun to surprise Megan with Sammy's new bowling skills. But honestly, he was still angry at her and his pride still bruised black-and-blue from the way she'd led him on or whatever she'd been doing. At the moment he couldn't have cared less about doing much of anything for her. Now his objective was solely aimed at Sammy. Getting Sammy better for Sammy in order to make him feel good. Practicing with him the same way his uncle Jake had practiced with him.

"You do like bowling don't you?" The thought occurred to him that he didn't want to be pushing Sammy into something he wasn't that crazy about.

"Yeah. I show you I like it."

Sammy aimed the ball exactly the way Mac had instructed him over the past weeks. Easy as anything, the orange orb went sailing down the ramp, splattering bowling pins in every direction. He managed to repeat that move successfully time after time, calling for some high-fives and drinks of water.

Mac had helped out with some baseball clinics over the past months and had even coached some kids at the beginning of his career—long before he'd gotten carried away with other "not so positive" things.

But working with Sammy brought out something in him that he'd never experienced in those other situations. Most likely because he felt so close to the boy. In fact, he felt like Sammy could be his own son. Which hurt. But felt really good at the same time.

"I'm proud of you, Sammy. Really proud." Mac bent down in front of him. "You try harder than a lot of pro players I know, you know that?"

Sammy's face shone with a look of awe. "I do?"

"You do." Mac nodded. "How old are you now?"

"I six."

"Only six? Buddy, you've got lots and lots of years of bowling ahead of you."

"But I be seven soon." Sammy struggled to hold up the correct number of fingers. "You come to my party, Mac? Maw-mee mail you invitation."

"Your party?" Megan had mailed him an invitation? Only for Sammy's sake, he was sure. But still, it could prove to be an uncomfortable situation. For him at least. Everything was pretty much a jumble inside of him. For one, he couldn't find a place to store up all his leftover feelings for her. And just the idea that he still had those lingering feelings made him angrier than he wanted to admit. "Well, Sammy, I. . ."

Mac stood up and began to hem and haw, started to hedge and come up with any number of reasons why he couldn't be there. But then he looked down at Sammy and knew he couldn't say no to the eyes gazing up at him so expectantly. Not only couldn't he say no, he didn't want to. Despite the surrounding circumstances, despite the fact that he and Megan didn't have a future together, he didn't want it to be like that between him and Sammy. So he said what was pressing on his heart instead.

"I'll be there, Sammy. For you, I'll be there. Always."

Chapter 20

Megan stopped inside her parents' foyer and peered into the gold-framed mirror hanging above the antique chest there. Evening sun poured through the palladium window above the front door, offering plenty of light, wrapping her reflection in an amber glow.

She swished her head from left to right, enjoying the feel of her freshly cut hair. Christy had done a good job as usual. Mac would be sure to compliment her. . .

If only he were still in her life.

"Hey, sweetie." Her mom came around the corner from the kitchen, waving a dish towel hello. "Your hair looks cute."

Mom! Forever her savior.

"Thanks, I thought I'd try something different. Go a little shorter. I needed a change." More like something to lift her spirits!

"Long or short. You can wear it both ways."

"You're my mother." Megan smiled. "You have to say that."

"Not really." Her mom slung the dish towel over her shoulder, settling her hands on her hips. Thinking her petite stance might look more formidable that way? "I tell it like it is when I have to," she said, before retracing her steps back into the kitchen. "I do, believe me."

572

"Oh yeah?" Megan followed behind, teasing. "And when would that be?"

"Like when I—when I— Oh. . ." She tossed a hand in the air, at a loss for an example. Reaching into the silverware drawer next to the sink, she drew out a fork. "Hey, try this for me, will you?" She pointed to a glass baking dish where Megan could barely see any cake for all the layers of whipped topping and sliced strawberries. "I just finished it up. It's angel food cake with crushed pineapple and strawberries. I wanted to bake something different for card club next week and thought I'd do a test run." She sank the fork into a corner of the dish and came up with a mouthful, which she pointed in Megan's direction.

Never one to turn down anything with whipped topping, Megan opened her mouth, happy to oblige while her mom tried to wait patiently before she asked with wide eyes, "So. . .what do you think?"

"Oh my gosh, Mom." Megan shook her head. "It's—"

"Bad?" Her mom's face crumpled.

"No, no. It's incredible."

"Oh, well good." Her mom gave a short sigh of relief then scuttled around the kitchen collecting a cake knife, plate, and napkin.

"Want to sit and have a piece?" she asked, even though she was already in the process of cutting a generous square, placing it on a plate, and handing it to her.

Not that Megan was about to refuse. She'd been eating far too many sweets recently, it was true. Anything to fill the void she'd been feeling inside. As if any of it could replace the person she was missing in her life. Even so, she sat down at her usual spot at the table, digging into her mom's newest dessert, savoring every whipped topping–laden bite. "Is Sammy with Dad? I didn't see his car out there."

"They should be back shortly." Her mom sat across from her. "Christy finished you up early, didn't she?"

With a full mouth, Megan nodded then swallowed. "Now, where is it they go again? Sammy and Dad? I can't remember if you told me."

"Oh, you know, around."

"Hmm. . ." she said, focused more on licking the fluffy sweet stuff from her fork than on her mom's answer. "This really is one of your best creations."

"I'll cut some for you to take home when you leave later." Her mom looked so pleased by her obvious enjoyment of the treat. "I'm sure Sammy will like it, don't you think?"

"He'll love it. I should also tell Janey about it."

"Oh, speaking of Janey. I meant to tell you, I saw her and Sean Shaffer together last Saturday night."

Megan halted the fork an inch from her lips. "Janey and Sean? Together? I doubt it, Mom."

But obviously her mom didn't have any doubts. She nodded vigorously. "Oh no. I saw them. At the movie last week. You know how they have the Moonlight Movies on the riverbanks? They were showing *Just Friends*. That really funny movie with Ryan—oh, Ryan—"

"Reynolds."

"Right. And, like I said, Janey and Sean were both there."

"Well, that I believe. But they couldn't have been at the movie *together*." She enveloped the fork-load of creamy stuff with her mouth, thinking she really needed the recipe.

It would be great for Sammy's birthday party. Or anytime actually.

Tilting her head, her mom's lips pursed, considering. "Maybe they didn't come together. But they sure *seemed* together," she said, not letting the subject rest.

Megan was well aware of her mom's track record when it came to sensing things between males and females, but really—Janey and Sean? On Saturday? No way. She shook her head.

"Mom, I just saw Janey for dinner last Thursday, remember?" And she'd talked to Janey on Sunday, too, giving her the lowdown about Volunteer Day since she couldn't make it that day. She'd also told her friend about the breakup with Mac. But Janey hadn't said a word about Sean to her. "Sean and Janey are miles apart. Not even close to being together."

"Well, it's true that Janey was sitting on one side of the amphitheater, and Sean was sitting on the other. But I saw them meet in the middle at intermission and, trust me, those two easily looked like they could be involved. I saw it in their body language. He was leaning close. She was smiling into his eyes. They were obviously smitten with one another. And, well, they looked so cute, standing side by side."

Always great criteria for a lasting relationship. Megan wanted to shake her head but there were still at least three more bites of her mother's angel food cake concoction to focus on.

"As a matter of fact, Janey and Sean looked the same way you and Mac do," her mom continued.

"Huh?" Megan's fork dangled in midair.

"You and Mac look like a couple. Like you belong together."

Megan hadn't wanted to get into telling her mom about Mac at the moment. She had hoped to get through the event on Saturday first. But with the way the conversation was going, the time was probably right. Unfortunately. She let out a sigh. Set down the dangling fork. And pushed the plate aside.

"Is it too sweet?"

"No, it's not that. It's surprisingly light actually. It's just that there are some things going on, and I—"

"What kinds of things?" her mom prodded.

"It's hard to explain because you and I. . .we're, well, we're so different from one another, Mom."

"Different? You and me?" The animation left her mom's face. She blinked, looking like a cross between bewildered and crestfallen. "I can't imagine what you mean."

Megan's heart wrenched. The last thing she wanted to do was hurt her mom's feelings. Actually, it felt like she'd been hurting too many people's feelings lately and not meaning to at all.

"Not in a bad way, Mom. There's nothing bad about you or what you do. Love and romance, that's all a part of your business. You're a wedding planner, for goodness' sakes. That's how you always look at things. When you see two people, you automatically see a match. A couple. I don't look at love that way at all."

"I see more than two people, Megan. Even more than a couple," her mom clarified. "I see a connection. A connectedness."

"Right. Because everything about you is 'love this' and 'love that.' Which is what I'm saying. We're different in that way." Oh, how had she started down this road anyway? She'd kept these thoughts to herself for how many years? More than she could count.

"And you're not about love? That's a crazy statement, Megan," her mom chided. "What about the way you love your son? And care about other people's special-needs daughters and sons? And what you do for a living—isn't that love? Your loving, caring touch helps people heal and get better."

"That's so different. I'm talking about *your* kind of love. The romantic kind, where you fall in love and get married. Which I did. And what do you know, it didn't work out, did it?" She wasn't even sure why she blurted out that bit of past history. Sounding so snippy. And pitifully sorry for herself. As if her mom had anything to do with it.

Yet her mom's reaction was exactly what she expected. She reached over and gently touched her hand. "Megan, what's going on?" she asked softly. "You really don't seem like yourself."

Oh, how she dreaded telling her mom. How she hated having to look her in the eyes and tell her the truth. But somehow she sucked in a deep breath and let the words flow out when she exhaled. "I broke things off with Mac."

"You what?" Gone was her mother's gentle touch. And her soothing voice. She flopped back in the chair, her eyes nearly as wide as her gaping mouth. "Are you kidding?"

Megan stiffened in the chair, feeling defensive. "Mom, seriously, did you really think it could work? Me and a pro baseball player? A national celebrity? Really? That's what I mean when I say we're different. To you, it's romantic. To me, it's not logical."

"Did I think it could work?" Her mom dipped her head. "Yes, Megan, I did think it could," she said emphatically. "And do you know why I thought it could work? Because it *was* working." She leaned forward, her eyes pleading to understand. "Why did you break it off? I don't get it."

"I didn't want him to have to choose." But even as she said the words out loud, she realized the excuse sounded weak.

"Choose? Choose what?"

"Between playing baseball and being with me. I love him too much, Mom. I really do. And I don't think it's right. He shouldn't have to compromise doing something he loves so much."

"Compromise? Did he say that's what you were asking him to do?"

"No. But I thought about it, and there are so many things that could happen. What if he got traded? What if it was to some team far away and he'd have to divide his attention between doing what he loves and trying to maintain a long-distance relationship with me? And Sammy?"

"Well, some couples do cope with situations like that, Megan. It's not that far-fetched."

"Yes, but they don't have to deal with paparazzi."

"Paparazzi?" Her mother raised her brows. "In Loveland?"

"Well, not paparazzi, but sneaky people taking pictures of us and Sammy when we don't even know it. And it's not only that, Mom, but what if women start chasing after Mac again? And what if he likes it? Then Sammy and I will just get hurt down the road. And you know what? I don't want to be the one to stand in the way of any of that. Not Mac's career or his fame, or other women or anything."

"Oh my gosh, Megan. Do you think you've thought of enough what-ifs? Hmm. Maybe if you try real hard you can come up with more awful scenarios for the future."

Her mother's sarcasm was shocking. Never had her mom spoken to her like that. "What?" Megan's head flung back.

"Megan, can I tell you something?" Mom asked, though it was apparent she was going to whether Megan gave permission or not. "When I look at you and Mac, do you know what I don't see?"

"What you *don't* see?"

"Yes, you heard me. What I don't see is a physical therapist. What I don't see is a major league baseball pitcher. But I will tell you what I do see, and I'm not being a gushy romantic doing my 'love this' and 'love that' thing."

Megan swallowed. So much for thinking her mom couldn't tell it like it is. "Mom, I—"

"No it's fine. I can see how you might think of me that way. But let me tell you, what I see with you and Mac are a man and a woman who love each other. Love each other very much. And I also see a man and a woman who both love a special little boy. And whenever I see that between two people, that intangible thing that you and Mac have, I pray that if it's God's will for them to end up together, that they will. And I also pray that if I can be of any help along the way, I'll be able to do that, too."

"I'm sorry, Mom. I am." She hung her head.

"There's no need to be sorry. But Megan, can I tell you

something else?" She touched her hand again. Wrapped her fingers around Megan's. Lifted her chin, and looked into her eyes. "There's no need to be scared either. Do you hear me? Don't be scared, my precious daughter, don't be."

Her mom drew her to her shoulder and caressed the back of her head. Megan hadn't been held like that since forever, and for a moment it felt like the safest haven in the world. The sweetest place to be. A place where she was known. And loved anyway.

Because without a doubt, her mom could always see through her. All the way into her heart. No matter how guarded she tried to be. How she tried to hide her feelings and put up facade after facade; her mom could always see through it all.

Her mom just knew.

"Oh Mom!" She burst into tears. Tears that ran beyond her control, feeling as if they'd been pent up, put away in reserve for far too long. "What if I can't do it?" She sobbed through the words. "What if the only thing I know how to be is Sammy's mom? I was okay seeing Mac and being with him, but now that I've fallen in love with him. . .I'm so afraid. What if I mess it all up? What if I've already messed it up? Or I'm just not strong enough?"

Her breaths came in gasps. "I tried so hard before, Mom. I tried to do everything right when I was pregnant and still—" She broke off, guilt weighing on her like it always did. "Sammy can't walk or run or talk like other kids. He never will. Even though I tried, Mom." Her voice broke. "I really, really tried."

"Oh Megan. . .Megan. . ." Her mother shook her head

emphatically, authoritatively. But even so, Megan could see the hurt for her in her mother's eyes. She saw it in her mom's glimmering tears. "You've got to stop. You can't keep carrying that burden around, do you hear me?" Her mom reached for her hands. "What voice in your head are you listening to, child? There's nothing you could've done any better. And we've got special little Sammy in our lives. He's perfect."

"He is perfect. I know that, I do. He's the only son I want," Megan said, meaning it with all her heart. "But then I chose the wrong dad for him once. What if I choose the wrong person to love again? Bring a man into our lives who walks out? I'm just so scared. So scared." She shook her head. "If it's just me and Sammy, I know how to keep us from being hurt. I know how to control our lives."

"But Meggie." Her mother squeezed her hands. "As much as you try, and I know you do, honey, you can't control it all. Because you're not in control." Her mom leaned in, saying gently, "God is, Meg. Our Father is. And as difficult as it might be to comprehend, I have to tell you, God loves Sammy even more than you do. More than you can imagine."

Someone loved Sammy more than her? Megan looked up, startled. Not in all her years of motherhood had she ever thought of God that way. Never.

"I know," her mom said, obviously noticing. "I'm a mother, too, remember? And it's hard—oh, it's so hard to not keep digging in, not keep thinking if you can only do everything in the world humanly possible, be the Super Mom of Super Moms, that everything will be all right for our kids. I know. I've been there. . . .

"But Meg honey," she said, her voice tender, "have you ever thought that Mac may be exactly the person God has been waiting to bring into your life? And Sammy's life, too? I know giving yourself to love can be overwhelming. It can make you feel out of control. I get it," she said soothingly. "But isn't it just as frightening to think of the joys you could miss out on? Do you want to take that chance? Do you want to take the chance Sammy could also miss out on that joy?"

Stretched out on the couch was usually a good place to be. But Mac couldn't get comfortable. Or interested in the mystery he was reading. Laying the paperback on his chest, he reached for the remote by his right hip, turning up the sound on the television. But even the ESPN highlights didn't appeal to him at the moment, so he muted the TV once more.

"Maybe we should get a dog. What do you think about that, Bitty?" he asked the cat lying at the opposite end of the couch by his feet. Bitty barely acknowledged his voice. Only lifted her head slightly and then huddled back into her own fluffy ball of fur again.

"I'll take that as 'a disinterested,'" he told her.

Lately he had been letting her come into the house more often. Even so, the homestead had still been feeling lonelier than usual.

Maybe because it wasn't the cozy haven it once was before all the renovations going on, with the mess and

furniture scattered about. But more than likely it was because he'd just gotten back from being at the warehouse
with Sammy, and truth was, he missed being with him already. Not to mention there was a prevailing emptiness he'd
been feeling knowing Sammy and Megan weren't stopping
by anytime soon.

Actually, outside of Event Day, quite possibly never
again.

Not that he could do much about it. Except maybe literally whittle away some of the extra time he had on his
hands. He was just about ready to take his melancholia to
the porch and do just that when his phone vibrated in his
jeans' pocket, startling him.

Taking it out, he stared at the screen hoping to see the
name of the person he missed more than anything, but of
course, she'd meant what she said. It wasn't her calling.

"Hey Hal. Getting kind of late, isn't it? Isn't it past your
work time?"

"Not in California."

"True, true." Mac chuckled.

"It's not only earlier in California. There's also more sun."

"But. . .we're here in Ohio, Hal."

There was a silence on the other end. Until Hal finally
spoke. "Not for long, Mac."

Mac sat up abruptly, feeling as if a boulder was lodged
in his chest. "Hal, cut to the chase. What are you talking
about?"

"You know that rumor about you being traded?"

Mac sucked in a deep breath. "It was more than a
rumor?"

"Uh, yeah. I didn't want to say more about it until I knew more but. . .being a Sacramento Miner wouldn't be so bad, would it?"

Shocked, Mac couldn't think of a reply. But as usual, Hal was never at a loss for words.

"Nothing legally binding right now because, of course, we have to wait until after the Series is over. But they'd really like you to come out next weekend for a little dinner and dancing."

"Dinner and dancing? Hal, could you be a little more serious here?" Although why should Hal be serious? It wasn't his life that was about to change.

"You're right. That wasn't funny. But they do want to meet with you next Friday evening. I had Sophie book a flight for you to leave Friday morning and return on Saturday. A little over a twenty-four-hour trip and could be the best one you've ever had. They're talking big bucks, Mac. And I think the timing is great. You're healed, you're well, and what else do you have going on in Loveland after this sports day thing is over, right?"

His head spun as he said good-bye and sat staring at the muted TV. After all these months of waiting, he had a new elbow. And a new team to go to. After all these months he thought he had Megan and Sammy, too. But there was no Megan now. And no Sammy.

Is this really what You want, God? He cradled his head in his hands. *Is this the path You want for me?*

Chapter 21

The first thing Megan heard when she woke up Saturday morning was Tim McGraw's baritone coming across the hallway from the other bedroom. The second was Sammy, chiming in with Tim singing "Live Like You Were Dying."

Obviously Sammy, who'd had an incredibly difficult time settling down and going to sleep the night before, was wide awake, and McGraw's song was the perfect one to be playing when his radio alarm went off. Even though Megan had assured him she wouldn't oversleep for All-Stars Sports Day, she had to smile when he insisted she set his clock for the special day anyway.

Honestly, she hadn't had such an easy time going to sleep herself. But it wasn't only because of Sports Day and hoping after all the months of planning everything would roll out well for their first annual event.

It was also because of Mac. She lay there in the dark for hours, only glimpses of the street lamp lighting her room, thinking about seeing him again. Thinking about all she and her mom had talked about. Thinking about her feelings for him. Feelings that just wouldn't go away. And sometime before finally falling asleep with a prayer on her lips and her own alarm going off, she'd made a decision. She wanted to talk to Mac, to explain herself, to ask for his forgiveness.

Yes, she really did want to look him in the eye and profess her love, to say it all.

She wanted to take a chance at love. At loving Mac. If only he still cared about her, too.

Flipping off the bedsheet with more fervor than usual, she bounded out of bed. The clock might've said she was on time, but she felt like she was running late for something. Every part of her finally ready and hoping so much to talk to Mac, to explain herself.

However, an hour later, when she and Sammy arrived at Mac's farm after eating breakfast and donning their red All-Stars Sports Day T-shirts, she spotted him standing by the roped-off entrance talking to a volunteer and could feel her nerve waning. Seeing him again, looking so ruggedly awesome in his usual T-shirt and jeans. Knowing inside and out that he was too good to be true. Could she really expect he'd want to listen to her?

She pulled the SUV up into her predesignated parking spot by the barn, turned off the ignition, and took a deep breath. For one anxiety-filled moment, she wished there was only a bull named Fu Manchu to face instead of Mac.

As far as she could tell, he hadn't noticed they'd arrived. But by the time she unloaded Sammy's wheelchair and got him out of the car and into it, all of that changed.

"Mac, we here!" Sammy called out to him, as if Mac had been waiting for them, and only them, to arrive all morning.

Mac ended his conversation and graciously walked toward them, his eyes glancing everywhere but at her.

"Sammy! How's it going, buddy?" he greeted her son. "You ready for this day?"

"I ready!"

Megan dared to look up at Mac but then instantly wished she hadn't. It weakened her resolve even more. Because she missed seeing the way he cared for her reflected in his eyes.

Missed the way he would've usually greeted her with a kiss. And how normally she would've had a breakfast sandwich or a coffee for him that she'd picked up on her way out to his place.

But there was little "normal" between them at this point. Now there was only an awkwardness and stilted conversation, mostly revolving around Sammy.

"He's more than ready," she said for want of anything better to say.

"I'm sure he is." Mac ruffled Sammy's hair.

"I ready to bowl!" Sammy exclaimed.

Mac chuckled at his enthusiasm while Megan reminded, "We got here early to work on some last-minute things, though, remember, Sam?"

"Like what?"

"Like the booths and games and. . ." she rambled to her son, but even as she did, her face burned hot. She knew what she wanted to ask Mac. Knew what she had to ask him. "Mac, can we talk?" she said in a rush, not even qualifying the question with a time or place the way she'd meant to.

He finally looked at her, but didn't seem the least bit comfortable about making eye contact. Scratching at his temple, he glanced away hurriedly, out over the fields. "If it's about the gate on the fence around the pond, I already know what you're going to say. But you don't have to worry. I sent Jason out to the hardware for a lock. It'll be fine, trust me."

"Oh?" She blinked. "Good thinking, thanks. But actually there was something else. If you have a few minutes later when all of this—"

"Hey Mac!" One of the red T-shirted male volunteers sprinted up alongside of them. "Rick Hall, your buddy from the radio station, is on my phone. He has a question about the opening ceremonies that I can't answer. You mind?" The volunteer handed Mac his cell.

"Megan! I'm so glad you're here." Another red T-shirt emerged by her side, this time a lady about Megan's mother's age. "Can you come over to the merchandise booth? We need your help deciding on which totes to put where."

"When do I bowl?" Sammy wanted to know in the midst of the conversations.

"At one thirty." Both Megan and Mac paused from what they were doing, answering him in unison.

For a brief moment their eyes met above Sammy's head. But just as quickly, Mac turned away.

Megan couldn't guess how many parents from Loveland and other Cincinnati suburbs had brought their kids for All-Stars Sports Day. She had tried to count cars at one point, but lost track once she got close to two hundred.

It had been a major scheduling feat, but all the volunteers got a chance to rotate shifts so they could have the opportunity to watch their own kids participate in the activities. Sammy had already tried a game of wheelchair basketball for his age division and had cheered on some of the older kids in a baseball game when it came time for bowling for his age group.

"I like basketball, Maw-mee. And baseball. But I love bowling," he kept telling her, over and over.

She wasn't sure why he'd say that. She could only figure it was probably because he remembered the first time they'd ever visited Mac's farm and Mac had the special bowling ramp built for him.

She couldn't blame him. That day had made an unforgettable impression on her as well. Even as she pushed Sammy's wheelchair over the rubber waffled sidewalk from the baseball field, past park benches a volunteer had donated for the event from their Loveland landscaping company, it lingered in her mind. It was the first time she and Mac had *almost* kissed.

"There Nana an' Pappy!" Sammy exclaimed. "Mac, too!"

Her parents had signed up to help with the bowling event, to set up and retrieve pins at one of the four ramps. And true to his word, Mac was already at the area. Standing next to her parents, he watched the older girls finish up their round of bowling. And, of course, reached out to help when one of the girls was having a hard time of it.

He was always so good with Sammy and the other kids. He believed in them. Actually, he believed period, didn't he? And just because she'd had trouble believing, she'd removed him from Sammy's life.

Oh, how she wanted to talk to him.

But it wasn't going to be easy. Not when he'd barely glance at her. Yet with Sammy, she could see Mac had no love lost there. His eyes practically shone when she pulled Sammy's wheelchair to a stop near the bowling ramp.

"Hey champ!" he greeted her son.

Sammy grinned widely. "Ima do good bowling, Mac."

"It'll be fun, buddy." Mac held out his hand, and Megan didn't know how Sammy knew, but the two of them went through the ritual of a secret handshake she'd never seen them do before.

Then it was time for the four boys to line up their wheelchairs at their respective ramps, nets surrounding each area in case of a wild bowling ball or flying pin getting loose. Each of the boys' families was obligated to keep score, as if they were bowling at a real alley.

Sammy was the youngest in the group, so Megan thought it was nothing but a fluke when the first ball he sent rolling down the ramp caused more than a handful of pins to topple.

But then when it happened again. . .and again. . .and even again, and she jotted down the high scores, she didn't know what to think.

She looked at Mac and her parents for an explanation. But they didn't seem as surprised as she was as they cheered him on. Twenty minutes later when Sammy won, and Mac was wheeling him over to shake the hands of his competitors, she couldn't do much of anything but stand and feel happily shocked for him.

"I bowl good," Sammy said proudly after being presented a blue ribbon for the event. "Didn't I bowl good, Maw-mee?"

"Better than good, Samster." She bent down to hug him. "I didn't know you could bowl so well."

"You surprised?"

"Well, you might say. . .yes, I'm surprised."

"I practice." He beamed.

"You practiced, huh?"

She wasn't sure what he was talking about. She'd never seen him bowl except for the day they'd been out at Mac's farm months before. But she hated to tell him his winning had probably been little more than beginner's luck, so she smiled and said, "Well, you know what they say, practice makes perfect."

"Uh-huh." He nodded. "I glad you surprised. We want to surprise you."

"We?"

Sammy nodded, uttering another, "Uh-huh."

She looked up at her parents who were standing next to Sammy's chair. Mac was still busy talking to the volunteer who had presented the ribbons. Or maybe he didn't feel right being part of the family's mini celebration, she wasn't sure.

"We who?" she asked.

Sammy's grin was extreme, as if he'd won the competition all over again. "We sneaky."

That still didn't answer the question of "we who?" She glanced up at her parents, who also wore dazzling smiles.

"I can't believe you never figured it out," her mom chirped.

"Never figured what out?"

"Well, all those times you came to pick up Sammy when

I was babysitting and he was off with your dad."

"*You* taught him to bowl?" She gaped at her father. She'd never known him to be a bowler.

"Me, bowling? Of course I didn't. Your mom's been working me over for years, trying to get me to play in a league."

"Well, then. . ." If it hadn't been her dad, and her mom was always at the house when she arrived, that only left— "Was it Mac?"

Her mom answered with a clap of her hands. Sammy giggled, and her dad let out a chuckle.

"And you were all in on it?" she asked.

"Oh yes, Meg. I've been *dying* to tell you," her mom answered all in rush, clearly eager to spill all she'd kept pent up inside. "Mac came to me months ago with a plan he'd come up with. A surprise for you. He'd asked if he could take Sammy to practice bowling on the nights your dad and I were babysitting."

"I not a baby," Sammy chimed in. "I almost seven."

"We know that, honey." Her mom grinned widely.

"So I'd run Sammy over to Ted's warehouse where Mac had everything set up," her dad explained with a lopsided grin, "and then bring him home when the two of them finished practicing."

"Oh my—" Tears pricked the sides of her eyes. She blinked, trying to hold them back. "Mac? Mac did all of that?"

"Maw-mee, why you cryin'?" Sammy frowned. "You not happy I won?"

"No, I'm very happy about that. Really I am, Samster."

"Mac, Maw-mee surprised and she crying," Sammy shouted.

Megan could see Mac's ear tilt in Sammy's direction at the sound of her son's voice. Clasping the volunteer on the shoulder, he finished their conversation then sauntered over.

"Did you call me, Sammy?" he asked.

"Maw-mee surprised an'—"

Megan butted in. "Mac, you taught Sammy to bowl? They just told me all about it," she blurted, sniffling back her tears, embarrassed for him to see her emotions running so high. "I—I don't know how to thank you."

"It's not a problem." He shrugged off her gratitude, barely looking at her. "I did it for Sammy," he said emphatically. "We're buddies, aren't we, Sammy? He's helped me immensely. I wanted to help him, too."

Her mom looked misty-eyed. Megan could only imagine all the thoughts going through her mind at that moment. "Your dad and I have to get over to relieve the Slaters," she said with a shaky voice. "Congratulations, sweetie." Her mom kissed the top of Sammy's head while her dad patted Sammy's hand. Then they headed toward their duties at the concession stand, but not before her mother had a chance to mouth, "Say something!" from behind Mac's back.

As if Megan didn't want to. But it wasn't easy when his words echoed in her mind, about how he'd done what he had for Sammy.

He may not even have feelings for her anymore.

The thought caused her words to falter as she asked, "Mac, can we—um, talk? Even if it's later, after we're through? I'd really like to talk to you."

"Yeah, sure," he said, looking more somber than excited about it. "There's uh"—he glanced down at his feet—"there's something I need to talk to you about anyway."

"Hey guys," a familiar voice chimed from behind them. "Guess who? It's your favorite photographer." Janey came around to face them.

Sammy the chatterbox spoke first. "You come to take picture of my ribbon?"

"Better yet, how about I take a picture of you, Sammy O'Donnell, the number-one bowler, holding your ribbon?" Janey smiled.

"Okay. And Maw-mee and Mac, too," Sammy insisted.

"Hey, it's your picture. You can have whoever you want in it." Janey adjusted the lens on her camera. "How about it, you two?" She looked up. "You in?"

Megan felt like it was taking Mac all the time in the world to get situated behind Sammy's wheelchair. And it wasn't lost on her how he finally claimed the opposite side of the chair, at the farthest point the two of them could stand from one another. Not so long ago he would've reached out for her hand. Or had his arm wrapped around her waist or shoulder as they leaned in toward Sammy for a picture. Now it was as if he was literally repelled by her. In the midst of what was supposed to be a celebratory moment, her head dropped at the sad thought.

"Um, could you look up, Meg? And could you all get a little closer? Like the three of you know each other?" Janey peered from behind the camera again.

Megan's heart pounded wildly as she and Mac stepped

nearer to one another. Especially when Mac's shoulder brushed against hers. Instantly without a conscious thought, she felt a surge of warmth rise up within her. No matter what, he would always be able to do that to her.

Standing there, cheeks on fire, trying to smile at the camera, she couldn't help but think how far they'd come since Janey had taken the first picture of the two of them together. And sadly, how far she'd managed to push them apart

Maybe it had only been twelve hours total. But in Mac's mind, it had been a crazy-long day of trying his hardest not to look at Megan.

Especially since for the past few months, looking at her had topped his list as one of his favorite things to do.

He'd spent the day turned away from her smile, not wanting to remember how it used to lift him up. Kept his eyes plastered on Sammy, or the ground, or whatever else he could find, so he wouldn't have to look into her eyes, knowing there wasn't a place for him there anymore.

Even with everything else going on around him, with the competitions and kids and all, it'd been tough not to notice how she was prettier to him than every other girl out there in her red T-shirt, dark hair tucked behind her ears.

So it had been better not to look as much as he could. Not to notice at all.

Until now. Now he had no choice.

Because after Rick Hall emceed the closing ceremonies,

giving praise and thanks for the day, and everyone had cheered about the idea of a second annual All-Stars Sports Day...

After carloads of participants took over an hour to pack up and wait patiently to exit the event...

After Laura and Kurt had driven off to take Sammy for celebration ice cream...

And every last one of the volunteers' cars had disappeared one by one from his farm...

After all that, it was only Megan and him and a setting sun, languidly spreading its pink-orange glow across the sky as if taking a long, slow bow at the end of its performance for the day. As if it, too, was about to depart.

Leaving them completely alone.

"What a day!" Megan let go of a happy sigh and sat on one of the loaner park benches. He noticed she'd positioned herself to the far right side, leaving plenty of room for him.

He felt a reckless surge, almost like he was giving in to a dare, when he decided to sit beside her. "A great day."

"Can you believe it? We did it. Well, us and dozens of huge-hearted volunteers."

He still wasn't keen on looking into her face. But he didn't have to. He could hear the pure joy in her voice when she exclaimed, "The first All-Stars Sports Day! Unbelievable."

"You've been dreaming about this day for a while, haven't you?"

"For years," she admitted. Sounding wistful, she continued, "See, somehow I thought I'd have to do it all alone. Somehow I thought I should do it all on my own. But that just wasn't true, was it? If I had worked alone, it wouldn't have turned out near as well." Her hair fell across her face when she leaned forward and turned her gaze toward him. "Mac, this entire day wouldn't have been possible without you. Without your help."

"Yeah, well." He sloughed off the compliment. "I really doubt that's true. With all your passion for the kids, I imagine you could do anything you wanted to."

And all very well without me, he wanted to add since she was the one who didn't need him in her life anymore. But he didn't say that. Why sound like a sore sport?

"Well. . .I wouldn't have *wanted* to do it without you, Mac."

So she wanted to do the event with him. Just not life. He ground his jaw. Whatever. He was trying not to hold it against her that she didn't feel the same way he did. But pride or no pride, it was still hard to believe. Hard to come to terms with.

"And now we've got the second annual All-Stars Sports Day to look forward to. I hope you won't mind helping."

Still feeling a little bitter—and more than a little put out with her—he got to the point. "Is that what you wanted to talk to me about?"

"Yes. Well, no, it was more than that. It was—" She instantly froze up. Seemed caught off guard like she needed another moment to gather her thoughts when she said, "But you mentioned you wanted to talk to me about something, too?"

"Yeah, yeah." He rubbed his hands together. "About Sammy's birthday party. I got the invitation and. . ."

Her eyes widened as she looked at him apprehensively.

Did she want him to say yes? Or no? He wasn't sure.

"I'll be there, but it'll be toward the end of the party."

He noticed she looked relieved. Surely for the same reason he was even going to the party—to be sure to spare Sammy's feelings.

"That's fine. We can always wait to sing and cut the cake until you get there."

"Well, don't feel like you have to. I'll do my best to get back to Loveland from the airport as fast as I can, though."

She clasped her hands together, rubbing her right thumb across the knuckles on her left hand. "You're—you said you're going out of town?"

"Yeah, I, uh—" He figured he might as well go ahead and tell her. People were going to start hearing things soon enough anyway. "A lot's happened since we talked last. My elbow got cleared, for one."

"I just heard that today, Mac. From Wendy. That's wonderful news. I'm really happy for you."

"Yeah." It wasn't the way he'd pictured telling her, but then lately nothing had been going the way he imagined it would, had it? "On the heels of that I got some other news. No one knows except for Hal, and now you, but there's a 99 percent chance I won't be here in Loveland next year to help with the All-Stars Sports Day."

"You won't?" Her brows furrowed.

"No. In all likelihood I'm being traded."

"Traded?" She frowned. "To where?"

"Sacramento."

"Cali—California?" She looked shocked.

"I know. Could they send me any farther? Obviously

nothing will or can be finalized next week. But they've got me flying out for a meeting with the team heads, and Hal says they've already come up with some numbers. So..." He paused, took a deep breath. "That's what I wanted to tell you. I'll be back on Saturday but I'll only be able to catch the last part of Sammy's party."

She sat staring at him, not saying a word.

"Can you explain that to Sammy for me?"

"Oh." She blinked then nodded. "Of course I can. Yeah, I will. But Mac, if it's a lot of trouble...you've already done so much for him. I can't believe how you made time to practice bowling with him. And then, he won. You're so..." She stopped herself. "It's something he'll never forget, Mac. I won't either."

He didn't know what to say. Even though there was a lot he could've said. Like how it was nothing. How he'd do anything for Sammy. For her. How once he started doing for them he'd never wanted to stop. Never thought it would stop.

"I didn't mind. He's a great kid."

They sat in silence for a moment. He looked out into the fields but could feel her next to him. Now her hands were unclasped. She rubbed them over the legs of her shorts.

"So are you glad about it?" she asked. "About the trade?"

"Well..." he drawled then finally turned to look into her eyes. "I have to be honest, I wasn't at first. But then I started thinking maybe it'll be a good way—and a good place—to start over. Far from past history here. Fresh. New team. New surroundings. New people."

"Well..." She paused, sought his eyes. "Good then. I'm

happy for you, Mac." She nodded, her lips curved in a slight smile. "You deserve to be happy."

He'd been fighting all day looking at her too closely. And now, having her stare at him that way, he'd thought of asking her to consider the two of them one more time. To ask what had gone wrong—or how he'd apparently misread her feelings so badly from the start. But then, why? He really didn't need the extra hit to his pride.

Instead he only asked, "So, what did you want to talk to me about?"

"Oh, that's all. Just, uh, about Sammy's party. I'll mark you down as a yes but coming late. And speaking of late. . ." She jumped up from the bench. "I bet you'd like to have this place to yourself. Mom and Dad and Sammy are probably finished with their ice cream by now anyway.

"So. Great day." She held up her hand to him like they were friends who normally high-fived, instead of like the couple they used to be who would squeeze each other's hands. Hold each other's hands. And touch each other gently. Lovingly.

"Yeah, big day." He nodded.

Part of him couldn't help but want to reach out and grab her hand, pull her into him like he had so many times before. But, of course, he didn't dare.

Even so, he hated that as he met her hand in the air, his fingers lingered on hers more than just a moment too long. Then once again, they parted. She was on her way. Gone.

Chapter 22

Ever since he'd been a toddler, Sammy had been fascinated by balloons. Such a simple thing, yet they brought out the biggest smiles in him.

That's why every year on his birthday Megan made a special point to go all-out on the balloon front. Or, actually her balloon planting began the night before his big day. That's when she'd sneak into his bedroom after he'd fallen asleep and leave a multicolored bouquet to surprise him in the morning. Downstairs, too, she'd have another group of balloons standing ready to bob around his birthday cake at party time. And there was always one special balloon—an extraordinary sort of one—she'd choose to tie onto the arm of his wheelchair.

This year, that balloon was Party Town's number twenty-seven. A three-and-a-half foot, bright yellow Happy Face, wearing a polka-dot party hat along with its traditional plastered-on smile.

With Mac another week gone from her life. . .and thinking about all the weeks and years ahead without him, Megan needed the Mylar smile to cheer her up. To help her get outside glum thoughts about the future. And to remind her to focus on the present. Namely, Sammy's special day.

Even so, she couldn't help but think about Mac each time the doorbell rang. Although he said he'd be arriving late, her heart involuntarily lurched in her chest—she bet as much as Sammy's did. Only she knew her son's heightened anticipation mostly had to do with Rachel.

"Think that her, Maw-mee?" he asked when the bell chimed again.

Due to sheer process of elimination, Rachel had to show up soon. Sammy's smiling face and his Happy Face balloon had already greeted most of the other guests earlier at the door—her parents, Allie and Greg and their crew, the Slaters and the Biddles. Janey, Rachel and Sean, and Mac were their only no-shows so far.

"It very well could be, Samster. Let's check it out."

Pushing his chair across the foyer, she noticed him patting his hair once more and really hoped that his first crush ever would be at the door, if only so he wouldn't have to go through the anticipation all over again.

Luckily, Megan walked around the wheelchair and opened the door to Rachel and Sean, and—

Janey?

"Hey, you guys." Trying to act as natural as ever, she hailed the three of them in out of the misty drizzle, all the while surreptitiously glancing over their shoulders out to the driveway. Janey's car had to be out there somewhere, didn't it? But she didn't see it in the drive or on the street, and though everything inside her wanted to know what was going on, she tried her best to pretend that the three of them arriving together was the most natural thing ever.

"Come on in!" she said, feeling like the Happy Face balloon's twin sister, a smile ingrained on her face.

"Happy birthday, Sammy!" Rachel exclaimed over the

adults' hellos. Clamoring across the threshold like a female thoroughbred focused on the finish line, she handed Sammy a gift wrapped in Spiderman paper. As Megan shut the front door behind her guests, she didn't think she'd ever seen his eyes glow quite so bright.

"Oh Sammy," Rachel squealed, "you have the best balloon ever." She gave the Happy Face a gentle bat.

"It have big smile," he said to his new friend and crush. "Want to see my cake? It have big smile, too."

"Sure." Rachel took over the wheelchair easily. Megan always appreciated how the young girl never hesitated. How she never let the hunk of metal stand between herself and Sammy.

After a moment, Greg came up and whisked Sean over to where the men were watching the baseball playoffs. Which left her and Janey. Staring at one another.

"So, you and. . . ? You two came together?" The mere idea was so improbable to Megan, so out of the blue, that she couldn't even manage to put their two names in a sentence together.

"Me and Sean." Janey's eyes glowed. "Yeah, we came together all right. Can you believe it? Crazy, isn't it?" Purse hanging at her side, she hugged her arms around herself, shaking her head in disbelief. "Oh Megan, I've started to call you a million times to tell you. I even wanted to mention it when you called the last couple of times to tell me about Mac. But then. . .I felt so bad about the two of you and how things were going. And, I don't know. I thought maybe I'd jinx something if I started talking about how much I've been starting to care for Sean. How it feels like there's something real between us. You know?"

Megan blinked.

Janey thought there might be something real between them? Evidently a lot had happened in the past few days. She tried to process that quickly. "My mom mentioned she'd seen you two. At the movie on the banks. But I didn't really think—"

"Your mom? Really? Did she say anything? I mean, did she, you know, get a feeling about the two of us?"

Her friend seemed so eager to hear that it almost made Megan feel envious, remembering how good it had felt to have feelings like that for Mac. Evidently, too, Janey was so head over heels for Sean that she'd forgotten she'd never put much stock into what her matchmaking mom had to say. But Megan wasn't about to remind her suddenly lovesick friend of that.

"Actually, Mom said that even though you both were sitting apart during the movie, when you met up at intermission, you two looked like you were together."

"She did? Your mom said that? Well, if she can see something special, then maybe it is real." She blushed, her eyes gleaming as she looked off into the distance, into the family room where Sean was watching TV with the guys.

"But how did you two hook up? I just don't get it." Megan almost had to wave her hand in front of Janey's face to get her friend's attention.

"I know, it's crazy. But not bad crazy. I think it's good, Megan."

"I'm sure you're right. It's surprising, that's all." Two weeks ago, Janey had been lamenting about Sean. Now she was talking about a real relationship with him?

"Well, before the movie even began, I spotted Sean sitting across the amphitheater," she said, her voice barely above a whisper. "I couldn't believe he was there. I got these butterflies in my stomach. The whole thing. It even got worse when he glanced around and noticed me. And then at intermission we sort of nodded to each other and met up and talked. And the whole time, I just kept remembering what you and Allie had said."

Megan remembered what Allie had said. But she was clueless on any advice she'd given out. She certainly wasn't in the position to give relationship advice, that was for sure.

"What I said?"

"Yeah. In the bakery that day. You said people change."

"And so you think Sean has changed?" As far as Megan could tell, Sean appeared to be the same nice guy he'd been in high school. But if Janey had thought he'd changed somehow and that led the two of them together, more power to the both of them.

So she was surprised when Janey said, "Actually, no. I suddenly realized that all along it wasn't Sean who had to change."

"It wasn't?"

"No, it was me. I needed to change."

"Well, don't change too much." Megan laughed. "I've grown accustomed to all your quirks and weirdnesses over the years."

But even as she said that, she could feel a twinge of envy resurfacing. There was a calm about Janey that she'd never witnessed before.

Janey laughed. "Oh, I don't mean that. Not things with

you and me. I mean with guys. I realized I needed to stop being in competition with them. Needed to stop making up stories about them to myself about who they are and what they're like before I even got to know them. And, Megan, oh my gosh!" Her cheeks flushed red against her creamy white skin again. "It's been so great. Sean and I have hung out every night this week. I can't believe how well we get along. I'd been carrying around a grudge since high school for no reason at all. It was so stupid." She waved a hand to the past. "And you know after we talked about it, we realized Stacy Littleton was the one who got us pitted against each other at the senior prom."

Megan remembered Stacy well. A girl who could have five guys liking her at one time but was never happy unless she was stirring up trouble for someone else.

"You didn't mention Red to Sean, did you?"

"I had to, Megan. I wanted to start clean. Be honest, like Allie suggested."

"What did he say?"

She laughed. "He knew it was me all along."

"But he'd asked me about the mysterious redhead."

"Figuring you wouldn't rat me out anyway."

Megan bit her lip. "He doesn't think I'm awful for not telling him?"

"No, just thinks you were being a friend. And he thinks I look good as a redhead, too." She giggled then looked around, sobered, and shrugged. "I didn't see Mac's truck out front. Is he coming?"

"He said he'd be late." She started to tell Janey the reason why but then stopped herself. Mac's business was his and his alone. If he wanted anyone to know his whereabouts or about changes in his life, that information should rightfully come from him.

"Oh! I have copies of the photo I took when Sammy won. I made five-by-sevens for you actually." She removed an envelope from her purse. "I thought you guys would like it. It'll run in tomorrow's Sunday paper, recapping the event and talking about next year's plans. Which was good I had a photo of the co-chairs anyway. I brought one along for Mac if you can help me remember to give it to him when he gets here."

"No problem, I can do that." Megan laid the envelope on the foyer table. "We'll put them here so we don't forget. Thanks, Janey. That was so sweet of you to make copies." She put her arm around her friend. "Guess we should join the party, huh? And go visit with that new beau of yours?" she said, not even bothering to open the envelope and glance at the photos of the three of them.

She couldn't at the moment. Not if she hoped to keep smiling.

Huge as it was, O'Hare's overcrowded airport terminal felt small and stuffy to Mac. Especially the designated section where he sat squeezed between two weary-looking travelers. He'd been sitting that way for over an hour waiting, which shouldn't have bugged him as much as it did.

After all, the quick trip out to California had been extremely worthwhile, and after meeting with the Miners' people the night before, he was heading back to Loveland, verbally assured he'd be playing ball next season for a stellar team and making more money than ever before.

But the day had been filled with delays. His initial flight held up because of a mechanical malfunction, and then further delays because of heavy thunderstorms in the Midwest.

For a while it didn't look like he'd make the connecting flight in Chicago, but after all the setbacks, he'd gotten there in the nick of time. With the hour time difference, he could make the tail end of Sammy's birthday party as planned.

That is, if his connecting flight got off the ground in the next fifteen minutes. Otherwise. . .

He hated to think about it.

Hated to think he'd made a promise to Sammy and had little to no control to make that promise come true.

Tired of not seeing any movement out the steam-filled windows and too agitated to sit still any longer, he got up and stretched his legs then picked up his carry-on and made his way over to the attendant at the boarding desk.

"Look, is there any reason we're not boarding yet? Isn't the flight scheduled to leave in the next fifteen minutes?" He knew he sounded huffy, but he couldn't help himself.

"Sir, I'm going to be making an announcement in just a moment."

"And then we'll be boarding?"

She looked at him but wouldn't give him an answer confirming or denying that.

"Trust me, miss, you can fill me in now. I won't tell anyone, I promise. It's just I have to get to a party."

"A party?"

"For a little boy. He's seven today." He glanced at his watch. "And I can still make his party if the flight leaves pronto."

Her face softened at the mention of a seven-year-old. "Well, I'm sorry to tell you, I'm about ready to announce that all the flights are being canceled."

"Canceled?"

She nodded. "Heavy mist. Poor visibility."

"Canceled temporarily or for the rest of the day?"

She shrugged. "We don't have any control over the weather, sir."

"I know, but. . ." Telling her how he had to get to the party again was a waste of time, he knew, and only made him sound ridiculous. "Of course you don't," he said instead. "Thanks for your help."

Lifting his cell phone from his shirt pocket, he went to sit down again. He plunked his bag on the floor and this time sat in a chair that faced away from the menacing weather. If nothing else, he could at least call Megan and ask to speak to Sammy and wish him a happy birthday.

He could. . .if only weeks ago he hadn't deleted Megan's cell number from his phone. He'd deleted her mom's cell number along with it, figuring it'd be too easy to reach out to her in a moment of weakness.

Tired and perplexed, he hung his head in his hands. Nothing seemed to be working out for them. Not a single thing. Every time he turned around there was something else keeping him from Megan, and Sammy, too, for that matter. First Megan and her out-of-the-blue dismissal of their relationship. Then the trade offer. And now a simple flight.

It must not be in God's plan, he decided. It must not be. And he'd simply have to get used to it. Even if he didn't want to.

"Aww..." he groaned into his hands and stayed like that for a while, a million thoughts jumbled in his mind.

Finally, he lifted his head and started to lean back in the chair and close his eyes. He might as well nap. It wasn't as if he was going anywhere. But before he could lean back, his eyes lit on a woman and a little boy. They were holding hands, walking down the aisle between the gates.

The two reminded him so much of Megan and Sammy that it made his heart ache. Reminding him of how much he'd wanted to be a part of their lives. Reminding him of how he'd changed for the better to the depths of himself, and Megan's heart still remained elusive to him.

But what was he supposed to do about it? Beg her?

Frustrated, he tried to tear his eyes away from the mother and son. Until a baseball hat fell from the boy's pocket and the pair kept walking, not noticing.

Jumping up from his seat, Mac went to pick up the hat. Over the pockets of travelers, he called out to the mother. "Excuse me. Miss? Ma'am?"

Somehow the woman heard him and turned. She eyed him curiously.

"Your son." He strode toward them, the cap in his hand. The little boy immediately moved closer to his mother, hugging her leg. "He dropped his baseball hat."

"Oh, thank you!" Gratitude shone in her eyes as she

reached for it. "He would've been so upset if he'd lost his hat," she told Mac. "Wouldn't you?" She looked down at her son who replied with a nod.

"Yeah? Is he a big White Sox fan?" Mac asked her, since her son appeared to be somewhat shy. "Did one of the players autograph it for him or something?"

The woman smiled. "Oh no. Nothing like that." She gave a slight shrug. "It's special because his daddy bought it for him."

Mac stood and watched the two of them for a moment, but they blended into the crowd and disappeared so quickly he wondered if he'd really seen the mother and son at all.

But it didn't matter. He'd seen what he needed to. Suddenly, he knew what he had to do.

He'd never given up in a baseball game. He'd always tried his hardest, to the bitter end. How could he give up on Megan when he loved her more than anything he had ever loved in his life? And Sammy—the boy was too much a part of him now.

Unfortunately, his pride had kept him from questioning Megan much that night she said they didn't have to see each other anymore. Even though it didn't seem like something Megan would do—to lead a guy on—his pride kept him from talking to her all the days that followed.

He'd been so hurt, he hadn't considered anything that was going on in her mind. Only in his own. He kept telling himself not to worry, to get over it. That he could have his pick of any woman.

But the truth was the only woman he really wanted lived in Loveland, Ohio, with her son.

And no, he wouldn't beg her to listen to him. He wouldn't beg her to tell him what all was going on in her head.

Unless, of course, he had to.

"Okay, God," he whispered under his breath. "I get it. I do. Thank You, Lord, for making me see. Thank You."

He glimpsed at his watch, set to eastern standard time. "Home" time. The party would be ending soon, and there wasn't a chance under the heavens that he'd get there for that of course. But Loveland was less than five and a half hours from Chicago. And if he didn't waste a minute more, he might be able to still get there before Sammy's birthday was completely over.

Picking up his carry-on, he made his way over to the boarding station again, realizing that despite all the good news from Miners' staff the night before, he really hadn't felt like smiling all that much. Until just now.

"Hey, one more question."

The attendant held up her hand to stop him. "Sir, I just told you there's nothing I can—"

He cut her off. "Trust me, I heard you. And I apologize if I was even slightly rude before. But now I need to know, where's the nearest rental car agency?"

Chapter 23

"D on't need to put jammies on," Sammy mildly protested hours after his birthday guests had gone home.

In contrast to his slight crankiness, the Happy Face balloon still bobbed and smiled widely at Megan as she pushed his wheelchair down the hallway.

"Honey, it's that time of night." She paused in the doorway of his bedroom and flicked on the wall switch. A ceramic lamp with a catcher's mitt base illuminated from his nightstand. "Time for bed."

"Buh Mac still coming. Don't want to be in jammies when Mac come."

Sammy was still wearing the bowling glove Rachel had given him and the cotton sweater vest Mrs. Biddle had knit for him while she'd been recuperating. He also had the photo Janey had taken on All-Stars Sports Day lying in his lap and would've been clutching the new bowling ball her parents had given him if she hadn't urged him to leave it in the family room with the rest of his gifts so they'd all be in one place in the morning.

Megan couldn't blame him for wanting to hold on to his special day awhile longer. But holding on to the notion that Mac was still coming wasn't as easy to deal with. It pressed on her heart.

"Sammy, Mac had to fly clear across the country, and

sometimes people get tired or delayed. There were a lot of storms everywhere today. You saw it raining here off and on." She pulled back the covers on his bed, not wanting to make excuses for Mac. But not wanting her son to feel dejected either. The part about the weather was absolutely true. Even though it could also be true that at the last minute Mac had decided not to come after all. Not that she could blame him. She'd given him every opportunity to excuse himself from their lives. Left the door wide open and practically pushed him out of it, giving him full permission to exit. To be gone from them forever.

"Did he call and say he not coming?" Sammy asked, his question more logical than anything she'd been thinking.

"Well, no, he didn't. But—"

"Then he coming. He told me he always be here," her son announced. "He be here," Sammy said emphatically. "Tha why I can't go to bed. Can't put on jammies. Say prayers later."

"Okay." She gave in. Against her better judgment. After all, how disappointed was he going to be when he woke up in the morning and found out Mac hadn't shown up?

But she was far too tired to think about all that now. It had been a big day for both of them. She'd simply deal with tomorrow, tomorrow. "Then how about you keep your clothes on, we take off your shoes, and then you can lie down and rest for a bit?"

"Rest till Mac get here." Sammy nodded agreeably with the new plan and didn't balk at all while she took off his shoes, picked him up, and laid him on top of his bed.

"Do you want the sheet over you?"

He yawned wide then nodded.

"And let's put this picture on your dresser first then, so it doesn't get wrinkled, okay?"

"Uh-huh." He nodded again, his eyes already drooping. "No wrinkle."

She removed the photo from his hands and placed it on the dresser before covering him with the sheet. Tucking him in, she leaned over and kissed his forehead.

"It was a good birthday. And you're a great birthday boy."

"Good birt-day." He yawned once more.

"I love you, my big seven-year-old."

A slight smile tugged at the corner of his mouth, though his eyelids dipped even more. "Love you, Maw-mee. If I. . . sleep. . .you wake. . .when Mac here?"

She stood up straight, wondering for a moment how she could answer him. But then she didn't have to say anything. Didn't have to make him a potentially empty promise. She could tell from his even breathing that he'd already fallen asleep.

Turning off the light switch, she paused in the doorway for a moment watching him. But the sight of him sleeping filled her with so much pleasure, she decided the birthday mess could wait.

A nightlight in the corner cast a dim glow as she settled into the rocking chair across the room from his bed. She hadn't sat in the cushioned rocker for a while. But through all the years, its familiar feel had always been the same, a comfortable place in the black of night where she'd rocked an infant Sammy to sleep. Or soothed him when he could still fit in her arms on nights a fever or a bad dream kept him from sleeping.

But how he was growing up now! She studied the length of him stretched over the bed, marveling at the boy he was on the outside. And on the inside as well. Intrinsically, his faith in people, and good, and God never wavered.

Oh, if only she'd had that kind of faith when she'd first met Mac. That kind of childlike faith that didn't only believe—but trusted earnestly. Then she wouldn't have second-guessed herself or him.

If only she had changed like Mac had—and even Janey. They'd both stopped letting their pasts dictate their futures. But she hadn't. She'd let all her fears of failing at love again overshadow the love she had for Mac. And she'd let all the lies she'd built up in her mind, all the what-ifs, dilute the blessing of Mac's love for her. She'd allowed it all to override the gift of happiness that God wanted to give her.

By focusing on the negative, she'd barely given credence to the positive. In every way, she'd looked at Mac's celebrity as if it were a frightening thing. But lying right on top of Sammy's dresser was proof of something bigger and grander than that. Something more than she'd ever imagined. A photo of her and Sammy and Mac that because of his celebrity might get noticed in the newspaper—and ultimately might change lives and give promise to so many others.

How could I have been so blind? She looked out the window. *How?* She searched the rain-dreary darkness. Finding nothing there, she turned back to the soft glow of the room, cradling her head in her hands.

"Oh dear Father in heaven, I don't want to be like this or live like this anymore. I don't." Her mind cried out like never before. Not even after she'd talked to her mom had she really understood and succumbed to His will. But now was different. Now it was all she wanted to do. With every part of her. "I don't want to try to be in control. I want to surrender. To You, dear Lord." Tears flowed from her eyes. Her heart wrenched with sorrow and repentance. "Please forgive me for my doubts, for not trusting. From this day forward, please know I trust You to lead me. I'm asking You, please, to guide me. I trust that when I close my eyes at night, You won't slumber or sleep and You will watch over my Sammy always. I trust that wherever You lead, I don't need to fear, because You will be right there with me. And I thank You for that, heavenly Father. I thank You for Your mercy and love and forgiveness always. I pray this in Jesus' name. Amen."

She wished she'd realized her mistakes sooner. She wished she'd seen them before now, when Mac was already gone from her life.

But she couldn't control the past any more than she could control the future. Only God was in charge of that. It was all in His hands. She knew that now. She trusted that. And for once in her life it wasn't an unsettling or a frightening thought. It was a comforting one.

Closing her eyes, she laid her head back on the chair cushion and rocked gently, a feeling of thankfulness washing over her as well as a calming peace she'd never known and had only heard about before.

At the time he'd been standing in O'Hare's overcrowded terminal, it had seemed like a good idea to drive from

Chicago back home to Loveland. And actually, the weather hadn't been all that threatening on the road. The five-plus hours had passed by rather quickly.

Yeah. . .it seemed like the right thing to do. To drive back for Sammy's birthday. Even though Sammy would most likely be asleep, it would prove to Megan that he was a man of his word. More than that, it was a chance to take hold of a situation he'd been too prideful to face before.

But once he pulled the compact rental car into Megan's driveway, his boldness disappeared, like it was stranded out on the highway somewhere. He sat with the engine idling, staring at the digital clock on the dash. It was 11:39 p.m. 11:40. 11:41.

All the hours he'd spent driving, he'd concocted a variety of scenarios. All about what he'd say to Megan. What Megan would say to him. In every one of those scenarios, he'd imagined her changing her mind, saying yes to him and declaring her undying love. He'd never entertained the thought she could say no to the idea of them trying one more time.

At least not until now.

Which caused him to pause. Scratch at the day-old stubble on his chin. And struggle with the choices he had.

He could pull out of the driveway and consider himself lucky he'd gotten home safely.

He could sit and watch the rain run down the windshield all night long.

Or he could do something more constructive than both of those.

He decided on his last choice.

Turning off the ignition, he bowed his head and began to pray. He asked for the right words to say. Words from his heart, that Megan would listen to and hear. Words that he meant, ones she could trust. He prayed for God's blessing over the two of them, and then he slid out of the car.

Trickles of rain pelted him all the way up Megan's walk. Standing at her front door, realizing it was midnight and assuming once more Sammy was asleep, he decided to knock instead of ringing the doorbell and taking the chance of waking him.

Once. Twice. Three times. He knocked over and over again, hoping she'd hear. Or maybe she had. Maybe she'd looked out the window and saw it was him and didn't want to come to the door.

It didn't matter. He'd driven a long way, and he'd stand outside in the rain all night if he had to. Ironic as it was, he felt proud of the fact that he'd managed to put his ego away. All in the name of love.

Startled out of sleep, Megan sat up in the rocking chair and blinked. She'd heard something, but what?

There it was again. A knock at the front door. What time was it? She glanced at Sammy's clock radio. . .11:47?

Heart pounding, she got to her feet, stealthily tiptoed out of Sammy's bedroom and padded cautiously down the hallway.

Standing at the edge of her entryway, she didn't know whether to be frightened or worried. She just hoped the knocking would stop. That whoever it was, would go away.

But it kept up. And then, she heard a voice. *His voice.*

And for more reasons than she could even name—hope, excitement, the possibility of disappointment—her heart began to pound all over again.

"Mac?" Rushing to the sidelight windows that flanked the front door, she peered out at his rain-soaked face. Immediately she unlocked the door and let him in.

"Mac, are you okay? Is everything all right?" It wasn't just that his clothes dripped with rainwater that alarmed her. It was the way he stood hunched over, like a man who'd been through something. Though she noticed his eyes glowed as if he might be nearing the other side of whatever that "something" was.

A hundred questions ran through her mind, but so many thoughts did, too. Like how she wished she could reach out and touch his rain-soaked hair. Or wipe the raindrops from his cheek. Afraid she might do just that, she only said instead, "Let me get you a towel."

Starting to walk toward the bathroom, he caught her arm. "Megan, wait. Please." He held on to her. Tightly.

"Mac, why are you here?" She stood facing him. "Sammy's asleep and—it's nice of you to come. But—"

"I know. It's late. I'm sorry." He nodded an apology. "All the flights were canceled. So I got a rental car."

"You drove? From Chicago?"

"I knew I'd be too late for Sammy's party. But I said I'd be here. And. . .I'm here."

He was at that. All six feet of him, filling her entryway the way his love had filled—still filled—her heart. And she wasn't sure what she was going to say. Or how she was going to say it. But this time she wasn't going to let a chance to talk to him pass again.

"Mac, I need to tell you—" she started to say.

But he pressed a finger to her lips.

"Don't. Please don't tell me to go. At least not yet, okay? I have to say something first. Something I realized at the airport today. I saw this mom and her son, and well. . ." He paused, as if to gather his thoughts. Maybe even his nerve?

"You know, when I played ball, for years I thought the measure of who I was as a man was only reflected in my stats. The same statistics that flashed up on the screen every time I pitched or came up to the plate. And the bad thing about that is those statistics can send you on a roller-coaster ride. Lots of ups and downs. With everyone watching. And it's not a good ride, trust me. It can make you crazy. Make you do crazy things." He hung his head before he spoke again.

"But Megan." He looked up, searching her eyes. "These past months, especially the months since I've been with you, let me know that's not true. Now I know the measure of a man is based on his faith. His family. The people he loves. And I love you and Sammy, Megan, I do. And I don't know what went wrong between us. If I did too much. Or not enough. I'm not too proud to say I'm not perfect. I make mistakes. And I made a big mistake that night that I let you walk out of my life without even trying to stop you. But with all that said, I realize it's late, but can we talk now? So I can know for sure there's not still something between—"

It was her turn to stop him. She pressed her finger to

his lips, halting him. She had to. She couldn't let him go on, looking in such agony, explaining himself. Especially when it should be the other way around, explaining herself to him.

"Something between us? Oh Mac, there was something great between us!"

His heart lifted with hope. He stared at her looking confused, and rightfully so.

"But then," she continued, "I put other things in our way. All that stuff I said about not seeing each other? I told myself it was best because I loved you too much. I told myself that it was only right to give you the freedom to let your career take you wherever you wanted to go. Not to make you compromise. But that was just a cover-up for all my fears. Fears from my past relationship. Fears of the future.

"I'm so sorry, Mac. I am." She bit her lip, searching her heart for more ways to explain. "I was afraid things wouldn't work out between us before I'd even given them a chance to. I wanted to duck out before Sammy could get hurt. Before I could. And well, I went completely overboard trying to control everything."

"You *can* be quite a mother hen sometimes." A smile tweaked at the side of his mouth. At his lips. "A cute mother hen, but still. . ."

"I don't want to be like that anymore. God brought you into my life, and I want to love you and be with you and accept all that comes along with loving you, MacNeill Hattaway. Whatever that is. I want to try. If you could only give me one more chance, Mac. Please?"

"You? One more chance?" He curled his hand over hers and drew her into his chest, wet shirt and all. She didn't care, it felt good and right and even warm cuddled in his arms. How had she ever dared to let him out of her life for one minute? What a fool she'd been!

"It'll be a tough job," he teased, pressing her close. "But I'm thinking I'm just the man for it." He looked down at her. "When do I start?"

"How about now?" She inched up on tiptoes, gazing at him, not closing her eyes until he bent his head to kiss her. And at the first instant she felt his lips on hers, tears filled her eyes. Tears of thankfulness. Of joy. And of course, of love.

Oh, what would she have done all her life, never knowing the feel of his arms. . .his lips again?

His kiss was slow, thoughtful at first, sending shivers through every part of her. A kiss her once-lost soul could melt into. But little by little, the intensity grew. His demanding lips caressed hers, recapturing all the love they'd almost lost between them. And then, softer again as if realizing the preciousness of that love. Only stopping long enough for him to say, "I've missed you, Megan."

She'd missed him, too. So much. And she could've easily stood there kissing him until the sun came up if it hadn't been for Sammy's voice calling from down the hallway.

"Mac. That you?"

Their kiss ended, but Mac still held her tight. She glanced up at him and smiled. "Seems you have another major fan besides me."

"What can I say? I'm a very lucky guy."

Holding Mac's hand, Megan led him down the hall. As soon as they reached Sammy's room though, she let go.

Sammy had his arms raised as far up as he could manage, waiting to hug Mac around his neck.

"You come on my birt-day," her son told Mac once he released Mac from his loving grip.

Mac sat down on the bed beside him. Megan followed his line of vision as he glanced at Sammy's clock. "Yes, I'm late. But it's still your birthday, isn't it? 11:58. Happy birthday, buddy." The two went all out with their secret handshake which was becoming less of a secret nowadays, Megan mused.

"I knew you come." Sammy grinned, looking wide awake as if he'd never been asleep at all.

"Yeah? How'd you know that, bud?"

" 'Cause you said so," Sammy said matter-of-factly.

Mac's eyes shone when he looked from Sammy up to her. She thought he looked like he'd just been given the world and everything in it.

"It's true," she told him. "He never doubted you. Never." Emotion caught in her throat.

And I never will either. I promise, God, I do. Not when You've given me what I'd never dared to hope for—a man I can love and a man I can trust with my heart. . . And as she glanced at Sammy she added, *and with my son—my life.*

Chapter 24

Did you know that Ohio's state motto is, 'With God, all things are possible'?"

Mac's eyes left the road only long enough to glance at Megan in the passenger seat of his truck. The mid-morning sun came through the windshield, lighting her face, warming the cabin Pretty woman. Nice end-of-the-summer weather. He'd remember this day always.

"I do know that, yes." Taking a tube of something from her purse, she dabbed glossy stuff over her lips. "Breakfast was really good, Mac. I love First Watch, don't you? Even if we did have to drive all the way to Montgomery, it was worth it."

"Uh-huh. It's great. Great pancakes," he answered, pausing for a moment, acting like he was studying the trees alongside the road when what he was actually doing was biding his time before feeding her more local trivia. "Oh, and do you know what they say about Ohio? They say, 'Ohio is at the heart of it all.'"

"Really? That's nice. I guess they mean the heart of the Midwest?"

It was an effort to act nonchalant, and to ignore the nervous twitch in his left eye. In his most professorial voice, he answered, "Yes. Yes, they do."

"Interesting." She nodded, even though she didn't

appear that interested at all. "Sammy loves the First Watch blueberry pancakes." She reverted to the topic of breakfast again. "But I'm sure he's not minding having breakfast at Allie's after his sleepover with Justin and Carrie."

"I doubt it," Mac agreed. Lucky for him after he'd talked to Allie, she'd made all the arrangements for Sammy to stay there, no problem. She'd contacted Megan, acting as if it was all her idea. "I bet he's having fun with them."

"I'm sure he is."

She turned to look out the window, and Mac waited a moment before he cleared his throat and continued. "And by the way, Loveland, coincidentally, is called 'the sweetheart of Ohio.' Have you heard that before?"

Megan turned her gaze from staring out the window and stared at him. "Actually, I'm pretty sure I have." She tilted her head, looking at him in a curious way. "Wow, Mac." She smiled. Teetered on a giggle actually. "I had no idea you were so 'up' on your slogans."

Well, at least now he had her attention. He might as well lay it on before she changed the subject again. Turning his sights back on the road, he rambled on. "Yeah, good old Loveland is an amazing town, for sure. A great community with great schools fingering into three counties. Lots of shops, restaurants, activities. Even has a castle, of all things," he said referring to the locally well-known Loveland Castle. "And plenty of history," he added, as his farm came into view. He flicked on the right blinker. "You do know how Loveland got its name, don't you?"

"Yes, Mac. Yes, I do."

But though she'd just said she knew the history, he

mowed right on just the way he'd planned.

"How Colonel Paxton came from Pennsylvania and first settled the area in 1795? But how later on, the name Paxton got replaced by Loveland because James Loveland was the area's first postmaster and an early shopkeeper, and the mailbag always got dropped off at Loveland's. You've heard that story?"

"As I just said, yes, I have," she answered. He tried not to notice the strain in her voice. "Now let me ask you a question." She glanced over at him.

"Shoot."

"Why all the talk about Loveland? I'm surprised you're not giving me fun facts about California. And Sacramento."

"You mean you're not fond of our little burg?"

"Well, of course I am. I've lived here all my life, silly."

A bit relieved at her answer, he pulled the truck onto the gravel drive and slowly made his way up to the house. Knowing the imminent moment grew closer, his stomach rocked slightly.

"I'm glad you wanted to see what I've done to the house. The renovations have taken forever."

"I'm happy you wanted to show them to me, Mac," she replied, but there was a question in her gaze. Which he could understand. He hadn't exactly been acting like his cool, calm self all morning. "I was never quite clear what all you were having done to the place."

"That's why we're here," he said. "So you can see."

Well, one of the reasons. He cut the engine and tried not to think about the other thing he hoped to accomplish as well. Instead, he hopped out of the truck and went around to the other side to help her out. She was already slipping down from the high seat and getting her bearings in her wedged shoes. She had on the same yellow dress he'd remembered her wearing the first time she'd visited the farm, but with a jean jacket over it. Though sunny, there was a slightly cool morning breeze reminding that summer would soon be departing for another year.

"Right this way, ma'am." He splayed out his hands, directing Megan to the new wide walkway that led to the back of the house. He couldn't have been more pleased when she readily noticed the change, oohing and aahing her approval.

"And a wheelchair ramp leading up to the back door?" Her eyes grew wide. "Mac, how wonderful."

"Yes, but that's not all." Trying not to wince at his own game-show host tone, he led her inside. For the next twenty minutes or more, he showed her all of the improvements that had been made, including widened hallways, sinks lowered to wheelchair leve,l and so on—everything that had been done to make the house more wheelchair accessible.

"I can't believe all the changes. It's awesome," she complimented him. "It's a shame, though, isn't it? After all this money and work, and now you'll be selling the place once you start playing in Sacramento, won't you?"

They hadn't gotten around to talking about the logistics of their relationship yet. They'd just agreed they wanted to be in each others' lives and somehow they'd make that work. But the more he had thought about it. . .

"I mean, a person has to go where life leads," she added matter-of-factly. "And California, here you come!" Her eyes shone and he knew without a doubt she was behind him all the way. "Sammy's going to love when we come to visit. He can watch you pitch. And after the games, we can take him to Disneyland. And Sea World in San Diego. He'll love it, don't you think?"

"Yeah, I..." He ruffled his fingers through his hair. And scratched at his chin.

"Mac, are you okay? You've been acting all jittery ever since we got here."

"Must've had too much coffee at breakfast."

"You only had orange juice."

"Oh yeah. Right."

He did wish he could calm down. His palms were sweating badly. Even worse than the night he first kissed her.

He sucked in a deep breath. "Can you come here a minute?" Taking her hand, he led her from the living room into the kitchen, over by the window. "See over there?" He pointed. "To the left of the baseball diamond? Where there's an open space in front of that grove of trees?"

Megan squinted. "Yeah. There's a lot of land. It's a very pretty setting."

"A nice place for a house, don't you think?"

"Well, sure. If a person wanted to build another home on this property. But it's hard to imagine a person would need another house. Especially when you've made this house so nice and cozy."

None of this was going anywhere. Not his chatter about Ohio and Loveland. Or talk of building a new house. She wasn't taking any of his hints. He had to spit it out, plain and simple.

"Okay, I can do this. I can do this," he murmured under

his breath. But obviously not quietly enough.

"Do what?"

"Do you mind sitting down? In the chair there?" He pointed to the kitchen chair.

"Are you sure *you* don't need to sit down, Mac? You look kind of pale all of a sudden."

"No, I'm fine." Which wasn't true at all. He was sweating worse than ever. Like he was on the mound, bases loaded, *and* he was about to pitch to the best hitter in the league.

But he had to man up. He wanted to man up. For sure, Megan was the one. The only woman he ever wanted. He'd known it since the beginning.

"Megan, I know we've been saying we're in for the long haul. But I—I want to make it official. I don't want you to go off and do something silly, like try to kick me out of your life again."

Megan laughed out loud. He smiled at the sound. "Are you going to be bringing that up to me for the rest of my life?" she asked.

"Uh, I hope so. Yeah. I hope forever."

It was the perfect cue. Dipping his hand into the pocket of his jeans, he retrieved a small jewelry box, and then dropped to one knee in front of her.

"Oh Mac!" Her eyes brightened with surprise.

He opened the box, feeling good that he'd spent the time to shop around to find the perfect ring at an antique store in Hyde Park. "Megan." He gazed up at her sweet face. "Will you do me the honor of marrying me?"

"Mac! Yes. Of course yes!" she said, no hesitation in her voice.

Relieved and thrilled, he started to take the ring from the box and place it on her finger, but then he stopped.

There were just a few more questions he needed to ask.

"And, Megan, will you build a house with me over in the field—that field I showed you?"

"A house for us in the field?"

"And also not mind if I never play pro ball again?"

She shot up out of the chair. He came up off the floor to face her.

She plunged her hands onto her hips. He snapped the ring box shut.

What now?

Her flushed expression had gone from ecstatic to concerned to totally confused and even slightly angry in all but a few seconds. "Never play ball again? Mac, what are you talking about?"

"Well, except for with Sammy. I'll always play whatever he wants with him. And with our own kids, if we have them. And with special-needs kids, too," he tried to explain. "Megan, you just said a person has to go where life leads them. And I prayed about it, and this is where I've been led. I want to build a new house for us—for you and Sammy and me in the field where I showed you. And I'd like to make Uncle Jake's house and property a place where special-needs kids can come all year long for sports. Not just one day a year."

He thought she'd melt into him at that. But she didn't. He tried to pull her close, but she stood her ground, holding up her hands to halt him.

"Mac, we've been over this before. You don't have to do that for me. You don't have to pick between what you love.

Or quit something you love. Sammy and I will be there, wherever you go. I've already told you that. I'll love you no matter what you do, I will," she promised. "My home is with you, Mac." She corrected herself. "Sammy and I, our home is with you."

He'd been in the limelight for many years of his life. But it never could compare to all the wonder and blessings he'd witnessed by following God's light. Like the blessing of Megan, whose presence in his life dazzled him each and every day.

"Then if it's okay with you..." He took the ring from the box and gently lifted her hand into his. "I say we stay right where we are, here in Loveland. Our home sweet home."

Chapter 25

"Thanks for dropping me off." Megan leaned against Mac's truck and peeked inside, talking to him and Sammy over the running engine. "You two guys stay out of trouble, you hear?"

"Trouble? What trouble can we get into?" Mac grinned in his signature way. All irresistible man with a hint of mischievous boy blended in. "We're only going to the hardware store to buy a border fence for the bulbs you're planting. Right, Sammy?"

"Right," her son affirmed from the rear bench seat. "Me and Mac be good, Maw-mee. No worry."

"Oh!" Mac leaned across the seat, as close to the passenger window as he could. "Tell your mom to tell your dad that we're a go for watching the OSU game tonight."

"Okay, will do."

"Oh—and there's something else." He crooked his finger. She inched her head into the cab again, closer to his. "I love you," he said.

She smiled. "I love you, too." Their lips brushed in a gentle, knowing kiss. "And I love you, Samster." She blew a kiss to her son.

The first part of their mission accomplished—dropping her off—Mac and Sammy pulled away, leaving her standing on the sidewalk in downtown Loveland. The same part of the walk where her feet had stepped hundreds of times before. Right in front of We Do! Wedding Planners.

Only this time felt different. Because it was. Quite different. She'd never had an appointment with one of the wedding planners inside. And today she did. With her mom.

"Hi, Mom." The door chimed with sweet familiarity as she stepped inside. Even though it was only her mother she was meeting with, the fact that she was meeting with her mother "the wedding planner" caused her stomach to twitter a bit.

"I hope you found a parking space. Lots going on downtown today with the beautiful weather. Plus, people are getting ready for the Bikes, Bands, and Bites festivities next weekend."

"It wasn't a problem. Mac and Sammy dropped me off."

"Oh, that's nice. What are those two up to?" Her mom smiled, her eyes gleaming the way they always did at the mention of her grandson and son-in-law-to-be.

"They're on a mission to buy a border fence for me. I bought some tulip and daffodil bulbs, hoping to get them into the ground in the next week or so."

"You're growing a green thumb?"

"We'll see. I didn't feel like I ever had time before to even think about a garden." But now with Mac jumping at every chance to spend some "guy time" with Sammy, she did. She realized she must have the same disease her mom did because the thought of the two of them made her smile, too. "Mac's made so many wonderful changes inside his uncle Jake's house, I thought I'd pretty-up the flower beds outside."

"Spring flowers are so exquisite!" her mom exclaimed, gathering up wedding albums from the reception desk. "Plant them in the autumn then forget about them. Then after a long, dreary winter, they pop up out of the ground and delight you in the spring. Which is a good thing because who knows how much time you'll have to garden next year—what with building a house. Getting ready for a summer wedding. Working and—"

"Starting All-Stars Sports Ranch."

"Whew, it's a lot. But I know you two will manage." She pointed over to the pair of love seats. "I guess we should get started with this preliminary appointment before your guys get back. Oh, and your dad and I were wondering, are you coming over tonight to watch the game?"

Megan nodded. "Oh yes. Mac said to let you know we will definitely be there."

"Great!" her mom said as they sank into the pink cushions alongside each other. "Well. . .I thought first we'll browse through these books, showing you some of the other weddings Pam and I have planned, just to get an idea of what you think you might like. And then—then we'll. . ." her mom's voice faltered. She dipped her head, put her hand to her mouth.

"What? Mom, are you okay?"

"I'm sorry." Her mom lifted her head, tears glistening in her eyes. "I'm sorry," she repeated. "I told myself I wasn't going to do this. Wasn't going to get all emotional. But, I can't help it. I've never planned such a special wedding before. A wedding for my girl. My daughter. Oh Meg." She sniffed. "I'm so happy you and Mac have each other! I'm so glad you found your happily-ever-after."

Her mom's tears almost made her own flow. But she kept swallowing them back, even as she plucked a tissue from the box next to the china tea setting on the table and handed it to her mom. Rubbing her mom's shoulder till she got a hold of herself, Megan glanced around We Do! Wedding Planners and realized for the first time ever she actually felt comfortable being there.

After all the years of rolling her eyes at her mom's romantic notions of love. . .after all the years of not believing in love's possibility for her life, she noticed that the candy heart pink love seats seemed to be just the right color. And all the tulle and satin, all the lace and pink bows, weren't overbearing at all. They were just perfect. And precious. As precious as loving someone with all of your heart could be.

"Mom. . ." she said wistfully. "When did you know?"

"Hmm?" Her mom dabbed at her eyes.

"About Mac and me? When did you know, do you remember?"

"Oh, that's easy." She clutched the tissue in her hand and sighed as if content. "It was the day of the Amazing Race. Your dad and I had finished the race and we were walking over to Nisbet Park to rest, and I noticed the two of you along the bike path. Mac was pushing Sammy's wheelchair and you were walking alongside him. And you both looked so—" Her voice cracked a bit. "Happy. Very happy and so—"

"Together?" she asked, to quote her mom.

"Definitely together." Her mom nodded. "Connected."

"Wow, so you saw that in us months ago?" Megan shook

her head. "You would've never forgiven me if I would've completely blown it with him, would you?" She smiled. "Actually, come to think of it, I wouldn't have ever forgiven myself."

"Oh Meggie." Her mom chuckled. "The thing is, what I love thinking about most, is that God knew you two would be together. Even before you were ever born."

"You're right. He did, didn't He?"

All those times when she'd plucked daisy petals as a young girl, dreaming of love and marriage. . .all the lonely nights as a young woman when she never dreamed there'd be anyone for her, He'd already had her happiness in place. He knew exactly the daddy He had in mind for Sammy. Exactly the man He'd created for her.

MacNeill Hattaway, former baseball star. Mac, her catch of a lifetime.

Jennifer Johnson and the world's most supportive redheaded husband have been happily married for over two decades. They have three of the most beautiful daughters on the planet and one amazing son-in-law. Jennifer is a sixth grade writing teacher in Lawrenceburg, Kentucky. She is also a member of American Christian Fiction Writers. When she isn't teaching or writing, she enjoys shopping with her daughters, hanging out with her husband, Al, or her best friend, Robin, and playing on Facebook. Blessed beyond measure by her heavenly Father, Jennifer hopes to always think like a child--bigger than she can imagine and with complete faith. She'd love to hear from you.

Cathy Liggett lives in southwest Ohio with her husband of over thirty years and two grown children. Her passion for all things involved in writing started at a very young age and still inspires her today. She is the author of both fiction and non-fiction.